All Roads Lead to Vegas

A. Milton Blankenship

ISBN: 0615831249
ISBN 13: 9780615831244

COVER ART BY: Christopher Standley of Las Vegas, Nevada.

EDITING BY: Bette L. Blankenship of Las Vegas, Nevada.
Interior formatting and typography by Createspace,
an Amazon Company.

To Lydia,

You are the angel on my shoulders.

ACKNOWLEDGEMENTS:

I would like to personally bestow my heart's profound thanks to each and every person who has enhanced my life, and moved me further. Special, specific—and well earned—thanks to the following:

- To my mother, Bette Louise Blankenship. Your editing of the novel made this all happen. You are the furnace that forged my pen.

- Joey's Tavern on Craig Road. Great warm-hearted place, I wrote some of the book there, you can just order the hot wings.

- To everyone who helped with the poster promotions, specifically: Jacob McCrocklin, Erik Maldonato III, Christopher Standley, Eugene Joe, and The Lady.

- To the Cities of Terre Haute, Mt. Juliet, and Las Vegas. Beauty is beauty, and trust me, it takes many forms.

- To Mo over at Discount Tobacco at Craig and Tenaya— The best cigar shop in town, and a true supporter of my work.

- Last, but definitely far from the least, to my parents, who without whose support this work would never have been possible.

PART ONE:

SUMMERLIN

Prologue

"I don't *care!*" the young woman shouted at the top of her lungs. A male voice could be heard soon thereafter, matching hers in volume, "I think that's been established! And I think that's the problem, darlin'. " The location was a beautiful gated community filled with nearly identical stucco-cloaked two-level apartment buildings soaking in the remnants of Las Vegas sunlight, and while Summerlin Heights unit #2145 looked peaceful and elegant from an outside perspective, it was filled with strife, which quickly begins to have physical manifestations—a door swings open with force, and a young man steps out; or rather, has been pushed. The large white-painted door had a lovely oval etched glass window in the front of it; Andrew Cadoret didn't have time to notice it, as it nearly took off his nose. He backs up several feet and looks overhead as if he knows what is coming. There is a balcony overhead, and the sound of a rummaging commotion began to echo from the open glass door above.

As Andrew watched, the young woman emerged, but she didn't seem to be coming to talk about reconciliation. She was moderately tall for a woman, and was slender with mild curves. Her long brown hair was currently flying furiously in the wind. A basket of his things was ejected out the window, and almost hit Andrew, who side-skirted the potential blow in the nick of time. "But Sarah, you said that what mattered was devotion. You said I did everything else *right.*" He had a very light Southern accent, especially when under duress. The woman scowled and said, "oh you *love* being right, don't you?" She huffed off only to return in an instant armed with more of Andrew's possessions-turned-projectiles. A box of books. A stereo still loaded with now-cracked CDs. "I don't have to be—" Andrew's words were cut off by another volley of items and the woman yelling, "define for me now how you're the one who is right and understands what's going on. Again! Olivia and Gina were so right about you." She went back inside the doorway, though this time with less force and speed than before. "Don't even get me started about them!" the young man shouted upwards to her retreating back. "I take it this is going to really make us working together difficult to handle for a while," the man said more calmly. The woman did not return to the sliding-glass door. Her voice, however, was immutably heard: "I wouldn't even think about showing up. We're through, and I can't handle this right now. Can't help you get the job, and I'm *sorry*." *Sorry*, Andrew thought, *What does she know about sorry? She's the one who is going to end the night with a job to look forward to, and a bed to sleep in!*

Andrew waited for a few moments, standing amidst the maelstrom which had become of his books, clothes and Atlanta Braves keepsakes. He thought briefly of staying, and trying to see if he could even begin to repair the damage to the relationship which had just occurred; yet, after surveying the physical status of some of his belongings, he began to slowly walk away from unit #2145, heading in a general path towards the gated exit of the apartment community. He was leaving several objects which mattered very much to him, as well as his clothing, but he didn't actually know where he was going or might end up; carrying things in tow seemed pointless.

Andrew had to wait for a car from the neighborhood to be departing through the gates before he could get outside of the place. There was a regular walking-traffic entrance, but he had never bothered to memorize the code for it. Once outside of the residential complex, he began to roam the endless streets of northwest Las Vegas. Lacking any companionship, or other pressing matters to keep him occupied, Andrew's thoughts are inevitably brought back to the chaos which had just ensued.

What glory is there in being "right," he began to wonder, *when it includes, amongst its many gifts, homelessness, loneliness and poverty? The question of* whether he had "won" or "lost" his cause no longer really mattered. He had entered a situation, he realized, which he could never have predicted—He was completely alone in an unfamiliar city. The "girl of his dreams", his Sarah, was from Steubenville,

Ohio. He, himself, hailed from a small town on the northern border of Virginia called Blacksburg. They had met when they had shared an entry level English class together at Virginia Tech during their freshman year. They had both wanted to be teachers; Andrew of English and Sarah of Art.

Their initial friendship blossomed over the following semester into a loving relationship, with Sarah moving into Andrew's Virginia home while they eventually planned their move. Guided by westward dreams and skillful research concerning regional demand and pay for prospective teachers, the two of them settled on moving to Vegas. The gambling and potential night-life didn't hurt the city's chances. They had decided to put college on hold while they both worked wage jobs to save up for the trip. It was their intention to take back up where they left off degree-wise by registering at UNLV once they had moved and found employment there—tuition prices were extremely expensive for non-state residents. It took eighteen months of such saving, accompanied with the usual frugal misery that pairs naturally with some endeavors. *Did hard times stop us? Did living on poverty just to get out to this sweltering place tear us apart? No. None of it seemed to do anything but galvanize our love,* Andrew thought as he continued to walk under the setting desert sun. Once they had moved to Las Vegas they both sought employment; Sarah landed a job at a local library branch, despite it having been Andrew's idea to apply there in the first place. Andrew did feel a bit confused as to how a person pursuing a degree in Art Education had been chosen for employment at a library over a person pursuing a degree in English Education, but he didn't complain about it. "I wasn't even jealous or worried when she told me she couldn't help get me hired on until the end of her '90 day probationary period," Andrew muttered softly to himself. His march to nowhere begin to feel truly just like that, a journey which started with at least the occasional coffee shop or gas station which served as small breaks in the monotony; but, now as the sky began to become a deep violet, Andrew found himself entering nearly-identical streets with nearly identical names, all honeycombed with seemingly-endless stucco-covered doppelgangers, each varying little from the last.

After what seemed like an epoch of trudging along the sides of roads and dodging Nevada-Plated cars, some of which offered him a single human digit as a present while honking, Andrew's thoughts began to shift to a more pressing, more pertinent matter: his footwear. *My shoes are startin' to show their age,* he began thinking, *my feet hurt. But that's not all bad. I'd rather have that to think about than this whole convoluted mess.* As he stared vacantly down the road, he came back to his world, he realized that the *reason* his feet were now aching and his throat was dry was because of his recent forced eviction.

Moving to Vegas had been the relatively easy part. Staying at a motel and waiting for employment while the bill on their green-striped "I-Haul" rental truck waited fully loaded in a parking lot. The point at which the relationship began to fade, in Andrew's eyes, was when old high school friends of Sarah's from Ohio renewed their acquaintance via the computer. They, too had moved to the city of the sand, and wanted to get in touch. "Oh boy, did they," Andrew spoke as he slowed his gait; his legs were beginning to feel as if they had been weighted down with lead. It had only been two months—of nearly constant days and nights filled with animosity and contention—since Sarah's "old friends" had contacted her. Andrew was busy wondering if the situation could have gone any other way, and failed to notice the reddish lights of a locals casino which he was approaching.

I.

As his head never rose, he was unaware when his feet crossed the property line. He continued to slowly shuffle through the matrix of similarly-constructed parked cars, too deeply mired within dejected contemplation to be aware of his surroundings. Suddenly, the sound of shattering glass brought Andrew back to reality. Andrew's head rose to see a tall, old Vegas-style hotel looming overhead. A reddish glow surrounded the entire place, aided by lights emanating the same color, running for long distances under the casino roof's eves. A large casino advertisement sign, complete with rolling lights and a digital screen, stood at the street corner; it had a massive lone star flag, and the words in oversized letters read "TEXAS PALACE HOTEL & GAMBLING HALL." A large statue of a cowboy, hat waving overhead while his horse bucked under him sat between lanes of incoming and outgoing traffic, which was heading towards the casino's main entrance, an area to Andrew's left was not fully visible. Andrew could also see, to his left, the beginnings of a Spanish-tiled canopy which was built into the front of the place. Andrew's eyes didn't tarry to admire the architecture; however, his prior-dazed state was roused to attention with the crash of another glass object—a bottle. This bottle's destruction rang deeper in

Andrew's ears than the first; this one came *quite close*. So close, in fact, he could taste a drop of cheap beer on his lips, which had sprayed his face when the bottle exploded near his feet.

Andrew realized several things at once: A, he had entered the auspices of a casino. B, he was within inches of the second broken bottle, and C, he had inadvertently entered the midst of a fight. "Cheat, liar and scum!" he heard, still feeling in a bit of a daze. "Aw, come on guys! With faces like those, I would have thought you'd have senses of humor." The voice sounded more like the smooth, enthusiastic yell of the ringleader than that of a normal casino patron. There was a nervousness to this fast-talking voice, yet it almost seemed as if the speed with which the man spoke was an over-acted affair, crafted for their benefit.

Andrew shook off his melancholic haze to take it all in: three men in semi-ragged apparel were verbally accosting the one other man present. The solitary man was moderately tall, and appeared to have at least *some* muscle, though he was currently walking backwards from the now-advancing trio of belligerents. He was clad in a very fancy looking blue suit with gold pinstripes. His short dark hair was currently mussed—the men had apparently strong-armed him out of the establishment against his wishes. Though obviously outnumbered, he still grinned like he was on the inside end of a private joke.

"You swindled us! You know it, you no-good lying sack of—." The leader of the triangle of men's words were cut short by the well-dressed man, "Fair's fair, and legal is legal. Give my regards to the Nevada Gaming Commission." Two of the three men lunged forward at the man, one armed with a billy club, the other with a broken glass bottle. The man who had stood at the center of the three stood his ground. He appeared to Andrew's eyes to be the leader of the other two. The suited man backed up slightly as he glanced from one potential assailant to the other in an oddly calm manner.

The bottle-holding attacker made an attempt to slice at the suited man's torso, but due to a quick dash of his target, ended up making contact on an old pickup truck instead. A few pieces of glass broke off of the bottle, clattering next to where the would-be victim had landed after his parrying the initial blow. "Now, you know, somebody's gonna have to clean that up," the well-attired one taunted as he dodged a swing from the other attacker's club. The man in the middle continued to watch the event with confidence. Due to the overhead light nearest the action being burned-out, Andrew couldn't fully make out his face; his body stance alone gave off an air of superiority. "Someone's gonna clean *you* up, card-sharking fuck!"

Andrew's mind became instantly clear upon his hearing the vocal outburst. He saw not persons, nor consequence; he bore witness, rather, to raw facts: an unarmed man was being physically intimidated by men who were armed, and did not look to stand much of a chance. That is, unless Andrew did something about it. At this point, he didn't feel fear, and part of him relished the chance to actually prevent a crime. Andrew walked towards the group and picked up a nearby beer bottle as he entered fearlessly into the fray.

The club-wielder managed to make contact with the well-dressed man's thigh. The man fell from the blow, and was about to be struck a blow upon his scull when a bottle came sailing through the night air, striking the leader of the trio's face as it landed. A horrified shriek of pain came from the leader as he collapsed to his knees. The man grunted in pain, and stood back up. He was clenching his face with his hand in an attempt to staunch the heavy flow of blood emanating from just above his hairline. "I don't think this is gonna happen, fellas," Andrew's voice called out. Everyone, both attackers and victim alike, turned. "Who the Hell are you?" the bloodied leader asked loudly. "Someone who ain't got anything better to do, and doesn't give a shit!" Andrew felt strange as the words came out of his mouth: being raised by his momma to be polite, he rarely in twenty-five years of life had found the occasion to yell, yet today he had done it twice. And cussing in public—well, even in the midst of a brawl Andrew mentally noted how lucky he was that his momma wouldn't ever know that it had happened. Feeling brave and perhaps a little further emboldened by the nature of his words, he charged forward at the two men who had resumed their assault upon the man in the three-piece suit.

Three on two still isn't fair. The ensuing chaos did at first favor the aggressors; however, Andrew joining the fight did grant the other man some respite. Andrew's instincts told him that the other man stood a far better chance of survival if a knife weren't added to his current troubles. Andrew wasn't large. Tall, yes, but by no means strong by any semblance of appearance. Yet he swung away and charged, and he struck back at his knife-wielding opponent with bare hands—his real strength was the pounding fury in his heart, which seemed, at the time, to be pulsing and flowing within his heart-pounding body. Andrew leveled the knife-wielder as he was charging at him and, in a bullfighter-like fashion, sidestepped him while grasping at the man's unarmed wrist. Andrew then swung the man in a whip-like motion. The knife dropped from the thuggish man's hand moments after his skull made contact with the flat, thick steel of a faded-yellow pickup truck from the 80's. The man limped momentarily before dropping beside the truck, collapsing upon the beer and urine-stained parking lot with a jiggle. Andrew retrieved the knife.

Sounds of further commotion reminded Andrew to turn and see what was happening between the two now leaderless combatants. As the man was still dodging their attacks, Andrew rushed to the man's aid. He felt that this strange man seemed chaotically at ease as he continued to parry their blows, which succeeded in merely tearing his clothes. Andrew, whose mind was still in the no-man's-land of self-doubt, boldly dove at the man with the club, toppling him to the ground. As he kept the assailant pinned to the ground, Andrew called out to the man whom he was trying to aid: "Here!" Andrew slid the now-unconscious leader's knife in the man's direction. The suited man pocketed the knife and seemed to stare at Andrew the entire time he was doing it. Out of nowhere, the former victim slid to his side and performed a drop kick on the other, non-pinned assailant, knocking him solidly on the head while he was busy staring at Andrew. *This guy's wily*, Andrew thought.

With his comrade's odds severely weakened and his leader out for the count, the man who had previously held a broken bottle—and now only held a remnant of the wine bottle's neck—looked at his compatriots and then at Andrew and the suited man and yelled, "I hear bikes Lenny, let's get out of here!" The former attacker tossed his bottle remnant blindly into the air as he ran—as fast as his feet could take him—in the direction of the property line, and the street beyond it. Andrew noticed this and decided to relinquish his physical control of the other thug, jumping off of him, stomping on his chest as he did. The unarmed attacker rose and ran wildly to catch up with his partner in crime. The leader remained motionless by the side of the pale yellow pickup truck.

The suited man's prior attackers did indeed "hear bikes"—The whirring of two bicycles being pedaled full force echoed around the corner of the building as two men wearing yellow shirts emblazoned with the word "SECURITY" came into view. Both men ground their mountain bikes to a halt ten feet from where the two men were standing and took off their white bicycle helmets before approaching Andrew and his now torn-suited acquaintance. "Bentley, you sure some explaining to do," the older and heavier of the two said, looking at the man whom Andrew had just helped survive. The man, whom the officer referred to as "Bentley," grinned and was opening his mouth as if to speak when the younger of the two officers walked up to Andrew. The officer leaned in to Andrew and spoke to him in a low volume, almost as if intentionally hiding his intent from his coworker: "Hey, what exactly happened here?" Andrew replied back to the officer in a similarly muted tone: "I don't really know—these three guys were chasing this man with broken bottles and a knife. Next thing I know, I'm almost hit with a bottle, and—" The older, plumper officer had walked up to Andrew and the younger officer. "What was that, Eugene?" the older officer asked the younger one. "Oh nothing, sir. Merely trying to ascertain what occurred," the younger officer replied. "What *occurred*, 54, is that our regular live-in nuisance is up to his old crap again," the senior officer chided while giving Bentley a frosty stare. " I don't think that's what we saw here, sir," Eugene, the younger officer with a clean shaven face and badge number 54, said. The older security officer ran his fingers through his salt and pepper goatee, his eyes never leaving the sight of Andrew and his new acquaintance. "I believe I'll be the judge of what we saw, 54," said the older officer who had finished his chin-strumming and placed his hand on his faux leather basket-weave utility belt. The older officer walked over to the side of the old Chevy truck and looked down at the man who lay on the ground beside it; the man was starting to wake. "So if you didn't do this, Bentley, who did?" he asked. Andrew's fighting companion was combing his hair, and didn't speak or acknowledge the officer until he was done, "Well, technically I didn't do that. Not directly, anyway...but, I have to tell you, this guy and some friends of his really did start all this." Andrew, still fueled by the power of "what the heck", couldn't help but join in: "They were drunk. You could tell." The senior bicycle officer turned to Andrew with a flash of anger in his eyes; his new acquaintance was laughing and loving it. The officer drew what Andrew perceived to be a deep inhale of pre-yelling air, but did not have the chance to speak–his subordinate spoke instead: "Well Mr. Bentley, I'm inclined to side with you, but we're gonna have to ask you to leave this and stay inside for the night." Andrew thought it odd that he and his new acquaintance would be allowed to leave such a scene so easily; he thought it *outright bizarre* that Bentley was told to "stay inside" rather than to leave for the night.

Bentley motioned with his hand for Andrew to come with him. As the two men were walking away from the scene, Bentley spoke, "So, to whom do I direct the thanks and praise for such unexpected aid?" Andrew answered back, "My name is Andrew. Why the hell were those men after you like that anyway?" "Bentley" was brushing himself off and meticulously noting the damage which his clothing had suffered. "They *suck* at poker. Wait," he stopped in his tracks and continued, "you didn't ask my name. And I definitely would remember someone like you. You sound like you've never seen anything north of the Mason-Dixon Line, and you strike me as half crazy, and half-likely to care. You don't *know* me?" The man's playful cerulean eyes widened as his thoughts rushed from his mind to his face with seemingly little or no filter between what he thought and how he appeared and spoke.

Andrew was a little hurt by what he felt the man was insinuating: that a good person should, in Vegas, need a *reason* for coming to a stranger's aid. Andrew turned to face him and said, "What do you mean by that? Nice people help one another when in need where I come from." "Don't be so upset," The man said, "I meant that I'm pretty well known around here, not that you aren't a decent person." Andrew resumed walking, heading in the direction in which he was previously being led: towards a side entrance to the right of the main canopy. The side entrance doors were dark oak with small glass windows near the top, and a lot less glamorous than what Andrew had always assumed casino doors looked like, even the side doors. The man called out from behind while walking briskly to catch up with Andrew, "It's Connor Bentley, by the way." Andrew slowed to a stop when he was within a few feet of the doors. He hadn't realized until then that this Connor Bentley would want to re-enter the place he was only just a few minutes ago chased out of unarmed and outnumbered and facing physical peril. Despite his willingness to help a victim or join Connor in mocking authority, Andrew wasn't in the mood to gamble. It wasn't a lack of courage, but merely that he had no money and zero interest in gambling. He was still thinking about the fight he had been in, and when that matter was mentally resolved, he still had Sarah to think and stress out about; for the time being, thoughts about enjoying gambling would have to get in line.

Connor Bentley caught up to Andrew and kept walking towards the nearby casino doors. When he got to the pair of wooden doors he opened the door to his left and took a bow while opening it. "Aren't you coming in, sir?" asked Mr. Bentley, in a bad attempt at a snobbish butler voice. Andrew looked at Connor's smiling face and said, "Why? I don't really gamble much, especially not tonight, if you don't mind." "Why?" Connor replied, "Because two against three is a risky endeavor, so you've already been a gambler tonight. And you seem to have too much 'don't give a damn' to have anything better to do." Andrew took a look through the open doorway to see an ocean of glimmering lights; from where he stood, about ten feet away from the doors, he could distinctly make out the incessant beeping and ringing of hundreds of machines which echoed from within the casino.

Nothing was in synch: all of the sounds and sights expressed themselves out of unison. A sea of ever-changing sounds lay within, the portal to which was being offered by an eccentric man whom Andrew had never met before. Andrew continued to stare, noting to himself how all of the symbols, sounds and lights within were designed to cater to the desperate. *Most of the people here probably feel a little like me, and come hoping to either have a win, or at the very least be temporarily distracted from their problems,* Andrew thought. He figured that the place would be at the very least a chance to escape his current thoughts, which were drifting back to Sarah, a chance to momentarily escape. A chance he was willing to take.

"So, how exactly did that whole thing end with you and I not going to jail?" Andrew asked as he followed the slow but steady walking pace of Connor Bentley. "Not all security is so bad – one or two of them like me yet. Now the swing shift supervisors, that's a different story," he added as he pointed a spot not far up their path to the left, "The Lone Star Bar, where you're never far from a cold beer or a broken heart."

They reached their destination: an old, dark stained oak bar with a heavily tarnished brass rail at the bottom which went around the entire bar. Old studded leather barstools sat in a line underneath the bar; of the bars twenty or so seats, only six were filled. In front of each stool was a video poker machine built into the bar. There were two wooden spindle-like pillars inside the bar's oval, one near each end. The pillars were covered with Texas-esque bric-a-brac. There was more Lone Star State décor above the bar which was parted for the occasional digital television. A seven-foot golden flagpole, complete with a gargantuan Lone Star flag sat in the exact center of the bartender pit. Connor had already hopped lightly upon one of the aged stools and pointed for Andrew to sit next to him.

Andrew sat down next to Connor. "Well, Connor Bentley, nice to meet you, but I just realized that I'm broke," he said while shifting his eyes from the booze racks which bookended the Texas flag to the blue video poker screen on the bar, whose buttons currently cradled his scratched up fingers. "Obviously, the drinks are on me, killer," Connor said. Andrew's chest was still heaving. "And besides–you seem just interesting enough to keep around for a while. And you can stop it with the 'Connor Bentley' stuff. It's 'Con-Man' to my friends and all the Texas Palace." Andrew didn't know if he should feel complimented or insulted, but he was inquisitive enough to ask: "Interesting?" Connor put a bill in the poker machine in front of him and replied, "Yeah, interesting. Not in a bad way, of course. You help people without asking their name without even knowing them. You've looked at liquor and gambling devices but used neither. I don't know, kid, you're just different, that's all. Heck, I bet there's more to that name of yours than just Andy." Andrew winced at the sound of his name's traditional short form; he felt that it was a bit feminine for a man and had a general dislike for the sound of it. "Ok, 'Con-Man', don't be usin' that on me. "And my name is Andrew Claude Bennet Cadoret." Connor flagged down the bartender. "Andrew Claude Be...ok, that's just never gonna work. Where you from, kid?" Andrew felt it odd to still be hearing the "k word" after 25 years of life. *This "Con-Man" could only be in his late thirties at the oldest,* he thought. He began to reply, "Virginia, I–." Connor waved his hands in dismissal as the bartender came up to the two of them and said, "I meant where in Clark County. Where in our fair valley?" The Con-Man was nice enough to accompany his words with finger gestures which made the shape of a box.

A short, stout, bartender with deep tan skin and a shaved head came over to Connor and Andrew's section of the bar. He looked first at Connor, who greeted him warmly, "Howard! How are you tonight you crusty old bastard? I'll take an Old Fashioned." The bartender laughed and replied, "Fine, fine," then turned his attention to Andrew, asking, "And you, sir?" Andrew replied with one simple word: "cola." Andrew turned his attention back to Connor and said, "Summerlin, I guess. But I'm not there anymore." Connor grabbed his newly arrived cocktail and took a sip. He wiped his lips afterwards and said, "Of course you're not there. You're here. Summerlin, eh? I think that'll do. Pass the pretzels, Summerlin." He leaned back and slung his right elbow over the rim of the empty seat to his right; he was a picture-perfect postcard of an odd man at ease. It was at that time that Andrew took a moment to notice what his acquaintance was wearing: it was a suit of high-quality cloth, and the buttons on his cuffs had black signatures on them, something Italian-looking that started with a V. "I don't like that, it sounds girly," Andrew protested. Connor took another sip from his drink and said, "A cat might hate being called a cat. It wouldn't change the name of the creature either way." Andrew sighed and thought, *With my luck a name like that is likely to stick.*

Andrew finished his glass of soda in a series of large gulps. His eyes dropped to his empty glass, and his mind left the brightly flashing buttons and ice cream truck melodies of the poker machine. Up until this point, Andrew had been occupied with pressing matters involving physical well-being; however, as the dangers of the parking lot had worn off, Andrews mind began to drift back to thoughts of loss and pain. Connor Bentley snapped his finger by Andrew's ear, yelling

"Summerlin! Summerlin!" as he did so. Andrew roused from his self-questioning and pushed away Connor Bentley's snapping fingers.

As he raised his head Andrew said, "I—I'm sorry." It was the best he could do; his mind was only then clearing enough for conversation. After a few composure-regaining moments, he cleared his throat and said, "I kind of got pulled away there once the chaos died down." Connor had a stern, concentrating look about him when he turned and spoke with a smile, "Well, it sounds like you need more chaos, then." He pulled a twenty dollar bill from his snakeskin wallet and slid it over towards Andrew. "What's this?" Andrew said as he pushed the bill back towards Connor, adding, "No thank you; I don't take charity, and I'll never accept money for doing something any halfway decent person would do." Connor took the bill and stood. He walked over to Andrew's left and placed his twenty into Andrew's machine, speaking as he did so, "Well then, consider it an investment. If you win you can give it back; lose and I'll take a toast as payment. You appear to be a nice guy, Summerlin, you just gotta learn to calm down. Before returning to his seat, Connor pressed the illuminated button labeled "Deal" on Andrew's machine. Once reseated, Connor put a twenty into his machine, and then placed a royal blue card into the machine's loyalty card reader; the program was called the "Palace Points Loyalty Club." He began to speak while pressing the buttons rapidly, "You seem like a nice kid who has merely landed in a little trouble. You helped me; heck, you didn't even know me, despite my obvious local fame. Maybe I could try to return the favor. What's your problem anyway? Lay it on me, man."

Andrew's first instincts are to outright decry "No. There is no hope for I". Pathetic. Poetic, but pathetic nonetheless. In the end, he decided that he might as well follow the night's trend of going with the unexpected, so he replied to Connor Bentley's offer, "Oh, maybe. I've lost the life that I thought I was meant to be mine. I've lost my muse, and I've lost myself." Andrew's words began to take on an irritated tone, with each syllable being more pronounced than the last. He continued,

"I had a plan; *we* had plans. I worked hard to help us achieve our goals. I honored her—" he was interrupted by a statement which began with an "Ah Ah Ah", like one would expect to hear from a child when an adult forgot to say the magic word, "I see what this is. Girl trouble." Andrew replied, "It's a little more complex than that—" His words were once again cut short; however, it was not due to Connor this time, at least not due to his voice. A group of adult men and women had cheered "Con-Man!" from the other side of the bar, near the Race and Sports Book area. Connor smiled ear to ear. He waved back to the group of six people and then leaned in towards Andrew and said, "Sorry kid. Occupational hazard. Go on." Andrew nodded and continued, "I lost more than just a girl. She is the only explanation of love my heart has ever wanted. In every meaning of the word. I lost everything that I had planned in my life as well. Look at me: I was in a nice apartment with a bed which I thought I'd see again. Now don't be offended, I'm having a great time and all," Andrew said in a sarcastic tone before continuing in his normal voice, "But I'm goal-less, homeless and broke. I've lost all prospects I had for gainful employment." After he had finished speaking, Connor retorted, "But you're still alive and seem to be relatively healthy. Actually, you're a lot stronger than you looked at first, anyway." Andrew ran his index finger around the rim of his empty glass. "I don't fight. I defend myself, that's all," he said. "I am not you. And you defended me," Connor chided. Andrew ceased is playing with the glass and looked directly in Connor's eyes and said, "What can I say, I was bored." He smiled afterwards and Connor laughed as he resumed his recline, extended elbow and all. The Con-Man continued to click the buttons on his video poker machine. "Bored or not, Summerlin, it shows that there must be something worth saving about you," he said while his machine played a short victory melody. Nothing is final except the river, kid." Connor gestured for Andrew to play his machine. Except for the first hand which was commenced by Connor, Andrew had been neglecting the remaining credits on the machine. He looked down at the result of the first hand—A would-be straight to the queen which was busted with a four of clubs. "Try it. At least you'll be distracted, right?" said Connor. Andrew was quick to respond, "With my luck? You'll soon be out a twenty." "Well, I won't be out a memory," Connor said, "Trust me, if your 'plans' are so important, or at all retainable, they will still be there after you take a rest." The bartender returned to the two men and served them another round of drinks. After playing another losing hand, Andrew glanced at Connor, who was taking a sip of his Old Fashioned and contemplating which cards to replace on the draw. Connor noticed that Andrew had stopped playing to observe him; he stopped tapping his buttons and said, "Rest from thinking about how you have 'nothing to rest from', then. For tonight and for now, just focus on the red and blacks."

Clicking buttons and making one draw after another lent well to passing time—soft, distinct classic rock, and a long, drawn-out discussion of the merits and detractions of the Designated Hitter Rule all but obliterated the worries that did so recently torment him, at least for the time being. Andrew even joined Connor in a drink, albeit a beer. An hour or so in, and twelve dollars the richer, Andrew looked up to see Connor talking to two giggling cocktail waitresses in leather miniskirts. *Who is this guy?* He wondered. When Connor finally returned to his seat, Andrew said, "I have to ask, what is it that you do? For a living, I mean." Connor rested his hands behind his head and spun in his stool slightly. "I do what I do. Nah, I'm just a gamblin' man; you know, ponies and poker, mostly," he replied. Andrew reacted to Connor's response with a wide-eyed jerk backwards which resembled that of a person being told that they are in fact the king of Neptune. "You gamble for a *living*?" he asked. "Or I live for gambling; same thing," the Con-Man replied.

Andrew sat back with a serious expression for a moment before turning back to Connor to say, "You know, Con-Man, there are so many questions which I could ask. Problem is, I am lead to believe by your nature that you've already been asked the questions before; probably often, perhaps too often." Connor's eyes widened and he said, "And its stuff like that which makes me need to further understand the oddness that is you." "Gee, thanks," Andrew spouted. Connor happily replied, "Hey, it might not be the best thing you could have going for you, kid, but you gotta take it where you can get it; a 'jacks or better' beats a rag-fold."

The two played for another hour, at which point Connor checked his wrist, which had several wristwatches and one or two other wrist-strapped devices, and rose from his seat. "Well look at the time. I had hoped to get some things done tonight. Can't always anticipate a mob of angry idiots. Anyhow, I'm thinking of hitting the King-Size," he said. Andrew was about to speak, but was cut off by Connor, "I know, I know. You're homeless. Luckily, the Austin Suite has an extra room, and you're outright interesting enough to let use it, Captain Lonely-Heart." Andrew sighed and thought, *Ok. Maybe Summerlin isn't the worst name, after all.*

Andrew followed Connor through the casino to the hotel elevators. At the far right of the elevators stood a glass door framed in whitewashed teak, with a brass sign upon it reading "TO THE SWIMMING POOL". In his opinion, the elevators took too long to arrive. The lobby was covered in Texas gilt and gold, and the inside of the elevator continued that trend. A large, thick, garish gold frame, done in French style, enclosed an oil painting of a field of soft rolling Texan hills in the sunlight with a line of old-fashioned oil derricks–the ones in the black and white movies—running from the foreground to the horizon. The classic rock of the Lone Star Bar had been replaced by 90's country. Garth, George Strait and Reba all had their turn on the elevator speakers before the elevator had finally been emptied of all of its passengers, save for Connor and Andrew, and an older Asian man reading a newspaper while humming along to "Why Haven't I Heard From You?"

With only two more floors until the one at the top labeled "Suites", Andrew felt too weary to endure standing and leaned his side against the elevator wall; he was leaning, yet he did not look relaxed at all. He looked weary and worn. Connor Bentley was also leaning against the elevator on the other side, but with a general élan about him. Two people can engage in the exact same activity, yet appear completely different when they do it. Such was the case with the two new friends as they waited for the elevator doors to open on the suite level. Before they reached the top, a grinning Connor said to Andrew, "Your shirt's torn. Kinda ratty." A very tired Andrew replied without turning, "We don't all wear Italian fancy clothes." He had pronounced "Italian" in his mild Southern drawl, as "Aye-talian", which caused Connor to wince in disgust.

A ding came from the overhead speakers, and the doors opened. The two exited, and they walked down a somewhat extravagant hallway; the carpet was thick and plush beneath Andrew's sore, weary feat. The walls had wooden moldings, and the ten foot ceiling had a beautiful white "popcorn" texture. Connor jaunted casually forward, and Andrew followed slowly behind him. Connor stopped at a set of double doors to their left. He pulled out a hotel keycard and slid it into the door, withdrawing it quickly, which caused the door to flash a green light and to click loudly as the door unlocked. The left door remained closed as Connor opened the right one widely and gestured in a host-like manner, bow included, for him to enter the room. As Andrew did so, he noticed that there was an oval brass plaque on the left door which had the words "The Austin Suite" carved on it instead of a room number. The doors across the hall had the words "The Dallas Suite" inscribed in the same fashion.

The white molded-panel door opened to a vast black marble landing that in turn led to a Great Room, which served as a game room, lounge and bar area within its length, which was close to a football field's.

"Home sweet home. At least for the past five years or so," Connor said as he walked through the great room, heading towards the archway to the left side of the landing. Andrew gazed upwards at the great room's ceiling, which was at least eleven feet tall—easily the highest hotel room ceiling that he had ever seen. White paint is supposed to be subtle, but there was no way that the décor of the Austin Suite, nor the man himself, could ever be subtle.

The walls were full of pictures and objects, most of which were related to horses. The largest wall hanging was on the wall directly facing–and visible from—the landing. It was a massive poster-sized framed photograph of the local Vegas newspaper which had a picture of Connor smiling while giving a champagne toast to the camera; the headline of the newspaper read "Prince of Ponies." To the right of the great room hung a large oak framed painting which had a brass nameplate engraved "Secretariat" at the bottom center of the frame. The rest of the space on the great room's walls were devoted to a mélange of personalized celebrity autographs and old-fashioned racing tack. Even in the room's current dim conditions, it was almost too much for Andrew's eyes to take. Several old-fashioned arcade games sat along the back wall of the game room. The great room's leftmost section was a wet-bar. It was a fully stocked bar with seats for four, complete with its own polished brass foot-rail, and two televisions overhead. The section of the great room which lay closest to the right archway was the lounge area, which had two studded leather chairs, four wooden bookcases filled with leather-backed tomes in varying states of condition, and a large aquarium with two rather large goldfish swimming in it.

The game room section of the great room was in the center of the room, directly facing the landing. This section of the great room was elevated above the others. The crimson-colored carpeting of the elevated platform continued off the platform and down the three small staircases—one facing the landing, one on the left side and one on the right.

Connor flipped a switch, and the room was illuminated by a series of low-intensity dome lights located not on the suite's ceiling, but on the walls about a foot below the ceiling. "Take a right and go down the hall–the third door down will get you there. Feel free to admire the interior décor," Connor said as he walked to the opposite side of the room, vanishing beneath the shadow of the archway. Andrew slowly, almost blindly stepped towards the archway to his right, glancing lightly at the walls and counting the doorknobs until he had reached the third. A rational-minded and well-rested Andrew would have had an interest in knowing what lay beyond all the doors, but he was too worn out to care.

Andrew didn't turn on the lights when he opened the door. He plunged into the room's shadows seeking anything relatively level to sleep upon. His hands found at last the velvety soft texture of a hotel-style bedspread. He lunged onto the bed and landed with a soft flop. Without even so much as reaching for a pillow, he was asleep.

2.

Country ears should never in a city-wise manner be awoken. It was not a radio, nor lights, nor a living human being next to him that woke Andrew, but the sounds of loud, large construction equipment clanging girders into place. There was little light, and it was only after a few moments of blurry-eyed mind clearing did he finally give notice to the décor of the room. It was money. All of it. Upon the guest room walls there was every adornment conceivable to man concerning the topic; so much so, Andrew almost swore he could smell the damned stuff. The framed art was a collection of everything from images depicting familiar bills, to actual pressed collections of monetary units so foreign to Andrew's eyes that he couldn't discern their origin. The rugs looked like greenbacks. There were several small paperweights and such on the desk near the bed with money-themed sheets. They were all enlarged reproductions of famous coins both golden and mundane. "I think I sense a theme here," Andrew said as he rubbed his neck after rising from bed.

Andrew looked at himself in the mirror; he was unshaven, bruised in several places, and his clothes bore several tears and other marks of battle. He entered the right side of the great room to find it fully lit—part by lamplight, and part by curtain-veiled sunlight. There was nobody around, *Not in the main room, anyway*, Andrew thought. It didn't seem right in his mind to go sneaking around to find out what lay behind the several closed doors, so he headed straight to the double doors at the end of the landing. It was the same as he had remembered from last night, except there was a brown paper-wrapped parcel with a white envelope on its face, hanging from a piece of twine on a brass hook which was positioned on the non-opening right door.

So, the oddness persists, he thought to himself, and he walked to the doors and retrieved the package, taking a seat with it upon a black wrought-iron chair which sat to the far left of the double doors next to a similarly made table for one with a pile of unopened letters upon it. The envelope read: "Profit waits for no man. Do your worrying-ass a favor, and just chill at the Palace. Enclosed is a new shirt—I know you consider my love of fashion to be excessive, but, you simply cannot go out in public with a torn shirt like that. It's rude. See you and the rest of the crazies at the Railyard, you'll know T.R.Y."

The "shirt enclosed" was a short sleeved silk button up with a left-breast pocket, which contained a folded twenty-dollar bill. *Who is this guy?* Andrew wondered.

The Texas-tacky elevator came within moments of a button's press. This time it was "Guys Do It All The Time" piped through overhead speakers. Ding. The doors slowly lurched open with a rubber-grinding squeak. And there it was, that somber yet delusional, hopeful land of monetary dreamers, made spiritually complete with endless deer-antler chandeliers lighting nearly-threadbare 70's carpeting, trod upon by those of every sort of fate. The cacophony of beeps, dings, clangs and "cash-out" sounds made it hard to focus, let alone grant a displaced Virginia man time to devise a strategy for his life. Andrew tried his best to keep his bearings, but it dawned upon him after only a few moments that due to the prior night's activities, and the sadness, weariness and alcohol consumption that it entailed, he had absolutely no idea where he was. His instincts told him to try to return to the "Lone Star Bar." *Yes. That's got to be the best option*, he thought. *Okay. Find a Lone Star flag. In here, where everything is screaming Texas so loudly that you almost have to formally request a break.*

It soon became apparent that Texas Palace had more than one bar. Five, he was told, when he inquired of a slot-technician passing by. "Go straight, past the buffet, then bear left and it will be past the Race and Sports area on your left," the technician said. Andrew tried his best to understand the man, and he certainly seemed nice enough, but possessed an accent so thick that he wasn't even sure which continent the man came from. "Sorry, could you say that again?" Andrew had to ask twice before finally garnering enough information to head out with a mild pace to the Lone Star Bar.

It didn't take long. It was vaguely memorable. The flag still stood tall and with distinction. The lung-filling miasma of pipe and cigar tobacco, fresh brewed discount coffee, and beer was twice as strong as he remembered. He walked up to the bar and took a seat at the stool which Connor had occupied the night before. The bar was at quarter capacity, at best. Only one bartender was present, and he was on the other side of the large oval bar. It wasn't Howard, either. Two of the televisions were showing a sports channel talk show, while the others showed a combination of live horse racing telecasts, Texas Palace's Keno results channel, and an odd channel which seemed to always be showing foreign drag-racing, whether day or night. The old leather stool bobbed slightly as he sat upon it, and he gazed ahead, towards the Race and Sports area, to see the long lines of paper and pencil holding gamblers. *They each have their own idea of what's gonna happen*, he thought. He then realized that he had little in common with those men and women—he *wished* he would have even some vague notion of what was going to happen in his life, whether it were good or evil. And such thoughts inevitably led to his thinking about Sarah. He pulled out his worn leather wallet and opened it. Sarah and himself, about a year ago, happily sitting together on a long log with green grass and trees in the distance. She had her arms lovingly placed around his neck, nearly kissing his cheek while smiling. Her long brown hair was relatively tame in the photo; *not a common occurrence*, he thought. *When did a year go from being an easily-metered, short span of time to an age untouchable, and utterly far in the past?* The photo was a memento from a visit to a local park near where they had lived—Andrew's place— for sixteen months of planning and saving before moving out west. To where the sky at night never fully turns black.

Andrew's eyes tingled with the sensation of oncoming tears when he was called back to earth by a tall tan-skinned bartender with a nametag which read "Fugi." "What can I get for you, sir?" he asked with a voice which had the slightest hint of an accent of dubious origin. "Oh, me?" Andrew said as he quickly tried to come up with a request, realizing that he was neither thirsty, nor in any great hurry to gamble. "So, Fugi, eh? Where are you from, sir?" he hastily inquired. "Detroit," Fugi replied, just as hastily. The bartender's demeanor had shifted from hospitable to scrutinizing; he spoke: "Is there anything I can get you, sir?" Fugi was looking down at Andrew's video poker screen. More specifically, he was looking down at Andrew's machine and noting it's unused status. "Oh, er, sorry. I forgot that this place is all business," he said. Fugi smiled slightly – and responded, "Actually, I just have to card you. You can play or not play, it won't really affect me." Andrew withdrew his driver's license from his wallet and handed it to the bartender. Fugi handed Andrew his card back and said, "You're fine by the law, so you're fine by me. You might wanna try cheering up though. A moping sad sack like you might drive off potential customers. Chill out. Drink?"

Andrew's stomach rumbled. He had forgotten to eat dinner the night before, and had been lately so driven by novelty and chaos that he had forgotten to stop for a meal. Andrew asked him, "Where is the food court from here?" Fugi nodded and said, "It's by the movie theatre; you know, in the 'Green Zone' that it's ok for kids to be in. Look for high schoolers sipping sodas and you're there." Andrew thanked Fugi and wandered off, keeping an eye out for signs to the movie theatre.

As he began his walk to the food court, Andrew thought he had heard a man's voice say the word "Wait," from somewhere behind him; however he was barely able to notice it through the casino's wall of electric sounds, and gave it little regard. *Who knows who that was intended for*, he thought. He continued his journey for food, following the overhead signs, following specifically the path for the movie theatre, which kept him going in the right direction the entire time. "Hey! You!" Andrew *definitely* heard it loud and clear that time. This loud yelling came from not far behind him. He slowed his gait, but kept moving forward. A cold chill ran down Andrew's spine as he felt an unexpected touch on his shoulder. Andrew stopped cold in his tracks. "Yes, you!" The man's voice yelled out, "Summerlin!" "It's *Andrew*," he uttered in a suspicious tone as he turned to face the man who had been trying so hard to get his attention. The young man was holding an index card; Andrew could make out, in large letters, the word "SUMMERLIN" on the card amidst a field of cursive which from his distance seemed like loopy gibberish. The man appeared to be in his middle or late twenties. His hair was light brown and fashioned into a spiky hairstyle. He had a bad-boy grin and a face which was shaven, yet had a few patches of unshaven stubble–hairs he had missed. Although this man's smile looked kind, there was a wild look to his eyes–Andrew sensed there must be something tempestuous dwelling deep within him. He was wearing jeans and a white t-shirt and a pair of black hi-tops. He had a black shirt with a red collar slung over his left arm.

"I was told by the Con-Man to keep a lookout for," he read the next part from his index card verbatim, "'a sad looking kid who won't be drinking or gambling.' I saw you there for a while and just assumed." The young man then looked Andrew over before adding "And dude, if that isn't you I'll eat the egg salad at the buffet!" "What's so bad about the buffet's egg salad?" Andrew asked. "Let's just say the eggs would have been as likely to hiss as to cluck," the young man replied. His brows raised inquisitively and he said, "Ok, just need to make note of something." "What's that?" asked Andrew. "You told me your name and we have talked without you ever asking mine, or why I was told to find you – instead you ask about the m-f'ing buffet! Strange, dude," The man replied. He looked a little angry, and Andrew could see the young man's eyes lock on him, as if he were enraged with Andrew for some reason. The young man then burst out laughing; Andrew breathed a deep sigh of relief and tried his best to smile while the man's laughing slowly dwindled. *This is apparently hilarious*, Andrew thought; *his* irritation and possible anger would not be nearly so staged.

"Ok, ok, maybe the joke at the end was too much; but I do think you're different, and that's not a bad thing," the man said. "People keep telling me that lately," Andrew added. "Ever wonder why?" the man asked as he started to walk and gestured for Andrew to follow. As he caught up with the man, Andrew said, "So, what *is* your name?" The man sighs and responds, "Xero. I'm Xero." Andrew was perplexed. "Zero? Like the number for nothing?" he asked. "No, Xero, with an 'x', like this lead-guitar playing, smooth-ass bar-back you're looking at right now," he said as his arms swept in an arc before returning to his sides. Andrew grinned and said, "Xero. With an 'x'. And I'm interesting?" For a moment that good old "chaos prevents me from worrying about life" feeling returned, and with it so did Andrew's smile.

"All right. I was supposed to find you; I accomplished that part. Now the next part is on you. Connor's instructions are that you are to 'relax your overly-worried ass at the Derrick Bar'. Do I need to give you directions?" Xero asked as he pointed to a location off to their right.

In the distance Andrew could make out a tall object which resembled a cartoon-style oil derrick with a circular bar beneath it. "No. I don't think that will be necessary. Thanks, though. Are you not coming with me then?" Andrew asked. Xero replied, "Yes and no. I gotta leave you for a moment though. Just go to the Derrick Bar." Xero lifted up his collared shirt, which Andrew noticed had a small Texas Palace Logo above a pocket on the upper right breast of the shirt, opposite where the nametag would be. *He works here?* Andrew thought as he watched Xero put his arms through the sleeves and begin to button it up as he headed off in the opposite direction of the Derrick Bar. And the man with the X in his name was gone. There were less seats at this bar than at the Lone Star; however, there were several small tables with chairs encircling the derrick. Andrew thought that the bar looked a little classier than its predecessor—well, less dirty-looking, anyway. He took at the bar facing the direction in which he had come, with the Lone Star Bar and the Race and Sports Book in the distance.

Once seated, he raised a hand up in the air in an attempt to summon one of the two bartenders tending the Derrick. One of them, a woman in her forties with frosted brown curly hair, was sauntering up to Andrew's spot at the bar, but she stopped and stepped back upon hearing a familiar voice, "That one's mine. Con-Man's orders." It was Xero, except his shirt was buttoned all the way up and now had a Texas Palace nametag bearing the name "Xero" on it. *I can't believe that he actually got the company to print that*, Andrew thought after he saw it. "I told you I wasn't leaving you. I just had to clock in. I love music and friends, but I'm no millionaire," Xero said. Andrew, still admiring the novelty of Xero's nametag, said, "So the bar-back/guitarist thing wasn't just for effect?" Xero replied while he finished wiping the bar top clean, "Well, on-call bar-back; hoping for full-time guitarist." Without

Andrew having noticed or asked, Xero had poured him a glass of soda while he was speaking. "Well, that's nice. I hope that it works out for you. How soon does Mr. Bentley's plan allow me to eat?" Xero laughed for a moment and replied, "He said you'd ask that first." Xero then reached into his right pocket and pulled out a dollar bill-sized piece of paper with a Texas Palace logo with "BUFFET" printed in large bold-scripted letters across the center. Andrew squeamishly glanced from the buffet ticket to Xero. "I thought the buffet was supposed to be awful," he said. "Just avoid the egg salad and you'll be ok. And don't steal the silver-ware," Xero replied. Andrew couldn't resist; he needed to know. "Ok, I'll bite—what happens if you steal the silverware?" he asked. Xero looked Andrew straight in the eye and said, "They make you eat the egg salad."

Andrew looked down at the video poker machine and briefly considered putting the twenty Connor had given him inside of the machine just for the fun of it. Before he had the chance, Xero returned from serving a nearby patron. He began to wipe down the bar top and said, "Gonna play?" Andrew looked dismissively at the machine and said, "Nah, not right now anyhow. By the way, you said 'Con-Man's orders' earlier. Why did I have to come here instead of just wandering?" Xero laughed lightly and then replied, "The Con-Man said you might need some looking after. He's usually right." A group of women waved for Xero from the other side of the bar. "Hold on," he said as he went to help them.

The buffet ticket showed a Texas Palace logo—A T and P with a lone star in the center— written in and encircled with blue on a white background. There was a faded red star in the center background. There were two rows of numbers on the lower left of the ticket, and each corner had the word "FREE" in glittery, golden letters. The reverse side of the voucher was a gold and white lithograph-style picture of Texas Palace from a Reata Ave point of view. *A little more uptown when seen in monochrome*, Andrew thought.

Xero returned from helping the bartender serving the group of customers. Andrew waited for Xero to be free before asking him, "Hey

Xero with an 'x', what exactly am I supposed to do at the Derrick Bar?" "Whatever you want to do within reason. Curing cancer might be difficult in a place like this," he replied. Andrew looked down at his buffet voucher. "I have no clue what I'm going to do later, but I do know what I want to do right now: I want to eat, and I'm supposed to go to the Rail Yard later" he said while looking from the buffet ticket to Xero as he finished speaking. Xero replied while leaning against the bar, "Everyone will be at the Rail Yard tonight, it's Friday." "Will you be there?" Andrew asked. Xero looked up from his wiping of the bar and grinned before replying, "Yeah, don't worry–you'll see me." Andrew got up from his seat and said, "Nice meeting you, number man. See you tonight, then." As he started off, he heard Xero's voice call out from behind him while he was inspecting an overhead sign, "Summerlin! Make sure you try the salsa!" Andrew walked to the buffet, stopping momentarily at a slot machine, giving the idea of playing it plenty of thought. He reached into his pocket to retrieve the twenty, but his stomach roared loudly, and Andrew returned to his original purpose, turning down his chance to play "Super Mega Insane Sevens" for the necessity of food. He was once again on his way.

The buffet had a huge wooden "Texas Buffet" sign over its two entry archways. The archway on the left had a small wooden "in" sign above it and a podium with a hostess just inside it, visible from several feet outside the place. The only thing that separated Andrew from eating was a long brass stockade, and the early-lunch crowd which at that point filled it. Mostly old people, and a few severely obese persons with fanny packs, clearly there to take advantage of the "all-you-can-eat" component of the buffet's lunch deal. There were signs for the lunch special, several featuring smiling poster models who were dressed to impersonate local everyday patrons, all over the place.

I just want a small, quick bite to eat, Andrew thought. The music playing overhead at the time was "Don't Stop Believin'." The song was over before Andrew got up to the hostess podium. A twenty-something brunette with a ponytail and a nametag reading "Judy" smiled and said, "How many, sir?" Andrew handed the hostess the voucher which Xero had given him and said, "one, please." She smiled and said "Right this way, follow me," as she led him to a table near the salsa bar. A normal Andrew who was not lovelorn would have noticed the hostess's youthful form—she was quite pretty, and had a lovely smile. Instead of noticing the powder pink ribbon which held Judy's ponytailed hair, Andrew noticed the stagecoach-themed pattern of the buffet's carpeting. It was auburn, extremely faded, and still bore the vaguest scent of tobacco smoke from back when smoking in restaurants was still legal in Las Vegas. Once the hostess had seated Andrew she said, "Your server will be around soon to give you silverware and get you something to drink. Tell Connor I said hi!" She was off before Summerlin had the chance to ask her any questions.

The booth was upholstered with dark brown leatherette which squeaked with every minor motion of Andrew's body. He looked around to see families, seniors, and a few persons whose largeness required an entire booth to themselves. It was a buffet, so there were no menus. His place at the table was actually bare; the plates and bowls were in stacks at each and every food station. After a few minutes of Andrew strumming his finger upon the white buffet tablecloth, the server came and gave him his silverware and took his order for a cola. Andrew now merely had to choose what he wanted to eat for the meal that he would call lunch for the day. He rose from his chair and walked out towards the sea of food stations; There were many different choices available, with each station having its own theme: Chinese, Mexican, BBQ, pizza, American, "fish of the world", salad, crepes, and dessert. The entire wall which faced the entryways and ran the length of the buffet was filled with back to back stations the entire distance. The breakfast, salad, crepe and dessert stations were all islands which stood closer to the table area than the others. In the corner nearby the "American" station, which from the entrance would be on the far right, there was a small, quaint-looking salsa bar with a carved-wooden sign that said "Salsa Loca! Andrew ended up settling on a slice of pepperoni pizza, a side of chow mein noodles, and, as per Xero's request, a bowl of salsa with two handfuls of chips; he chose the mild flavor.

The food was decent; however, Andrew found the salsa to be a little too hot, especially for a product being marketed under the label "mild". He did not steal the silverware. He left a tip for the drink server and departed. He decided to take a stroll around the place; *Maybe there'll be a 'Help Wanted' sign up somewhere*, Andrew thought. He walked through the countless rows of video poker and slot machines of varying themes and denominations. He didn't notice the machines so much as he did their beeping and ringing as he attempted to get a general feel for the layout of the place.

After less than two minutes of walking with a clueless expression his face, Andrew reached the theatre. Another stockade-like serpentine led to a counter with black and red digital signage above it, and two teenage girls with nametags that said their names along with a company logo, a trident, with the words: "TRIDENT CINEMAS" superimposed behind their names. The name of the theatre flashed on the screens overhead every twenty seconds or so—Andrew took to counting the timing of it as he walked past the Theatre towards the Arcade, and noticed a single pair of simple wooden doors near the door-less arcade entrance. Andrew had thought such institutions of American youth to have been extinct; he hadn't seen a genuine coin-op video game arcade in years. It was, to Andrew's eyes, as if a perfect replica of an arcade from his early childhood had been presented to him. There were over thirty machines, most in the well-known cabinet-style which most people associate with arcade games; there were a few table-style games, and a few skee-ball lanes next to two basketball throwing games in the back. There were also three vehicle-style games: a helicopter, a jet fighter, and a Formula One racecar. There were change machines near the entrance which converted dollars and quarters into arcade tokens. Dim fluorescent lights twitched every so often overhead as he peered inside. *Too many kids. Can't get a quality Galaga score with lots of yelling kids around*, Andrew thought as he saw the machines overrun with unaccompanied minors.

Andrew continued walking. He passed by the Bingo hall, which was on his left; he gave a quick glance inside without so much as slowing down. His brief viewing through the wooden door's small windows gave him a look at a sea of blue hair, and a loud voiced man who called the bingo numbers with such volume that Andrew could hear from outside the place. He then came upon the Keno area.

The Keno area was tucked into the wall on Andrew's right, a sight of aged green vinyl chairs and filthy moss-green carpeting which had been mended with duct tape in several places. A bar-like counter separated customers from the person performing the actual dealing of the game. Beyond the counter lay the massive see-through globe which had many white balls with black numbers on them tumbling perpetually within it. There was a large illuminated grid of the numbers one through ninety-nine above the counter; a few numbers were already lit. The worn green armchairs were populated by a strangely diverse group of people: five or six elderly, depending on one's definition of the word, three men in their early thirties and four Japanese tourists wearing shirts whose logos indicated the various well known casinos on the Las Vegas Strip that they had visited. There was one other person, a man, whom Andrew had failed to notice until his second scan of the Keno area's populace. This man had been hard to find because his face had been obscured from view by a local Vegas newspaper—he was asleep. Keno seemed far too laid-back for a mind which was struggling with fears of loneliness, loss and unemployment. Andrew went onward. He passed several restaurants, and finally got a glimpse of the remaining bars in the place. *They must really, really love their hooch here*, Andrew thought. A restaurant came up on his left as he continued his walkabout of Texas Palace Hotel-Casino. It's tinted glass doors had a frosted relief of angelfish on them, and a sign overhead which said "The Coral Room Seafood and Delicacy Experience." The sign had a fish and a pearl-holding clam, but was conspicuously lacking in any depiction of coral whatsoever. Exiting patrons provided Andrew with a glimpse of long tables with fancy white tablecloths and several nautical statues, all under a subtle, soft blue light. Having just recently eaten, Andrew was nowhere near hungry, yet he liked the look of the place and noted its location for possible later patronage as he kept on walking.

Once again, Andrew found himself navigating a maze of video and slot machine rows and clusters. Eventually, the walkway he was taking through the machines led to a cluster of slot machines. The six-machine cluster sat on an elephantine wooden dias a foot and a half in height; the machines alternated between two machine titles: "Faery Fortune" and "Dixie Dollars". The first game held no interest for him, but the second, Dixie Dollars, made Andrew slow to a stop. He looked over the machine: The canopy and bottom front of the machine had cartoon Rebel soldiers charging at Union officers with moneybags in their hands on a grassy set of hills. *Go for it*, Andrew thought as he retrieved a twenty from his shirt pocket. He started to flatten the bill, but shrugged his shoulders and put the bill back into his right pocket. "Now that's a bold move followed by a weak decision," said a familiar voice coming from somewhere off to Andrew's left. He turned, and saw the Con-Man, leaning with his right elbow out against one of the many large wooden square pillars present throughout Texas Palace. He was dressed in what was, for him, relatively normal attire: dark jeans and a black t-shirt, on which was printed upon, in large white capital letters, "IT IS WHAT IT IS." Andrew lowered his head and took in a few breaths before asking, "Ok, I'll be your huckleberry; what's 'it'?" Connor looked down at his shirt and then waved his hand over it in an up and down motion; he then proceeded to stride around the floor in a long runway-like manner, turning back and striking a pose before returning to his normal gait. Upon seeing this, Andrew thought, *He's smiling with what looks to be–pride?* "What 'it' is, clearly. I had assumed that you could read, Summerlin, I mean, you *sound* different, but it has always resembled English," Connor said with a jokingly serious tone, adjusting his hair by using his reflection off of a video poker machine's glass screen. *Never saw that one before*, Andrew thought. Upon finishing the revision of his coiffure, Connor sprayed himself with two spritzes from a blue cologne bottle.

It was then, when Connor was finished adjusting his appearance, that Andrew noticed his friend's choice in footwear. *Holy Cow!* Andrew thought as he beheld them: They were grey and white tennis shoes with black Velcro straps; except, the shoes had what appeared to be a ring of half-inch thick neon tubing which ran the perimeter of each shoe's bottom from heel to toe. The illuminated tubing in each shoe changed colors each time that a shoe made contact with the ground. Neon shades of blue, pink, orange and green were displayed from Connor's shoes in rapid succession as he walked up to Andrew. "Why did you call my decision weak earlier?" Andrew asked with a mildly irritated expression. The Con-Man's face became uncharacteristically serious for a moment. He looked Andrew dead on in the eyes and said, "Why? Because you had just acted weakly. You wanted to play the Dixie Dollars quarter slots, didn't you? You even went so far as to take the money out of your pocket before deciding to let cowardice dictate your actions. You kept yourself from doing something that you wanted to do. Not an act to be proud of, Summerlin." Andrew looked down for a moment before clearing his throat and responding, "I—I decided that I might need the money to buy food or something. I *am* unemployed, you know. And I can't let you give me any more than you already have; I was raised better than that," Summerlin countered. Connor, who had been grinning throughout the entirety of Andrew's statement, spoke immediately after Andrew finished speaking, "Well, Summerlin, how about you let me completely cover you, monetarily-speaking anyway, for one day and one night. After that, then even this wonderful, generous—I might add stylish—young man will be forced to let you swim on your own insofar as matters of finance are concerned. The info and sage advice are free, so I'll be able to keep those going as long as you like. You can thank me later, Summerlin." Andrew thought it through and was about to ask him what exactly that would entail, but Connor started speaking again, "That way, you'll be able to eat, see the local house band—best in the valley, I might add—and, hopefully, learn to cheer up and relax a little, for the love of God." Andrew immediately rebuked Connor, "Hey there buddy, don't be takin' my Lord's name in vain."

Connor put his hand on Andrew's arm as if he were about to brace down a struggling man and spoke to Andrew in a calm, soothing tone, "Woah there, woah. I am very sorry to have insulted your religion..." Andrew replied calmly and with a smile, "We're fine. Are you—Are you an atheist?" Connor's face looked perplexed. "Am I a what?" he asked. "An atheist," Andrew said, stressing every syllable in his modest Southern accent. "I'm sorry, I'm still not getting it, kid. Some kind of a regional language barrier or something," said Connor apologetically. And at once, Andrew had become the hard-to-understand slot technician from earlier. *Figures*, Andrew thought, *only in Vegas could the tables be turned with such speed.* It was an ironic and funny enough thing to realize for Andrew that he just had to laugh out loud before even attempting to answer Connor again. "An A-T-H-E-I-S-T," he finally replied, looking with hopeful eyes at Connor, and hoping that his friend "got it".

Connor rolled his eyes and replied, "Oh, *that*. Sorry, you speak very well. It's just, well, Summerlin, your voice is a bit, how shall I say it? *Suthrun*." Connor had emphasized the last word by saying in what *he* probably thought was a grand and fine impersonation of a Southern accent—to Andrew's ears, it was not. "And as to religion, it's not that I don't believe in God—it's more an issue of me not adhering to any specific organized religion. I believe you could sum me up with the word *deist*, if I'm not mistaken in the word's meaning, that is. I'll take the Supreme Being, but hold the side of dogma which structured religions tend to create. One really shouldn't make a practice of inquiring as to what religion someone is; it's a little rude and usually starts an argument at some point. For the record, though, I respect your Christian choice, and truly meant it when I apologized. You need to allow yourself to be happy, and part of that has to do with allowing yourself to do what you want—within reason, of course." Andrew turned and faced Connor and replied with a slight touch of bitterness to his words, "Oh? What do you know? I mean, don't get me wrong, I don't intend any disrespect, but you're only a decade older than me, if even that." Connor winked and replied, "Trust me, kid. I don't know everything, but I've lived through enough ups and downs to know that for anything to get better you gotta get relaxed." Andrew looked back at the Dixie Dollars machine and then began to walk back to it. "I admire the enthusiasm, Summerlin, but there's no time for that now. Do it later," Connor said before Andrew could reach the machine. He turned from the machine to look back at Connor and asked, "Why?" Connor replied, "Well, since you're here, we might as well go to the Derrick, take in a few fermented beverages and get ready for the show." Andrew sighed and said, "I'm guessing that if I say anything about not going you'll counter with 'you have nothing better to do, so we might as well do it your way." Connor grinned and said, "You learn quick, kid."

They walked together with Connor leading the way, stopping ever often to say "hi" to someone he knew, or to give a Texas Palace employee a high-five. On the way to the Derrick Bar, Andrew decided to fill the silence by asking Connor something which he had been wanting to know all day, "Hey Connor, what was with the odd placement of the word 'try' in the note you left me?" Connor replied without missing a step, "That's 'The Reason Why', the house band I mentioned earlier. The

'Y' obviously represents the interrogative word; clever, huh?" Andrew nodded and said, "Oh, I get it."

Although it came upon him abruptly, Andrew's current schedule being scripted for him for the moment was a welcome relief; having less choices meant having less worries, in his current mind state, anyway. Instead of worrying about Sarah, employment, or even how many credits to bet per line, Andrew had the pleasure of following someone else's path. *At least the people seem interesting*, Andrew thought as he caught random glimpses of various persons along the way—In Vegas, one is never too far from a millionaire or a bum. As the two of them neared the Derrick Bar Andrew thought, *And the house band at a casino called "Texas Palace" is bound to play country, right?*

The two men arrived at the bar and took their seats. Andrew hadn't fully sat down before a fifty dollar bill was slid his way. "What's this for? I still have money from before, and you know it." Connor gave him a dismissive look before hailing the bartender and saying, "Just adding to your allowance, Summerlin." Andrew realized that he had agreed to do things Connor's way. He put the fifty into the blue-screened video poker machine. Connor took a sip from the Old Fashioned which he had ordered. The bartender slid Andrew a bottle of beer. He raised the bottle towards Connor and said, "Thanks." He took a sip of the frosty brew. After a few such refreshing sips and the "ahhh" which followed them, Connor glanced down at his video poker screen; He had three aces, a seven of clubs, and a two of diamonds. He then took his eyes off of his hand and looked off into the casino pit. Andrew saw a long conglomeration of table games: craps, blackjack, roulette and Pai-Gow tables were set in clusters along both sides of a grand walkway which lead up to the main casino entrance, each bearing a placard denoting what the minimum bet at that table was. The casino pit appeared to be having a busy evening; almost all of the game tables were staffed and in use by patrons.

Andrew's gaze returned to his poker hand and he held the aces. He was about to press the deal/draw button when Connor's words roused him to the non-gambling world. "You doing alright there, Summerlin?" he asked. "Oh, I'm about even," Andrew replied. "No, not that," Connor

35

said. Andrew's mildly happy expression was gone, and in its place was a sad look of hopelessness, one Connor had not seen on Andrew's face. "Oh. Well, I'm still unemployed, and my girl has changed her number," Andrew replied. Connor grimaced and said, "I don't even need to ask how you know that. It's obvious that you are going to need further help in learning how to let it all go." Andrew attempted to change the subject by speaking, "And how was your day?" Connor replied after a sip of his cocktail, "I'm down a High Society on the tracks, but I royal flushed on a dollar progressive machine, so I'll be alright. *Jeez, what would a man like this do with real problems?* Andrew thought. After a few moments of quiet, Connor broke the silence by asking, "Problem, Summerlin?" Connor inquired. "I just don't think we will understand each other's problems. You obviously aren't in love with a lady; not a specific one, anyway. Your problems seem, to me at least, to be the problems of the rich," Andrew said before taking a deep gulp from his beer. After putting his bottle back on the bar, he added, "I mean no harm, you've been very kind 'n all, I just—" He was once again cut off by Connor. "Kid, kid. Kid. Calm down. I simply commented on my day's work. You asked. I *do* enjoy love every once in a while, I'm just as human as the next guy. And as to rich..." Connor paused and rose from his stool, looking left and right and across the bar. His head stopped at the other side of the bar on Connor's left, facing where the casino pit ended. There was a huge set of dark red curtains which were closed, but a doorway was fashioned out of a parting of the curtains at the bottom. There was a large metallic sign hanging several feet above the portal which read "The Rail Yard Music & Dance Club". Connor regained Andrew's attention by speaking, "Rich? Me? Nah, I'm just a gambler on a really good beat. You want to see rich? Look over there," He then pointed in the direction of where his head had stopped a moment before, and said, "at him." Connor was referring to another bar patron, a younger man, perhaps two or three years younger than Connor. The man was dressed in a light green dress shirt. The man wasn't gambling, and was sitting alone. He seemed distracted—and appeared to be *talking*. There were two glasses of white wine in front of him...

3.

The tall, lanky man in the green shirt had pale skin and short, semi-combed brown hair which stuck up in a few places; his hazel eyes looked melancholy. He was looking down at the wineglass which was closest to him. The two glasses were each filled a third of the way to the top. "You don't need to take it so badly," said a soft, dulcetly toned voice coming from his left. It was a young woman dressed in a shimmering gold dress, with deep green eyes and the face of an angel. Light brown and blonde curled tresses frolicked wherever they would upon her neck, back and shoulders. She was short, but not too short to match the man to her right's face; if they stood back to back, her crown would reach his jawline. She was blessed with soft, plump cheeks and a small, pouty set of lips. "I'm sure they only called because they meant well," she finished. The man was now cradling his head in his hands with his elbows on the bar. "They *only* call when they are worried about me. It makes me feel like they think I'm somehow doing something wrong. What'd I do *this* time to set them off worrying?" The man's voice dripped of sadness and misery with a touch of politeness.

"You know," the young woman began, in a tone which was almost musical in nature, "you should count your blessings. Not everybody has someone to annoy them by caring too much." With a warm smile, she reached out with her hand and gently stroked his cheek. She continued to smile as she leaned in towards him. He shook slightly in regaining his balance, taking her in his arms to keep her from falling after he had adjusted his seat to be closer to hers. He was wearing khakis and penny loafers; she was wearing a simple pair of gold-colored heels.

"I just wish that they would listen to you for once and leave me alone for a while," the man said. His spirits were starting to improve—he had even raised his head. "I tried baby, several times. It just didn't work out," the young woman responded, stressing, with effort, her syllables so that they came out in a form most caring and kind. The man sipped on his wine and then said "I suppose I can count my blessings that I have you, darling. That's a good thing I can count on, as sure as tomorrow's sunrise." The woman gave him a gentle but reproachful look and said, "We all love you Tommy, *all* of us. And I'm proud of you, always have been," she continued as she adjusted his collar and kissed him upon the cheek, "Look at you. My little millionaire." She giggled and reached for her glass of wine...

"What's going on with him?" Andrew asked Connor after observing the man across the bar who was having a conversation with no one. Connor took a break from his video poker screen to reply, "Ah, that's a friend of mine, his name is Thomas but his old friends call him Tommy. He's been a little troubled as of late, but he's still a great guy." Andrew's eyebrows arched and he said, "Okay..." his tone rose as he said the word as one's does when asking a question. "He loved a girl, too. Was gonna marry her and everything," Connor said; a dark look had overcome him. Andrew wasn't entirely eager to hear the end of Thomas's story, but deep down, he had to know; he asked Connor, "What happened?" Connor finished his drink and spoke after placing the empty glass on the bar, "His girl, his Sylvia. They met as kids, and after knowing one another for eight years, were engaged to be married. But a drunk driver on Maryland Parkway had different plans." Andrew looked crestfallen, yet Connor continued, "This all leads me to what I was trying to prove. You want to see a rich man and his problems? There he is. Whether his problems qualify as 'rich people problems' or not, I'll leave up to you."

Andrew was looking perplexed. "His plans of starting a business—a Laundromat, no less—turned out to be wildly successful. That, Summerlin," he pointed at Thomas, "is what happens when your greatest dreams come true—And then lose every reason for having dreamt so hard in the first place," Connor somberly finished. "Oh God," Andrew said in horror, not even realizing that he had spoken the words aloud. Connor took a glimpse of the basketball game which was airing on two of the televisions overhead; Los Angeles was leading Miami by ten points early on in the third quarter. "Well, like I said, he's still a great guy," Connor said as he got up from his seat and walked over to Thomas. "C'mon," said Connor as he gestured for Andrew to join him in greeting Thomas. Before he got up from his seat, Andrew looked down to press the "cash out" button so that he could receive his ticket, but saw that he had still had the three cards held and had never pressed the button to draw. He did, and jackpot music played loudly from his machine. He watched as the money climbed to over five hundred dollars before stopping. He pressed the cash out button, took his ticket, and walked at a quickened pace to catch up with Connor, who was already halfway around the bar.

Andrew found himself feeling awkward as he approached Thomas. *I have no idea what to say or, heck, even what to do when in the presence of someone who has seen such grief,* he thought. Five college aged girls stopped Connor to shake his hand; two of them kissed him on the cheek. Connor arrived mere seconds before Andrew, who had closed the gap between them while the Con-Man had been flirting. "Hey Tommy Salami!" Connor yelled out in a very poorly done Italian accent. *This Thomas must be part Italian,* Andrew thought. Thomas slumped when he heard Connor's salutation. He then turned to face Connor and Andrew, who sat in stools next to him. And although Thomas had until just then been talking towards the seat to his left, that seat was actually empty. Andrew presumed that the seat to the left of Thomas had been vacant the entire time. Thomas had been sharing a drink with open air, apparently; Andrew didn't know whether to feel scared of the man, or to feel sorry for him. The general oddness of Thomas's behavior would normally incline Andrew to avoid the person, but there was a polite sincerity present in Thomas—something Andrew couldn't quite put his finger on, but felt strongly nonetheless. Thomas had large bags under his eyes, but otherwise appeared to be in fine health—physically, at least. Thomas looked at Connor and replied to Connors greeting, "Connor Stephen Bentley. The Man who's luckier than the little guy holding the pot of gold on the cereal box." Thomas then pulled his right arm up and stretched it out, landing it upon the back of his chair in a manner that almost perfectly mirrored that part of Connor's stance. The Con-Man looked at Thomas with immediate disgust. "Goodness! You're doing it all wrong," he chided as he moved to stand facing Thomas directly. He then proceeded to do a motion which was almost identical to Thomas's, culminating with his extended right elbow gliding to a stop on the top of the bar. "*That* is how it's done," Connor's sentence was accompanied by a grin and two clicking noises. Andrew watched in a mixed state of amusement and confusion. "How are you doing today my dear Laundromatier?"—Connor pronounced the ending of the last word as if it were a genuine word of French origin. Andrew noticed Thomas's face wince at the sound of the word; *He liked it about as much as I did*, he thought. The only thing genuine about the Con-Man's foreign sounding word was the way he pronounced it—His counterfeit French accent wasn't actually that bad—*Perhaps the only one he's done so far that actually sounds believable*, Andrew thought. Hearing it led Andrew to remember how much he had hated having to learn French in high school and college. Both levels of education had required that he study a foreign language; after three years of lessons, Andrew still couldn't conjugate an –er verb without being helped. "That is *not* a word, Bentley," Thomas said before Andrew even had the chance to say it. "Okay," Connor said sarcastically, "How are you my dear friend who owns four establishments within the Las Vegas region where you can wash your pajamas?" "Ha ha," Thomas said lightly; he seemed a different person altogether from the man whom Connor and he had been observing from across the bar moments earlier. "We are fine," Thomas replied, "just enjoying a glass of the good stuff, seeing the sights." Andrew didn't have it in him to question the "we", and if it was noticed by, or bothered Connor, was anyone's guess, for if it did, he didn't let it show.

Thomas finished his glass of wine and waved for the bartender, who was busy serving a group of people watching basketball and ordering multiple rounds of booze while doing so. "Who's the kid? Some new gambler trainee or adherent?" he asked while facing Andrew. "This is Summerlin. Summerlin, this is Thomas." Connor replied. Andrew managed to say, "It's Andrew," before Connor reiterated: "He is Summerlin. Trust me." The bartender came and replenished Thomas's glass, and served new beverages for Connor and Andrew—An Old Fashioned and a beer, respectively. "Well, Summerlin, it is a pleasure to be of your acquaintance," Thomas said while offering his hand to Andrew for a shake. Andrew took Thomas's hand and shook it, adding, "...Apparently, it's Summerlin. Pleased to meet you as well." Thomas nodded and then turned to Connor, who had taken to playing a nearby video poker machine. "I take it you are here late on Friday for the usual reason?" Thomas asked him. "You're damn ri—" Connor took a look at Andrew and then changed his words, "You're darn right." Thomas laughs. "Darn? From *you*?" he asked Connor. The Con-Man gave Thomas a confident, self-defending stare and hastily explained, "I'm just trying to be sensitive to the feelings of 'Oh-Way-Down-South-In-Dixie' over there." Connor had turned to look away in an overly-dramatic manner; he had feigned embarrassment for the last part of the sentence. Andrew gave Connor a stern look and said, "Fearing the Almighty isn't just a Southern thing." Connor gave a sarcastic look of wide eyed enlightenment, as if he

41

had just become aware of that fact, before returning to his prior form of semi-serious smugness. "You won't find that many 'God-fearing folk' in our fair city. Though I'm sure there are some," Connor said; he had added the latter sentence after he noticed Andrew's gaze was locked on him. Andrew nodded to the Con-Man and then said, "I'll just have to be content that you admit I'm not the only one. Something tells me that with you, that's actually considered progress."

After ten minutes, Connor's drink and video poker balance were both empty; He placed a ten dollar bill in the tip jar, which sat beyond the video poker machine, and rose from his seat. Both Andrew and Thomas looked at Connor as he rose. "Well easy come easy go—both for the money and the sauce. Well, Summerlin, I have one or two small errands which need tending. You got him, right, Tommy? He's nursing a broken heart." Andrew sighed and Thomas took a sip from his new glass of wine. "Errands?" Andrew queried. Connor was standing and gazing towards the Lone Star Bar. He turned back to the other two and said, "Well, you know, can't be a gambler and *not* make next-day sports bets." Thomas laughed and said to Andrew, "I love the weird 'rules' of Connor, don't you?" Andrew replied, "I've only seen a few, but bless his heart, I feel like a person might need to carry a notebook around to understand the man." "Don't give him any ideas, young one," Thomas retorted with speed. Connor smiled and patted Thomas's shoulder. Thomas tried Connor's "elbow glide" again, and failed; Connor suggested that he drop the issue for the time being, and then hustled over to the Sports Book counters. Andrew turned to face Thomas, who had returned to his conversation with the empty seat to his left.

"So I'm being babysat?" Andrew inquired. Thomas had taken to viewing the foreign drag-racing channel. "No. You can do whatever you like. Have a ball. We're just here in case you need us. That being the case, if all goes well, you and I won't meet again until tomorrow, since you are going to attend the show, and I will not," Thomas replied. Andrew couldn't tell if Thomas was serious, or kidding. "Oh?" Andrew said as he leaned against the bar, "Not a 'The Reason Why' fan?" Thomas coughed and laughed, replying, "You know them quite well for a person who has never seen their act." Thomas grinned, but after a glance to his left his expression changed to a guilty look. *Now that's curious*, Andrew thought upon noticing the change and its apparent cause. "They're fine, I'm sure. It's just not my cup of tea on a Friday night. We'll be here for a while, then we'll probably turn in early for the night. We did, after all, just get here. It took forever to lock up everything at home," Thomas said. Andrew finished his beer and said, "I'm not going to presuppose anything about the band, I'm just gonna give the show a chance."

Andrew decided that he would play some of his ticket at the bar while he waited for either the Rail Yard doors to open, or for Connor to return. He pulled out the white piece of paper and was reminded of its worth— $530.00! Andrew remembered hearing a winning hand sound before he cashed out and received the ticket; he did not, however, remember the win having been so substantial. Andrew smiled as he looked around to see where he could exchange the ticket for cash. "Looks like some-body's having a good night," Thomas said. Andrew looked once more at his winning ticket and responded, "Yeah, I guess so." "So you're not gonna play it after all?" Thomas asked in between sips of wine. "Can't let my dreams get too big," Andrew began, "I'm from Blacksburg, Virginia; I was raised to believe that old adage about a bird in the hand, you know. The only hand I could hope to attain which would pay more than what I got would be the Royal Flush." "True," Thomas conceded before returning his attention to the foreign drag racing channel. As Andrew studied the overhead sign's directions to the cashier before departing, he could hear Thomas say behind him, "Make sure you have fun—And don't ever let the Con-Man hear that you didn't go for a Royal Flush." Andrew was too far away to reply without yelling. *I'm sure I'll see him again*, thought Andrew as he continued to move farther away from the Derrick Bar.

It didn't take Andrew long to reach the Cashier's cage. *Ha, it's just like in the movies*, Andrew thought as the area came into his view. The entire cage area was done in polished brass, and a large sign that read "CASHIER—CHANGE" in letters which were composed of myriad glittering lights. Andrew looked ahead to view the line's length as he joined it; he laughed and thought, *Great, another stockade* as he noticed that indeed, almost every attraction inside Texas Palace had a corresponding stockade to endure. As the minutes rolled on without the line making any progress, Andrew found himself observing the people ahead of him in line to occupy the idle time. There were nine people ahead of him: six of them were holding varying amounts of casino chips in their hands; the other three were holding envelopes, which Andrew supposed were paychecks.

Twenty minutes later, Andrew finally reached the end of the line—he was next to be called up. Now that he had actually reached the cashier's cage, he could see one of the reasons for the slow service: of eight brass-barred windows with "cashier" placards, only two were open. Andrew was waved up for his turn. When he got to the window, Andrew found a dark, overweight woman with a disgruntled scowl wearing a blue Texas Palace collared shirt with a nametag that informed him that the woman's name was "Serenity". *How ironic is that?* Andrew thought with a grin. Despite the intimidating nature of his cashier, Andrew smiled and presented his cash-out ticket to Serenity and said, "Howdy. I'd like this cashed if y'all don't mind." The woman sighed and, trying to hide her irritation, said, "Gladly, sir. Next time, you don't have to get in line and wait to get up here if all you're doing is cashing in a ticket. Just look for a ticket redemption machine, there are several on the casino floor." Andrew was pleasantly surprised by the woman's demeanor. "Oh, I didn't know that," Andrew replied. Serenity checked the authenticity of Andrew's ticket twice before her cash register drawer popped open. You're not from around here are you?" she asked Andrew in what he thought was a kind enough manner. "No ma'am. I'm from Virginia. Been here about two months, and I'm kind of just floating around for now, I guess," he replied. Serenity counted out his five hundred thirty dollars; Andrew pushed a ten dollar bill through the window. Serenity genuinely seemed a little amazed to have seen a bill pushed back. "Do you—Do you need change, sir?" Andrew replied, "No. I need you to take that, and to have a nice day." *She surprised me with kindness when I expected duress, it's only fair that I return the favor in kind*, Andrew thought. She took the bill and said "Thank you," and Andrew placed the money into his wallet, keeping a twenty in his pocket in case he decided he wanted to gamble later. *It's just a money holder for now*, Andrew thought as he saw the picture of Sarah facing outwards. He looked for a moment before flipping it over to the other pictures in the wallet—there were four family pictures behind the professional portrait of Sarah. A picture of his mother and father sitting outside in the shade from Andrew's youth was opposite Sarah's portrait. On the back side of Sarah's photo was a picture of his older brother, Bradley, in his Army Graduation photograph, looking proud and proper. After that was a picture of Andrew's sisters, Dakota and Courtney, who were both older than he, posing in swimwear on the beach. Andrew hadn't seen either of his sisters in years; Andrea moved off to Florida for a job, and Courtney married a lawyer from Connecticut. Brian had been deployed to a post in Germany two years ago. The last picture was of his uncle Charles, who had taught him how to play chess. *Ten years and I still haven't had a victory*, Andrew thought as he smiled and returned his wallet to his right rear pocket.

After accepting profuse thanks from Serenity, Andrew turned from the window to once again face the casino floor, which still didn't feel familiar to him. He relaxed when he remembered that all he had to do to find the Rail Yard for the 9pm T.R.Y. show was to follow the signs to the nightclub, which led him past the table game, or pit area as it was described in the overhead signage. While the pit was not visible from every point of the building, it was large enough to be comfortably located from afar, and served as a great landmark in Andrew's eyes because it was it was the most congested area in the casino.

It was at that moment, when a checkup on the time would have proven most prudent, that Andrew noticed that there were no clocks to be seen, anywhere in the entire place. There weren't any windows, either. After several fruitless glances, he decided that it would simply be easier to ask someone who was using a cellphone or wearing a wristwatch. He saw a security officer in the distance. It was one of the two officers who had confronted Connor and he the night before—the older, bearded one. He asked the officer what time it was. The man checked his watch and replied, "about 6:30." The officer's eyes widened and he said, "Hey—weren't you with Bentley last night?" *The man's reputation proceeds him*, he thought. "Yeah, why?" Andrew inquired. The officer let out a loud and hearty "Ha!" Andrew stared at the officer inquisitively, and asked "What was that about?" "Oh, nothing," he replied. The fact that the officer had an opinion of Connor meant that he might also know about him. "Well," Andrew began, "How long have you known the guy?" "He was already living in the suite when I started as an outside officer. Though he didn't used to be half as successful, nor one tenth as annoying." Andrew couldn't help but grin as he realized that the officer with whom he was speaking had doubtlessly been the butt of many of Connor's jokes. "How long have you worked here?" He asked the officer. He replied, "Almost two years. Good luck—And I hope sanity isn't something you cherish too deeply," he said before giving off a chuckle and walking off in the direction of the theatre. Andrew didn't take note of the officer's name, but remembered that the officer had been wearing badge #68. Andrew couldn't help but wonder what Connor would have been like when he "didn't use to be half as successful". *Even when penniless, he probably still had that odd swagger about him*, he thought.

6:30—Wow, Time flies when you're in a land of no clocks. The casino probably likes it that way, Andrew thought as he turned from

46

the Rail Yard area and began wandering aimlessly about the floor. He had remembered that the entrance doors to Texas Palace were heavily tinted; *The owners of this place must love it when patrons lose track of time, especially if they go so far as to hide the Sun*, he thought. As he walked, he remembered the restaurant that he had seen earlier, The Coral Room, and decided to set out that way. He found the restaurant to be a ghost town in the early evening—He was seated promptly and politely. The clam chowder at the Coral Room was satisfactory; the roasted halibut was exceptional.

It was nearing eight o' clock when Andrew finished up his meal and paid his bill. He left the twenty Connor had given him with his shirt as a tip. While he was not particularly worried or stressed, Andrew did find himself using the overhead signs to direct him back to the table games, knowing that such direction would indeed deposit him in a place with a prime view of the nightclub. As he was passing the gift shop, he heard sounds of a commotion. A group of indoor security officers were putting handcuffs on a man who was yelling out nonsensical sounds. "The Cadillac ate my monkey machine!" the man screamed as the security officers dragged him off into a holding cell within the casino's inner chambers. Andrew could hear the poor wretch yell "Sammy, where's my sausages!?" as they dragged him through a pair of steel doors in the distance marked "Employees Only". Andrew rolled his eyes and thought, *What a place* as he sighed and continued to follow the overhead signs.

When Andrew arrived in the gaming pit, he found there to be assembled a surprisingly long line of motley clothed individuals all waiting to be granted entry into the Rail Yard for the T.R.Y. show. Two velvet ropes bordered the line for the last thirty feet. *At least they don't force this line through a stockade,* he thought. In front of the nightclub's entrance stood a large white sign, which bore a black and white photograph of the band with a T.R.Y. logo overlapping the photograph. The sign had words written in black capital letters: "The Reason Why. 9:00pm show: Twenty-one and older please. Entrance = Women $10; Men $20. No entry after 8:59 until 10:30pm. Karaoke after midnight— No cover." *Twenty dollars? I sure hope they're good. If this is a Texas-themed place, I might even get to hear some country*, Andrew thought as he joined the line.

As before, Andrew took to counting and analyzing the persons who stood before him in line. There were at least fifty people—Some were standing calmly in line, and others formed mini-clusters of friends talking loudly. Many of the people were wearing black and white t-shirts emblazoned with the band's acronym-based logo, which just happened to also be the word "try". *Clever*, Andrew thought as he realized the play on words. A few fans near the entrance were dancing in place to the music piped in overhead. The odd formation of the line made it impossible for Andrew to truly discern how many persons were actually ahead of him. The line didn't start to move until 8:30. Andrew could hear the sounds of microphones and musical instruments being turned on and set up coming from beyond the black curtains.

Twenty or so of the people in line appeared to Andrew to be at least in their middle forties. *Maybe I'll luck out and get to hear some country after all*, he concluded as he noticed that most of the older patrons were wearing leather jackets and boots. As the line crept ever forward, Andrew gave a moment to read the smaller print which was near the bottom of the T.R.Y. show sign; he noticed the phrase "classic rock covers and band-made favorites." *Dear goodness, what "classics" will they be doing covers of?* he cautiously wondered. "Well," he began speaking in a soft voice as the line drew him ever closer to the entrance, "I have to go either way—I already said I would." Andrew had become used to the steady crawl into the Rail Yard, and was easily startled by a voice calling out, "Hey man!" Andrew turned to see Connor Bentley, standing just outside the line. He was wearing the same clothes as before, except he was now wearing a black sports jacket with diagonal pinstripes, and had a pair of aviator sunglasses tilted above his eyes. Connor waved his arms, indicating that Andrew should join him on the other side of the ropes.

Andrew realized that Connor would not stop waving at him and yelling his name until he abandoned his place and joined him. "Howdy," Andrew said, perhaps a bit more rapidly than usual, "I got here with time to spare." Connor reacted to Andrew's statement with the same reception one would expect to receive after telling a friend that you are in fact, Batman, or king of the watermelon kingdom. "Kid, kid, kid—We don't wait," Connor replied. Andrew began to reply, "But I was just thought—" before he was cut off by Connor, who said, "It's ok, kid. Tonight, you're with me. And I am *with* the band." Andrew's eyes widened and he thought, *Wow.* "Oh," he managed to say, "nice. Thanks Mr. Con-Man." Connor grinned as he led Andrew towards the Rail Yard, adding, "Don't mention it. You don't need to thank me for anything tonight, remember?" Now jump that rope and lets go, Summerlin!" Andrew, still feeling a little out of place amidst the lights, sounds, and crowd of the place, did as his friend requested.

Andrew followed Connor as he walked straight up to the entrance of the nightclub and walked in like he owned the place. Connor led him into the nightclub without even stopping to be checked in by the host who was standing at a podium. The Con-Man stopped only briefly to wave hello to a few patrons who were apparently "fans" of his work; after bestowing his gregarious nature upon his followers, the Con-Man walked up to an unmarked door which was next to a bar that sat to the left of the Rail Yard's stage. Andrew did his best to dodge thoughts about how out of place he felt; he was sure that Connor wasn't breaking any rules, but Andrew simply was not used to being treated like a high-roller. Andrew noticed that once he and Connor had entered the club, the sea of noise which had been the casino floor had somehow been reduced to the point where he almost forgot what sort of business lay beyond; the lights, too, were gone. The carpet of the nightclub was black, and there were several round tables with chairs sitting before the bar. A backward glimpse provided Andrew with a view of a movie-theatre style balcony, which was capable of holding at least a hundred persons, and was becoming filled with more humanity with each passing second. A wooden-paneled dance floor, which could easily accommodate forty or more, lay directly in front of the stage. There were five people on stage setting up the equipment; Andrew recognized the tall young woman adjusting the center stage microphone from the T.R.Y. picture on the nightclub sign. He was actually kind of interested in watching the people whom he assumed to be band members prepare for the show, but Connor Bentley obviously was not—aside from a few kind parade-style waves to people he knew, Connor led him quickly to the bar, which was flooded with people grabbing their pre-show beverages. "Shouldn't we take our seats before we get drinks?" Andrew inquired. Connor gave the bar a gentle knock to grab the attention of the goateed bartender who was frantically serving the patrons drinks and replied, "We have reserved seats. Calm down, Summerlin." The bartender failed to notice Connor's original attention-getter; he knocked again, this time adding in a loud tone, "Jack, Jack! You got VIPs over here." The bartender stopped in the middle of the cocktail he was preparing and rushed over to face Connor, and greeted him with a loud, boisterous "Con-Mannnn!" Connor and the bartender exchanged a few words and what seemed to be a series of high-fives. "And whom do we have with you tonight?" the bartender asked. "This is a little wayward soul from Dixie. We call him 'Summerlin.'" Andrew smiled and shook the bartender's hand and said, "It's *Andrew*. And it's a pleasure to meet you sir." The bartender replied, "The nametag says Jack, but call me Charles. And likewise." By this point in time, another bartender had appeared to aid Charles in serving the other patrons. Connor ordered an Old Fashioned, and when prompted, Andrew requested a shot of Tennessee Whiskey with a side of soda. Andrew downed the shot in one go, and wiped his mouth after returning the empty shot-glass to the bar. Charles and Connor gaped at him. "What, just because I don't order drinks from the nineteenth century doesn't mean I can't drink." Connor nodded and added in a polite tone, "Indeed!" Charles looked to Connor and, while clearing the bar top of unwanted empty glasses said, "So are you two going in the back?" Connor grinned after a sip of his cocktail; "Yep. I'll be taking little Summerlin for a stroll. Gonna show him some killer music along the way, too," he replied. Andrew looked at the five persons who were arranging things on the stage and then glanced back to Connor and Charles, saying "I'm beginning to get this bad feeling that this concert isn't goin' to involve *any* music regarding Texas at all." "Relax," Connor replied, patting Andrew's shoulder while moving away from the bar. He then walked towards an unmarked windowless door which was directly in between the bar and the stage, which had at that moment just become fully lit. The curtain fell on the stage as Connor held the door open and motioned for Andrew to follow.

The door by the bar gave way to a labyrinthine set of passageways which Andrew assumed to lead backstage. *We're going to the band?* He wondered as he followed Connor. The Con-Man's path took the two of them to the deepest depths of the theatre, depositing them in the backstage dressing room area, which was a long rectangular room with several smaller individual dressing rooms connected to it. The communal area of the dressing room had a cheap wooden paneled floor. Andrew approximated the floor planks to be easily older than he, as they were heavily scratched and lacked the luminous luster of the dance floor. In the center of the room there were two couches positioned back to back; one was brown vinyl, the other was an old, severely faded floral print which appeared to have seen better days.

Connor leapt upon the vinyl couch and reclined leisurely on its cushions as its frame creaked beneath him. Andrew glanced about the room and wondered what the purpose of it all was. He turned back to Connor and said, "So, our reserved seats are *behind* the stage?" Connor smiled as he lazily stared toward the ceiling. "Give it time," Connor responded, briefly checking his wristwatch before returning his gaze upward.

Andrew remained standing as sounds of rustling and commotion came from behind the door at the opposite end of the room. Connor sat up as the door opened and the men and women who had graced the stage moments before entered the room, laughing and conversing boisterously. While four of the band members were unknown to Andrew, the young tall man who had entered carrying a Fender guitar he recognized instantly: it was Xero. *So that's why he grinned when he said I'd see him at the show,* Andrew realized. "Gonna kill it bro," Xero said to a shorter, more full bodied man with curly hair; "They look prime and ready," the shorter young woman added. Upon seeing Connor on the couch, all five band members cheered "Bentley!". Connor rose from his seat and gave a laid-back smile while extending his arms wide and saying, "Whaddup fellas? And Jail-Bait?" Connor's gaze lingered on the taller of the two women. They all greeted him and exchanged handshakes and half-hugs. The young woman whom Andrew presumed to be "Jail-Bait" smiled and looked towards Andrew and said, "Well, who do we have here?" Connor took no delay in replying; he was like a child at show and tell: "This is Summerlin. He's got a case of lonely hearts syndrome." Andrew sighed as Connor went on: "And Summerlin, I have the sublime honor of introducing you to Sin City's best house band ever, The Reason Why. Xero was dressed in an entirely different outfit than earlier: gone were the slacks and collared Texas Palace shirt, and in their place was a pair of ripped jeans and leather biker jacket with an orange t-shirt underneath topped off by a miss-matched pair of Chuck Taylors. A quick scan of the band's attire gave Andrew the notion that the members favored individual style to a uniform attire; no two were dressed even remotely similar to one another. Connor continued in his introduction: "There's Blake Blanchard, lead vocals and rhythm guitar." Blake gave Andrew a wave. He was a full figured man in his middle thirties, bearing an equal combination of fat and muscle, with a head of thick curly hair. "And on keyboard and *occasionally* the four string, the illustrious Jail-Bait Jones!" Connor gave a grin during his introduction of the taller young woman. Jail-Bait said "hi" while she gathered together sheets of paper from a table near the wall. Xero yelled aloud "8:49" in the background as the introductions rolled along. *"Jail-Bait?"* Andrew inquired. The young woman walked over to where Andrew and Connor were standing. "It's Jasmine, and I'm *twenty-four*. But, with Connor Bentley around I might as well not even try." She was dressed in a dark purple sun dress layered over blue jeans and a pink camisole. Andrew wasn't one hundred percent certain, but he thought he noticed army boots beneath the dress's hem. Connor then gestured towards the tall, dark-skinned man who had remained near the door and was tuning the strings of his bass. "Then there's Trent, artistic lead guitarist extraordinaire—" Connor was cut off by Trent: "I thought we'd agreed on 'sensual guitar Cassanova'." He was laughing. Now that he had stepped a little closer to address Connor, Andrew caught a more complete look at him. Trent was tall and muscular with striking chestnut eyes and a laughing smile that would make even a stranger want to join in on the joke, regardless of what it was; he was easily the youngest of the five, save for Xero. Trent's dark skin was contrasted heavily by his choice of white vest and slacks, with white-buck shoes to match. "Hey Summerlin," Trent said to Andrew, stressing and drawing out the last syllable of the name as he did so. "It's Andrew. And it's nice to meet y'all," he replied. With one simple word, Andrew drew the attention of all six of them; Xero grinned and added in a phony southern accent, "We got ourselves a regular son of Dixie among us!" Andrew thought Xero's version of a southern accent to be nowhere near believable. "I know, I know, he's different—but he's just so *interesting*!" Connor said. Blake gave Connor a quick look of disapproval and addressed Andrew, "There's nothing wrong with the Southland. From Arkansas myself." Connor dismissed the topic and went on with his introductions. "Xero you have already met," Xero made a "gotcha" type pointing gesture at Andrew, and Connor continued with his intro, his voice resembling a broadcast radio personality voice as he went on, "And that leaves last, but not least in any way but size, Samantha Greene on Drums, with no vocals whatsoever." Samantha nodded, twirled her sticks and said "hey." Jail-Bait finished gathering her papers and walked over to the doorway and addressed her band mates: "It's 8:56 guys. You know we love introductions, but we *do* have to play. You can finish the rest of your introductions and such *after* the show. You know Connor, that is the entire point of a backstage pass, that you use it *after* the performance." Connor had been trying to get a word in edgewise, but only managed "I—" before Jail-Bait continued. "S'all good, Con-artist!" she said in her best Connor Bentley impression as she hustled the rest of the band back towards the stage. "Game on! Game on!" she was yelling as they left. Blake, Connor, and Andrew remained in the room. Connor and Blake were standing next to one another and conversing between themselves when Jail-Bait's voice called out from the hallway: "Blake Blanchard! Co-band leader and *supposed* responsible one!" Blake winced and said, "Uh oh, gotta run" before running out the door to catch up with the rest of the group. Andrew looked to Connor and said, "Now what do we do?" Connor started for the doorway which they had used to enter the dressing rooms and added, "Now, Summerlin, we go to our seats."

Andrew followed Connor back to the Rail Yard. The show was due to start any moment, and Connor's pace increased to almost that of a run. Noting the increase in pace, Andrew thought *How can a man hurry while still looking so calm?* It was the fastest Andrew had ever seen the man move.

Although there were no tables or seats on the dance floor, the table at which Connor seated himself was the closest to the stage one could be without being expected to rhythmically move one's feet. Atop the table was a crisp white notecard which read, in grandiose calligraphy, "Reserved", that served as the table's centerpiece. No glasses, nor silverware—just the card. Andrew sat down next to Connor. Nobody was on the dance floor or at the bar anymore; everyone had taken their seats. The nightclub's house lights went dim, and a hush came over the audience. The curtain began to slowly rise, and the stage lights came on in unison.

"Ladies and semi-well-behaved men!" a male voice said without being visible to the audience—Andrew recognized the voice as Blake's. The voice continued, "It's nine o' clock. You're at Texas Palace, and you're feelin' rowdy." The crowd began to cheer. Blake went on, "No no no. We don't need to ask. We already *know*—" Four extra lights came on, and a bluesy set of chords began to echo through the nightclub. Blake walked out to front center stage, carrying a microphone in his hand. His curly locks gave off a mild reflective sheen from the lights. He leaned out towards the crowd and pumped his microphone holding fist into the air. The crowd responded by loudly screaming "The Reason Why!"

The audience's cheers were greeted by the rushing melody of a piano playing *fortissimo*. The lights all went out as the piano played on. The crowd went wild, a lot of them were rhythmically chanting the band's name. After a few moments of chaos, the lights came back on; all five band members were now present on the stage. Andrew could now see that it had been Jail-Bait Jones who had played the ivories with such expert precision.

The band went straight into a song which was not familiar to Andrew. After two rounds of the chorus, he deduced that the song's title was "Don't Break." *Must be one of those "band made favorites" the sign mentioned*, he thought. Nearing the end of the tune, the melody progressed into a guitar solo by Trent. Blake walked the length of the stage while talking in an eloquent voice: he introduced each band member, taking a pause for each person to play a riff on their respective instrument between introductions. Samantha Greene was announced last, which led to her playing a drum solo while the stage lights flickered in strobe fashion overhead. *Wow. Good Heavens, she's good*, Andrew thought as her solo came to an end; Jail-Bait was looking at her wristwatch in a playful fashion as the audience cheered ever louder.

The Reason Why went on to play several songs from the 80's—mostly rock songs which were so well known that even country music loving Andrew found he knew most of the words. There were two more songs which Andrew recognized to be "band made", one titled "That's Just Life", the other "Shut Up and Hold the Wheel." People were dancing near the table when Andrew realized that Connor Bentley was absent from his seat. The band had begun a cover of the Allman Brothers Band's "Ramblin' Man", and Andrew found Connor where he had least expected to locate him: the man was in the center of the dance floor, and dancing with two attractive women. At once. Andrew sighed and looked down at the table. No matter the abundance of pretty women before him, Andrew could only think of Sarah. The bad times, the good times—his mind even drifted to ways in which he might have been wrong. This lead Andrew to dwell in sadness; his head hung low as his eyes fought the temptation of oncoming tears.

The band played with a high level of skill. *They almost don't belong in a place like this*, Andrew thought as he watched the show. *They should be having concerts and getting a record deal, or something—not playing at an off-Strip casino nightclub*, he thought. The Reason Why had a way of having fun on stage that made everyone in the crowd feel like they were a part of it—the adoring fans chanted lyrics to their home-made songs, and held fan-made signs, which varied in message from simple signs with the band's name to signs saying "Jones for President 2020". Andrew noticed that there was a section of the audience which was full of young women wearing what appeared to be wedding veils. They were seated nearest Xero's position on stage right. Three young women held a large orange and black banner reading "BRIDES OF XERO." At one point, the band's music softened and Jail-Bait Jones approached the center stage microphone stand and, instead of singing backup vocals, she spoke: "Okay guys, you know what time it is!" Her gaze was aimed primarily at those in the balcony overhead, but she also gave a quick smile and wink to those who had filed onto the dance floor. Xero laid his guitar gently upon the stage and walked up to Jail-Bait. Those who were dancing stood still and gave the band their undivided attention. The audience roared after Jail-Bait pulled out a hacky-sack from her pocket and handed it to Xero in a dramatic fashion. The stage lights flickered rapidly in a burst of color as Xero hoisted the hacky-sack into the air. The rest of the band began playing an electric version of *The Flight of the Bumblebee* as Jail-Bait waved her hand in Xero's general direction, as a magician would do upon saying "voila!" and returned to the keyboard which sat at stage left. Connor Bentley kissed each of his dance partners on the cheek once their dance had been ended by the theatrics on stage. One of the young women had leaned towards Connor in hopes of receiving a bigger kiss, yet she was left hanging as Connor broke away from her and arrived at the table before Jail-Bait made it back to her keyboard.

Once Connor had resumed his seat, Andrew turned his eyes from the stage and asked, "So, what exactly is all this?" Connor pointed at the stage as if to remind Andrew that what was occurring was of some grand importance. Xero was pacing the entire length of the stage back and forth while carrying the hacky-sack overhead; a spotlight followed him the entire time. "It's Xero's weekly showing of skill in all things sack," Connor replied. Andrew noticed something moving in the darkness behind Xero towards stage left: it was Blake, and he was pushing a big screen television which sat atop an old, metal wheeled cart. Once he had pushed the television to rear stage center, Blake returned to his acoustic guitar, which sat at rear stage right. The television screen turned on, and a large white zero appeared on a black screen. "What exactly does that mean?" Andrew inquired while Xero walked to his former spot at center stage. "Well, allowing for his odd form of showmanship—his strange pre-stunt presentation and all—he will make up for it in production value, in *spades*. He's about to be a one-man army, just watch," Connor replied. Xero knelt and checked his shoelaces before rising and tossing the hacky-sack ten feet into the air.

And so, Andrew watched as the hemp-knitted ball rapidly returned to gravity; it never made it to the ground. What Andrew witnessed was nothing short of a callisthenic miracle: Xero proceeded to kick and self serve the hacky-sack to himself in a rapid progression of volleys, pitches and stalls of the object, each different and more implausible than the last. Each time the hack was caught and re-ejected by Xero, the number on the television behind him increased by one. The band began to increase the tempo of their music as he passed the fifteen-hack mark. Xero performed a no-look behind the back kick for number twenty. The crowd loved it. Even Andrew found himself amused enough to put his worries aside, at least for a while. Connor gave Andrew a nod of approval as they watched Xero's hacky-sack total surpass thirty.

Xero made it to thirty-four before the ball hit the stage, and the song stopped. The audience was applauding and cheering "Xero! Xero!" while he picked the hacky-sack off the ground and returned to his regular spot at stage right. Xero picked up his bass, and the music returned. The remainder of the set was devoted to 90's pop and a few covers of modern country hits. The band brought the show to a close by performing a cover of Elton John's "Tiny Dancer." Jail-Bait and Blake sat at a piano which had been rolled in by Trent and Xero, and Andrew found their version to be a spirited, emotionally-vested portrayal of the piece. As Jail-Bait's fingers played the final notes of the melody, the lights went out. Trent's voice could be heard on microphone saying, "Thank you, thank you. We are The Reason Why, and we love you." The group left the stage, and the audience began to raise lighters aflame over their heads. The group returned after about thirty seconds of cheering and flame holding.

Blake approached center stage with an acoustic guitar, and Jail-Bait joined him, carrying a violin. The duo played a tune titled "Don't Mess With Texas" while the remaining three band members worked to clear the instruments and speakers from the stage. It was obviously another band written composition, but it still amused Andrew—he'd been expecting a song about the Lone Star State; what he got, however, was a song paying homage to Las Vegas locals, pimps and crackheads, with the recurring chorus "Every little thing is out of sight in our special little Texas land." Andrew couldn't tell for certain, but he thought he even heard a reference to Mr. Bentley in the song's third and final verse.

Upon the song's conclusion, the band took a bow and exited the stage. After a few moments, the house lights came back on, dimly at first, gradually returning to full brightness. The people who had been dancing slowly made their way to their seats. About a third of the audience departed immediately; the rest remained in their seats as if waiting for something to happen. Connor had returned. A group of two girls in shimmering mini-dresses and one man in a lavender suit exchanged pleasantries with Connor before walking across the club to find their seats. The bar crew had begun rolling out and powering up the karaoke equipment when Connor rose unexpectedly from his seat and said, "let's go back." Andrew followed the Con-Man through the backstage entrance by the bar. Connor led him through the same passage as before the show, which led them towards the communal dressing room area.

4.

A ndrew collided with Connor; as he rose he said, "Ow. What's up?"
Connor responded by putting a finger to his mouth and going
"Shhhh." There was a loud voice coming from within the backstage
room—a male voice unfamiliar to Andrew. Connor crept to within
inches of the cracked door, and Andrew joined him moments later. The
two men stood semi-crouched and listened. "So, you're dissatisfied
with us, *again*?" they heard Blake say. His voice was raised, but not
in the angry manner in which the unknown man had been speaking.
Blake continued, "Tell me *why*, again, you insist on keeping us under
contract, when we have repeatedly asked to be released, *and* you are
always so unhappy with our work?" The yeller replied, "You will fulfill
your contract. You will listen to club management, that's *me*, or else you
will be found to be in breach of contract, without pay, and hearing from
my lawyers." Samantha could be heard moaning "Aww *man!*" from the
other end of the room. "Here are my grievances, which you are bound
to mend," the angry voice began in a somewhat calmer, yet still negative
tone, "As you have been told before, there is to be no curtain up while
your group sets up the equipment. The curtain is only to be drawn for
the show." Trent and Xero started to speak in protest but were silenced

by the stern man's steady verbal barrage: "Your group skipped over my official song request; again." "Wait—You mean you're mad at us because we didn't play 'Your Cheatin' Heart'?" Trent asked with a tone of accusation. The unknown man replied, "It was an official request from club management. Yet again, *me*. Instead you insist on playing that 'Texas' song, which you know full well I *hate*!" Scoffs were heard from throughout the room. Jail-Bait's voice responded to the chiding, "Okay, with all due respect, Mr. Moroni, we leave our curtain up while we prepare because the fans *asked* us to, it lets them feel like their part of the show—and 'Don't Mess with Texas' is a fan favorite. If you delete our songbook, aren't you breaching the contract yourself?" Her points were quickly countered, "Don't you dare roll your eyes at me! That song is a disgrace. And speaking of you, Ms. Jones, I believe management has notified you and Ms. Greene, several times, that you are to be dressing in a *more feminine* manner." "Hey," Jail-Bait began, her voice indignant, "I wore a dress." Mr. Moroni then glared at Trent and Xero and said, "And you two—Do not entice bottle throwing, women exposing their chests, or the use of marijuana! God!" Trent replied, "Isn't it wrong to use God's name like that? It's not nice, you could offend someone." A creaking of old furniture springs indicated that Trent had taken a seat upon the aged cloth couch. Andrew and Connor then heard a thud, like that of someone falling upon the floor. Then came Xero's sarcastic voice: "Sir! Sir? Please sir, Please don't let my little children starve great sir! Please?" Mr. Moroni responded, "Get *off* my suit! *Very* funny, you little miscreant." He had enunciated the final words like they were evil. "You will comply. You will act like you like it, or," Mr. Moroni paused, "you won't get paid. And I have ways at my disposal, let's just say, to make it very difficult for your little group to ever find work in this city again." Mr. Moroni stormed out of the communal dressing room, pushing past Andrew and Connor without a word as he headed out towards the nightclub. He was a short, older man with perfectly combed salt and pepper hair dressed in a plain black suit. Andrew looked back at the club manager to get a better look at him, but Connor pointed towards the dressing rooms and said, "Come on."

The two walked into the communal dressing room area. When they arrived, they found the band members sitting in various places, all quiet and with dissatisfied looks upon their faces; Xero was the only one standing, thought he was really leaning against the wall. Trent was flipping errantly through an issue of *Playboy*. "Con-Man and my southern brother from another mother, welcome back," Blake said as the smallest of smiles returned to his face. "Summerlin, was it?" Jail-Bait asked in a friendly tone. Andrew replied, "Yeah, I guess that's gonna mean me for a moment." Blake pulled out a portable radio, turned it on and began to tune it. "No radio! You don't want Moroni coming back do you?" Jail-Bait chided. Blake countered with a grin, "Do I have to answer that responsibly?" "Yes!" she replied—her answer closely mirrored that of a mother informing their child that they still had to bathe after a rainstorm. Blake turned the radio off meekly. Connor took a seat on the old cloth-covered couch; Trent moved his legs to make room for him. "Can you believe the nerve of that guy?" Samantha spoke out. "Mr. Moroni?" Trent began, "he's evil. Money driven, blood drinking evil." Trent had made a creepy gesture with his hands before finishing his thought and resuming his perusal of his girlie magazine.

Blake got up from his seat near the table on the wall, and began to address the group. His voice was loud, yet was filled with enthusiasm, not anger: "That's why we have to do like Jones and I said, guys, we need to keep expanding in ways that he can't prevent. It will only be a little longer before we get enough attention to get noticed by somebody." Xero chimed in with a spirited "Yeah!", and Blake went on, "Until then, we're going to have to try to do some, *but not all*, of the petty man's requests." Jail-Bait sighed and began to gather and pile all of the band's sheet music. Connor waved for Andrew's attention. "You see, Summerlin," he began to speak, "you shouldn't feel too bad about your options changing. Even if your current state doesn't even bare a resemblance to what you had planned; even if your world has changed to the point where you can't see your future." The band members had hushed and began to listen to the Con-Man's discourse. "I don't know what to even say about that," Andrew replied, "But perhaps you, a gambler, wouldn't understand—I wanted a *degree*." Connor stood up and appealed to the group: "Okay, guys, I hope you don't mind, but my young friend here is really confused on the whole 'life goals' thing. I'm gonna need your cooperation for a moment—I think we could fix something here." There was a general consensus of nods. "You see, Summerlin, what you plan to do has very little bearing on what you *are*, or what you are to become." There were nods again, except from Andrew. Connor continued, "Look at Jail-Bait here," he said as he walked to face her directly. She leered at Connor for the use of the nickname, and Connor went on, "She has a degree." Jail-Bait smiled and said, "English education." "And tell me, Ms. Jones, what do you do for a living?" Connor asked in a tone usually reserved for investigative reporting. Jail-Bait gave up on her paper stacking and replied, "I play here, as you know, and I DJ at the Shake House on Tuesdays." Connor made a clicking sound and walked next to Blake. "Mr. Blanchard," Connor said, "What do you do professionally speaking?" Blake replied, "Why sir, I'm a carpenter; proud member local union 205." Connor leaned in as if he were holding a microphone and said, "Not hammering any nails today, Blake?" "Nope," Blake replied, sounding almost happy with the fact. "But why is that?" Connor's journalist voice probed. "It's feast and famine out there, I'm afraid," Blake replied.

"Starting to see a trend, kid? Well, either way, let's go on," Connor said as he walked over to the wall and stood beside Xero, who was now smoking. "Xero," Connor laughed for a second before returning to the subject, "Xero had a very 'interesting' essay on his college entrance exam: the entire lyrics to The Rivington's 'The Bird's the Word'." Xero took a puff off of a joint and replied with a grin as he exhaled, "I have a fundamental love of education." Andrew looked Xero, Jail-Bait and

Blake over and then turned to face Connor. "And the drummer? Am I to believe she's an out of work doctor or something?" he inquired. "Nope!" a voice answered in a pitch that was higher than what Andrew had expected. "Banker's daughter and spoiled rotten," Samantha said as she smiled and winked. "You see kid," Connor finished, "what you are has little to do with what you will be—and what you plan on being has even less to do with the matter. Take that as Lesson One, Summerlin." The group relaxed; the Connor Bentley show had ended. Andrew couldn't help but ask what to him had become the obvious: "Connor—What did you grow up wanting to be?" Connor winced and responded, "Woah, unauthorized name usage. Well, I'll be nice and still answer your question. I never intended on being anything but me." "Figures," Andrew said with a sigh.

Within minutes, the band mates were buzzing with conversation, mostly about their prior performance. "Thirty-four, man!" Xero could be heard yelling from his wall-perch. Connor and Trent went on for several minutes about the difference between College Rock and Alternative. The group began to splinter into two groups: Jail-Bait, Blake and Trent gathered near the doorway of the room; Xero and Samantha passed a joint back and forth while Connor and Andrew sat on the floral print couch, which faced them. Connor turned to Andrew after a while and said, "So how was your Vegas day, Virginia boy?" Andrew didn't respond right away. Rather, he looked up on a poster which hung on the wall near Samantha—an autographed poster of, according to the words printed thereupon, "Rockabilly legend Jackie J. Jackinson"—whoever the heck that was. He then thought, in as neutral of a manner as he could, of his day and what he had experienced: His odd wakeup, meeting Xero with an "x", the five hundred dollar jackpot, the buffet, and of course, The Reason Why. Andrew succeeded in attaining a feeling of benevolent impartiality. He had gone an entire hour without thinking of Sarah or unemployment, and when the topics were brought up by his new friend, it hadn't hurt as much as it had before. *It can't be a matter of time healing wounds—there must be something to this place,* he thought. "Taking an epoch there, Summerlin," Connor broke in. Gonna get there anytime soon?" Andrew broke his attention from Jackie Jackinson and replied, "Sorry, Yeah, I can answer right now, actually. This has been, by far and wide, one of the strangest days I have ever had." Connor appeared to be mulling Andrew's statement over in his mind. Andrew felt the need to further explain his comment: "Don't get me wrong, I meant it in a mostly good way. Vegas? Was that Las Vegas? I didn't see anything remotely like what I've seen in the movies." Connor's eyes widened. "Ah, that's a common misconception. The Vegas of which you are speaking is a pre-packaged, monopoly owned affair; not a bad place if you want to see some killer architecture, or need to find someone with blow. You've been in the real Vegas, kid. You got to meet some real people, too." That much was true, but Andrew was troubled by the use of the word "real". "No offense," he began, "but I've heard that word used as a marketing tool—a lot. 'visit the *real* New Orleans'; 'see the *real* Miami.' Sounds a little repetitive, huh?" Connor laughed and replied, "Well, that accent of yours is wielding some big words there." "What can I say...I always fancied book-learnin'," he said, purposefully playing up his southern drawl while doing so. Connor smiled and said, "Well it's good to see you can laugh amidst your 'woe'." Andrew replied, "I can't say that it doesn't hurt to think of it at all, but I'm doin' alright. Might even get it all back someday." His tone was defensive—deep down, Andrew wondered who he was trying to convince more: Connor, or himself. Connor took a deep breath and exhaled. "Okay, there's error number two." Andrew became concerned; worry lines appeared on his brow, and his eyelids trembled ever so slightly. "What? Why?" he asked. Connor resumed his seat upon the cloth covered couch, and motioned for Andrew to join him.

"The thing is, kid," Connor began, "I've found, that when sorting your life out, it is of highest importance to attend to your own matters before you go off and try relating to another person." Connor made efforts to keep speaking, but Andrew waved his hands in an attempt to speak: "What do you mean attend to myself first? I'm right in this whole thing; I'm trying to forgive." Connor sat up and took a dignified stance while attempting to educate his protégé. "Let me get this straight—she threw you out, broke your stuff, and even went so far as to make you unable to get the job you wanted," he said. Andrew began to feel irritated. Now the memories of Sarah came back, but this time in the form of a mild fury; tears began to well in his eyes, and he clenched his fists as he fought the severity of his emotions coming over him.

"Don't get mad. It's the easy path of least resistance which deters a sound mind to anger. *Understanding* is a far more lofty, not to mention doable, goal. Look at you, Summerlin: the mere mention of a woman's name has you falling apart." Andrew began to breath slower, and began to regain his composure. Connor continued, "You need to get to the point where things, especially words, can't bother you so much. Besides, you need to give this girl some time anyway; trust me. Women need time to recover, too—you'd be surprised how similar we really can be." Andrew listened intently, and when the Con-Man had finished, asked, "So, what's the point?" Connor shook his head in disbelief and said, "My Point? Ah, my point," Connor rose from his seat and continued, "Come with me to the Austin, and I'll get to my point." Andrew shrugged his shoulders and rose, adding, "fair enough," and noting in his mind that going up to the suite did *not* necessitate him staying there, or accepting further charity from Connor. The two said their goodbyes to The Reason Why, and left the communal dressing room.

"My point, dear Summerlin," Connor commenced his speech while he and Andrew were walking across the Pit, towards the hotel elevators, "I have an idea." Andrew's interest was piqued; "Go on, strange

Yankee, go on," Andrew responded. "Well, my idea is this: You are outright interesting to say the *least*; helpful when one is in need for certain. And the fact that you are in need yourself is equally as evident," Connor said. Andrew felt the desperate need for a rebuttal, but only managed to utter "I w—" before he was cut off in a fashion with which he was becoming increasingly familiar. "Don't deny it, country boy. It's not polite—to yourself." Andrew was vexed enough for Connor to go on: "Have you given any thought to the notion that your interests might best be served by following a smooth, easygoing gambler like *moi*?" "Huh? What do you mean?" Andrew inquired as they reached the elevators. Connor pressed a large rectangular button marked "Suites" once they had boarded; all of the rest of the floors had buttons which were roughly the size of a quarter, and became illuminated upon being depressed. The illuminated buttons reminded Andrew of the lit-up buttons he saw on the video poker machines. Martina McBride's *Independence Day* played overhead as the elevator began its ascent. They were alone in the elevator this time around. After the song hit its middle eight, Connor reprised his train of thought from the lobby: "I think we may be of use and assistance to one another. Your help to me being already understood, I venture to say I can help straighten you out—real quickly, I'm sure."

Andrew was confused. "Wait—What do you mean it's understood. What exactly would you be getting out of all this?" The Con-Man sighed and answered him: "The knowledge that I have helped someone who aided me *sans* regard? The entertainment 'y'all' provide? Something for my bored ass to do?" Andrew bestowed Connor with a look of awe—*Who is this guy?* he thought. Connor didn't give him the time to figure it out. "I intend to help you, mentor style. Follow me for a little bit. It's not like you have anything better to do, kid," he said as they exited the elevator. After they got out, they headed down towards the suite on the left near the end of the hallway. As they walked, Andrew thought the idea over and began to speak, "Okay. Let's say the idea has merit. I *could* 'follow you'; but I'm not taking any more money or free stuff. That was the deal, remember?" Connor gave him a glance which dripped of regretful acceptance, and nodded. "Yes, a deal's a deal, and you made your point; however, my wisdom won't cost you a nickel—just time and willingness to learn. And heck, you already have pocket change, I hear," he said. Andrew nodded and smiled. "Yeah, I got four aces," he replied. "Must've had a kicker with it," Connor responded. "A 'kicker'?" Andrew queried. Connor spoke without breaking his stride: "Aces, kid. If you are lucky enough to assemble four of them, your desire is to have the 'fifth card' be a two, three, or four—also known as 'kicker cards'. If your fifth, non-ace card is one of those, your jackpot gets increased significantly. Standard payout for four aces on a quarter machine with max coins bet is two hundred; five hundred with a kicker. Increases the payout, my man." He had done the entire sentence in a butler-esque voice; Andrew felt tempted to call him "Jeeves". *You learn something new everyday, if given the chance to notice*, he thought. "Oh," he said, "I don't gamble much, so except for those penny slots I saw, I don't think I'll be fixin' to gamble much more; money-wise, at least. I can pay you for the use of your guest room while I straighten up." They reached the double doors of the Austin Suite. "Don't even worry about it, kid. Just keep the room clean, and no eating the buffet egg salad and coming up here for the restroom—no way. That stuff stays down there for the professionals to clean up," Connor said, opening the door with a quick-draw of his room key. Andrew laughed and followed Connor as he walked into the landing.

"So here is my plan, 'phase one', at least. You are to wake when I wake, and shadow me; I'll provide all the rest for instruction. You will chill out, and you'll probably keep having good luck—you give me that kind of feeling," Connor said. Andrew nodded and replied, "Your plan seems to match my resolve—to get my life back." Connor quickly retorted, "Hey, there's no guarantee on what life you will someday have; yet, you can try to get a degree or get a girl. Always remember Lesson One, kid—You can have the best intentions, but that still won't give you knowledge of the future, nor lock in place your fate." Andrew was beginning to feel too tired to argue his point. "Fair enough," he replied, "With that, I believe I'll be going to sleep then—I'm beat." As Andrew walked to the guest room, he heard Connor say from the great room, "Well okay, but starting tomorrow, I won't allow for such an early tap-out, for I'm off to the floor; late-night blackjack awaits!" Andrew was shocked that someone could still be alert enough to gamble after what had been, for him at least, a very full day. "You sure you don't want to reconsider? We could play at the five dollar tables; not mandatory to your 'resolve' or my plan, but it'd be good times." Andrew stopped and turned around and rolled his eyes as he replied, "No. Thank you, but no. I'd really like to relax and get some sleep, especially since I apparently won't be afforded those options again anytime soon." Connor replied, "Haha. You're killing me, Summerlin. If you should find yourself in need of deeper relaxation than a bed or chair can afford, there's a sauna to your left, and there's a hot tub one door from your room to the right, if that's more your thing." Andrew replied before going down the hall-way, "thanks, Con-Artist." Connor called out behind him, "You've been talking to Jail-Bait too much!" Andrew went to the hot tub as Connor went to his room for a pre-blackjack change of clothes.

Andrew found the hot tub to be beyond relaxing; he spent his warm soak contemplating the day he had enjoyed, and little else, save for the bother of ending the hot tub and physically getting to the bed while feeling so soothed. His walk to the money room was done half-asleep. Andrew slept well in the room of money that night.

5.

For the second time in as many days, Andrew woke to the sounds of high-rise construction in a room which had replicas of money everywhere. This time, Andrew actually went to the window by his bed and parted the curtains, which looked like large, cotton C-notes, to take a look and see if he could locate the source of the unnatural noises which had woken him. It didn't take him long to find it: Not far off in the distance, *perhaps on Rancho Drive*, he thought, there was a skeleton of a building. Andrew squinted his eyes for a better view, and guessed that it had to be at least ten stories tall, with no sign of it being near completed in height. *I wonder what that's gonna be?* he thought as he noticed two cranes adjacent to the skeletal building frame. Andrew closed the curtains once he felt his mind had cleared from post-sleep delirium. *A shower would be a great way to start the day*, he decided.

As Andrew turned from the window, he remembered something: he didn't have a fresh set of clothes to change into after his shower. He was still in his boxers from the night before. *Can't ask Connor for clothes. The no-charity rule is something I'm not comfortable bending on; not to mention who knows what sort of textile horrors await within his closet*, he thought. Andrew went about picking up his clothes from the guest room floor; he was actually amazed that he had remembered to bring them with him from the hot tub the night before, as he barely remembered getting into bed. He was reaching for his last needed piece of apparel—a sock—when he noticed something had been slid beneath the guest room door. *What is that, a postcard?* he pondered; it appeared to be an small white card with a string wrapped around it which trailed back under and beyond the door. *Oh goodness, what is it now?* Andrew thought as he approached the card and picked it up. The string gave resistance; he kneeled and looked at it. It was a Texas Palace souvenir postcard which had a small note in Connor's handwriting upon it. The card read: "Don't pull me. Just open the door." He did, albeit cautiously. He found the string to be attached to a brown paper parcel which was knotted upon the outer door knob. *That man sure has a strange sense of humor*, he thought as he smiled and untied the package from the door-knob. *At least some of his eccentricities are predictable*, he thought as he carried the package to the bed and opened a white envelope which was taped to the brown paper. The envelope contained a crisp white card which was inked in what appeared to be fine calligraphy; the words were Connor's, and read: "I know we have our 'no-charity- rule' going on and all; but your clothes, especially those jeans, have to be filthy by now. I had an idea: take the clothes laid herein, and leave your old clothes in the bag—you can give me a dollar for each exchange, if it makes you feel better. I'll wash and sell the clothes, or something; being that there are no donations, such a system will, even in your eyes, con-stitute a fair exchange. When you're ready, join me at the Poker Room. Oh, and feel free to enjoy my excellent taste in threads, my man." It was simply signed, "Con". Opening the package, which was roughly the size of a six-pack of beer, exposed an outfit only a gambler nicknamed "Con-Man" could love: A bright red soccer jersey covered in orange stars which had "VICTORY" in large reflective letters across the chest. Beneath the shirt lay a pair of grey nylon running pants which had a thick mirror-like strip running down the sides of both legs. Andrew gave the shoes that followed an awkward glance—*Are these bowling shoes?* he thought. Whether or not they were intended for athletic use, the black, matte leather shoes had red stripes running horizontally, and reminded Andrew of a place called "Colonial Lanes". The first three parts of the ensemble had been so visually grating to his eyes that when he got to the last object—a neon green pair of socks—he didn't even notice the oddness of their hue.

After taking several skeptical viewings of himself from the wall opposite the bed, Andrew finally ventured out of the guest room. As the door to the Austin Suite closed behind him, Andrew became cognizant of the fact that he didn't have a hotel key to get back in. He took a desperate look at the door, and began to think of what he would need access to within the place. After a moment's contemplation, Andrew calmed down when he came to the conclusion that he didn't own anything; he had nothing to return for. *I'm sure my buddy Connor would find a way to turn that into a lesson about remaining calm under any given set of circumstances*, he thought as he continued his stride down the hallway.

The elevator doors chimed open; however, Andrew found it to be a different one than he had ridden in the past. This one had a gilt framed oil painting of a cowboy riding triumphantly upon a bucking bronco. He began his ride down alone, but was joined by an older couple on the sixth floor. The remainder of the way down was seamless and pleasantly quick. Andrew had neglected to visit the Poker Room in his exploration of the casino the day before, but he was informed by a passerby that it was located between the High Limit Lounge and the Race and Sports Book area. He remembered that the Race and Sports area was easily viewable from the Lone Star Bar.

Andrew walked at a relaxed, easygoing pace; he felt too awkward in the Con-Man's garish clothes to think about his lost girl or lost job. As he cut through the Race and Sports area, Andrew noticed the double doors of the Poker Room; he looked at the decades-old, faded wooden sign that hung over the doors as approached. A security officer scrutinized Andrew closely, and checked his Virginia driver's license three times before finally allowing him entry. *Either I look too young, or word of Mr. Bentley's acquaintances travels fast*, he thought as he stepped inside the room.

The Texas Palace Poker room was wooden-paneled, and smoke-filled. Eight rectangular felt tables sat upon an old, tattered green carpet. The three tables closest to the back were in use; the other five tables sat with black and white signs reading "Table Closed" upon them. Andrew walked past the vacant tables, noting that despite their worn deep blue velvet, he could still fully see white stars at every seat position. He spotted Connor sitting at the table in the middle near the back wall— while the other two tables were half-filled with patrons, the Con-Man's table seemed to be where all the real action was; there were three men waiting for the privilege of joining. Connor had noticed him, as well: he waved his hand overhead and called out, "Summerlin! Yo, Heart 'o Dixie! Over here!" Andrew lowered his head and walked over to Connor's seat at the table. Connor was quite salient amongst the other gamblers, who were mostly gray-haired; His red, white and blue sequin suit didn't hurt his salience, either. "Take a seat, kid. It's early Saturday—No Limit Hold 'Em buy-in is only $60 before noon," he said, sounding like he had read it directly from a brochure. Andrew looked at the full, bustling table, whose center was being loaded with chips by players anticipating the next round. "There's no space, Con-Man. All seats are occupied," Andrew replied—deep down, he was kind of glad that they were. "Ah ah ah," Connor said as he anted in, "no chickening out on me, Summerlin. This is part of our deal. Go buy in at one of the other tables, and I'll leave you be until I'm done putting these guys to shame." There were a few snickers from his opponents. "Fair enough," Andrew semi-growled as he grabbed his wallet and headed towards the table to Connor's right.

There were several seats available; Andrew took a seat directly across from the dealer. After another ID check, he found himself in possession of his very own chip rack, loaded with sixty white chips, each with a Texas Palace logo and the word "POKER—ONE" upon them. After he looked the rack over, he placed half of the chips in on the white star on the table in front of him. Luckily, this was not Andrew's first rodeo; he and his high school buddies used to play Seven Card Stud and Texas Hold 'Em on weekends. He wasn't terrific, yet he was far from unskilled. *Just keep to your presentation—the actual hands mean nothing*, he reminded himself. He wasn't Connor Bentley, but Andrew was determined to make his sixty dollars last at least an hour.

Andrew anted up, and was dealt pocket eights. A glance to his left revealed that Connor had just won a hand—he seemed to be applauding himself, much to the consternation of the other players. Andrew felt that his eights of Hearts and Diamonds would hold up well in the final two rounds of betting; after seeing the Eight of Spades fall on the Turn, he held three eights. The other two community cards were the Ten of Clubs and the King of Spades. He decided to bet all of his remaining chips that were on the table on the final round. *That's thirty*, he thought as he saw the final card, "the River", fall: the Two of Clubs. The betting froze at the River; everyone "checked", or passed, the final round of betting. An old lady in a Mumu wearing thick glasses had a full house, Kings over Twos. *Damn*, Andrew thought as he watched the woman giggle with glee as the dealer pushed the winnings to her.

During the next half-hour, Andrew found himself betting with more prudence than he had during his first hand. *Gotta be careful, apparently, out here even the ones that look like sheep are ruthless*, he noted. He was near even money when he heard Connor's voice. "Coming over, kid," he said as he sat down in the vacant seat to Andrew's right. "How's it going, killer?" he asked Andrew enthusiastically. Andrew counted his chips and replied, "I have forty-two dollars. You?" "I think I'm around two hundred seventy-five. Of course, I bought in at sixty, so I'm really at two hundred fifteen." The next twenty minutes were entertaining, to say the least. Andrew watched as Connor the dominated the game: bluffing, table-talking—the art of chattering about the game to mess with other players' minds; he even went all in while holding a two and a seven unsuited—and won. Andrew's chip count grew to a hundred fifteen, a fifty dollar profit when all was said and done. After a losing hand, Connor tipped the dealer and said. "I'm about done here." Andrew looked up from his chips and asked, "Oh? So where to now, o wise leader?" Connor pulled back his left sleeve to check his various devices. After playing with buttons on a mini-tablet and giving one of the watch-faces a glance, Connor responded, "I do believe that a visit to Race and Sports Book is in order." Andrew shrugged his shoulders and said, "Okay. Can't hurt." "Can't hurt?" Connor asked with rising intonation before continuing in a calmer, more *instructor-like* manner: "It's all part and parcel to the process, kid. We can't tell how we're gonna get you to a stable future just yet, so we don't want to go throwing away any possible components before we ascertain if they are to be of use." Andrew's apprehension mixed with confusion. "I'm along, I agreed to this. But, did you just say 'component'?" They both laughed as they gathered their chips and got up. "My point is," Connor began as they exited the Poker Room, "what if Race and Sports Book somehow leads you to your destiny? You can't say that you know for a fact that it won't." Andrew felt the logic a bit harsh—"That kind of logic could lead you *anywhere*," he said. "Exactly," Connor replied, cool as a cucumber the entire time.

Connor led Andrew through the Race and Sports Book area. The seats were filled by gamblers eagerly watching the large screen televisions which hung high above the counters. The seats on the Sports Book side were a mix of dark green easy-chairs and college-style desks, complete with cup holders. Andrew found the seating in the Race Book side to be far more upscale: each leather-backed, wheeled office chair was positioned with in its own wooden-paneled booth. The cherry panels were tattooed with decades of Vegas locals' graffiti and a variety of scratches, intentional or otherwise. Every booth had within it a shelf which was stocked with scratch paper and mini-pencils, and a ten inch color television that looked like it had been borrowed from 1993. Many of the booths had tattered and pen-marked copies of racing track forms and discarded losing tickets. Cigar smoke permeated the massive room, so much so that Andrew felt that oxygen was the additive there, and tobacco smoke the norm. Connor pulled several folded sheets of paper from his jacket pocket and grabbed a clutch of mini-pencils from a can on the counter, clicking one of his wrist devices as he made notes on the papers and took a glance at the white dry-erase boards which were directly behind the Race counter.

There was a collection of white posters taped upon the dry erase board; they were printed in black and white, and were each the size of a theatre movie poster. The posters varied principally at first sight by the names of racetracks which were printed in all capital letters on the top of each one. Andrew noticed a wide variety of track names: some, like Santa Anita and Churchill Downs, were known to him. Others, like Fingerlakes and Hollywood Park, were not familiar to him. He smiled when his eyes caught the sight of Mountaineer Park—He remembered the time when his uncle took him to the West Virginia racetrack when he was twelve. He was roused by the Con-Man, who tapped him on the shoulder and added, "Come on, kid. You can't make a move standing out in the open. It is time to conduct *business*." He waved in the general direction of the booths, and took a seat three rows in.

Andrew took a seat at an adjacent booth and rolled his chair near Connor's. The television was tuned to a race simulcast. There was a copy of the large "Track Form", which to his eyes appeared to closely resemble a newspaper in color and format, sitting next to the television; it was opened to a section with bold type reading "PRESQUE ISLE" upon it. Connor's television had a different race broadcast than his. "So, what's your game here?" Andrew asked Connor. The Con-Man lifted his eyes from the Track Form to reply, "What do you mean?" He didn't wait for a response; he delved immediately back into his furious note taking. Andrew was undaunted, and further pressed his inquiry: "I mean, you said 'the ponies' were your favorite; and, you're a professional gambler—So I gotta assume you'd have some sort of method or procedure with the whole thing..." Connor scoffed and once again raised his gaze from his "paperwork". Connor's brow creased, and his voice raised, not in aggression, but rather the will to inform. He said, "Racing. Don't trifle an art with a hobby's definition. I'd love to teach you, kid, but we're gonna skip the study of the supreme science and keep it simple for now. We're gonna focus on that whole fix your life thing for a while." Andrew stared in awe; *the simpler goal is fixing my life? How hard can betting on a race be?* he thought. Connor gathered his papers and got up from his seat. As Connor rose, he asked Andrew, "Are you going to place any bets?" Andrew got up and replied, "How can I? I like them as animals 'n' all, but I've never bet on a horse before. Hey—Seein' as how that 'science' of yours is a little heavy for my tastes, what would you suggest I do?" Connor placed his fist to his chin as he thought; *Great, it's Rodin's "The Thinker," only he's in a sequined jacket,* Andrew couldn't help thinking. Connor caught a glimpse of Andrew's grin and replied, "Well, maybe the best 'trick' for the uninitiated would be to have no trick at all; try guessing out of the blue, or pick a horse with a name that you like. Andrew replied, "Okay, I s'pose that could be fun." He followed Connor to the line for the Race Book Counter.

As they slowly advanced to the Race Counter, Andrew heard a loud voice coming from the Race attendant behind the counter when Connor arrived. "Connor Bentley! A little late for the Belmont, aren't we?" the Attendant said. Connor retorted, "The P-Man's in the house!" The two men laughed, and Connor added, "It's okay, I've found a few plays for Hollywood Park instead." Connor continued speaking with the attendant, albeit in a hushed tone. After about a minute, the Con-Man slid a few greenbacks across the counter, and took a few white tickets from him before walking back to his booth. Andrew didn't have the foresight to listen in on his bets. When his turn came, he found the

Race Book attendant to be a pale, rather portly man with a gray goatee. He was smiling, and seemed to be rather easygoing. Andrew noticed the man's nametag said Patrick. *Well, that explains who "P-Man" is,* Andrew thought. "Batter up, new better please," Patrick said as he waved Andrew up.

Anxiety began to take hold of Andrew—though he had visited a track before, he was a kid at the time, and mostly remembered liking the sounds of the galloping horses. He had never placed a bet on a sporting event in his life; at least not a legal one that didn't involve his brothers' friends and a six-pack of beer as the vig. He looked over the various posters until one for the fifth race at Hollywood Park caught his eyes— He had just heard Bentley mention that track. He pointed his finger to the poster and said, "I'll take that one—Number seven, 'BetyouIcan'." Andrew was beaming: he had accomplished the feat of placing a bet without looking awkward or sounding novice. He handed Patrick a crisp five dollar bill from his wallet, and eagerly awaited his ticket. Patrick looked at Andrew like he had just produced a Bald Eagle from his nose. *Uh oh*, he thought, *somethin' tells me I didn't get it right, after all.* "You want *what* exactly?" Patrick asked. Andrew was dumbfounded; he felt out of place and was struggling to say anything comprehensible. "Look, you're with the Con-Man, and you seem to be new. Need help there, Deep South?" Patrick said, seeming to possess a little bit of a southwestern accent himself. *Oh great, they all do it*, Andrew thought. "Yes I do, sir, but I'm afraid I don't know with *what*," he responded as he looked again at the Hollywood Park race five poster.

Patrick instructed Andrew in the concept of Win-Place-Show betting, which pleased him immensely, and irritated the motley crowd of gamblers who were waiting in line behind him. Andrew thanked Patrick emphatically, and placed a bet for "two dollars across the board", which he had just been informed equaled a six dollar bet, and would cover him if "BetyouIcan" came in first, second, or third place. He thanked Patrick again, and gave him a ten dollar tip for his troubles after receiving his Race Ticket. Andrew turned from the counter and made for his seat when he saw that Connor was standing with a proud look on his face—he had been watching the entire time. "Channel nine, Summerlin," he said to him, pointing at the television in Andrew's booth as he took his seat. He turned on his television and turned it to nine. The fourth race at Hollywood Park was about to be underway; the horses were being loaded into the gates. "So, what do we do now?" Andrew asked. Connor replied without moving his eyes from his television screen, "Well, obviously, we're gonna wait for the fifth race now, aren't we? I know for a fact we both have a bet in that one." "Care to elaborate on what your picks for the fifth race?" Andrew asked. "Wouldn't you and half of Clark County love to know, kid. You gotta remember the calming down part. We'll probably stay around for a few races. I don't need to see all of Hollywood Park's remaining races, though. We can always check the Race Results Board," Connor said as he pointed to a glass encased bulletin board with several sheets of paper upon it that adorned the back wall near the Poker Room. "Just stay seated, try to enjoy yourself, and maybe you'll learn something," Connor added with a grin. Before returning to his television, Andrew had one more thing on his mind: "And I have to ask, gamblers do eat don't they? I haven't seen you eat yet, and lunch time seems pretty close to me." The Con-Man laughed, and for a minute Andrew accomplished the impossible act of distracting his view from the race. "I eat when I wake, far earlier than you, I might add. And as far as lunch is concerned, that will have to wait; Saturday lunch, for me, is a special experience. And for special experiences, one has to aim for feats 'above the bar'. So we're gonna have to kill some time first before we can do what I have planned." "Why's that?" Andrew immediately asked. "You ask too many questions, kid," Connor replied before turning back to his television.

Then came the fifth race. Connor was reclining in full relaxation, while Andrew had butterflies in his stomach as while he watched his horse, the brown one with a maroon saddlecloth bearing the number seven, slowly cantor into his gate. Connor seemed amused; his heels were now upon the desk-ledge of his booth as he grinned. *If he seemed any more at home here, I'd swear he was built with the place*, Andrew thought with mild frustration. He couldn't comprehend how anyone could be calm while their cash was being risked upon something as random as a horse race—not to mention how someone could do something like that so often as to constitute a profession and all the while remain undaunted was beyond him. Andrew's attention jerked back to his television when he heard an announcer say, "and they're off!"

Three lighter colored horses broke off to an early lead; Andrew's horse led up the rear of the pack well past the first two furlongs. *Number seven is definitely not Secretariat*, he thought with dismay as the horses reached the half-mile mark with "BetyouIcan" making very little forward progress. He heard Connor calmly mutter "go baby, go" from the next booth over. Andrew watched in anticipation as his horse broke from the pack and charged towards the three-horse cluster near the front. Anticipation became disappointment as he watched "BetyouIcan" prove that he, in fact, *could not*—the number seven horse finished fifth out of the twelve horse field. Andrew looked over at Connor, and found that he did not appear to match his mood, nor demeanor. *He must have won a little*, Andrew thought as he saw Connor rise and approach the betting counter with one of his white Race Tickets in his hand, all the while having a chipper sort of spring to his step. Andrew reclined and rolled his eyes, noting that he had never really liked the color maroon, anyway.

The next half hour or so was spent watching the sixth through the eighth races at Hollywood Park. After race seven, Connor made another visit to the Race Counter, ticket in hand. The Con-Man seemed to stride more calmly than before, however—*He must have broken even*, Andrew assumed. The eighth race was viewed with mild interest by Connor, and no interest whatsoever by Andrew. As he didn't go to the counter at the race's conclusion, Andrew noted that Connor must not have prevailed in that one.

"All right," Connor began as he checked his wristwatches, "It's a quarter of twelve; we should be able to obtain our seating." He got up and looked to Andrew, adding, "And while we wend our way, here's some knowledge for that currently empty plate you have: I know you lost. How, in your judgment, do you think I did?" Andrew thought carefully for a moment before answering: "I think you won two races. I make this call because I saw you go up there. Twice. And one time you seemed much happier than the other, I'd reckon." Connor replied in a professor-like tone, "And, Mr. Summerlin, which of those racing conquests profited me more?" "The first one, obviously," Andrew replied with haste. Connor looked like he had a point to prove; he stood and began to walk, gesturing for Andrew to follow him as he continued his instruction, "Oh? And why's that, kid?" He bit his lip in contemplation; Andrew sensed that his companion was about to expose a flaw in his logic, but he couldn't discern a way to precisely predict it. Andrew responded, "You seemed to have a way bigger smile on your face on your first trip back from the counter than on your second one. Connor nodded and said, "that may be true, but one's feelings of life shouldn't be viewed by just one or two circumstances, even if they be positive ones. For instance, I submit the case of *me*, back there, just a few minutes ago: I won seven thousand dollars—on my ticket for race *seven*. Race five was a win by the favored horse, number three, on a Win-Place-Show; it profited me five dollars, Summerlin." Andrew gave Connor a nose-squinted look of defiance and replied, "Okay, that only means you were aware that I was observing you, and you reacted accordingly in a manner to suit your future 'lesson'." Andrew was too distracted with the topic at hand to realize where they were in fact going—he merely followed and kept pace with the Con-Man. The two of them had been talking so intently that they had already reached the elevator lobby. Connor pressed the call button and continued speaking: "No, that's not it at all, Dixie-child. I don't change how I act, whether for *lessons* or not. That's part of how my honesty and my teaching work. It is also the spine column to which Lesson Two adheres: Only rational judgments matter—fear and wishful thinking are to be left at the door. Once you learn it well enough, you'll be able to call it 'just be yourself'. " Andrew contemplated the fact before giving a sigh and replying, "You know, for some strange reason, I'm actually inclined to believe you. I doubt you could be anything but you." Connor winked and said, "good." They boarded an elevator, joining two other passengers, a teenaged boy playing with some sort of iDevice, and an old man, who tapped his cane to the beat of Billy Ray Cyrus' *Achy Breaky Heart*, which was playing from the speakers overhead. Andrew saw Connor push a button, but didn't notice which one; he had assumed that they would be eating room service in the Austin Suite, due mostly to the fact that Connor had alluded to his Saturday lunches being "special experiences". The young man disembarked at floor three; the older man's cane tapping grated Andrew's ears until he got off on floor twelve. Andrew approached the doors in anticipation of the elevator stopping on the Suite level—it did not.

Andrew was dumbfounded. He glanced at Connor with extreme curiosity. "I was wondering when you'd become curious as to where we were going," Connor said. He gave Andrew an opportunity to speak; however, he was too agape to reply. The Con-Man went on, "we are going to the top-most level of the Texas Palace: to the 'Executive Level'." "The 'Executive Level'? What are we goin' to do there?" Andrew inquired. "Why, eat lunch of course. Didn't we go over that part before?" Connor replied rapidly. Andrew decided it would be easier to just go along with the whole thing than to ask.

Connor and Andrew exited the elevator, and entered a long white hallway with elegant wood moldings, and plush red carpet. There were, as well, the occasional, obligatory pieces of Texas-related art: paintings of cowboys, horseshoes hung on nails, ranching tools, and the like. After they had gone about twenty feet in silence, Connor said, "The point I was making, Summerlin, is that you don't act cool and collected during a loss because it's the 'cool or 'mature' thing to do. An experienced and well-informed soul plays it cool because they have learned how to be in control of their emotions—for their own betterment, I might add. If you learn not to *not* let a lot of small things bother you, you will become calmer, and have a clearer mind with which to mitigate any new incoming stressors. You'll handle everything better, both the good and the bad, kid. Or if you want the short form version: you'll take things as I do the moment that you learn to not allow anxiety to affect you in any direction; don't sweat the minutiae of life." Andrew was silent, far too deep in thought to speak—the wisdom of a professional gambler, while lacking the grace and conciseness of Socrates, had been poignant nonetheless.

Connor came to a stop in front of a large set of double doors with impressive brass knobs. The knobs were different from the ones on the rooms and suites, in that they were lacking a hotel card-key reader—the right knob, instead, had an old-fashioned keyhole. "And, what is more," Connor continued his discourse, "learning to be slow to react will enable you to give situations the extra time they might have needed before even being attemptable." He jiggled the doorknob, and the door opened smoothly and wide before them. "Consider all that Lesson Three. And with that, we may relax."

The room that lay before the two men was marvelous: it was a spacious meeting room, with massive windows and royal blue carpet; it was furnished with a well-polished mahogany table which had enough Victorian chairs to seat fourteen, counting two extra seats for the end of the table. A massive video presentation screen sat at the far end of the room. "I give you the Texas Palace Executive Conference Room—our dining room!" Connor cried out in joy as he walked up to the table and ran his finger gracefully upon the length of the table's edge. "Take any seat you want, kid. I recommend the window view, consider it Vegas

Alfresco." Rather than ask what in the blazes that *was*, Andrew took a seat with a view, two chairs to the left of where Connor sat.

It was all perfectly elegant, yet there was no food in sight. "I hate to be a fly in your ointment here, but how exactly are we going to order food up here?" Connor had established a deep recline in his stiff-backed chair, and deployed his right elbow upon the nearest ledge—in this case, the table—which resulted in his chair pointing to the table at an angle, a sight with which Andrew was becoming increasingly familiar. "Be calm. Things happen when they are supposed to happen. See what you made me do? Lesson four was meant for after the meal," Connor replied, ending his phony complaint with his customary grin. Andrew knew better than to ask any more food-related questions, and instead asked himself one: *Calm. How the heck is someone with my lot in life supposed to be calm? I don't have any clue on anything right now*, he thought. Connor had taken to glancing out the window in quiet contemplation.

After an idle ten minutes had passed, a knock came upon the doors. "Room...Room service?" the voice was heard, sounding quite unsure if they had the correct place. Connor sat up and replied, "Come on in, guys." Andrew turned in his seat to face the opening door. Two young men dressed in suits entered, pulling a service cart draped in white linen behind them. *Oh, Goodness, what is this all about?* Andrew thought as he watched the men pull the cart within inches of Connor. One of the two men pulled off the linen to reveal two covered silver dining trays, along with a few assorted dining accoutrements on a third, uncovered tray. Andrew watched the spectacle, becoming very interested in what the possible contents under the silver lids might be.

The room service attendants placed the covered serving trays on the table, one for each man. Next, two elegant white teacups were placed before each of them: Andrew couldn't see what filled Connor's cup, but instantly recognized the smell and sight of hot, fresh-brewed coffee coming from his. The serving tray lids were drawn precisely in unison, to which Connor added a mild, "voila". Andrew noticed Connor's meal first: a large plate of noodles with a light-colored sauce upon it, with a small saucer to the side with an unopened bag of fruit chew candy atop it. Andrew's tray held a meal which was far more normal in his eyes. It even seemed "down-home", if such a thing were even possible in Las Vegas—bacon, eggs and grits, with a piece of pecan pie. *These grits are real!* He thought in astonishment as he savored every bite. He, being a Southerner by birth and rearing, *hated* "instant grits", and he could quickly detect their presence; these were slow-boiled, and delicious. "I gotta admit," Andrew said to Connor after finishing a gulp of bacon and egg, "these are darn good. What the—pardon—what the *heck* are you eating, if you don't mind me asking? Connor swallowed his mouthful, and wiped his mouth clean with a napkin before replying, "It's Beef Stroganoff, and the other is a locally made candy, 'Wallbangers'." From anyone else's mouth, Andrew would have doubted the credibility of the bag of candy's name; from the Con-Man, it seemed believable.

They continued their meals, and Andrew treasured every bite—it was the first meal with bacon that he had gotten to eat since Sarah's "No pork" phase, which had started a year ago. Though his discourses on life seemed to make an odd form of sense, Andrew realized there was no hope to figuring out the eccentricities of Connor Bentley. *When in doubt, ask*, he thought before placing his fork down and asking, "So how did you know I—" Connor had finished his Stroganoff, and cut him off, "I knew you were coming because of the deal; that, and I couldn't resist the opportunity to amaze. And I knew you'd like that saturated-fat-fest because you pronounce the word 'here' without an 'r' sound." Connor was smiling, genuinely amused. *"Nice,"* Andrew replied with sarcasm. "It was to your liking though," Connor noted. "Very true," a contented Andrew answered moments before another knock came upon the Executive Conference Room's doors. Andrew looked to Connor, hoping that he'd shed some light on what appeared to be the next part of his plan—it wasn't. "Now *that* I didn't call for..." the Con-Man said slowly and quietly, barely above a whisper. Andrew's eyes widened as he began to wonder if his friend had led him into the Executive Level under pretenses that were less than official. "Come in, come in!" Connor said in his best fake-Arabic accent. *Great, we might getting in trouble, and he thinks he's a Sultan*, Andrew thought.

The doors swung wide open, but this time with enough force to rattle the door frame. Three persons, two men wearing badges and the beige, police-like uniforms of an indoor security officer, and a short, pudgy ,brunette woman wearing a purple blazer with a scowl on her face and a snub-nose revolver on her hip. The woman walked straight to Connor, and glared him in the eye. "Connor Bentley," the woman said in an icy tone. "Allison Schwartz," Connor replied in a playful manner. Something of a rebellious nature sprung from deep within his soul—his friend was about to be picked on, and Andrew couldn't help but jump in; "Should I...Do I get my turn too?" he asked with a bright mocking smile, "I'll do my own, I'm Andrew Cad—" Connor cut him off in his usual fashion while extending his left arm towards Andrew, "He's Summerlin." The three people Andrew assumed were members of the security staff were scowling at Connor. Andrew relented to Connor's using of the girly nickname; he decided to save his energy for more important endeavors, and simply waved to the officers.

Allison Schwartz put her hands on her hips and asked demandingly, "What are you doing here, Bentley?" Andrew began to feel like he had become invisible; nobody was looking at him, nor did the woman seem to notice his crack at her authority. "Well," Connor began mockingly, "I *was* coordinating a 'we love Allison the overweight assistant security supervisor' parade—but you just had to come up and ruin the surprise. It's for the best, anyway, it turned out that a one-thirtieth scale float of you was deemed 'too large for road use' by the DMV...*and* the fire department, of course." Allison's scowl turned into a tomato-red, teeth-gnashing grimace of pure hatred. "Whether or not you think you are amusing, you are a guest at this hotel, and do not have the authorization to be in here. The Executive Level offices and Conference Room are for the expressed use of commercially registered business guests and company personnel. You are *neither*. I believe you have been informed of this fact in the past. By *me*." Connor was genuinely amused by Allison's rage, and fighting the earnest desire to burst out laughing; the woman was playing into his able hands. *It's like watching a shark near bloody water*, Andrew observed. He felt too scared to speak, and believed that he and his friend would be ejected at any moment, possibly with force. "Yet here I am, inside the room, and we managed room service, to boot. Odd huh?" Connor mused. Andrew noticed one of Ms. Schwartz's back-up officers fighting the urge to laugh.

"How did you get that door open without a security officer or company executive?" Allison demanded. Connor twisted in his chair to face her directly; he looked like a kid in a candy store. "I must be even more important than I look, huh?" Connor added before taking a leisurely sip from his coffee cup; Andrew finally noticed that his friend's cup was filled with sparkling grape soda. "Who'd you bribe, Bentley?" Allison asked. The assistant supervisor's backup officers continued to stand near the door, arms crossed, with a look of pride, which one can only possess while being a "guard" of something. "Well," Connor began to reply, "according to *you*, this mystery person that I bribed must have been an executive, or a member of your proud little security force." If explosions could be people, Allison was Krakatoa in a utility belt. Again, one of the backup officers was having problems keeping a straight face. Connor finished his bag of candy, and wiped his mouth with his napkin once more before looking back at the security staff, and rising from his seat. "Kinda through with the place anyway, though. Do you want us to leave the tip for room service up here on the table, or do I hand it directly to you?" he casually inquired. The officers behind Ms. Schwartz were able to hide their laughter because their jobs had depended on it; with Andrew, that was not the case—he was laughing quite freely. "Out! Now!" the woman ordered. "Coming, Summerlin?" Connor asked as he brusquely passed by Ms. Schwartz. Andrew jumped up to quickly follow in his footsteps.

The officers were locking up the Conference Room while the duo headed for the elevators. "You sure got up there fast, Yankee," Andrew said as they stepped inside the elevator. Connor replied, "Well, sometimes a cause can outlive its usefulness. We were done eating, anyway. So, by irking that wretched harpy, and filling our bellies, I say job well done on our part, as far as lunch is concerned." Andrew laughed when he realized what Connor had actually just said. "You seem pretty laid-back around most people. What did she do to get you so aggressive. Funny, but aggressive nonetheless," Andrew said. "She's the kind of *officer* who gets offended when you use a boardroom table for shuffleboard: no sense of humor in life whatsoever," Connor replied.

The elevator began its descent. Andrew looked to the familiar painting—good ol' oil derricks on a rolling Texas hills—before turning his attention back to Connor. "So you knew from the moment they arrived that we wouldn't be staying. So, we stayed for reasons of...?" Connor winked and replied, "It was simply a case of knowing when to fold. We played one heck of a good hand in the meantime." *I suppose he has a point, though I gotta admit Connor's idea of entertainment is cavalier, to say the least*, Andrew thought as he laughed a little, remembering what had just passed. "So, back down to the casino then?" Andrew asked. "Well, through it, to be more precise," Connor replied. Andrew knew he might be made fun of for asking too many questions, but he couldn't resist—"Okay, I have to ask: *through* it?" he inquired. "Yes, Summerlin, through it. We are going to the west side valet. Near the front, kid," he responded as they reached the lobby, and the elevator doors squeaked open.

Andrew followed Connor as he walked briskly towards the casinos main doors. As they crossed through the Pit, Andrew said, "At least I'll get to see what kind of car you drive." Connor opened a door to reveal a view of Reata Ave basked in late-afternoon sunlight. "You get to see *one*, kid," he added as they walked outside. They crossed two lanes designated for guest and visitor drop-off, both of which were under the massive front canopy. Connor waved his arm high overhead as he looked to the valet booth, which was built into the far left "pillar" of the canopy. A man in a tan collared shirt exited the valet booth and waved back at him. "Number seventeen today, please!" Connor called out to the man, who re-entered the booth and quickly returned with a set of keys before running past the canopy and into the valet car lot.

Connor strolled to the curb by the valet booth, and Andrew joined him a moment later. "So, where are we goin'?" he asked while they waited for the valet to return. Connor was looking off in the distance, and replied without turning, "We are going to several places. The first and most important stop will be for clothes." Andrew felt the need to immediately rebut: "Hey—I thought we agreed that there'd be no more charity goin' on." A loud engine revved in the distance, and Connor replied, "Not charity, kid. I am buying some clothes; can't live a life like mine without poppin' tags every now and then. Granted, you *are* in extreme need clothes-wise; however, I figured we'd just keep to the exchange you have already signed off on by wearing that lovely shirt.

As luck would have it, we're the same size." *Sheesh, I wonder how long it took for him to come up with a generous plan I couldn't cancel out?* Andrew wondered. "That would depend, gamblin' man—will all the outfits look like this?" he asked Connor while he did a wave over his clothes with his left hand. A sports car pulled up. The term "sports car" would be putting it lightly—the car that the valet parked inches from the curb was a sleek, loud-engine revving, two-seater convertible coupe, covered in metallic, reflective paint. It looked as if the vehicle had been carved out of mirrors. "Well, not all of my threats are as chill as that set, no," Connor said as he jumped into the driver's seat without opening the door. Andrew opened the passenger door and got in while the Connor handed the valet a twenty from his seat. The car roared to life; Connor yelled "Thanks, Zak!" as he and Andrew drove off the property, first onto Reata Avenue, then onto the highway heading north.

While they sped upon US Interstate 95, Andrew decided to turn on the radio, and tuned it until he found a Country music station. *"Really?"* Connor asked—Andrew grinned as he reclined and let Waylon Jennings do his thing. Within twenty minutes, they arrived at a strip mall with several small boutiques, most advertising men's fashions. "You gotta love options, Summerlin," Connor said as they got out of the car. "Options—Actually I'm not liking too many of those lately," Andrew lamented. Connor shook his head in dismissal and said, "That's because you've failed in availing yourself of a better set of options." Connor led Andrew towards a clothing store called "Top Drawer Menswear".

The front signage of the store looked old, cracked, and irretrievably worn-out; however, the contents of the inside of the establishment were all posh and in pristine condition, from the flawless hardwood floor to the mirror-polished oak shelves and clothing racks. Top Drawer Menswear was brilliantly lit by a conglomeration of fluorescent bars. Shoes, shirts, slacks and suits were all artfully displayed. "Sergio, good to see you, old man," Connor said as he eyed the cashier upon entry. Sergio and Connor talked quietly near the cash register. Meanwhile, Andrew saw a happy couple shopping together near the back of the store. It was a young blonde in a ponytail, holding hands with a tall, tan man with broad shoulders and a cheerful smile on his face. The woman was holding a shirt on a hanger against her companion's chest, comparing its size against the man's frame. Andrew then, for the first time that day, thought of Sarah. Years ago, he and Sarah had been on a trip similar to the happy couple he had just observed. Their shopping trip had been to the New River Valley Mall in Blacksburg, but the rest of the details were almost identical—Andrew vividly recalled the pastel collared shirts she had picked for him. He had detested the shirts intensely; yet, in his current state he would have traded all he owned to have just one of them back. *They're with all my old Braves shirts now, in a dumpster somewhere I'll reckon*, he thought.

Andrew had reverted to his pre-Connor form of emotional dejection, and collapsed his head into his hands. "Hey, Mr. Counter-productive!"

Connor's loud voice woke Andrew from his grief. He looked up to find Connor and Sergio, each holding a handful of clothing, and clothing-related items. "There's no time for that. Plus, if you break your little Tuscaloosa heart in every store we visit, you're never gonna make it, kid. Now try these on," Connor said as he handed Andrew a silk shirt and a pair of ash-gray slacks. "Tuscaloosa's in Alabama," Andrew replied. "Whatever," Connor said with a slight smile as he pointed him towards the dressing room in the back.

The next two hours were devoted to visiting a multitude of similar men's clothing shops, and therein obtaining an entire lot of clothes. Most of the purchases had been made with Connor's "clothing exchange" in mind; however, one bag of clothes in the trunk of the mirror-coupe had been separated from the other purchases—"Those are too good for the uninitiated," Connor said when pressed for information by Andrew. The sky was blue-black, and most of the stores were closed when Connor and Andrew exited a shop entitled "The Superior Male", and got into the car.

"Okay, now that you have the proper attire for our fair city, where would you like to go?" Connor asked. "Me?" Andrew asked in disbelief—he had become accustomed to simply following the Con-Man, and hadn't given any genuine thought as to where *he* would choose to go. "Yes, you," Connor replied, "It's part of that whole letting yourself be happy thing. Remember the slot machine earlier? Do what comes to mind within reason, kid." Andrew sat back and stared the passenger seat sun-visor while he pensively debated what he'd want to do. He had hoped that, as earlier, his next activity would have been pre-planned for him. It had become easy in the last two days to ditch the responsibility of making plans and simply follow his new strangely-dressed friend. *What's fun when you've bottomed out?* he asked himself. He finally had an idea, and turned to face Connor with it: "I don't suppose there's a honky-tonk around here?" he asked. Connor bit his lip and thought for a minute before responding, "Well, we could go back to the Rail Yard, if that's what you want." Andrew shook his head in protest, "Not exactly what I had in mind, Yankee." Connor turned his eyes to Andrew with a serious look on his face; "You don't need to be calling me names, you know," he said. Andrew glared at him and hastily replied, "*Summerlin? Really?*" "Good point," Connor admitted as he turned the key to start up the mirror-coupe. "So?" Connor said before revving the engine. Andrew looked out towards the horizon and replied, "Okay. Let's go somewhere I've heard of. Show me Las Vegas." Connor grinned and said, "You want *Vegas*? I'll show you Vegas." The mirrored car sped off wildly towards the highway.

The highway led the two men to an off-ramp which was bathed in a sea of perpetually twinkling, multicolored lights. Andrew didn't see any buildings fashioned after Wonders of the World; he didn't see any edifices named after a famous Roman emperor, either. "Where are we?" Andrew asked Connor as the night air ripped through his hair and the car slowed at a stoplight. "This," Connor began to speak dramatically, "is the fabulous city of Las Vegas!" The light turned green, and they began to roll forward. "Las Vegas Boulevard and the Fremont Street Experience," he added. Andrew was steeped in confusion—"What about the Las Vegas that's in all the movies, though?" Connor pulled to the side of the road and slowed to a near stop. "*What?* You've never seen a James Bond movie, Summerlin?" he asked with a bewildered look. Andrew then noticed that the pull over had not just been for dramatic effect: Connor had steered the car into the valet lane of a large casino which sat at the intersection of Las Vegas Boulevard and Fremont Street. Andrew had been too distracted by the lights to even notice which hotel-casino they had stopped at. A valet attendant wearing a bright red jacket with brass buttons took Connor's keys and handed him a valet ticket—Andrew couldn't be sure, but he thought he saw him hand the valet a twenty dollar tip.

After the men had exited the vehicle, they walked out to a side-walk, where Andrew could see what could easily be a million lights, most twinkling on and off beneath the starless Las Vegas sky. "You see, it's all about perception," Connor said to Andrew as they walked beneath a massive steel dome which had a digital television screen built into its underside, "the official limits of the actual city of Las Vegas end going southbound on Sahara Avenue. 'The Strip' isn't even in the city, Summerlin. It's unincorporated Clark County—well, most of it, anyway. There's also Windsor, Enterprise, and Paradise...don't get me started." "I won't," Andrew quipped as he walked down the sidewalk to get a better view of what lay beneath the dome. Connor stood where the sidewalk met the valet area, and looked deeply concerned for a moment—"Did you...Did you just make a *joke*?" Andrew heard Connor say from behind him.

Andrew was dumbfounded by the raw, mechanical beauty that was old Vegas. He had never seen anything like it before, nor would he have even expected to. And then he saw it: lights began to come on, almost *aflame*, at the other end of the long dome. As there was no car traffic on Fremont Street at this part of the city, Andrew didn't feel the least bit frightened to follow his impulse, and run towards the lights. "I'm goin' to look at that!" he yelled as he ran while looking overhead. "Attaboy," Connor said softly with a smile as he walked slowly behind him.

The light show was fantastic, at least in eyes of Andrew Cadoret. He never looked back for Connor, but spent the entire show looking as the images changed overhead: there were montages of beautiful landscapes, high-definition aerial dogfights, and two music numbers by noteworthy artists, all interspersed with screen-wide flashes of brilliant hues that only a casino could love. *That was nice*, Andrew thought as he finally looked down. When his eyes finally adjusted back to natural light, or

Vegas' version at least, Andrew noticed that there were many people who had gathered with him under the dome for the light show. Men and women of every age, size, race, wealth and status had been joined, even if only for a moment, as a common people, all sharing the same vision and same happiness. *How strange that a common human denominator would be found here, amidst the hustlers, hookers and dice pits,* Andrew thought.

Andrew turned in several directions, but failed to locate Connor anywhere. *He wouldn't—He wouldn't leave me here, would he?* Andrew worried. A cold sweat covered him as he became drenched in fear—he *had* only just met the man days before, and though he had seemed a genuinely good soul, Andrew had the deep fear that he might have misplaced his trust, after all. *Have I been too naïve?* he thought, *I hope I'm not the textbook yokel who got taken by "Sin City."* He backtracked his steps, and approximated the path he had taken since he was separated from the Con-Man. Andrew saw a valet attendant, and recognized the red jacket with brass buttons—he had, after several minutes, at last arrived at where he had or started out from. He walked up to the valet booth window, and a person who was playing video games on a small TV sprung to his feet and dashed up to greet Andrew. "Hi," the baby-faced man said. Andrew countered with his usual "howdy." "Has the guy I came here with come back for his car yet?" he asked the valet attendant, who, according to his nametag, was named Steve. "Do you have a ticket, sir?" the attendant asked him. Andrew looked down before replying—he already had an idea as to where this topic would lead: defeat. "No. I'm 'fraid not," he answered. The valet shook his head and said, "I'm quite sorry, sir, but I'm not permitted to divulge the status of a vehicle to anyone, unless they have the ticket; it's the law." Andrew let out a sigh and said, "Oh. Well, thanks anyway."

Backtracking had gotten Andrew nowhere; he decided that the only option he had at his disposal was to go the opposite direction down Las Vegas Boulevard—*If I can't find him by going towards "Old Vegas," maybe I'll locate him by going away from it*, he reasoned.

After walking only a few steps southward, Andrew heard a voice call out from behind him, "Excuse me!" He turned in an attempt to locate the voice; within a few frantic glances, he found it. It was a tall, physically imposing man clad in a suit under a red frockcoat with brass buttons, with a matching captain's cap on his head. *He must be a bellman,* Andrew realized as he noticed that the coat matched the valet's color scheme, and there was nametag upon the man's breast. The bellman did a slow run to catch up to Andrew. "Sir, are you a man with the nickname 'Summerlin'?" he asked. With look of mild annoyance, Andrew sighed and responded, "Yeah, I guess that's me." The bellman—whose nametag bore an embellished B.N. above the name "Lorenzo"—gave a sigh of relief and smiled ear to ear. "Mr. Bentley gave me a—let's just say a *generous* donation for me to find a man matching your description with the name 'Summerlin', and to bring him back to the casino," he said. Andrew took a deep, relaxing breath: he had been delivered from his chaos. "Lead on, well-paid man, lead on," Andrew said with a relaxed smile. As they walked back towards the valet where Connor had parked, Andrew thought, *I'd love to tell Connor what I was worried about back there, but something tells me I'll be deluged with a lesson about judging books by their covers, and I'll never hear the end of it.* He followed Lorenzo back to the valet and beyond it, through a set of tinted doors with gilt handles which were about thirty feet up the street.

As he followed the attendant through the casino floor, Andrew coughed a few times with increasing frequency as they moved deeper into the place. It was the second time in as many days that he, a man who had been raised by a family of smokers but did not himself smoke, was driven to rapid coughing—The other had been Texas Palace's Lone Star Bar. *I can handle a cigar smoker or two, but this place seems they manufacture the darned things here,* he thought as he rubbed his eyes. It was only after this that Andrew finally looked away from Lorenzo's back long enough to notice his surroundings. The gaming floor of the B.N.—Whatever that stood for—was massive, and, save for a few changes in decor, looked remarkably similar to that of Texas Palace. The smoke was thicker, perhaps, and there was a faint musty smell to the place, which only a century of gambling, drinking and fighting could produce. Andrew continued to follow the bellman as he led him into the Pit. *Wow, it's huge!* He thought as he saw the gigantic, faded, glitzy glory that was the B.N.'s table game area. Although it seemed a little ragged, there was an undeniable *Old World* charm about the place, with the ever-present clicking of Roulette wheels, the constant yelling of far off gamblers, and the occasional thud of dice hitting the backside of a craps table. Lorenzo came to a stop at a Blackjack table in the center of the Pit. "Ah, it *is* late-night," Andrew said to himself when he saw a relatively joyful Connor Bentley seated at the middle of the table. Lorenzo nodded at Connor and went on his way. "There's a seat free if you're feeling brave," Connor said. Andrew replied, "Oh? Blackjack isn't necessary for my well-being?" Connor glanced down at his chips before looking back at Andrew. "With a shoe this cold, nothing's necessary except extra fall-back cash for later and a stiff drink," he answered. The Blackjack dealer gave the Con-Man a stare; he tossed her a five dollar chip as a tip, and added, "Not your fault though, sunshine." Andrew watched as Connor played several hands, with the eventual result being the loss of all his chips. "I guess that's why they call it gambling," he said nonchalantly as he rose from his seat and joined Andrew, who had been waiting a few feet from the table. "Now what, gamblin' man?" Andrew inquired. "Now, I'll show you the *real* Las Vegas."

Connor led Andrew around the entirety of downtown Gaming District. Andrew followed him inside every casino they passed, and Connor described each building's history and legends with a surprising amount of historical detail, and a multitude of facts relating each edifice to the cultural subtext of the city. Their jaunt ended when they reached the Art District, which began near Charleston and Fourth

Street. Connor urged Andrew to "take in all of the skyline" as the two of them gazed southward, and then back towards downtown; after a short speech by the Con-Man concerning "the positive outlook for Vegas-born industry", Andrew smiled and nodded He *did* appreciate the skyline; however, he had no idea what industrial goods have or ever would be made in Las Vegas. They had a round of locally brewed beer at a small bar called "The Dizzy Lady" before beginning their walk back to the mirror-coupe. Their return placed the two men at the valet booth of the B.N.; however, Connor didn't stop there. He led Andrew beyond the valet area, and down the street, where he turned right.

Though he had no clue where his gambling mentor was going, Andrew followed without question. Within twenty minutes, they arrived at the intersection of the Boulevard and Seventh Street, where Connor came to a stop in the middle of the sidewalk. He turned to face Andrew, and pointed to a four-story building across the street. It was a dingy structure with a seven foot sign near where the property met the curb; it was an old marquee style sign from the Sixties, which had yellowed with time and had words upon it reading "22 DOLLARS A NIGHT. WE HAVE COLOR TV"; both of the "o"s in "color were long-gone. Upon reading the sign, Andrew turned to Connor and remarked with a grin, "Now am I to believe they are bragging that they have *a* television?" Even the Con-Man couldn't fail to see the humor; he laughed and patted him on the back. The building itself was concrete, and all of the windows had their old-fashioned shades drawn. "This is the fabulous 'Golden Old Nevada Inn'. Truly a gem, really," Connor said. Andrew gave the place a skeptical look and replied, "A gem? I know that *betters* can't be choosers 'n all, but doesn't this place look a little run-down to you?" Connor sprang quickly to the distressed building's defense: "Run down? I'd hardly say so—you haven't seen the inside of the place yet." In thirty-seven steps, he did.

The interior of the Golden Old Nevada Inn appeared as if it had been teleported there directly from the 1950's, complete with an old innkeeper behind an oak counter, with a large assembly of antique wooden pigeonholes behind him. Andrew noticed that each hole held room keys—*actual keys*—each having a neon-colored, diamond-shaped tag with a room number on it. There walls were stucco, and covered with gold-mining-related artworks; nothing about the place looked like it had seen a sunrise since Elvis had played at the International.

Connor stepped up to the counter and waved at the gray-haired man who stood behind it. "Greetings. Two rooms, please," he said. Andrew walked up to Connor's right; *No nametag*, he thought as he looked over the innkeeper—he was short, frail and had a beard that would have easily won him a prize at a ZZ Top lookalike contest. He spoke up and said, "Make sure you'll be chargin' us separately," before the man had a chance to gather their keys. The old man nodded and retrieved two keys from the pigeonholes behind him. Andrew handed the innkeeper twenty-five dollars, and was in turn handed three dollars change and the key to room 403—the top floor. Connor did the same, and was handed the key to room 405, which the innkeeper stated was one room down on the right from Andrew's.

There was no elevator at the inn, so Connor and Andrew had a midnight stroll up four staircases which were bordered with wrought-iron railings, and strongly resembled fire escapes. "Why, again, did we choose this one?" Andrew quietly asked before sticking the key into the doorknob. "Convenience and atmosphere, Summerlin. Trust me, the bedrooms are awesome," he replied. Andrew felt his "trust" in his friend's accommodation choices waver a bit; his brow rose in apprehension. "Sleep, kid. You won't believe this place in the morning," Andrew hadn't believed the place at *night*, and not in the ameliorative way that Connor had meant the expression.

Each door opened, and each door closed. Andrew didn't even bother flipping on the lights—he was too tired to criticize the anticipated ramshackle nature of the room. That could wait until morning. Andrew got into the bed, and after having a few fading recollections of the day which had passed, he fell fast asleep.

6.

Andrew awoke to the loud voice of Connor outside his door—he was currently doing a personal rendition of the song *Viva Las Vegas*, pausing to knock between each verse. *Ugh, maybe the construction sounds were better*, he thought as he rose from the still-made double bed beneath him. The bed occupied approximately half of the room. Andrew noticed the décor as he walked towards the door, and the bad singing it was hiding: There were several thinly-framed floral prints— the sort of decorations one usually finds in a dentist's office. There was an old floor mirror near the door; as he passed it, Andrew caught his reflection, and realized that he hadn't shaved in more than two days. The cuts and bruises from the Thursday night altercation, though, had healed somewhat. He was wearing a rust-colored short sleeved shirt and dark tan slacks. Andrew had convinced Connor to allow him one concession during their shopping spree the day before: a trip to a store called "The Boot Coral" for a set of *proper* footwear. In his request, Andrew had found one of the few types of stores—Western/Country apparel—that the Con-Man *didn't* know the location of in town. Andrew found it in the yellow pages, and bought a pair of handmade black Ropers that fit him to a tee. He got to the door by the time Connor had begun crooning something about women living wildly and not having any regard.

"What time is it?" Andrew asked through the door before yawning. "Nine o' nine," a surprisingly fully-awake Connor replied. The door opened. "Coffee, kid?" Connor offered Andrew a hot paper cup with a white plastic lid that had puffs of steam emanating from it. Andrew nodded and took the cup as they headed downstairs. "Behold! My city awakens!" Connor cried out in a dramatic fashion; only Andrew, in all his southern sensibilities, couldn't tell if his friend had been serious, or kidding. The morning sun kissed the old downtown warehouses, bail bondsmen, and low-rise hotel-casinos near Seventh Street and Las Vegas Boulevard. Most of the buildings that Andrew could see were still closed for business. *It's early Sunday*, Andrew noted as they reached the ground level. Connor took a deep breath and said, "Can you taste that glorious, desperate, ambitious Vegas air? It's the fuel of the kingly and the miserable." After taking another look at the neighborhood, Andrew responded, "You choose here—the non-gaming part of downtown, when all the shops are closed, to get poetic?" Connor gestured for Andrew to keep walking. "Well, I suppose that brings us to Lesson Five: never let a place, or circumstance limit what you choose to be. If you think about it, it sorta goes along well with Lesson One, that what you plan has no affect on what's really gonna happen, huh?" Connor said as they reached the Fremont Street Experience, heading in the direction of his car.

"Back to Texas?" Andrew inquired after the valet attendant went to get Connor's reflective ride. Connor nodded and replied, "Yeah, we can't miss the track today, it's why we woke up early. It's bad enough we missed early Sunday Morning Bingo." "Correction," Andrew rebutted, "*you* woke up early for that. *I* was woken up early by *you*. Oh, and don't quit your day job, by the way." Connor laughed as the two got into the car, and drove off for the highway. "You keep cracking jokes like that, and I'm gonna make you walk," Connor countered playfully. Andrew grinned and replied, "Judging from our whereabouts, that makes me inclined to remain polite." They both laughed, and the mirror car rolled on.

Connor and Andrew arrived to find Texas Palace relatively busy. "Bonus Point Day," the Con-Man noted as they pulled into the valet lane. "Is that something we're doing today, too?" Andrew asked. Connor scoffed and replied, "Nonsense, Summerlin. That's for Slots and Video Poker only; today, we're off to go a-racing." And to Race and Sports they went.

Unlike their last visit, the seats in the Race Book were completely filled—it was standing room only. Connor ran off towards the main casino floor, waving his arms and yelling "Cory!" In a short time, he returned to Andrew, and a tall, wide-shouldered man with dark hair, chestnut eyes and a three-piece suit was with him. "Mr. Bentley, it's always a pleasure," the man said. The voice in which the man addressed his friend, along with his perfect state of dress and placement near the casino floor's center gave Andrew a professional vibe; but he didn't see a nametag, or any other Texas Palace ID upon him. *Maybe he's high up, like that assistant supervisor Connor called a harpy*, he figured. "And how is the host with the most?" Connor asked enthusiastically. The two men did few rounds of chummy fake punches and then turned to Andrew. "I'm doing great, my guest with the best. And who do we have here?" the man Connor identified as a host asked. Connor made a clinking sound and gave a wink. Andrew's eyes had drifted to the multitudes of people passing by their three-man cluster on their way to the betting lines, but his attention returned to his mentor when he heard the accursed nickname. "This is a good hearted wretch I rescued from a sea of *romantic woe*; everyone calls him Summerlin." *You have got to be kidding*, Andrew thought. He shook his head at Connor's theatrics before giving the host a wave. "Summerlin," Connor began, "this is the best customer relations liaison in the business: Mr. Cory Detwiller. Cory offered Andrew a handshake, and he took it. "It is an honor," the host said; Andrew replied, "Likewise."

Connor's face became distressed upon taking a glance at the Race Book seating situation. Beyond the seats, the betting lines for the races winded to within feet of where the men stood. "Hey, Cory, that brings me to why I called you: think you can pull me a VIP?" Connor asked him. Cory pulled a small leather covered notebook from within his suit pocket, and flipped through several pages before landing on one that caught his interest. After a moment of contemplation, Cory answered Connor, "It's a Sunday full house, but I can get you in." He left, walking past the Lone Star Bar, and completely out of view. "What's that all about?" Andrew inquired. "Give it time," Connor replied. After a few minutes, Cory returned.

"Right this way, Con-Man," Cory said as he lead him, Andrew in tow, several feet behind the main seating area of the Race Book, to an area which was cordoned off with a red velvet rope. Beyond the barrier Andrew saw five Race Book booths; however, these were nothing like the ones he had seen below: the booths were made of similar woodwork to the others, but were far larger, and lacked the scratches and graffiti of their pedestrian counterparts. There was less smoke, and the carpets were flawless lush green Berber. As Cory led them to the furthest booth back, Andrew realized that each booth had not a television, but a personal theatre screen which wrapped around the viewing area, which had two brass-studded Corinthian leather chairs on brass castors. Each booth had shelves that came pre-stocked with new Track Forms, erasable pens, and a mini-fridge; there was a large red call button with the words "Press for Attendant" on the right corner of the lowest shelf.

Andrew stood in temporary awe at the difference a player's status can make. "How did we get here?" he asked Connor. "The same way you get to Carnegie Hall, kid: practice, practice, practice." Andrew couldn't help but laugh; *you gotta hand it to the guy, he's always ready. What for? That I don't know if I'll ever know,* he thought as he looked about the VIP booth. He noticed the personal VIP Race attendant—a short, voluptuous woman with tan skin, and almond eyes—she was sitting at a small desk on the other side of the elevated floor. The woman was reading an e-reader while twirling her hair. Connor once again brought his companion down to earth; "You stay here, Summerlin. I'll go get the updated race sheets from the counter" he said as he got up and left the booth.

Andrew squinted in an attempt to look down at the now far away dry–erase boards; they were too far away for him to read the particulars, but he guessed from the abundance of posted sheets that the day was going to be a busy one. He saw headers in bold above the clustered groups of sheets, names which were becoming ever more common to him: BELMONT, MOUNTAINEER PARK, and PRESQUE ISLE—and numerous races were scheduled at each. Rather than look around for interesting horse names, Andrew decided to stand and wait for Connor to return, so he could at least see what a race sheet looked like. He'd thought that the newspaper-like Track Forms contained all the information a human being could ever want to know about the races; however, he reasoned, if a pro like the Con-Man left his booth for them, they must have some purpose.

Connor returned in a few minutes, clutching a pile of eight inch by eleven inch papers, about the thickness of a phone book. *I'm guessing he took a sheet for every race at every track*, Andrew thought. He placed the pile onto the shelf near the viewing screen, and said, "Not using your prior technique today?" "Nah," Andrew replied, "I don't walk dogs that don't hunt. I figured I'd just be a fly on the wall; I know you won't teach me your techniques 'n all, but I thought I'd look at the stuff you use, just for fun, if you don't mind." Connor slid smoothly into one of the deep leather chairs and responded, "That's cool by me; however, don't ever ask my my picks, or how I got 'em. I used to try to help people out, but it went downhill when the odds started shifting. Some people can get very angry with that sort of thing, not to mention the fact that all the winners have to split the pari-mutuel share. Can't make money helping everyone but yourself, kid." "Wow, is that Lesson Six?" Andrew ambitiously inquired. Connor shook his head from side to side calmly and said, "No, just consider that a piece of worthy supplemental information, that's all. And no more talking; you're great, kid, but this is business. I can and will send you out to Xero if need be." Connor rolled over to his stack, and began systematically sorting them upon the ledge. A serious look came over him as he attended his notes. Andrew grabbed the remote control near Connor's left and turned on the television, if a sixty-inch set could still be called that. He flipped through the channels: there were no regular channels, just races, and a channel that was airing a boxing match in Portuguese. "Hey, turn that to eleven," Connor requested. Andrew did so before occupying the other chair.

Channel eleven was a broadcast of Presque Isle, currently about to have its third race of the day. "I like the haunches on that one; great conformation," Connor noted as a russet-colored mare wearing a red cloth strutted alongside her stable mate. Andrew was about to make a note of the horse on a piece of scratch paper when Connor added, "but, that's race number three, they're about to be out of the gates. The Con-Man took the initiative to write down several numbers and observations upon a piece of paper. "If it's not wager-able, why write stuff down?" Andrew inquired. "I'm not looking at the horse for today: I'm looking at her for the future. I want to see what she's got." Andrew nodded and said, "Oh. Clever." Connor spoke without lifting his head from his sheets, "And you broke the rule, which means I'll see you at the Derrick Bar, Summerlin." *Wow, for a laid-back guy like him, that sounded kinda harsh—Well, at least he said it in a polite way. I better split,* Andrew thought as he began to walk away. "See you in a while Yankee," he said while still within earshot. "See you then, southern son," Connor replied in his best Southern, which Andrew rated as being one percent better than Xero's. Andrew whistled Dixie, *literally*, as he went off to the Derrick Bar. *At least the big ol' derrick is easy to find*, he mused. As he exited Race and Sports, he gave a casual glance to the overhead televisions which were showing races; he noticed the screen for Presque Isle: the horse Connor had taken interest in had won. *Wow*, Andrew thought; he shook his head in disbelief, and said to himself with a smile, "that odd, strange man, and the logic he lives by..."

When he arrived at the Derrick Bar, Andrew took a seat at the bar which lay close to the massive derrick's wooden skeleton. Xero was there in uniform, though his collared shirt was unbuttoned, giving view to a shirt that was identical to the one Samantha the drummer had been wearing at the T.R.Y. show: it was dark orange, with a solid black star in the center, with the words "TEXAS WORLD" vertically sandwiching it. The young bar-back turned guitarist was assisting Fugi the bartender as he filled two cocktail waitresses trays at once. *Connor's not the only one who loves a race day, I suppose*, he thought as he noticed the women labored with their full trays towards the Race and Sports area. Andrew waved to Xero and said "howdy." Xero noticed him, and patted Fugi on the back before walking out of the bar, and taking a seat next to Andrew. "Are you allowed to sit there while on the clock?" Andrew asked him. Xero shrugged his shoulders and made a waving gesture to Fugi before adding, "If I were on the clock, no. My shift ended two hours ago; just couldn't let a buddy down when in need." Fugi slid a bottle of beer to Xero, who opened it and took a long draught. It looked like a normal glass beer bottle, but it was blue in color, and had a label he Andrew had never seen before: *X-Treme Ice*. "Where'd that come from?" he asked Xero. "Summerlin. Ha! That's funny *and* accurate!" he said before taking another swig with relish. "Then I guess I'll have one of me," Andrew called out to Fugi, who had been walking over to attend to his side of the bar. "Make sure to put a note in the machine, standard policy for free brew, my man," Xero reminded him. Andrew withdrew a twenty from his pocket and put it into the machine before him, which hungrily gobbled it up. Andrew had never been to an actual casino before his interlude with the Con-Man; and, if one were to not count a five dollar bill that he put into a video poker machine at a gas station near the state line, he had *never* played a gambling machine before Texas Palace. He'd come to the realization that he hadn't paid for any of the beverages that Connor and he had ordered at the Lone Star Bar, but he was unaware of the "free drink for gamblers" policy; he had just figured his buddy must have had an enormous tab. "Thanks," he said to Xero upon receiving his X-Treme Ice. "Don't mention it," Xero replied. They toasted their bottles, and Andrew smiled as he leaned back and tasted the ale. *Not bad stuff, actually. At least the place makes good beer*, he thought. As Andrew began to play video poker, Xero cut in, "So, what's up, Summerlin?" Andrew swallowed and replied, "I talked twice while in the VIP race booth." Xero looked like he had heard the story before Andrew even told it—he laughed lightly and said, "Yeah, that'll happen; try not to do that. I think that might be the only place he's ever taken seriously in his life." Andrew nodded with understanding and became somewhat relieved: *At least it wasn't anything negative about me specifically, then*, he thought. "So, what about you though?" he asked Xero, who had been eyeing a younger red-headed cocktail girl from across the bar. "Me?" he began, "I'm just chillin' after an eight hour shift." *Eight hour shift? How is that even possible?* Andrew thought. "Weren't you just off shift last night? How can you be just finishing a shift now?" he asked Xero. The young man winked and replied, "I'm an on-call employee: gotta take the sheckles where I can get 'em. Besides, don't worry about me, I'm fine. What are you and the Con-Man doing after he's done doing his businessman thing?" Andrew paused his poker playing and gave the matter thought before replying: "I honestly have no clue. Unless I get to choose, in which case it will be to find a dartboard and a beer I recognize." Xero replied, "That sounds fun. How's that problem you have working out?" Andrew glanced up to see a golf tournament on two of the televisions that lay overhead. *Ah to be playing a sport in fair weather*, he thought before turning to Xero and replying, "I have no idea, yet."

Xero flagged down Fugi and ordered another round. By this point, Andrew's on-machine balance was at five dollars and twenty-five cents. Then, the victory music played: he had held the Jack of Spades, and received the other three jacks on the draw. The machine's balance raced quickly until it reached sixty-five dollars and twenty-five cents. "Good hit there, Summerlin," Xero said upon noticing Andrew's success. "Yeah, call me crazy, but I think I'm goin' to take my money and run," he replied before pressing the cash out button. "Ah, I see the master may instill some Vegas sense in you yet," Xero said as he glanced at a television overhead which had the ubiquitous European drag racing channel playing. "Always pull out when you get ahead of the machine, they say. I don't play 'em much; but, I have enjoyed the Poker Room before, though," Xero added. Andrew tried to picture Xero and the Con-Man playing at the same table—*there would have been a lot of personality for just an eight-person table*, he thought. "I did alright in there, not my kind of thing, usually, though," Andrew said. Xero watched Andrew put the e-ticket into his wallet and said, "Perhaps you're right. The machines seem to love you, anyway." Andrew smiled; he felt grateful that he was good at something, no matter how random of a skill it truly had been.

The two men sat at the bar and continued to drink for a while—Andrew was waiting for Connor, and Xero was there because, as the Con-Man would say, he had nothing better to do. At long last, Andrew heard Connor's voice from nearby. "No, no no. You're wrong Lenny; I hate telling such a stand up pony-man like myself when he's erred, but you're far off base," he said in a loud, though polite, tone. It was Connor, alright, and he had brought an acquaintance with him. The man was short, bald, and hale despite appearing to be an octogenarian. The two seemed to have no genuine animosity towards each other—this seemed more like a spirited debate amongst good friends. "I'm telling you, you little jack-sprat, I was *there*! Nobody, but nobody could ever beat Secretariat," the venerable man replied to Connor. Xero and Andrew turned to face the two gamblers simultaneously. "Oh *brother*," Xero said, "don't tell me you old-timers are on about that old chestnut again."

"And that brings us to the children. Xero you already know; the other one with the drawl's my personal side project: a desperately broken-hearted l'il thing we call Summerlin." Connor pointed out Andrew to his Race Book buddy. Andrew waved and let out a sigh; *I got a bad feeling that the descriptors are only goin' to get worse, and the nickname will never die*, he thought. "Summerlin, this is Lenny; though you can call him 'Old-School' if you want, he won't mind," Connor said with a grin. "Won't mind, my *ass*," Lenny replied. He shook Andrew's hand and added, "You got yourself a good friend here, but he's completely lost in terms of historical equine perspective." Xero was amused; he put his beer down and started watching the two older men engage in heated discourse. "You're wrong, and that's all there is to it. Need I quote Captain O' Kelly again?" Connor said. Andrew switched his eyes to Lenny in anticipation of his response. "I know, I know, you're going to say 'Eclipse first and all others later, or whatever it is," Lenny answered. "So if you know," Connor playfully said, "then why would you even dispute it? Eclipse ran undefeated through eighteen races that were Grade III stakes equivalents for the time." Lenny scoffed and retorted, "Well I don't think races from the Eighteenth Century should count!" Connor replied, "But they do, and you *know* it. They don't call the best Thoroughbred award the 'Secretariat Award', now do they?" *Ooh, Lenny might be beaten*, Andrew observed—thought he could have never predicted it beforehand, he was actually becoming somewhat interested in Connor and Lenny's debate. "Your horse from the late seventeen-hundreds was clocked and calculated to have run at 25.04 feet per stride. *Big Red* was clocked at 25.41 feet per stride. Advantage Secretariat!" Lenny proclaimed. "Yeah, about that: Secretariat was great—a freaking *legend of the track*, even—but, my British buddy, Eclipse was charted to have run at eighty-three feet per second, and the fastest horse in American history, whatever size he was, only ran at a lightning fast *fifty-four* feet per second. Case closed," Connor countered. Andrew and Xero continued to observe the conversation; Xero was grinning, but Andrew, who had never seen one of Connor's inter-pony-bettor debates before, was watching with jaw agape. "Well, to that," Lenny began, "I only have two words: *Triple Crown.*" Connor sneered. "*Knew* you'd bring that up, *again.* Triple Crown was a little too early for my favorite, but he ran undefeated eleven times at the Kings Plate—a comparable, if not more difficult feat to achieve. And I might add that Secretariat, though awesome, *lost* races during his lifetime. Eclipse never knew what it was to place, show, or 'also-ran'." The Con-Man looked smug. "*Whippersnapper,*" Lenny spouted with an angered look on his face. Connor followed in suit, bearing an almost-evil looking grimace as the two men stared each other down; then, they laughed heavily and exchanged a hug. "See you the same place as always, you scoundrel!" Connor said, winking at Lenny. "Ever as always you little scheming *chalk player,*" Lenny replied as he walked slowly back towards the Race Book. "Well, now that we've done *that,* greetings gentlemen," Connor said as he patted Xero and Andrew on the back and joined them at the bar.

"So, did you hit 'em hard today?" Xero asked Connor once he was settled with an Old Fashioned in hand. "They aught to give me a trophy, man," Connor replied before gingerly placing a hundred dollar bill into the poker machine in front of him. He glanced over at Xero and added, "You're not playing?" Xero replied, "Nah, I'd rather just pay for my sauce. I'll gamble on how drunk I can get tonight." Connor nodded and then directed his attention towards Andrew; "And Summerlin?" Andrew beamed with pride and responded, "I already *got* mine." He patted his pocket for emphasis. "Ah, the student has progressed..." Andrew was confused; "I thought you weren't goin' to teach me the whole gambling thing?" he asked. Connor took a sip of his drink and responded while playing video poker, "Well, it's completely understandable for me to have pride if some of my talent accidentally rubbed off." Andrew noticed that Xero was laughing, like he'd seen the conversation play out before. "And our next lesson, besides the severity of your rules while in the VIP race booths?" Connor replied cheerfully, "Hey—business is business. And tonight? Well, we're not doing much, except our monthly tradition: it's the second Sunday of the month." Andrew couldn't help but to ask: "And what's that?" Both Xero and Connor replied at the same time, "The worst food in the valley."

After an hour of beer drinking, television watching, and Connor gambling, the group slowly made their way to the west side valet. "Are we taking the 'Attack Van'?" Xero asked Connor. "Nah," he replied, "that'd be a little rough for the kid. I was thinking of something a little more modest." When they had exited the front doors, Connor did his wave to the valet shed, as before, only this time he requested the car in space number six. Xero played a furious air-guitar while the Con-Man checked his wristwatches. Andrew merely looked up to notice a few lace-like clouds, most of which were nearest the western horizon. A sky-blue car with classic curves rolled to a stop in front of the three men—it looked like it had rolled directly off of a classic car calendar. Andrew anticipated Connor jumping into the driver's seat and taking off with the same quickness as he had the day before; however, he did not. Connor was talking on his cell phone.

At a second glance, the car seemed strange somehow: the paint and body were in pristine showroom condition, but the automobile had a third headlight positioned in the center of the grille, and the engine had sounded somewhat louder than normal for a V-8 when it pulled in.

"What in your deepest peculiarity is *that*?" Andrew queried. Connor put his phone to his shoulder for a moment to in order to respond, *"Respect. It's my Tucker; and it's epic."* Andrew walked towards the front passenger seat, but was beaten to it by Xero, who yelled, "'gun is mine!" and opened the door, promptly taking his seat. Andrew resigned himself to sitting in the back, and reached for the door handle. "Hey, not yet, kid. We're short one." *Ah, that must be who he was talking to on the phone,* Andrew reasoned. "So, who's our fourth?" he asked Connor. "Tommy. You met him on Friday." Andrew instantly thought of the gaunt, polite, sad mess he had seen at the Lone Star Bar before the T.R.Y. show; *Oh, he's coming,* he thought. A glance to Xero informed Andrew that he was too busy playing an imaginary guitar to be of any conversational value. Connor handed Zak the valet a twenty, and looked to the front doors of the casino. "Hey, Tommy the slowpoke, let's move!" he called out. Sure enough, the tall, somber man walked across the guest drop-off lanes to join them. He was wearing a navy seersucker suit with a metallic silver dress shirt beneath; he looked striking, and his eyes resonated with a quiet depth that made Andrew want to show reverence—though he wasn't quite sure why. Thomas waved at Andrew and Connor, and brusquely turned his face away from Xero as he noticed him. He opened the right rear door to the Tucker and took a seat; Andrew joined him. "Andiamo, baby!" Connor cried as he brought the ancient vehicle's engine to life, and peeled out in the direction of the highway.

On this voyage, Connor drove them north on the US 95—Andrew could tell instantly from the change in scenery. The trip didn't last long. They took an off ramp marked "Cheyenne Ave", and the light blue hot-rod from the past slowed to a stop at a red light at the intersection of Cheyenne and Rainbow. The lots on the northwest side of town were cleaner, and newer looking than the ones Andrew had seen downtown;

they were less densely packed into their lots, as well. A glance at Rainbow Ave reminded Andrew that he was now closer to Sarah's apartment than he had been since meeting Texas Palace's most notorious citizen. There were three commercial plazas visible from the intersection: a grocery store sat next to several clothing boutiques and an "everything's a buck" store. Across the street, on the west side, there was a massive Super Dollar World "megastore", which Andrew had actually been inside before—these were places he had only remembered once he had started to think of Sarah. *It's so easy to take such simple things for granted*, he thought as he fought off the urge to get weepy.

The blue Tucker slowly wheeled into the massive parking lot of the Super Dollar World. Connor parked the car near the end of the lot, in a diagonal position so that no other car could park within ten feet of his. They got out and started walking towards the superstore, but veered a little to the right as they got closer. Halfway through the lot, Andrew realized their intended destination—a very small restaurant, occupying but one "stall" in the strip-mall complex. From where he was, he could see how the limbs of the plaza arced out from both sides of Super Dollar World, forming a giant "U". The sign above the small edifice was a small back-lit rectangular marquee, with the words: "A Taste of Sin". *I guess that's supposed to be clever*, Andrew thought as they arrived at the door. Thomas held the door open until everyone was inside.

The restaurant was exceedingly small: Andrew counted eight tables in all. He could hear the sounds of clashing dishes and clattering silverware coming from a kitchen in the back. A short, curly-haired woman in a black apron came up to the group. She smiled and said, "Hey there. You want the usual, guys?" "Yes ma'am. And an extra plate from the usual, for the boy," Thomas added. *The boy?* Andrew thought with mild irritation; *well, maybe I have been a little bit of a child lately*, he admitted to himself. The woman led the four men to a square table next to a window by the door. They took their seats, with Connor and Xero occupying the chairs closest to the window. Andrew sat next to Xero, resulting in him facing Thomas. "No menus?" Andrew said. "He sure does ask a lot of questions, doesn't he?" Thomas noted. Connor took a moment from unfolding his napkin to remark, "Yeah, he really does. But he'll be okay." Andrew raised his head to say, "guys, I'm *right here*." Xero, Thomas, and Connor all replied, "We know."

The woman later returned to the table, first to deliver silverware, and then to bring them their drinks—they were all served tea, without having even ordered it. Andrew gave the table a cautious look—he didn't even know why they were there, when there were so many fine restaurants in the valley; and he definitely didn't understand why their server hadn't asked what they wanted to drink. "We always get the same exact thing when we come here, Summerlin. It's part of the tradition. So, a menu here would make about as much sense as a pogo stick in a parachute, now wouldn't it?" Connor said softly. "Fair enough," Andrew replied, keeping his head up this time. Eventually, the woman returned again, this time with a large serving tray with four steaming hot plates of pasta on it. She carefully placed a plate in front of each of them. "Sally's baked ziti. It's a little-known legend," Connor explained as he prepared to take a bite. "The no-menu policy will also keep you from accidentally ordering something else," Xero added—he had already dived in and eaten several massive forkfuls. Andrew found Xero's statement funny, but a little bit harsh, especially since the woman who had just served them was still within earshot. He looked to Xero as if he were about to teach him a lesson in manners, but Sally cut in: "It's ok, he's p'rolly right." She went about cleaning the unoccupied tables, adjusting the flower vases that sat upon each table as a centerpiece. "But her ziti is the *bomb*," Xero noted as he continued to hastily consume his portion.

Everyone else had devoured half of their meal by the time Andrew decided to dive in and try it. The ziti was surprisingly good; cheesy, yet covered with a red meat sauce which vaguely reminded Andrew of the not-that-authentic "Italian"-style red sauce which he had become accustomed to back home in Virginia. He ate all of it, and nearly reached Xero's breakneck pace while doing so. The tea was decent, but in Andrew's opinion didn't light a candle to real southern sweet tea. Xero

115

and Connor discussed the new upcoming T.R.Y. playlist, and Connor debated the merit in purchasing a new car with Thomas. Andrew simply remained quiet and tried his best to fit in; he had never been invited into a long-time tradition before, and felt pleased to be a part, albeit a mostly silent one.

Eventually, Connor wiped his mouth with a napkin and asked, "Ready to go, guys?" Thomas and Xero nodded, and after a moment, when he realized the other three men were awaiting his opinion, added, "Yeah." They all thanked Sally, and Connor paid the bill at the cash register near the front. Xero and the Con-Man had already departed when Andrew and Thomas walked to the exit. Andrew saw Thomas place a freshly minted hundred dollar bill on the table as a tip before patting him on the back and saying, "Come on, young one, time to join the crazy men in the odd-mobile."

After they had boarded the vehicle—Xero once again beat Andrew in calling "shotgun"—Connor drove the Tucker onto the highway heading south. "So, where are we going?" Andrew asked him. "Back 'home'; we got things to do." "Oh, alright," Andrew replied. Xero turned on the radio and tuned it to a heavy metal station. Andrew tried his best to become lost in his thoughts: he didn't want to spend the whole return trip listening to electric guitars wailing and screaming voices. Fifteen minutes later, they arrived at Texas Palace, and returned the vehicle to where they boarded it, several feet from the valet booth. A female valet with a nametag reading "Melissa" received the keys and returned the car to spot number six. It was only as he was watching the car pull away that Andrew finally noticed the vehicle's license plate: "CONTKR". He couldn't remember what had been on the mirror car's plates: he never had made a point to look.

All four of them walked to the front doors. Andrew noticed that Xero, Connor and Thomas stopped short of going inside, so he did the same. "Well that's done for March, then," Thomas said in a businesslike fashion. Xero looked genuinely offended. "You don't have to treat it like it's a trip to a graveyard, you know," he said to Thomas, who replied,

"I can treat it however I wish. A tradition's a tradition, and a promise is a promise. But don't ask me to enjoy it—especially *your* presence." Andrew noticed that Thomas's words were clearly spiteful, and aimed right at Xero. *There must be more to why Thomas doesn't watch The Reason Why perform*, Andrew thought. Thomas didn't seem to mind Andrew or Connor's presence at all; in fact, he even gave the impression he might have been enjoying their company from time to time. Thomas did *not* enjoy being in the company of Xero; however, and that was more than evident, even to an outsider like Andrew. "Hey, hey, *hey*. No need to get nasty, fellas," Connor said while calmly raising his arms like a referee trying to separate a pair of boxers out to kill one another. Thomas sighed while looking in the general direction of Xero, and then smiled when he turned to Connor and Andrew, saying, "Been real. We'll see you later, Con, Summerlin." Thomas then departed, going into the center pair of deeply tinted doors.

The sun glimmered upon the door's etched Texas Palace logos as they closed behind Thomas. "You goin' to stay, or do you have somewhere to go?" Andrew asked Xero. "A better question," Connor's voice powered through Andrew's inquiry, and interrupted any possible talking until he was finished, "would be am *I* gonna chill and stay here. The answer, of course, being no. I'm gonna have to split, gentlemen." Andrew felt confused, and a bit saddened upon hearing the news. "Hey kid," Connor added, "I'll be seeing you by tomorrow at the latest. Be good, or be good at it." Andrew felt drawn to defend his quality of companionship: "Is it more racing stuff? I promise I can be silent. I—" He was muted by another classic Connor cut-off, "It's not about that. Calm down, kid. I merely have things which I have to do. Things that involve me not being near you two guys. Don't feel offended, you wouldn't gain any lessons where I'm going, and you'd probably hate it, anyway." Xero was back to his air guitar, and remained silent. Andrew couldn't resist the urge to ask what came to his mind, "So, is this a thing with a girl, then?" he grinned, feeling he had finally figured the Con-Man out. Connor replied, "If I were seeking companionship of that kind, it wouldn't just be with one person, kid. But I digress; I don't have to divulge info about my private affairs." He grinned before adding, "Before I go, do you need anything, guys?" Connor pulled out a wad of hundreds that was thicker than a deck of playing cards. Xero shook his head, but remained silent; his gaze had fallen upon a pretty young woman in a red dress who had just dropped off a car at the valet, and was heading towards the doors. "Ahem," Connor said, and Xero turned back to face him. Andrew laughed at the sight. He also shook his head against the monetary offer. "Well, sadly, for various circumstances, two of the three involved in the Sunday tradition always rapidly depart when it's over, and today it must be three," Connor stated. Andrew turned to address Xero, "You're leaving too?" He nodded and added, "Yep, I have to. I got an extra shift available tonight." Connor leaned in and cupped his hand to Andrew's ear, and whispered, "He doesn't sleep much. I wouldn't make too much of a fuss about it." Xero, without losing a beat, chimed in, "If and when I ever need sleep, I get it." Xero then pulled out a pair of sunglasses and put them on. "Later *Ignos*—Gotta go put on the charm and earn a little '*Monet*'," he said before hustling off through the left-most pair of doors. *Must have been because of that girl he saw,* Andrew thought as he tried to figure out why a man he knew had disdain for authority would ever rush to get to his job.

"Hey, before you go—where in blazes do I sleep tonight?" Andrew asked Connor, who was heading back to the valet booth. Connor replied without breaking stride, nor turning back, "That's up to you, kid. I know I'll never convince you that it's ok to crash at the Austin while I'm not in it; if you want to, you can though. Registration desk's always open, too." As Andrew departed, he heard Connor cry out to the valet, "Gimme number twelve!"

Andrew did *not* feel right about sleeping in Connor's suite; he felt that it would be better to seek a more modest—and self-paid— accommodation for the night. He headed for the registration desk on his way in, so he could book a regular hotel room for the night. The registration area turned out to be beautiful—deep-colored, wood paneled walls were encroached by a thick, bar-like counter, which was made of stained oak, with elegant moldings upon it. There were four similarly styled pillars, each about two feet wide, which appeared to support the grand, popcorn-textured ceiling above. The floor was made of an intensely reflective gray marble. Texas Palace, too, had wooden pigeonholes behind the counter, but these empty recesses were merely harbingers of days gone by. Andrew stood behind a couple dressed in Hawaiian-style shirts, and advanced to the counter once they had received their room keys.

Once it was his turn, Andrew was greeted by a doe-eyed brunette who wore a nametag inscribed "Megan". She was a little overweight, but had a pretty face. "How may I help you, Sir?" she asked. He requested a regular, non-smoking room. For forty-nine dollars, he was given the key to room 602. He put the key into his pocket, and turned to face the casino. As he departed the registration desk, he overheard Megan say to one of her coworkers: "He's from the *South*!" in a giggly, blushing high schooler voice. He smiled, and thought, *Now what do I do?*

Having no plan nor schedule set upon him, Andrew found himself wandering through the casino Pit, unsure of where exactly he wanted to go. It was then that he remembered something he had said to Xero earlier in the day: he began a slow, steady quest for a dartboard and a domestic, massed produced beer. He found his desired activities to both be present at a small side-bar near the Convention Center hallway, which itself was near the gift shop, a two minute walk from the Derrick Bar. Andrew *loved* using his landmarks.

The small bar was essentially a wooden semi-circle built into the casino's wall, and tucked into the architecture in such a way as to be easily missed by all but the most scrutinizing eye. Unlike the other bars, this one lacked an overhead sign declaring its name. Upon taking his seat and asking the bartender, he was informed that the locale was known colloquially as "the Billiard Bar". Upon looking to the right of the bar, Andrew noticed that there were indeed three pool tables in the corner, with an old television mounted overhead. The pool tables, and dartboard, were on a small section of purple-carpeted floor which was elevated by three steps, and shared a wall with the bar. All three pool tables were currently vacant, as was the dartboard. Andrew gave the bartender his request: "A plain, regular, well-known domestic beer, please." Upon receiving his beverage, he thanked the man and tossed a ten and told him to keep the change.

Andrew walked over to the dartboard, and realized that there were no darts sticking in it. He bore a look of perplexity; *What do I do now, buy and bring my own?* he wondered. "You ask the bartender for them, Summerlin," a familiar voice called out. It was Trent—Andrew hadn't taken care to notice that the Billiard Bar had three other patrons. *Trent must've been there the entire time,* he realized. Andrew walked back to the bar, this time standing near the bass player's seat. Trent had been watching the golf tournament on the nearby television, and was half-way through a Pilsner glass of ale. He was wearing an old jean jacket with a Texas World shirt beneath, and a pair of khakis which hung neatly over his white bucks. "You wanna play?" Andrew asked him. "Yeah, I'll play," he replied before waving at the bartender. "Yo, Chris! I'm gonna need some pointy aerodynamic objects to teach this kid a thing or two." A tall, tan-skinned man with a clean-shaven head and a large genial smile walked over to them and handed each man three darts; Andrew got red ones, Trent received green. They walked back to the dartboard, and did a quick game of rock-paper-scissors to decide who went first. "What game do you want to play?" Trent asked him. Andrew replied, "Any competition's fine with me as long as it's darts, and not singing. I've heard myself sing, and trust me, you wouldn't want it," he replied. They both laughed. "Cricket it is, then," Trent declared.

Trent and Andrew ended up playing five games of Cricket, with beers and Texas Palace-related toasts in between each round. Andrew won the first four matches, but was outmatched by Trent in the final game, in which he lost by a hundred twenty points. "Good games," Andrew said when they had at last finished their fifth match. "Not bad, not bad," Trent replied in a happy voice, "And don't be thinking you got the best of me, either. People only remember the most recent winner of a championship, after all." They both cracked up laughing. Trent departed soon thereafter: he had noticed the time when his cell phone went off; "Eight o' clock. Yeah, I have to go, or my girlfriend is going to *kill* me," he said, patting Andrew on the back as he did so. After returning the darts to the bartender at the Billiard Bar, Andrew wandered around the floor a bit. He had decided that he was feeling tired enough to head up to his room, and headed towards the hotel elevators.

Six people exited the elevator before he boarded it. *Wow, Sam Houston*, Andrew thought as he eyed the portrait which graced the elevator wall. The music playing overhead was a country-western instrumental which he didn't recognize. He was alone; the doors gave their customary "ding" before the doors closed, squeaking all the way. Room 602 was two left turns, and five doors down on the right. Andrew did the hotel key push-and-pull, which caused a green light to flicker, and the door to unlock. Upon opening the door, he saw his room for the night: the walls were taupe, and adorned sparsely with western-themed lithographs; the royal blue carpet was old, but in good repair. At the back wall of the room sat a double bed, covered in a standard multi-color bedspread that looked exactly like every other hotel bedspread he had seen in his life. Across from the bed sat a wood veneer entertainment stand with a relatively modern twenty-seven inch television. A small nightstand with a lamp and a beige phone was next to the bed's right side. There was a small cardboard advertisement for the "Texasland Café" propped up next to the phone. "Not a suite, but not bad; not bad at all," he said to himself as he walked into his room, letting the door slowly glide closed behind him.

There was a small bathroom immediately to the door's left; directly to the right of the bathroom there lay a small, door-less closet which was filled with hangers that couldn't be pulled off the bar. A simple black desk sat in the room's far right corner, fully stocked with Texas Palace stationery, and adorned with bouquet of plastic flowers. Andrew walked over to the window beyond the bed, and pulled the curtains open, which exposed a dark city before him, and the strange purple hue of the strip not too far off in the distance. He glanced towards Las Vegas Boulevard, taking special note of a bright white beam of light which seemed to shine up to the heavens. *I still want to see it*, he thought as he enviously imagined what sort of adult playgrounds lie within. Andrew closed the curtain and turned the air conditioner which lay beneath it onto "medium cold". After grabbing the remote control from the entertainment center, he turned on the television and laid down on the bed.

Andrew kicked his shoes off the side of the bed, and turned the channel to a sports network. After watching various professional sports scores roll by—the Braves won by three—he closed his eyes, hoping for the luck of drifting easily to sleep. *I can shower in the morning*, he thought. Forty-five minutes, and a TV program and a half of "postseason predictions" went by, and sleep had yet to find him. Andrew sat up and rubbed his eyes. "Now, why can't I get to sleep?" he asked himself aloud. A few more minutes of "Postseason Roundup" made him rise from the bed, and head to the restroom, intending to take a shower.

While basking in the high-powered water jets from the shower-head, Andrew did his best to let go of everything and just relax in the warm water. As with his previous desire for quick sleep, his aspirations of attaining an uncluttered mind faded quickly. It was obvious to him that his mind was needing to be put to rest, and that the only method Andrew knew to accomplish such a feat was to think all of his issues through, at least as far towards conclusions as he could accomplish in room 602 on a Sunday night. It had always been that way for Andrew during stressful times, as far back as he could remember; he had gotten used to the Con-Man keeping him up until absolute exhaustion prompted a proper slumber. This time, he was on his own. He finished his shower, and climbed back into his clothes to lie down.

The television remained on; however, Andrew lowered the volume substantially. His eyes stared directly up at the ceiling while he took a series of deep, slow breaths.

Where did this mess all begin? Andrew wondered. His thoughts drifted back to when Sarah and he had moved to Las Vegas. They had stayed at a motel, taking only what was essential for living inside, and took turns looking out for the loaded I-Haul truck, which was locked with a padlock and chain in the motel parking lot. *Lean, but happy times for the both of us*, Andrew thought wistfully. Then he pictured in his mind how happy Sarah had been the day that they signed the lease for their apartment at Summerlin Heights. They moved in that very day. It took nearly two weeks to unpack all of their boxes; the I-Haul rental, including all of the unexpected days, ended up costing them four hundred thirty-five dollars. "To being broke!" he remembered the two of them toasting on their empty living room floor on their first night.

Things had gone great for a while at their Summerlin apartment. Sarah and he were living on love and savings money while they both hunted for employment. Their ideal workplace, a northwestern library branch, hired Sarah about two months before Andrew's "eviction". *Oh, how quickly things can change*, he thought. Sarah's employment meant that the bills and utilities could be fully paid; this, in turn, enabled them to finally have their phone line and internet access turned on. This became a problem for Andrew when, by random chance, Sarah was contacted by her old friends through one of those "social media" websites. "That was the advent of the devils in our midst," Andrew said to himself. The "contact" turned out to be a girl whom Sarah had known in high school before moving to Virginia for college. This friend, named Olivia, lived—believe the luck of it, near another former Ohio girl whom a teenaged Sarah had known, named Gina.

Andrew's mother had always raised him to be polite, and his father taught him growing up that he should always "give people a chance". He was arguably *not eager* about any of his prospects; but, to his recollection anyway, he did all he could. At least, in the beginning he did. When

Olivia and Gina first visited, he greeted and treated them with as much politeness and charm as he could humanly tolerate. He acted interested in their stories about shopping and boyfriends gone by; he even laughed amicably when Olivia and Gina tossed in occasional references to the supposed quaintness and simplicity of southern folk. Andrew even tolerated the gradually increasing amount of "girl time" that caused him to eventually *barely see* Sarah. It didn't bother him at first; but, slowly and surely, Andrew began to rarely see his girlfriend, whom he felt had become more of a roommate. Sarah's attitude towards Andrew began to slowly mirror that of Gina and Olivia: no longer did she laugh and consider his Virginia ways "cute", as she always had—she didn't seem to have any patience during stressful situations in which he was present, either. The two of them had always been able to talk things through in the past; yet, as the days rolled on it became increasingly difficult for him to communicate with her.

Andrew also felt that he failed her, though. He was old enough to be honest with himself, and admit that he fell right into Gina and Olivia's trap: by allowing himself to get irritated with their obvious disdain for him, he was unable to communicate with Sarah about the hypnotic effect that her friends had over her without his irritation making him sound like he was selfish. *Now that's a game of checkers I wish I had to do all over again*, he thought. Andrew's mind then drifted to that evil Thursday. He was immensely grateful for all of Mr. Bentley's generosities, and they were many. He was actually having—at some moments—a good time, even. Despite all of his good luck and fun excursions with the Con-Man and his interesting friends, Andrew still felt the pangs of recent separation, and he was on his own for only the second time in his life.

Andrew let out a sigh, and came to the conclusion that he'd gone as far as he could go—at least while alone in a guest room, anyway. The fact that he was able to admit some of his own wrongdoing enabled Andrew to feel he had made sufficient progress to be able to relax. The sports channel had begun airing an infomercial about "Instant Hair 4 U". At long last, Andrew's mind slowly began to drift off into delirium.

PART TWO:

A BEGGAR AND
A PRINCE

7.

A phone rang. And rang again. Andrew's eyes were merely half-awoken slits when his arm groggily reached for the telephone's handset. *Ugh, not another early one*, he thought. "Hey man, it's time to wake up! Get up, get up, get up-up-*up!" When did I accidentally set myself up for a daily Las Vegas version of revellie?* he thought. Andrew had only managed to get a few hours of sleep, and did not want to even roll over, not to mention actually rise and vacate the bed. Andrew could hear an energetic Connor's voice still yelling, though the receiver had slid several inches from his ear. "*Fine,*" he said in an aggravated tone as he sat up drearily and then stretched forward as he rose.

Andrew had hung up the phone before he had thought to inquire as to where he was to rendezvous with Connor. The "bucking cow-boy" elevator took him, along with three teenagers in swimsuits and towels, quickly to the lobby. He exited the elevator to find Connor lean-ing against a buffet advertisement sign which stood directly in front where the elevator doors opened. *How did he know my room number if the staff keeps names confidential; better yet, how did he know which elevator I'd be coming out of?* Andrew thought. Rather than admit to his awe and add heaps of grist to the Con-Man's mill in the process, he kept the questions to himself. "What, no coffee?" he asked Connor as he stepped out.

"Nope, I'm afraid not. Java wouldn't really match the morning profile, anyway," Connor stated as he began to lead the way. "And what exactly would that be?" Andrew inquired. "Martini Monday, kid. We're gonna get a little stiff, and then head out to the Pai Gow tables," he replied, leading Andrew towards the food court and movie theatre area. "Maybe *you're* gonna get stiff. I'll take a soda. And what the *heck* is 'Pai Gow'?" Andrew countered. "The game of champions, kid. Anyone can win. Of course, anyone can lose, too." Connor winked, and, strangely enough, piqued Andrew's interest. *I'm still not drinking this early*, he thought. "We are goin' to eat first, though. Right?" he asked. Connor responded without turning his head, "Again, I'm afraid not. We gotta do this right. You'll see. Sorta."

They shortly arrived at "Martiniville", a bar which was less than a football field away from Trident Cinemas. A sign with the bar's name and a few "buildings" made out of artistically rendered martini glasses hung above the entrance to the bar, which sat on a sunken-in platform that formed a dimly lit alcove which was tucked in between the theatres and a Tex-Mex restaurant named "Rio Grand*er*".

There were eight modern-styled stools at the bar, each being alternating colors of purple and crimson. Only three televisions hung above the Martiniville bar, though there was a Karaoke stage with a free mic in the far corner of the alcove, which was elsewise populated with low-lying square tables and Asian-styled cushion seats that matched the barstools. Connor hopped with glee into one of the crimson-fabric covered stools, and flagged down the bartender. Andrew sat to Connor's right, spinning in the purple fabric-covered stool as he did. He noticed a multitude of neon signs behind the bar, and upon the two massive faux-brick covered pillars that sat within the alcove: almost all of them were advertisements for alcohol. *Funny how the state of Texas vanished and got replaced by Milwaukee*, he thought with a grin. An average height man of a full build with prematurely gray hair and a gracious smile walked at a hasty pace to greet them. "Jim!" Connor cried out. The bartender cried out with equal jubilation, "Bentley, my main man, how's it hanging?" Connor gave his usual nonchalant grin and replied, "Doing fine, doing fine. This is my new pal, Summerlin." Andrew started to speak, but only managed "It's And—" before cutting *himself* off. *Aww, the heck with it*, he thought, as he gave up even trying. Summerlin leaned back in his chair and gave the guy a wave. Jim waved back heartily and said, "So, boys, what'll it be?" Connor pointed to the four tiered shelf of liquor which sat beyond the bar; "The Monday usual, please," he said. "Sure thing, no problem. I'm going to have to check the child's ID, though," Jim replied. *Child? Jeez*, Summerlin thought as he reached for his driver's license, knowing full well that his out-of-state ID would make him endure an extra round of scrutiny beyond that to which he had grown accustomed since turning twenty-one. The bartender eyed his license for two straight minutes before handing it back to him and saying, "That's a good fake, kid, what'll you be having?" Summerlin had to look to Connor to tell if he had been serious—judging from the laughter coming from the Con-Man, he was *not*. "He'll be taking the Monday, too. Whether he likes it or not," Connor said as he rolled his eyes and took out a thick cigar with an ornamental band near its tip.

Jim went about making their drinks. "What, dare I ask, is the 'Monday usual'?" Summerlin queried. "It's a martini, obviously. I thought we had covered that," Connor replied. Summerlin looked at him, waiting for a vaudevillian *rim shot* that never came. "The better question would be, what did you do last night?" Connor asked. "Last night?" Summerlin said. "Yeah, kid, last night; it's what comes between yesterday afternoon, and before today morning. Don't tell me you got depressed and ran to room 602 before the sun had fully set even," he replied. Jim slid a traditional martini in front of each of them. Connor reached into his white sports jacket and pulled out a fifty for the bartender. "Okay, I'd *really* like to know how you knew which room I stayed in, by the way—especially since they seem to be so touchy about confidentiality in this town." "Simple, kid," Connor replied with an ear to ear grin, "I'm *me*. And don't change the subject." Summerlin took a reluctant swig of his cocktail, and said, "Actually, I can honestly say I didn't do that." Connor looked surprised; "Oh? So may I ask what you did do then?" Summerlin mimicked his companion and grinned before adding, "I'm 'fraid not. *Private affairs* and all, you know how it is." Connor put his drink down, and sat wordlessly for a moment in a mixture of shock and amusement. He soon regained his footing. "Brilliant counter, protégé; however, the topic at hand concerns how you have been spending your time, which, of course, directly impacts how you are living your life. And, by that rationale, it becomes a necessity for me to know," he countered. *Does he practice this stuff?* Summerlin thought before consigning himself to the obvious: you can't out-kid a kidder. "I played some darts. That lead guitarist of The Reason Why, Trent, was there," he responded. Connor seemed pleasantly surprised. "Good, good. Are you any good at it?" he inquired as he finished his glass. Summerlin had barely touched his drink; he had never found alcohol to be tempting during daytime hours. Connor, he reasoned, was probably only aware of daylight half the time, and didn't share such an inhibition. "I'm fair, I s'pose. I was the best in my high school; those college boys I played against back home were pretty good, though," he replied. Connor nodded in comprehension. "Me, personally, I don't play the non-casino games that much, but we'll have to play sometime." Summerlin said, "Sure."

The two men had already ordered another round—a martini for the Con-Man, and an orange soda for Summerlin—when Allison, the assistant supervisor of security, came into the Martiniville bar area. She headed straight towards Connor. This time, she was not accompanied by indoor or outdoor subordinates: a tall man with a sleek, oiled back blond haircut in a charcoal business suit was walking beside her. He, like Allison, had no nametag on, but Summerlin noticed that he was wearing a security badge and a snub-nose revolver on his belt; *I s'pose that's all the credentials you need*, Summerlin thought. The man leered at Summerlin and Connor through a pair of thick, nerdy glasses.

Allison and her tall coworker stopped within inches of the bar. The man was about as tall as Connor, and dwarfed the once-again tightly pony-tailed and purple-blazer wearing Allison, at least in terms of height. Next to the fit-looking man, the assistant supervisor looked even more overweight than before, very much resembling a round ball with arms, legs and a head.

Connor turned in his stool to face the badge-carrying duo, and Summerlin reluctantly did the same. *Let's see what the crazy Yankee does next*, he thought, half in fear, and half in sheer enjoyment. "Oh, security! And you brought the supervisor. Good, good," Connor began, "what brings you finest—" he coughed dramatically before continuing, "*and* largest that the field has to offer here this fine Monday morning?" Both supervisors leveled stern looks upon him. "Mr. Bentley," the man began, "we have heard that someone around here has been selling these," he pulled out a bundle which he had been holding in his right arm: it was two shirts, one of which Summerlin instantly recognized as a Texas World shirt; the other was a black t-shirt with white lettering reading "2 IGNO 4 U". *There's that word Xero used again—what does it mean?* he wondered. "Do you know anything about these?" Connor appeared to be looking over the shirts meticulously, as if he had never even seen a Texas World shirt before. Summerlin was once again finding it hard to keep a straight face while his friend was messing with the security staff. "Me? Nah. You know me, Lonnie, I'm not into clothes much...not that you could prove that I was if I were," he replied nonchalantly. Connor's response made Allison begin to tremble; Summerlin noticed that her clenched fists had turned bone-white. She pulled the Texas World shirt from her boss, and thrust it, collar first, into the Con-Man's face. "The inside of the collar has a stamped logo on the back side. '*Con-Wear*'!" the pudgy woman declared. Connor was laughing heavily—few things seemed to delight him as much as a good horse race, and annoying the security personnel was definitely one of them.

Both supervisors folded their arms and gave Connor a look of scald-ing condemnation. "I know. I'm *not* the only one who finds t-shirt tags offensive, huh?" he proclaimed. Summerlin couldn't help but laugh aloud. "All right, let's go, *Calvin Klein*," Lonnie said coldly, like a father to a son who had just broken a window. After a sip of soda, Summerlin attempted to spring to his friend's defense. "Hey, it's not exactly like he's using your logo or somethin'. Can't you give the guy a break? Or are you always looking for ways to get in a bad mood?" Allison didn't even turn her head to acknowledge him. Lonnie gave Summerlin a brief glance, and spoke once he had turned back to Connor, "That's irrelevant. Mr. Bentley knows that he's been infringing on our logo policies. He has been ordered several times to cease and desist in his creation of those mockeries. I'd strongly recommend that you keep quiet, son."

Lonnie pulled out a pair of cuffs, to which Connor amicably raised his wrists together, remaining cool and collected the entire time. "Hey kid, it's gonna be just fine. Don't give them a reason to tie you up as well," Connor said as Allison tightened Lonnie's handcuffs on his wrists; she seemed to want them to click together even tighter than they could. "That's enough out of you," She said with glee as Lonnie and she began to pull him away. "Summerlin yelled out, "Connor! What am I supposed to do? How do I bail you out?" Connor responded in an elevated volume, without losing one modicum of calmness, "Nah, don't worry about it. I'll be fine. This happens from time to time, they're just gonna annoy me with questions in the holding cell until my lawyer shows up." Summerlin had been following the supervisors, but at this point Lonnie turned and said, "leave, *now*, or I'll call the cops for obstruction." Summerlin was crestfallen. He did perk up a bit when he noticed that despite all their best efforts to mute and censor him, Connor had began to sing the T.R.Y. song *Don't Mess With Texas*, and continued to do so until he was far from view.

"Woah, that was harsh," Jim said to Summerlin as he returned to his section of the bar; during the entire event, the bartender had faced Connor's direction, but defiantly avoided making eye contact with the security supervisors. Summerlin nodded and said, "Yeah, I'd say so. Though knowing what I do of the man, he's goin' to annoy them so much within the confines of that cell that they'll wish they'd never cuffed him." Jim laughed and added, "That's our Con-Man. Can I get you another drink for your troubles?" Summerlin shook his head and said, "No. Thanks, though. I'll just settle up here and look for somethin' to do besides drink or gamble." "Alright, then. Just stay away from the buffet's egg salad." They both laughed, and Summerlin pocketed the unlit cigar Connor had left on the bar top and paid his tab, plus a ten dollar tip, before leaving Martiniville.

Andrew didn't initially have any clue as to where he should go. Once again, he had gotten used to the comfort of a predetermined schedule, and once again, he had been cast into a situation where he had to live without it. *Still not a big fan of infinite possibilities—not yet, anyway,* he thought as he walked away from the food court and theatre area. He gave a slow series of glances to and fro as he found himself walking through the Pit.

After checking his wallet, Andrew noticed that he still had about five hundred dollars to his name. He stood near a Roulette wheel, and considered playing it for a moment. *Nah, it's probably not really worth it right now; Connor may need me, and I can't go wasting time just for gambling. It's not going away soon or anything, I can always play it later when I'm in the mood,* he thought. He took a twenty out of his wallet before returning it to his back pocket. For a brief moment, Andrew thought of the room he had spent the night in; he had remembered seeing a small ad for a café, but didn't remember where it was. "Now," he said under his breath, "where is that 'Texasland Café'?"

Summerlin eventually located the Texasland Café between the bowling alley and the conference room doors, which were on the deep east side of the casino, past the live Keno area. Though it was relatively old-fashioned and a tad "low-scale" in terms of décor, Summerlin found the service and food—a cheeseburger with fries—to be quite good. *Extremely tasty,* he thought. Summerlin hailed a waitress so that he could pay his bill. While waiting, a thought began to nag at him, and slowly grew to become a worry: *Connor told me not to let fear or condition influence my decisions. I didn't want to play Roulette. Was I scared? I just didn't want to play; but, what would the Con-Man say?* he thought. He vividly recalled being interested in watching the metallic marble bounce upon it as it spun, yet he made a choice to not play it, just as he had done with the slot machine days before. *Did I allow myself to be free?* he wondered. The waitress returned with the bill, tucked neatly into a small leatherette folder. Summerlin breathed easier a few moments later when he came to the conclusion that he hadn't declined to play the game for the same reasons he had on Friday—his recent choice had been motivated by hunger and a concern for lost time. *Besides*, he thought, *All I really know of the game is what I've seen in movies. I'd be far better learning how to play it from a guy like Connor.* Summerlin got up, and left the money for his meal, plus a five dollar tip, on the table before departing.

I suppose a nice walk outside would be nice—I haven't even seen a tree since I met Mr. Bentley, Summerlin thought as he walked through the Pit. It had, in fact, been several weeks since he had enjoyed an outdoor walk; *the several mile hike from last Thursday didn't count,* he thought as he walked towards the theatres. He had remembered seeing a single pair of wooden doors near there. Summerlin had seen the view of Reata Avenue from the entrance before; his only other view of the property had been one he experienced in the midst of a fight, and he wanted to see a *different* view of the property.

The lightly-stained wooden doors swung open with a gentle nudge, and Summerlin felt the refreshing feeling of fresh air kissing his skin.

Once outside, he was greeted by the warm sting of the scorching desert sun. There lay before him an ocean of cars of every hue, make, and model, all reflecting brightly in the daylight. Summerlin glanced upward to see what was, the sun notwithstanding, a starkly azure sky. A yellow-shirted security officer was riding a bicycle through the lot, row by row. He took a deep breath and stretched out his arms and back. There were a few birds nearby, mostly pigeons, were clustered on both sides of the entryway he had just exited. *People must leave food for them*, he thought as he decided to follow the sidewalk which wrapped around the building.

After a five minute stroll past some slow-moving Bingo grannies and the occasional hobo, Summerlin passed under the massive entrance canopy. Two minutes after that, he saw another set of doors in the distance. By the time he was reaching out for the door handles, he realized that he was standing about two hundred feet away from where he had met Connor Bentley for the first time, and where his new, hopefully temporary, life at Texas Palace had begun.

Summerlin looked down the lot to see the general area where the three-on-two altercation had occurred. A mild laugh escaped his mouth as he remembered the flashy, cavalier words his friend had brandished that night, even in the face of imminent death. *Pure Connor*, he thought before he turned and reentered the casino. On his way inside, Summerlin's path was impeded by several people, all of whom were rather well-dressed. He recognized one of them as Lonnie, the security supervisor that had taken away Connor for "questioning". The others were not involved in security as far as Summerlin could tell—they lacked badges or holsters.

"Of course, this will only be our precursory viewing; the number-crunchers and the county are sure to have their say before any interested party would have the right," one of the men said. "Correct. It is also to be noted that my client will need further ratification by—" Summerlin had passed by the group by squeezing through. Lonnie avoided eye contact with him. Two others—a tall tan-skinned man with a goatee, and a short, younger man with a beer-gut—seemed to find his awkward creep amusing, and grinned as he passed them. The other one of the group, a tall, clean-shaven man in a black suit, gave him a dirty look as he danced near him on his path to freedom. *Now there's a group you don't see in a local's casino every day*, he thought before heading to the casino floor.

After he had walked through the rows of slot machines, Summerlin stood on his tippy-toes and tried to locate one of his "landmarks". In looking off to his right, he found one: the Live Keno area. The seats were nearly all filled. There was a white and blue backlit sign reading "DRAWING #", with a red LED display showing the number "7,502". *They've played seven thousand games this week? It's only Monday*, Summerlin thought in disbelief. He had assumed that the "drawing number" was a weekly total because, in his mind, there was no way it could have been a daily number, especially this early in the day.

The white, golf-ball looking Keno balls oscillated wildly within a large fishbowl as Summerlin passed the Live Keno area. "The seventh number is ninety; once again, ninety," he heard a voice yell out from behind him as he headed towards the bright casino-style twinkle light sign reading "CASHIER—CHANGE" which lay before him. About fifty feet from the cashier's cage there stood an wooden octagonal podium. A security officer sat in the middle of the oaken structure; the badge-wearing woman elevated several feet above the floor by means of a hidden staircase, Summerlin supposed.

Perhaps it was an informed decision, or a stroke of luck; or, maybe it was just left over "don't give a damn", but Summerlin couldn't resist approaching the security podium. He didn't recognize the middle-aged female officer who was on duty, but he could read her badge and nametag: Martha, officer seventy-six. The woman turned as he walked up to the counter of the podium; however, a ringing telephone pulled the officer's attention away from Summerlin, and he found himself silently observing the cashiers at the casino cage while the podium officer was talking to someone on the phone about a lost and found item.

Though he had been there briefly one time before, Summerlin had failed to notice the security presence about the casino cage the first time: there were so many black plastic security camera domes surrounding the place that he could easily detect their presence, despite being at least four car lengths away. There was no line at the stockade this time, though only three of the "windows" were currently open for business. A large man in a Hawaiian shirt walked away from the second window from the left, thumbing through a wad of cash as he walked past Summerlin and toward places unknown, whistling all the way. "Sir?" a female voice said—it was the podium officer, Martha.

Summerlin turned to face the woman and said warmly, "Howdy." The woman's face stayed neutral and emotionless; "How may I be of assistance, sir?" she asked in a placid manner. He smiled anyways. "Yes ma'am. I was wondering if, perhaps...Say one of my friends were to have been taken to the security department—where would that be?" She squinted at Summerlin, though it seemed to have little to do with visual adjustment, and more to do with intimidation. "The security office is located just beyond the employee entrance corridor. You can't go back there unless you are the person's legal representative, or a medical professional. Something tells me you're neither, sir," she replied. It was at this time that Summerlin realized although he had showered recently, he had gone over thirty-six hours without a proper change of clothes or shave. *Darn it, I supposed I should've endeavored to look more presentable; I gotta get up the Austin Suite so I can change*, he thought. But, for that, he'd need Connor. Summerlin's silent pondering resulted in additional words from the podium officer: "You can't go back there. Period. You *can* leave a note for the party, and he or she will receive it if and when they are no longer being held. Nevada Revised Statute. Now you have a good day." *I know I hear her wish it, but something tells me she didn't exactly mean it*, Summerlin thought in reaction to Martha's response and send-off.

"Thank you, ma'am, but a note won't be necessary. I'm led to believe 'the party' will be out quite soon; besides, something tells me he will find me," Summerlin said, maintaining a congenial attitude. The officer frowned before turning her attention to the black and white security monitors which sat near the telephone. He walked around looking for anything which looked like it could be the "employee entrance". *It would be best to locate it, just so I can have a place to await Connor,* he reasoned as he strolled through the High Limit Slots lounge and into the Pit beyond.

Summerlin remembered that he had seen a door with the sign "TO THE POOL" on it nearby the hotel elevators. Seeing as how he had yet to ever *see* the pool at Texas Palace, he decided that a jaunt in that general direction might shed some light on where exactly the employee corridor was. After arriving at the door for the pool, Summerlin opened it to find a long hallway; there were several wooden signs with the word "POOL" and red arrows to guide potential swimmers to their destination. It wasn't the promise of water; however, that caught his interest: he found a door labeled "ACCESS CORRIDOR" halfway down the hall. After a moment's contemplation, Summerlin decided that it could be worth the effort, as he had never gone in that direction in the casino before.

The linoleum-tiled corridor emptied out onto a shining gray marble floor, identical to that which Summerlin had seen near the registration desk. *Wherever I am must connect to the registration desk,* he reasoned. He followed the floor pattern, and within less than a minute Summerlin could see the bell desk and guest registration counter in the distance. Before he got there, though, he saw a pair of ornate, etched glass doors with cloth curtains on his left. There was a simple carved wooden sign suspended by brass chains above the doors, reading "S.F.S.". Summerlin could barely make out the silhouette of an attendant standing just beyond the closed doors.

Summerlin moved on. He passed the bell desk, and turned left to return to the casino Pit once the triple set of main entrance doors appeared on his right. Once again, Summerlin found himself slowing to a stop near a Roulette table. He thought to himself, *You know what? Screw it!* and tossed a twenty dollar bill from his wallet onto the table. After the dealer handed him four red chips, he placed them on the betting square for "red". *Rattatattat.* "Number nineteen, red!" the dealer called out once the ball had landed. Summerlin then found himself to be the possessor of forty dollars in chips. The bow-tied dealer gave Summerlin a look; he was waiting for him to place his next bet. Summerlin declined, and shook his head, adding, "I put twenty on the table, and this outcome gives me the chance to leave with forty dollars—well, thirty-eight." The dealer looked confused; "Thirty-eight?" he politely inquired. "Yessir," Summerlin said as he left the dealer a two-dollar tip before departing to cash in his chips.

Summerlin arrived at the cashier's cage to find two other people waiting before him in line. He had advanced to become next in line for service when his entire body felt the cold chill which often accompanied unexpected physical contact—someone had just tugged on Summerlin's right cuff from outside the brass stanchions of the stockade. He turned in immediate reaction. It was Connor Bentley, freed of whatever bonds had dared confine him. "Hit it lucky, kid?" he asked; he was now wearing shades. "I'm twenty dollars richer," Summerlin replied before advancing up to the counter for his turn. "Go get 'em, tiger," Connor cheered as he walked up to exchange his chips.

After Summerlin had pocketed the money from his winnings at Roulette, he rejoined Connor, who was then currently making a series of funny faces at the Martha the podium officer. "Goodness *gracious*," Summerlin said to Connor after watching quietly for several moments. "Oh," Connor said in surprise, "Sorry if I didn't notice you at first, she's too much fun, that one." "Whatever," Summerlin replied, shaking his head in disbelief before laughing. Summerlin pulled out Connor's cigar, which he had been keeping in his breast pocket. "Thanks, kid," Connor said, before lighting it and blowing a thick wall of cured tobacco smoke towards the security podium. The two of them then walked away from the cashier's cage in the direction of the main pit.

"So, what are the plans now, Yankee jailbird?" Summerlin asked. Connor gave a defiant smile and countered, "*Ha.* I was merely interrogated. Security could indeed prove that I was involved in the shirts' creation, but I had nothing—" Connor *coughed* the word "provable" before continuing, "to do with their distribution." Curiosity began to consume Summerlin concerning the seemingly ubiquitous dark orange shirts—"Hey Connor, what is 'Texas World'?" he asked as he began to, as usual, follow the Con-Man blindly. "It's this thing we're into. Call it 'people restoring the glory of Texas Palace," Connor replied. "*Glory?*" Summerlin asked skeptically; they had just arrived at the elevators. The Con-Man replied, in response to Summerlin's skepticism: "Look, Summerlin; first off, Texas Palace is awesome. It's got real flavor—it's the *Awesome Sauce* straight from the tap. You don't even *understand* it's hustle." Summerlin replied with a grin, "Well, if you keep talkin' like that, I won't *understand* anything." "Nice. I'd come up with some sort of retort regarding your homeland, but we have more important things to do," Connor said as he pressed the "up" button. *I do get his point; this place has a charm all its own...but what in the scorchin' blazes of Hades is "Awesome Sauce"?* Summerlin wondered as they boarded the elevator.

As the Sam Houston elevator began to ascend, Summerlin said, "So why are we goin' upstairs?" Connor replied, "We need to change our clothes to suit tonight's cause—especially you. You could've bought a gift shop t-shirt or something, for goodness sakes." Summerlin nodded and said, "I somehow knew you'd bring that up; I didn't think my clothing plans through." The Con-Man was smiling; "That much is obvious. And that leads us to Lesson Seven: Always craft your appearance to suit your goals. A good idea to aid you in this process is to think about what it is that you want to accomplish, in any act, public or private." Summerlin was confused. After the elevator doors opened on the Suite level, he turned to Connor and asked, "But what about Lesson

One? What if you plan for a soiree and get a heavy metal concert?" The Con-Man replied without hesitation, "That's easy, kid—you go with the flow, and roll with the punches. You're not ready for the last two lessons, but it will all begin to make sense; well, that, or you'll go clinically insane." Summerlin laughed; he hoped his friend was kidding about the last part.

As they approached the door to the suite, Summerlin struggled to maintain Connor's pace. "So, what would be "the cause" we need to get gussied up for?" Connor replied, "In this particular instance, it would behoove us to be vested in fine apparel. Sophisticated activities await us." Summerlin wondered what his horse-betting, cigar smoking friend would find *sophisticated*. "Sophisticated gambling, o wise teacher?" he asked as Connor withdrew his room key from the Austin Suite's door, to which Connor replied, "Sophisticated *living*, my good southern man."

The two men entered the suite. "Your clothes for the night are in the gray bag on the bar," Connor said as he vanished into the hallway on the left side of the great room. Summerlin cautiously approached the gray cloth tote-bag, which had gothic script-style lettering reading "Alpha Male Unlimited" upon it. The contents turned out to be a suit; a gray, silken one, with a steel blue dress shirt to be worn underneath. "At least I can keep wearing my boots," he said to himself at almost a whisper. "Only if you polish them to parade shine!" Connor's voice cried out from his hidden side of the suite. *How on earth did he hear that?* Summerlin wondered.

Summerlin polished his boots to as high of a reflective sheen as he could accomplish. *My brother Bradley would approve*, he thought. Of course, Lance Corporal Bradley Cadoret was expected to have parade-gloss boots—Summerlin had never anticipated having to need the skill, but was now grateful that his older brother had shown him how when he was still in high school. Connor came out of his left-side hallway wearing a suit which matched a tuxedo in every cut, fold and hem, but was made in zebra-stripe patterned fabric. *Now there's one he didn't buy while I was around. I love the support and lessons, but even I would have screamed aloud seeing a person purchase that,* Summerlin thought. The Con-Man twirled in circles in front of a floor mirror, and then strutted to the marble landing. "You ready to hob-nob *'Vegas style'*?" he asked Summerlin. "Do I get a choice, *'Prince of Ponies'*?" he eagerly requested. Connor's response echoed through the hallways as the two of them headed towards the elevators: "Love the use of the name. And, not a shadow's chance on Fremont Street, kid."

There was no hailing of a valet when Summerlin and Connor exited the main doors. A Connor Bentley car was already sitting in front of the valet shed—Summerlin didn't need to ask the owner of the vehicle, as he thought upon seeing it, *This has to be a "Con-Man car"*. It was a large, solid black car which looked like it belonged to a mob boss from one of those old "film noir" gangster movies he'd seen on late-night TV: the vehicle was long, and somewhat boxy by modern standards, with curved, old-school fenders and a classic chromed-out grille. The head and tail lights were circular, and the car only had a rear license plate, which read "MAYBAC1". A deep, powerful rumble informed the ears of all who stood within earshot that the automobile was running. Zak, the valet, stood next to the driver's side door as if in the pose of military attention, with his elbows bent and his hands behind his back.

Connor tipped Zak and hopped into the driver's seat once the young valet had opened his door. "Coming, Summerlin?" he asked; but, in turning, he found that Summerlin had not been directly behind him—he was still on the other side of the guest drop-off and pick-up lanes, staring vacantly in the direction of a motorcycle shop which sat on the other side of the intersection of Lake Mead Avenue and Reata Avenue. "You gonna be okay there, kid?" Connor's voice broke through Summerlin's deep, pensive state. "Oh, yeah," he replied, looking still a bit distracted while doing so. The "instructor" voice of the Con-Man returned: "The word you're looking for is '*Maybach*', and no, you may *not* drive it." He had gestured with his fingers to suggest a name bracket or underlining of the term as he had said it. Summerlin nodded in appreciation; *I suppose if anyone were to spend the kind of money it would take to obtain such a vehicle, they may as well be proud of it*, he reasoned.

Summerlin was still eyeing the ancient, yet pristine nature of the car when Connor said, "Okay there, starry-eyed wanderer, it's time to get in and go. It will just be us this evening." Summerlin found himself the proud owner of an exit strategy—he could avoid Connor's emotional probing, at least this time, by saying that he had been waiting to see who would be joining them. *He doesn't know I was thinking of the girlfriend—he thinks I was waiting for Xero, or Tommy*, he reasoned. Summerlin opted to go with the simpler choice, and in doing so, he nodded to Connor and said "Okay, let's go then," before getting into the front passenger seat. Summerlin found the Maybach's interior to be quite spacious, and luxuriously upholstered in butter-soft black leather. "Nice wheels, Con," he added as they left the property. "I know," Connor replied with a grin.

The Maybach slowed to a crawl once the men had arrived downtown. "Symphony Park, the home of some of the finer sculptural works our city has to offer, the Smith Center, and, more importantly, the Akerman Legacy Symposium Hall. Very chic," Connor said before turning onto a driveway, which lead the two of them past a multitude of dark, unlit buildings and into a clearing with trees, grass—*actual living, green grass*—and a large cluster of buildings further down into the park area. The building complex which sat amidst a seemingly midwestern knoll was a strange mixture of old and new: A blind arcade ran almost the entire length of the building cluster, but sharp asymmetrical glass towers jutted out from within its center. There was a plethora of black vehicles surrounding the drop-off area, which had a wide white stone walkway that lead towards the lit buildings beyond. Summerlin had become accustomed to the sight of limos, coach-sedans, and all things livery after spending less than a week with the Con-Man. *It's lookin' like there's a bunch of fancy people here tonight*, he thought as he glanced from the luxurious vehicles to the throngs of well-dressed persons walking along the walkway. Connor stopped the car when signaled by a special event valet wielding a flashlight with an translucent cone on the end of it. After the Con-Man had slipped the silver-vested valet attendant a large tip, Summerlin and he began their way down the stone path.

As they made way for the group of people congregating around the entrance, Summerlin turned to Connor and whispered, "So, what are we doin' here?". "Be with the people, kid," the Con-Man replied as the duo neared the four sets of doors currently being held open by tuxedoed doormen, "You really do ask too many questions. We're gonna be with people; just act like you've just done something really cool, and you won't look different enough to be noticed. No matter who you see, just remember that they are just as normal as you or I. Just feel proud of yourself, and you'll be fine." Summerlin *wanted* to inquire as to how normal he could actually consider a professional gambler, but didn't get the chance; Connor and he had reached the doors.

Upon reaching the massive doorway of the Akerman Legacy Symposium Hall, Connor and Summerlin had to take turns walking through a metal detector. After that, most of the people entering were asked to present their tickets—Summerlin became confused when he noticed that a few people were being granted direct entry without further scrutiny. When asked for his ticket, Summerlin made a confused expression, and shrugged his shoulders. A backup officer, who had been watching from places unseen, walked up to join in his coworker's inspection. "Hey, he's with me guys," Connor exclaimed as the rather large backup officer stood inches from Summerlin. The guards gave Connor a glance: he was holding out a piece of parchment paper with a gold embossed seal at the bottom. There were several lines in calligraphy upon it; "*And one*, See? It says 'and one.' He's my 'and one'." Sure enough, underneath the bold words "By exclusive invitation only," was Connor Bentley's name. After the two badged men looked at one another to confer—they nodded—The original guard responded in a burly voice, "You two are clear to go. Enjoy your night, and forgive the formalities" "It's no problem, gentlemen," Summerlin replied, cutting off Connor's chance to mock them. *As much as I love the 'Connor versus the Security' shtick, these guys seem good enough, and have never met him, so they don't deserve it*, he thought.

As they passed the security staff, Summerlin noticed a cluster of people holding cameras. Panic began to pound through his veins as he realized what was happening. Oh my word, those are *Paparazzi—what the heck is Connor doing, and why am I here*, he worried. Summerlin did not look forward to walking into the limelight; he had never fancied himself a future celebrity, and always felt revulsion at the notion of having to deal with the entire world looking at him. However, Connor had different plans. One of the camera-wielding horde called out, "Con-Man! Mr. Bentley! Give us something good!" Connor then strutted in a triumphant posture, and at an incredibly slow pace, taking pauses to wave at certain persons, and blow kisses at the cameras. *Bastard*, Summerlin thought as Connor pulled him in for a few standing-still shots. He tried his best to smile, but his heart was racing, and he was on the verge of nausea.

Once the men had cleared the paparazzi, Summerlin saw a massive reception room, elegant in every regard. There were crystal chandeliers overhead, though they were well out of reaching distance; there was thick red carpeting from wall to wall, and the room was populated with men and women dressed to the nines in opulence. There were shimmering gowns and tuxedos everywhere; only Connor had thought of—and been willing to wear—a zebra tuxedo though. Summerlin looked about the clusters of people, recognizing an Academy Award winning actor, and he realized that he had no idea what Connor had gotten him into.

Several people of note, both at a local and international level, were present. The mayor of Las Vegas was present near the back, arm in arm with her husband, who was happily sipping a glass of gin as the group posed for a photo with a few showgirls. Connor poked Summerlin in his ribs and whispered, "Don't gawk. *Normal people*, remember?" He was sure that Connor had some strange reason for making him endure the culture shock, but that was of little comfort. With every flitting glance Summerlin seemed to recognize more and more of the people there; though he was certain that they would not recognize him. There were actors of blockbuster movies, local Strip mainstays, and even a couple of models present. *I am so going to get him back for this*, he thought. He sighed when he came to the conclusion that there would be no way to truly *get* Connor back; the concept of which would necessitate the Con-Man being capable of being embarrassed—Summerlin knew all too well that that was not possible.

"Why didn't you and some of the others not need to show credentials?" Summerlin asked as Connor and he skirted the wall. "Well, Summerlin, no offense intended, but would you card a celebrity attending your event?" Summerlin rolled his eyed before conceding, "Good point." Connor grabbed a glass of punch from a table which sat at the far right of the enormous room. As Summerlin reached for a cup, Connor said, "Hey kid, don't freak out or anything, but I gotta go talk to a few people. Hold out near here, you'll be fine. I'll be back when I'm back." And, with a pat on Summerlin's shoulder, Connor scampered off before he could stop him. *I can't help but feel that this stunt here is somehow tied to my not letting him mock the security officers*, he worried.

Minutes came and went, and Summerlin remained near the punch table the whole time. *It's not that I don't think they're not real people— heck, some of those actors' play in movies I don't like. It's just weird, that's all*, he thought as he tried to see how many people he actually admired in their various arts. His count stopped at two—a Heisman Trophy winner from a year back, and a western novelist he enjoyed— when he lost count: several of the mini-clusters of celebrities had converged at a point near the center of the room. Within minutes, the group erupted into raucous laughter; someone was in the center, entertaining the glitterati while they themselves were being adored. A *Forbes 500* automotive tycoon walked towards the punch table, exposing a gap within the cluster; then he saw it. The attention-darling was *Connor*; he was currently laughing at an actress's joke, holding his half-drank punch glass high in the air. *Well that just figures*, Summerlin thought before reaching for a refill. *I got a feelin' this is goin' to be a long night,"* he decided.

Watching Connor work the room enveloped Summerlin in curiosity and despair. He stood still, with his head lowered as he flushed in shyness. It made him remember the time he had met Chipper Jones as a child—he vomited within ten minutes of getting his picture and autograph. "What's the problem, Summerlin?" Connor had snuck up on him, without him noticing. "What's wrong?" he replied, "What's *wrong*? You know, normal people don't set people up for an ambush like you did." Connor clinked his glass against Summerlin's and replied, "Well, that all depends on your point of view. Did I ambush you? Or, did you fail to adequately anticipate your future?" Summerlin had to actually stop and think about that one; "Both, I guess," he replied. "Kid, kid, kid. If you're rolling with me, you know I'm not gonna sugar-coat *anything*. If I have something to show you, I'm not going to show you the kiddie-pool version. One thing about that whole debacle you told me was that you allowed those two friends of your girl to get you all riled up, is that not correct?" Summerlin nodded. "Well, then," Connor began after momentarily pausing to raise his glass and wave to the group he had departed, "You need to see this for what it is: an opportunity, albeit by baptism through fire, to learn how to not let people affect you in any way, good or bad. Consider it another offshoot of Lessons One—and, Lesson Three really: 'give situations time before you react to them'." *Dammit...he has me again*, Summerlin admitted to himself; he couldn't help but laugh at how predictably unpredictable his friend truly was.

"Just come with me kid. Think of it this way: the worst that can happen is that you will experience the worst anxiety in your life—so, once you reach that point, you won't be capable of feeling any worse. After feeling *that*, you'll be surprised how mild any other hindrance will seem to you. Summerlin had to admit that Connor had a point. "Alright, I'll go. Just don't expect me to like it," he said. Connor nodded and spoke as they approached the throng of well-dressed elites, "You'll thank me later, Summerlin."

Summerlin was nervous the entire time. His overall anxiety level *did* lessen as time passed. Everyone that Connor introduced him to, whether Summerlin recognized their notoriety or not, introduced themselves to him with in the same normal manner that one would a neighbor or friend. *My mind tells me to feel awkward, but I can't—how could I treat such polite people with anything but friendliness?* he thought. As Summerlin found himself becoming calmer, his thoughts returned to what they had been before entering Akerman Hall: *Why are we here?* There were no signs up in the reception room, and though he had heard conversations regarding the hopes for a good time, he still had absolutely no clue as to why Connor and he were there. Connor could have brought him to the presence of celebrities at any point he wished to—there is always an abundance of them in Las Vegas at any given time; even he knew that. There must have been a specific reason; however, after a few minutes of devoted inspection without any results, he realized he would just have to go with the flow.

Meanwhile, Connor Bentley fit in with the hob-nobbers like a quarter in an old-school slot machine. He was the teller of many tales, most being humorous in nature. Summerlin kept himself to short responses, but smiled amicably throughout.

About ten minutes later, the doormen, who had been previously standing at the entrance to the hall, walked into the room and began the process of opening several ornate wooden doors on the end of the room facing the entryway. "Show time," Connor said; he kissed the gloved wrist of an Indie ingénue before promptly grabbing Summerlin by the hand, and leading him through the doors. "Yes, but what kind?

Theatre, speeches, music—what?" The Con-Man didn't need to respond; the Heisman Trophy winner did it for him with a smile: "Hey man, you ask too many questions!" Even Summerlin had to laugh.

What followed was an hour-long performance of Classical-style music which had been written by modern musicians. *At least the place is nice*, Summerlin admitted to himself as he yawned. Truth be told, he had been apprehensive about the show from the moment the large velvet curtain rose to show a stage full of instruments. Sarah had begged him to attend a performance of *The Magic Flute* when they were sophomores, and he remembered two things about it: one, that it wasn't in English, and two, that he found it very hard to focus on anything but the fact that men were parading the floor in tights while holding swords. *Good Lord, don't let it be* opera, he thought before they began to play. He had fallen asleep during the performance, but Connor was too busy tapping his feet enthusiastically to the beat to notice. A voice announced through a set of overhead speakers which were hidden from view: "Attention, ladies and gentlemen, we will now be having a brief intermission before continuing on with part two of the program." *Part two?* Summerlin wondered as everyone began to rise from their seats and head for the doors. He really wanted to know what 'part two' was going to be, but was too afraid that someone he had seen on the big screen might tell him he was asking too many questions.

It was on their way through the doorway that Summerlin finally noticed it—a small, elegantly designed poster made of stock paper which bore the words "The Akerman Legacy Symposium Hall is pleased to present: The 4th Annual Springtime Musical Benefit for the Las Vegas Performing Arts Fund." There was a smaller set of words near the poster's bottom, "Made possible through an endowment from our friends at Palace Casinos." By the time he had finished reading the sign, Summerlin turned to find that Connor had already gone back into the reception room, and was nowhere to be seen. *He did it again, dar-nit,* he thought before sighing and heading for the punch table.

Once he was back in the massive reception room, Summerlin found that the invitees had once again formed into a collection of people-clusters. He spotted the Con-Man in the far back corner opposite the punch table—he was playing rock-paper-scissors with the mayor's husband. Connor noticed him from afar and waved for Summerlin to join him. *I better just do it—who knows what he'll do if I don't*, he thought before ambling slowly over to join him. "Hey kid, got some real fun people to introduce you to," Connor said upon his arrival. The Con-Man doled out introductions, and Summerlin happily greeted the people in the mayor's group. He was actually glad to shake the mayor and her husband's hands; they seemed like genuinely friendly people.

When there was a break in the conversation—which had been about increasing digital signage on the Strip—Summerlin whispered in Connor's ear, "So, are we goin' to go soon?" Connor replied, "Why? Are you not having fun?" Summerlin shook his head mildly and said, "No, it's not that; I just figured that since we've seen the show already, we'd be leaving. The people are great and all, but this 'Classical music benefit thing'—it's not exactly a place where my Hank Williams-lovin' ears fit in." Connor scoffed; "Nonsense. *Every* place should be your kind of place. Don't let the surroundings determine your attitude, remember? *You* are the only one who should determine that," he added. "The show is done though, right?" Summerlin asked. "Yes, the musical performance has come to an end; however, the most important part of the night has yet to come. And don't even ask because I won't tell you; enjoy the moment, let life hit you, kid," Connor replied.

And so, Summerlin followed Connor in the ensuing minutes. By the time the doormen reopened the doors, the Con-Man had introduced him to nearly everyone who was present for the event, doormen and servants included. Everyone slowly milled their way back to their seats within the auditorium. Once seated, the house lights dimmed and the curtain rose once again, exposing a single microphone with a spotlight aimed at it. A serious looking man in a white suit approached the microphone and began, "Ladies and gentlemen, on behalf of the Palace

Casinos Corporation, I would like to thank the Las Vegas Symphony Orchestra—money indeed well-spent." The audience applauded. "But seriously folks," the man continued, "great show. For those of you who don't know me, I'm Tyler Lancaster, founder of Vegas Palace on Charleston, our flagship property at Palace Casinos. And, as you may know, our family has always been committed to helping the local community, with our city's devotion to the arts being no exception. I am also pleased at this time to be the bearer of some rather exciting news. Palace Casinos is proud to announce the creation of a new, *exciting*, Palace Casino, coming this winter to Rancho Drive and Lake Mead Avenue! Construction on 'Rancho Palace', some of you living or working in the local area may have noticed, is already underway."

Connor leaned back in his chair once Mr. Lancaster had finished with his 'exciting news'. For the first time since Summerlin had met him, he looked distressed—possibly even angry. Mr. Lancaster continued speaking, "But, for the really good parts of it all, I'm going to hand over the mic to Bob over here..." Though Mr. Lancaster had been smiling throughout his entire speech, Summerlin sensed that a more severe man loomed behind the smile; *I can't quite put my finger on it, but there's something odd about that man, and not in the T.R.Y. or Connor sort of good-guy way, either*, he thought. Mr. Lancaster gestured to a pot-bellied man in a gold pinstriped suit, who walked up a small flight of stairs to join him.

Mr. Lancaster handed the rotund man the microphone, and walked down to take an unoccupied seat in the first row. "Good evening, everyone. Some of you may know me from my work as the Assistant General Manager at Vegas Palace; but if you don't, I'm Robert Ruckford, General Manager for the development of Rancho Palace!" The audience was astir with *oohs* and *aahs*, which were followed by applause. Mr. Ruckford paused his words and smiled triumphantly for dramatic effect. It worked: camera flashes went off in abundance, and the applause grew progressively louder. All Summerlin noticed was the bright gold tooth that sat front and center in Robert Ruckford's used car salesman-like smile. The crowd's excitement began to calm down, and after the clapping died down, he continued, "Yes, you heard me right, *Rancho Palace!*" He pointed to a gargantuan high definition screen which was slowly descending behind him.

Once the screen had finished lowering, it turned on, displaying an artist's rendering of the casino-to-be: It was a tall, glass-faced building which was surrounded by a colony of one story facades and mini-towers. Some of the facades and small structures had restaurant logos upon them, while some were casino entrances. The entrances signage was very similar to the old-Vegas style street sign, which stood near the corner of the property line, and was a third as tall as the casino itself. After inspecting the large map-like image, Summerlin noticed that the tall central building was actually a set of three glass towers which were bound together at the base; each one had a different height, with the western tower being the tallest, and the eastern the shortest of the three. It vaguely reminded him of the Sears Tower in Chicago he had seen in movies and magazines, only it was a massively shorter building, and had neon and LCD signage *everywhere*. The logo on the massive neon structure was a palm tree surrounded by three glass towers— artistic interpretations of the hotel's *actual* proposed three-towers-in-one layout, no doubt—with the massive words "RANCHO PALACE" in bold blue letters surrounding the graphic image. And then came the realization—he had seen this casino before. Rancho Palace's construction had been the cause of two soothing nights' rest brought abruptly to an end. *Another Palace Casino so close to Texas? Why would they want to do something like that?* he thought. Connor looked livid.

Summerlin turned and was about to speak when Connor rose from his seat and said, "We can go now, Summerlin." Though he was curious as to why a casino would build itself new competition, he realized that his companion did not look like he was currently in the best of moods; he nodded and rose, following Connor out the doorway while Mr. Ruckford began spouting off about the casino's future amenities.

Both the trek to the valet and the pursuant ride back to Texas Palace were silent affairs. Connor seemed distracted and distant on the elevator room up to the Austin Suite. The only thing he said to Summerlin before vanishing off into his personal side of the suite was, "You know where everything is. If you need anything else for the night, call room service. Not mad at you, kid, but I *need to be alone* right now." And he was gone.

Summerlin stood on the landing for a moment, and looked in the direction of the pool table which sat beneath the "Prince of Ponies" print; to the far left, he saw it: a dartboard. There were several darts with white and black flights. He walked to the bar, and climbed the short set of stairs to stand on the elevated gaming area of the great room. He plucked the darts—six in all, and walked back away from the board. His eyes spotted a thin line made of red electrical tape about six feet from the board, and took aim with his left hand. *Let's see how many bulls I can get*, he thought before tossing all six darts in rapid procession. He hit the bull's-eye twice; other than that, he hit a twenty, an eight, and two fourteens. "I guess that's good enough to rest on," he said to himself. He walked down the hallway, seeking sleep in his money-themed room.

Waking beneath the bright lights of the ceiling fan the next morning made Summerlin grumble and squint his eyes. "What the hell?" he said disgruntledly. "Ah ah ah, you shouldn't go using such *filthy* language," the voice was Connor's, and he had extra relish when saying the negative adjective. Summerlin rose and saw Connor standing next to the light switch with an impish grin. He was wearing what, for him, would amount to business casual: a forest green sports jacket which had its edges lined in sequins; a simple white t-shirt lay beneath. "Are you... are you wearing jeans?" Summerlin asked, somewhat in shock. "Indeed

I am, young pup, I am. But don't go thinking I would dwell in lesser fabric: these are from *Portugal*," the Con-Man replied. Summerlin gave a nod and added, "I'd ask by whom, but I'm sure it's something I won't be able to pronounce." Connor shook his head and said, "Jealousy is such an ugly color on you, Summerlin. At any rate, get your knowing-what-hominy-is butt up and get dressed."

Summerlin rooted through the generous selection of the "clothing exchange" which Connor had stocked inside the guest room closet. *At least I get to keep the boots*, he thought as he winced upon seeing the collection of shoes Connor had assembled; there were neon ones, light up when you walk ones; one pair seemed to be made entirely of synthetic fur. He happily placed his boots onto his feet after putting on a pair of gray slacks. "And that leaves a shirt," he said softly while tracing his finger along the hanger rod. Summerlin expected to have a hard time picking a shirt that he actually fancied. He did not, however, expect that Connor would reply, "I'd go with a burgundy; and make sure you wear a sports coat." *How does he do that?* Summerlin wondered as he put on the burgundy shirt and looked for a sports jacket that didn't scathe his retinas. He settled on the one he found the least visually offensive: a pure white cotton jacket with red trim around the collar and pockets. He wandered out into the great room to find it empty.

The two men reconvened at the elevators. *Ding*. The "oil derrick" elevator took them on a non-stop trip to the casino. Connor led Summerlin to the fancy looking doors near the registration desk—the ones curtained off from within, with the carved wooden "S.F.S." sign. Summerlin looked up at the sign which, due to the faux-calligraphic style letters, seemed foreboding to him.

"So what's a Las Vegan do here?" Summerlin inquired. Connor turned back to him and answered, "Well, relax, obviously. But beyond that, I have found in life that when one is in need of focus, it is always best—and more fun—to do it in a place of class. Besides, a place like this, you never know who you're gonna run into." When they reached the ornate doors, Connor was greeted by a silver-haired doorman in a tux. He brandished a royal blue card, the kind which Summerlin had recently seen by countless gamblers in the past few days; it said upon it, in big metallic letters, "ROYALTY". The doorman opened the door politely and said, "Wonderful to see you again, Mr. Bentley." Summerlin followed close behind, but was halted by the doorman. "Player's card, please," he said. "I don't have one," Summerlin replied. Connor looked horrified.

"Okay," Connor began as he turned around and walked back to face Summerlin, "I could understand it if he stopped you for not being "Knight" level or above, but you never even bothered to get a player's club card, even though you've been gambling this whole time? There's signs for the darned things everywhere, and I know you've seen me use mine." Summerlin's eyes widened; the truth was, he had seen the advertisements for the player's card program—the "Palace Points Loyalty Club"—he just never really felt the need to wait in another stockade for a card that he hoped he would only be able to use for a few days. He knew that his logic had been wishful thinking, but he figured that Connor, the "seeming" king of positivity, would understand. "What can I say, Con-Man; you got me. I just didn't think it would be that big of a deal." Connor shook his head and replied, "You could've been earning points the entire time, kid. Trust me, points are a good thing, you want 'em. I just—" For once, it was not Connor doing the cutting off, but the doorman, who said, "It actually isn't 'that big of a deal' at this point, gentlemen. As you pointed out just a moment ago, Mr. Bentley, your friend here, even if he had a card, has not attained "Knight" status. No guests or players are allowed into the Six Flags Club without having achieved Knight status or higher. Now, I am more than pleased to admit you entry, sir." His smile seemed genuine, but his tone gave off hints of irritation; *I bet his rules have gotten in Connor's way before,*

Summerlin thought with a laugh. He knew too well how the Con-Man treated those who got dared get in his way with rules.

Connor stepped away from the Six Flags Club entrance, and took Summerlin with him, tugging his left cuff the entire way until they found themselves several feet into the Pit. "What's going on, Con?" Summerlin asked as they made their way through the pit, heading towards the movie theatre area. Connor replied as they entered the food court, "Okay, kid, I got several pieces of news; but, for the sake of brevity, I'll just say 'follow me'. This can all be more properly explained at the source. I'll let you go if you promise to actually do what I have planned." Summerlin asked in apprehension, "Do I get a choice?" Connor laughed and added, "On the 'follow me or be tugged there' part? *Yes*. On the activity? No." *Quintessential Connor Bentley*, Summerlin thought before adding a defeated, "Fine, Yankee, release me. At least then I can have something to pull my hair out with." Connor turned his head and winked before releasing Summerlin's cuff and saying, "You learn quick."

The hike through the casino floor ended at a semicircular counter which was built into the wall to the right of the food court dining area. There was a large brass sign with the words "CUSTOMER REWARDS CENTER" suspended several feet above the counter on high tension wire. Behind the counter were two older women, both were wearing glasses. "Chrystal, Emma, I got a new one for you. This poor lost soul didn't even realize he needed a player's card," Connor said with a smile as his elbow slid out to kiss the heavily varnished counter. Summerlin walked up to the counter; *he must really love the rewards program*, he thought. "All this fuss to get me to sign up?" he queried. Connor replied, "Well, kid, there's more; but, you can't even get to step one without your card. I'll save the news and subsequent irritation from you for *after* that. The Con-Man was beaming, like he had just won a grand debate. "Howdy ladies, it looks like I'm goin' to need one of them there cards," Summerlin said with a polite smile. The woman on the left, with the nametag reading "Emma" looked up at him and replied, "Well that will be no problem sir; I'm just going to need a photo ID." He handed her his Virginia license, and she started to rapidly click on the keys of a computer which was hidden under the lip of the counter. "Can I ask now, then?" Summerlin asked Connor. "I'm afraid not. You see, it's gonna be for your own good, but you're not gonna like me for it—and I'd hate for you to get impatient around a lady—it just wouldn't suit you, really. He shook his head and waited patiently for Emma to finish clacking away at her keyboard.

Though he had directed his attention to Emma, it was Crystal who rose from her seat to grab Summerlin's player's card and hand it to him. "Thanks girls, you are absolute angels," Connor said before Summerlin had the chance to thank them; he nodded and gave a "thumbs up" instead. He looked at his new card, which was still warm to the touch from being freshly printed. His looked identical to Connor's, with two exceptions: his was white, and it lacked the metallic lettering; the card said "Pilgrim" in red lettering. There was a faded Palace Casinos logo— several stacks of gaming chips topped with a crown—that was the in the background; *I didn't even notice that on Connor's card, it was too blue to see it*, he thought. Summerlin turned to see the Con-Man leaning against one of the ubiquitous faux brick pillars.

"Okay, now what's all the fuss about?" Summerlin inquired. "Well, kid, it's good news or bad news, depending on how you look at it. Seeing how I am acquainted with you, I'm pretty sure you're gonna take it as bad," Connor replied. "Let's just get it over with: what is it?" Summerlin asked. "The thing is, kid, for our little life-fixing arrangement to be of any real value, I'm gonna need you to be able to follow me wherever I go," he began. Summerlin nodded and said, "okay, go on…" Connor began to walk, and jerked his head forward as a signal for him to follow.

"As you may have noticed, I have earned the right to—feel no shame in enjoying the finer things that our fair city has to offer. There is a roadblock in your path to doing so—you can't access any of the premier services within the Palace Casinos empire. And that, we're gonna have to change," Connor said. Summerlin's eyes widened. "Exactly how long would that take? You've lived here for years: I just got here. I don't even know what the name of the tier above 'Knight' is, let alone how much time and money it would take to achieve it," he replied. Connor laughed before continuing, "Well, that's not such a bad trait, kid. Because we don't need to get you to the second teir; 'Serf', by the way, we need to get you to the third tier: 'Knight'." *Knight? That does not sound like something which can be easily attained by a novice*, Summerlin thought. "Okay, you are obviously wanting me to ask 'how', so I will. How?" Connor cracked his knuckles and then replied with a grin, "That's the interesting part about all this. Just follow me." He did; his mentor led him to an ATM which sat right outside of the Poker Room doors.

"My child, today you are going to survive a baptism by fire," Connor began as he slid a card into the machine, and covered the screen while he entered his PIN, "There is an old Vegas trick to attaining 'tier three' at a casino. It's a tradition older than Caesar's," he said as Summerlin became distracted by what was becoming a massive pile of hundreds in the withdrawal slot. "Hey, eyes up here, hot-shot," Connor said to regain his attention before continuing, "It boils down to this: casinos never want to turn away millionaires, kid." Summerlin was officially confused; "I don't know how much money you think is in that l'il box, but I know there isn't a million in there," he quipped. Connor replied, "Ha, ha, *ha*. You're killing me here. What I *mean*, dear child, is that a casino never wants to run the risk of giving potential VIPs anything but the best in amenities, freebies, and so forth. Now, usually, the millionaire—or billionaire—would gain their recognition and status by gambling a lot of money, no?" Summerlin nodded, but still had no clue where Connor was going with all of this. His friend continued, "What if a potential big spender—or, '*whale*', to Vegas insiders—was only visiting for a day, or a few hours even?" Summerlin had no clue. "I honestly don't know. Do they call the host you introduced me to?" he replied. "Good guess; *wrong*, but good guess nonetheless. No, too many people would try to lie, and besides, there is a more accurate way of figuring out which wheels deserve the extra grease, so to speak." Summerlin asked quickly before Connor had finished, "When are you getting to the point of all this? What is it I'm not goin' to like?" Connor grabbed the money from the ATM, and handed it to Summerlin. "Be patient, I'm getting there. Long ago, a group of very smart casino operators came up with a solution: the twenty thousand point day," Connor said. "The what? If you're talking about those "player points", the most I've seen you rack up on your screens is a thousand, and that was after three hours," Summerlin replied; he was beginning to feel nervous as to what his friend was going to ask him to do. *What in crazy Connorland is he goin' to suggest?* He thought, half with excitement, and half with trepidation. "It's all a matter of pacing yourself. But, before you ask again, here is the task I am laying before you: You are to play until you have accumulated twenty thousand player's points within a twenty-four hour period. The reason is this—if a player scores that many player's points within a single day, the computers and their algorithms will interpret you as a player who has gambled at a VIP rate within a short amount of time, and thus, a high-tier player. Sadly, the tiers above 'Knight', 'Nobility' and 'Royalty' respectively, are not able to be reached using the twenty thousand point day system. Well, I've heard rumors that the Italian place on the Strip has a one hundred thousand point week, but I can't verify that...," Connor said. "Wow," Summerlin replied with a smile. The Con-Man looked shocked and replied, "You're happy? I thought that twenty hours of video gambling and slots would piss you off; the eye-burn from the screen and the cigar smoke and whatnot." Summerlin beamed and said, "No, don't get me wrong, I'll complain about that in a second. I'm just happy I finally found something out about Las Vegas that *you* don't know." Connor laughed and responded, "You got me there kid. But I'll be able to find out before you get to ten thousand."

Summerlin hoisted the money back towards Connor, but he made a pushing gesture and shook his head, adding, "No, you're going to need that more than I today, I'm afraid." Summerlin gave him a grave look and said, "I thought our deal had been laid out pretty well by now: *I don't want any of your money.*" Connor put his card back in his wallet, and then responded in a calm, collected manner: "Well, good then, kid, because I'm not giving it to you—I'm lending it. You are to play at all times, taking only breaks for biological necessities; also, don't go thinking you're gonna burn this away rapidly in a ten-dollar slot machine: you are to play no machines that have a denomination of play higher than twenty-five cents. You can play 'max bet', of course. I'm not cruel." Summerlin raised an eyebrow; "Are you sure?" he said sarcastically.

"How exactly am I supposed to pay you back all the money I'm goin' to be losin'?" Summerlin asked. "Well," Connor began, "this is a special type of loan; I don't expect you to pay me back the full amount, just whatever you have left when you've completed the two objectives. If it helps you to remain calm, just think of it as me playing the game from a different level. In fact, since I noticed you watch baseball a few times at the Lone Star, let me put it to you this way: you'll be the position player on this one, and I'll be the manager. If you lose some or all, I'll hold no grudge whatsoever, and you'll be off the hook for the investment capital. But don't go thinking it will be that easy, Summerlin: it is mathematically impossible to lose two grand in a twenty-four hour period by playing only quarter-or-less games. I'd go into the calculus of it with you, but that would necessitate me getting very drunk." Summerlin didn't know what to say to that type of logic; "alright, looks like I'm not goin' to get out of this. Where do I contact you should I actually pull this whole thing off? And what did you mean by 'two objectives'?" Summerlin said. Connor lit a cigar and replied, "Ah, I thought you might've noticed that. Your two goals? Obviously, the first is to obtain the points. The other would be to endure a full day of Vegas turmoil. Consider it part of that lesson about overcoming your surroundings. And where will I be? Well, I'll be around, doing my thing. I'll check in, but I have some bets and financially risky behaviors that I need to be involved in . Any last questions before I send you out to your challenge?" Summerlin actually had a ready-made response to this one question: "Yeah, where can I find a 'Dixie Dollars' machine?"

160

8.

T he 'Dixie Dollars' machine was located at Bank 432, by the Coral Room; It did not really shock Summerlin that Connor had known the location of his desired machine. *That guy lives here—literally,* he reasoned. He had placed the wad of hundreds in his pocket, and disliked walking around with it. It wasn't the obvious security risk of having such money on him in public that bothered Summerlin; it was more of a comfort issue. The bulge of freshly minted bills made the simple act of walking an uncomfortable, asymmetrical affair. *Popular game, I guess,* he thought upon seeing that three of the "Dixie" machines were currently in use. A glance to the large LED screen above the bank of machines with the words "Progressive Jackpot:" hinted as to the cause: the progressive jackpot was currently nearing three thousand dollars. Summerlin took a seat at the unoccupied machine and put one of the C-notes that Connor had given him inside it. Upon accepting his bill, the machine played a garish instrumental snippet of the song "Dixie" while the screen showed his dollars being converted into machine "credits".

Summerlin began to play the game, betting "max lines" and "max credits per line", which amounted to a dollar-fifty per pull of its lever.

The "dollars" must refer to the prize, and not the denomination of play, he thought. He had noticed that there was a button for starting each spin, but he had always seen people pulling the handle of the "one armed bandit" in the movies, and couldn't resist the novelty of it all. Summerlin continued to pull the arm and await the results; countless flags, cannons, and cartoon union and rebel soldiers spun in rapid succession, and he found himself praying for the game's highest possible jackpot—three United States flags—which would trigger the progressive jackpot.

Summerlin was down thirty dollars by the time a short-skirted cocktail waitress came by offering free beverages to players. He ordered a cola, and kept on playing. By the time the cola arrived, he was down by sixty dollars. Despite his belief that it should only take five minutes to receive a drink, he still tipped the woman a dollar. After losing the entire hundred without so much as a bonus game or minor hit, Summerlin got up from the Dixie Dollars machine, and went to look around the casino floor for the next machine that "spoke to him". He, being aware that all gambling devices are truly random in the nature of their payouts, *knew* that any machine was as good as another; however, in his mind he figured, *I might as well find one that sticks out; a false feeling of hope is better than none at all.*

His quest for a salient machine brought him to a "Game Queen Multi Game" at the Lone Star Bar; he had won a jackpot there before, and the odds couldn't be any worse than on the floor machines. Summerlin put another of Connor's bills into it, and selected the game called "Deuces Wild". *Haven't played this one before—might as well have some variety,* he figured. He played there for what seemed like hours, though he couldn't have been sure, due to the clock-less nature of the place. The only thing that he seemed to be accumulating was a free soda and 3,045 players points. The bartender came up to him and asked if he needed anything.

It wasn't Jim or Chris; It was Fugi, the eccentric bartender whom he had first met during his first morning at Texas Palace. "Howdy there Hoss," he greeted Summerlin, who gave him a friendly wave. "How are you doing today?" Fugi asked. Summerlin gave Fugi a nod and said, "Doin' great. Hey, I got a question." Fugi placed three empty margarita glasses next to the mixing machine and looked up. "I may have an answer, try me," he said with an odd accent and a witty smile. "Why don't I ever see my buddy Xero at this bar?" Fugi began to wipe down the bar and replied, "That's because he is a young one, an apprentice, or 'bar-back' as we call them in the trade. They assist at the Derrick and Rail Yard Bars, mostly. Oh, and they get to test their skills as bartenders when one of us calls off sick, or there's an early hour shift that needs filled." Summerlin pointed to the beer tap and said, "That makes sense then. I wager it's gotta be evening somewhere, all this gambling's making me need a drink." They both laughed, and Fugi poured him a Pilsner-full.

Summerlin was taking a sip from his glass when his machine gave him four threes on the deal. He held the threes and hoped furiously for a "kicker". He got the Jack of Clubs. Even though he was essentially playing with someone else's money—he was playing for points, not money, even—Summerlin still found a jackpot to be enjoyable. That is, until he realized that his natural four of a kind was relatively *worthless* on the Deuces Wild game. He found himself the proud possessor of fifteen credits—a profit of three dollars and seventy-five cents. *Something tells me I did somethin' wrong here; I better change back to regular,* he thought as he pressed the menu button and selected "double bonus" from the game list. Summerlin didn't know—or care, really—what the differences between the payouts were on the various "regular" draw poker games. He remembered that he had been playing the "double bonus" versions on both of his first two video poker hits, and figured it would just be for the best to focus on holding the correct cards as his player's points slowly rose.

"I guess that's that, then," Summerlin said as he rose from the seat, having just sent two hundred of the Con-Man's dollars into oblivion. He left a ten dollar bill from his own money in a glass for Fugi, who was currently on the other side of the bar. As Summerlin walked past the bar, he heard the bartender talking to a group of patrons, "Me? Cleveland."

A semi-wrinkled note was quickly gobbled up by the "Triple Nine Slot-o-Rama" machine. Summerlin had decided that a slot machine would be a good break in the monotony, and he found one which "spoke to him" at a bank of machines near the doors of the bowling alley. The slot machine had old fashioned mechanical reels, just like in old movies. It only had three modes of betting, one quarter, two, or three, and the payouts were based on how many coins were being played. *None of that 'lines played' or 'credits per line' stuff; I'm supposed to be gambling, not doing algebra*, he thought with a smile as he gave the machine's arm a crank. Despite the machine's venerable age, there was a small LED "Player's Points info screen," which had been retrofitted to the upper left of the machine's cabinet. He glanced at the red LED every so often to check his progress—he was currently standing at 6,202 points.

Boredom started to ensue; he was neither winning nor losing, but rather, proving his friend right about the fluctuations of two thousand dollars on quarter machines. For every six hundred he lost, there was a two hundred to five hundred dollar payout. Lacking the fear a player usually has when wagering their own, often hard-earned money, Summerlin began to notice the ebb and flow of the currency—it was almost a stalemate. As earlier, the only thing he seemed to be gaining was free beverages and player's points, with the latter seeming more and more to be growing at a glacier's pace.

Three groups of bowlers passed Summerlin on their way into "Metroplex Lanes", and he was still playing when they made their way out. He gave the LED screen a look; *7,340?Man alive—How long will this take?* he began to wonder. Summerlin got up and walked over to a bank of poker machines that were next to the Conference Rooms. There was a large display mounted atop the bank of six video poker machines.

After taking a seat, he closed his eyes for a moment in an attempt to ease the irritation he felt from what had to be at least five hours of straight gambling. He removed another hundred from his bulge of Connor's currency. While he was fumbling to put the greenback into the machine's bill reader, Thomas passed by his seat. He was dressed to the nines in a navy blue suit with polished brass buttons. Thought he appeared to be alone, he was having a conversation.

"I hate to bring it up, baby, but when exactly do you think you might be going back?" the young woman in a little black dress said. Thomas turned to show her a disgruntled look as they continued to walk. "Darling, not now—*please*," he said as he increased his pace. As he looked to see if he had out-walked his companion, he saw that he was in the clear. "Now I know you're not silly enough to think you can escape me, love," The curly-locked woman chided him, appearing directly in front of Thomas when he turned his gaze forward. Thomas sighed and stood facing her.

"I only ask because you honestly seem to do better when you're at work. You seem so sad when we go out lately, honey," she said. For a brief second, Thomas looked like he could burst into rage; but, upon seeing the sweet smile on the young woman's face, his irritation was wiped from his face, leaving only a weak smile behind in its place. "My love," he began, "It's just too difficult to deal with others right now. At least this place has happy hints of what once was. I just don't feel I can reconcile myself with the world right now. And could you honestly say you blame me?

The young woman linked Thomas' arms in hers, and began to walk him towards Rio Grand*er*. "Look, darling," she began, in an almost-motherly tone, "that's just it: you don't seem to be getting anywhere near calm. I *really* wish you were. 'Always look for something to amaze you in life,' like I always told you, remember?" She slid her hand down to hold his hand, her fingers intertwined with his as they slowed their walking pace. Thomas at last began to breathe a little calmer than he had been, and he smiled as he felt a squeeze upon his right palm. He squeezed back. "Why must we waste time discussing my inevitable return to our business?" her eyes widened with eagerness, and she hastily replied, "Because, there is no such thing as time wasted! Besides, it's a sound request—and trust me, you'll learn to know I'll be proven, in time, to be right." Thomas nodded with reluctance; "You do know best—we'll work on it. But for now, filet mignon with pico de gayo?" She nodded enthusiastically and gave him a kiss on the cheek before they approached the host podium that sat before the restaurant.

Summerlin leaned back in his chair and stretched his arms widely. He had achieved 9,100 player's points, and was gradually beginning to grow a dislike for gambling machines. *Connor, where are you?* he wondered as he changed seats, preparing to play the machine to his right. Summerlin had just lost several C-notes in his most recent machine, and wanted a change of venue that would not necessitate a cross-casino hike. The plan didn't help his bottom line—after losing another hundred, Summerlin pulled out a wad much thinner than the one Connor had handed him hours ago. *One thousand, one hundred and eighty,* he thought as he placed the last twenty-dollar bill upon the top of his pile. Throughout his day, Summerlin had visited ticket cashing kiosks after any hit of two-hundred dollars or higher—most of his wins came from high-numbered four of a kinds, though, which netted sixty dollars. He didn't like the idea of a white piece of paper being worth several hundred dollars. Also, Summerlin feared the possibility of losing said piece of paper and having to face Connor, who would be sure to accuse him of doing it on purpose to get out of the challenge. He placed the wad, minus a fresh twenty, back in his left side pocket. The twenty went in without a hitch.

"Portrait of the gambler as a young man," a voice said smugly from behind him. "Took you long enough," Summerlin replied without even turning around. Connor jumped into the seat to his left, and put a bill—and his player's card—into the machine that Summerlin had been playing a little while ago. The two men played wordlessly for several minutes until Connor at last broke the silence: "You're not asking me where I was, kid." Summerlin took a soothing breath as he held two aces and pressed the draw button before responding, "I've learned that when I ask questions about you, my friend, I can't *unlearn* the answers." Summerlin grinned and did his best imitation of Connor's arm glide; his elbow ended up knocking over an ashtray. *"Nice,"* Connor said sarcastically. "By the way, how'd 'Dixie Dollars' work out for you?" Connor asked. "The South lost; *again,*" Summerlin replied with a sigh.

"I had a few things to do, but I thought it prudent to check in with you so you wouldn't end up going insane or anything," Connor said as he continued to play his machine. Summerlin looked back at his screen; he did not get the other two aces. He did; however, get a straight flush. "Hearts, king high. And it's not that bad. Bad enough to complain, yeah, but not horrible enough to lose sanity. *That* occurs when I look at your wardrobe," he said as he turned to face the Con-Man. "The shark has *fangs*!" his friend replied, except, it wasn't in anger, but with a look of beaming pride. "You keep thinking on those toes, kid, and we might fix you up just yet," he said. Summerlin glanced at the player's points LED screen and said, "Oh, and I have 10,976 total player's points, too." Connor smiled and continued playing, adding, "Well done! You could actually get to sleep tonight."

Summerlin's stomach rumbled as he drew a busted straight. "Sounds like someone needs food. Want me to go get you something?" Connor said as he got four queens. He waited until the machine he had put over two hundred dollars in finished giving the Con-Man a victory melody to answer him. "Yes, I'd like some of the buffet's egg salad. They don't have slot machines in the hospitals here, do they?" Connor hit cash-out and pocketed his ticket; "I'll have them bring one into your room," he said slyly. "*You* might," Summerlin retorted. They both laughed. "Well, it's good to see you're not insane yet, anyway. I have a few more things to do. In my line of work, one has to endeavor to live life to the its fullest," Connor said as he rose, patted Summerlin on the back reassuringly, and departed in the direction of the Pit.

Food was a good idea, he thought. Summerlin hadn't wanted to tell Connor that he had been hungry. He didn't want to find out what kind of ribbing asking for a favor during a "challenge" would elicit. The machine still held a balance of seven dollars; he decided it would be quicker—and easier—to just play off the remaining balance. *Going to a kiosk to cash a single-digit ticket would be like kissing my sister*, he reasoned with disgust. His first hand resulted in a loss; his total was then five seventy-five. The next hand dealt him two pair, which he kept, and resulted in a push. He endured a similar result after that, two kings, and his money back. Two more losses lowered the on-screen balance to three dollars and seventy-five cents.

With such a small remaining balance to play off, Summerlin decided to just keep pressing the "DEAL/DRAW" button in rapid succession until the money had been cleared; *I'll get the same player's points either way*, he reasoned. The only problem was, the game stopped taking his command. Summerlin had tossed five cards and received a Royal Flush, in Clubs, on the draw. In his hunger, he had still failed to notice it; Summerlin drew a sigh as he reached for the red "Call/Fix" button which sat on the far left of the machine's other buttons. Then he finally saw it.

Summerlin's heart began to race as he came to the realization that the sign mounted atop the machine must have been a Progressive Jackpot sign—the machine's balance grew by over seventeen-hundred dollars. *He's never goin' to let me live this one down*, Summerlin thought. A quick glance to the red LED screen on the machine cabinet's upper left corner informed him that he had, so far attained 12,306 player's points.

"That's good enough for a food break," he said to himself with a smile. After hitting the cash-out button, he took the ticket and redeemed it at the kiosk near the Poker room. The wad had grown *larger* than it had ever been; he counted it to be sure, the result being two thousand, four hundred sixty dollars. Hunger drove Summerlin to quickly pocket the money, and head in the direction of the food court.

Summerlin ate at a food court table with a triumphant look on his face. Certainly, an order of hard-shells from *Taco Taco Taco* might not have been the epitome of haute cuisine, but he was too happy with having satiated his hunger and seeing a real Royal Flush. He'd heard many people mention the term casually in the past several days, but had personally never gotten closer than three cards towards the danged thing. *It's not even my money, really. I just can't believe I finally saw one, and it was because of me...*his thoughts ground to a halt when he realized that he wouldn't be able to brag about the hand without exposing the reason for his shock. *I only got the darned thing by trying to rush the game. I didn't hold anything*, he thought. A few seconds later, he washed down the rest of his meal with an ice-cold cola. *Still—I think that Connor would tell me 'what's the difference in how you win?'* he concluded. He grinned; his friend's logic may have seemed convoluted at times, but it certainly did have a way of smacking him in the face with truth when he least expected it to. He dumped his garbage into a trash can and placed the empty red plastic food tray atop it before heading back to the 'twenty thousand points in a day challenge".

He plodded through several hundred hands of video poker with moderate interest at best. As paying attention to the individual hands slowly became lost to Summerlin, he began to find himself looking his machine's screen less and more at the sights and sounds around him. Cocktail waitresses went from machine to machine, carefully—and cleverly—balancing their massive beverage-laden trays with stunning precision. There were a few people who walked past his field of vision with the starry-eyed look of hope that only a novice gambler can provide. And, he also saw a couple men and women walking dejectedly towards the nearby exit door, doing the loser shuffle with their heads hung low. An older woman in ragged clothes went from ashtray to ashtray, collecting half smoked cigarettes in her pocket before a uniformed security officer asked her to leave the property.

Summerlin had officially reached the point where he didn't care what type of machine he was playing anymore. Rather than walking around looking for a machine that struck his fancy, he began to simply move to the nearest machine to his right after every loss of funds or a win above two hundred. Eventually, Summerlin reached the point where he didn't even care what game he was playing at all: he found himself accidentally playing "Five Card E-Keno", and just kept on playing anyway.

After a period of machine-hopping, Summerlin found himself at a small bank of digital slot machines which sat in front of the main entrance. Before he took a seat, he looked through the heavily-tinted doors; it was not easy for him to tell through the tint, but Summerlin he was pretty sure from glowing streetlights that was getting dark outside.

Time rolled on at an unbearable pace; Summerlin glanced at the the red player's point screen—14,052—and wondered if he would ever want to play a slot or video poker machine again in his life. *To think, I actually couldn't wait to try one of these things*, he thought, giving his current slot machine a light kick as he did so. Until a few months ago, such things—gambling devices—had been, to Summerlin, props in movies and television shows. *My mama always did tell me that 'if you hang out in the kitchen, the food will lose your favor.' Smart* woman, he thought before taking a sip from a nearly empty soda. As Summerlin watched his player's point total rise to 19,992, took a deep breath and pressed the draw button rapidly until he saw the number on the LED advance past 20,000.

Jubilation overcame him once Summerlin had finally crossed that lofty number. His happiness was brought on by the fact that, come Hades or high water, he would not have to play anymore. He couldn't tell how many hours it had taken, and contemplated if he would have really wanted to know, if such information would have been possible to attain. *Heck no*, he thought as he pressed the cash out button. After snagging—and pocketing—the cash out ticket for his remaining balance on the machine, Summerlin headed to a kiosk, and cashed in the ticket. He placed the money into his left pocket without so much as counting it. *Time to find out if they keep the Customer Rewards counter open this late*, he thought as his feet raced towards the movie theatres.

The Rewards counter was indeed *still* open; however, Emma and Chrystal were long gone; a large man with a nametag reading "Morris" alone sat behind the wooden semi-circle. The man looked up from an e-reader to greet Summerlin, "Hello, how may I help you tonight?" "Good evening, Morris, I need to have my player's card updated," Summerlin replied. Morris clicked his computer mouse twice and then responded in a voice almost as southern as his, "No problem, sir. Just let me have your card for a moment so we can get a look-see..." Summerlin smiled; familiar sounding voices had so far been few and far between. "What part of the south you from?" he asked Morris. "The *south*? What made you think I'm from there? I was raised in Evansville, Indiana!" he replied, not in anger, but extreme confusion. *Okay, you don't have to take it like it was an insult. Though it goes to show that you shouldn't assume anything about anyone in the Silver State. So many people come here from so many places*, he thought. "Oh, sorry, I must've misheard you. Beg your pardon," Summerlin said with a smile. Morris burst out laughing; "*Man*, you're fun! I'm from Atlanta, Summerlin!" *Summer—what? I don't get...huh?*" He was beyond

171

confused. The Indiana joke he got—Morris had been messing with him. The remainder of the Customer Rewards representative's words left him slack-jawed, however. "How did you know my name?" he asked, still in shock. Morris's chair gave a squeak as he leaned back in it. "Relax. The Con-Man knows everybody 'round here. He told me a few hours ago that 'someone who sounded like y'all'—gotta love his jokes—would be coming with a "Pilgrim" card and have enough player's points to skip two tiers. And he said that I was to under no circumstances admit to being from anywhere than the Hoosier State until I fooled you," Morris said. "Very Funny," Summerlin replied sarcastically. Morris returned his eyes to the computer before him; he gave the keyboard several rapid clicks and tossed Summerlin's white "Pilgrim" card into a bin with the words "To be shredded" written upon it. "Maybe he wanted to see what would make you crack—who knows with that one," Morris said as he got out of his seat heading for the card printer. "Or maybe he wanted to see how you took it,"—Summerlin jerked at the sound of a voice to his immediate right.

Connor Bentley was leaning against the nearest faux brick pillar. "Really?" Summerlin said. "Yes, really. You get a B for effort, my lad. Not bad; but we can get you to 'greater'," the Con-Man answered. Summerlin's eyebrow raised; "I think I'll go with a B. That's not that bad of a grade, after all—*Wait!* What do you mean a B? I did everything you said, followed your plan through the whole thing," he said before reaching in his pocket. He handed Connor the new-and-improved wad and continued, "And, what is more, I even turned your gamblin' man ass a profit, too." Connor nodded solemnly. He placed the wad on his left palm and raised and lowered it gingerly; he then looked at Summerlin and said, "About three thousand, I'd wager." *Okay that just isn't right*, Summerlin thought as his eyes set new world records for wide-openness. "I'm not even going to ask how you know that by weight," he wryly replied. "Oh, come now, Summerlin. That's just not like you. I will even explain your grade," the Con-Man said with a smooth voice, sounding remarkably similar to a game-show host. "Here you go, sir," Morris said as he handed Summerlin a fresh, still warm player's card. It was still a card with his name and player number on it, but his new card was silver in color with large red letters reading "KNIGHT" in front of a faded Texas Palace logo background. "I know the weight of any wad, kid. That comes from experience" Connor said. "Fine, I get that part—but only because it's you; tell me about the rest. A deal's a deal: speak. Why'd you give me anything but an A-plus?" Connor looked over the casino floor before gesturing for Summerlin to follow; "C'mon, kid, walk with me, talk with me," he added.

As they walked through the main pit, Connor began to speak, "You did everything perfect. I pinged you for complaining about my awesome sense of humor. The real reason for all of this is simple: the 'Challenge' was actually a *test*, kid—one of many to come. You think I couldn't honestly get you into that club? *Please*, I'm *me*. I paid Ronaldo to reject you, no matter what you or I had to say. I won't tell you how much I had to pay him, but let's just say he's smiling while on unpaid leave—possibly permanently. The real name they have for the 'twenty thousand point challenge' on the Strip is '*The Gauntlet*', kid. I needed to see if you could start holding it together throughout unexpected stressors; I won't always be there to reign you in when the Olivias and Ginas of the world are at your throat. And, I wanted to see how much attention you've been paying. Do I need to recite the tenets I've stressed?" Summerlin shook his head violently; "No no no—I'll be fine. I see your point. I *hate* it. But I see it, nonetheless," he answered. Once they had reached the elevator lobby, Summerlin stopped in his tracks and said, "okay, I was challenged by different expectations, conditions, and appearances. And you said I did it well, so what's your point?" Connor stood facing away for a moment before turning to respond, "My point is simple: stop caring if you're right. All I ever hear from you when you're sad is about how you were *right* —and once you heard you got anything less than a perfect grade, you couldn't let it go. Want the truth, kid?" Summerlin nodded, trying his best to hold his temper and give the man a chance to explain. "The truth is, Summerlin, it doesn't *ever* matter in life who was wrong and who was right—*ever*! What really matters is what you do the next time, regardless of fault. File that under 'Lesson Six'." *Wow*, Summerlin thought; he was at a loss for words. Connor continued, "And if you're mad that I set you up for unneeded gaming, well, I only have one defense to that—would you have said yes to playing that long on purpose?" Summerlin had to laugh; "No. Not only no, but *heck no*... Dammit..." Summerlin's battle was lost, and he sighed before patting Connor's shoulder and adding, "As before, I understand, and also concurrently, don't have to like it." Connor nodded with a proud smile and then raised up his hand out of nowhere, gesturing for Summerlin to "give him a second".

"Almost forgot," Connor said, "you gave me too much earlier," handing him a mini-wad that was mostly twenty dollar bills. Summerlin grabbed the wad out of instinct, and tried to hand it back, like a hot potato the moment he had received it. "What's this?" he asked Connor. "That," he began, "is not mine. I lent you two thousand dollars. You gave me three thousand." Summerlin nodded and waited until he had finished speaking to contest, "The deal was that you'd get it back." Connor grinned and deployed the *arm glide* upon a ticket-cashing kiosk to the left of the elevator lobby. "Actually, if you use that bright mind of yours, Summerlin, you'd remember that I said you wouldn't be held responsible for losses. I never said anything about what would happen in the event of a surplus. And, I *believe* I remember someone being very vocal about not accepting or charity or something like that. And I know that if I'm made to honor your requests, then you should honor mine. So obviously, I can't accept that," the Con-Man replied, beaming with pride. *And checkmate*, he thought. "Okay, I get that I'm just goin' to have to surrender on this one. You're making my head hurt, Yankee," Summerlin replied. Summerlin reluctantly put the extra money in his wallet. "Well, kid, I think you've been pretty good lately at holding that irrational tendency of yours. You're obviously all tested-out for the night, and can do as you please. But, before I give you a key to the Austin Suite, may I interest you in some late-night Blackjack?" Connor said. Summerlin smiled and replied, "After 'the gauntlet'? No thanks." The Con-Man shrugged and pulled out a hotel room key-card which looked identical to the green card he had seen Connor use. "It's yours: you earned it—just don't wreck the place. Sweet dreams, Appalachian friend," he added. Summerlin replied, "Thanks. For everything. Especially the parts I don't understand yet." Connor winked and made a clicking noise before departing towards the Pit.

As he rode the elevator, Summerlin could think only of sleep. A gentle calm came over him as he walked down the hallway towards the Austin Suite. His trembling, weary hands slid the green room key in and then lumbered into the landing. Summerlin headed in a beeline for the guestroom bed, desiring slumber perhaps more than he ever had before in his life.

When Summerlin finally awoke, he felt well-rested and amazingly refreshed—it was the first time since meeting Connor Bentley that he had managed a full, uninterrupted night's rest. He got out of bed, and stretched contentedly upon rising. Summerlin listened intently for the familiar sounds of nearby construction, but didn't hear a thing except for the distant sound of cars speeding by on Reata Avenue. *It must be late afternoon already*, he thought upon seeing that the sun was already nearing the western horizon.

Summerlin took a steaming-hot shower and then shaved before resigning himself to choosing his clothes once again from Connor's "clothing exchange" items. He settled on a *Texas World* t-shirt, and a pair of indigo jeans with French Seams. "Bless my boots," he said aloud with joy as he grabbed them from the closet floor and placed them at the foot of his bed.

When he sat upon the bed's edge to put on his boots, Summerlin noticed that there was an old-fashioned bell style alarm clock on one of the entertainment center's lower shelves. He had never noticed it before. *I'd normally accuse myself of being unobservant, but it's pretty hard finding a specific money-themed item in this sea of all things Federal Reserve*, he thought. The clock's hands revealed that it was 2:55. Summerlin noticed that there was a white card propped up against the rear of the clock; he walked over to the clock, grabbed the envelope and tossed it on the bed. Summerlin put on his boots after getting dressed. He gave the crisp white envelope a skeptical look as he opened it.

The note enclosed was in Connor's usual calligraphy-like script, and read: "I thought I'd let you take a day, kid. You suffered enough yesterday. Tomorrow will be a different matter altogether. And, before you even think to ask—Don't bother. Just relax. Go out, do something fun. The valet is awaiting you; I personally recommend car number two." The letter was signed, "Sincerely, Con." *Car number two is probably a Model T*, he thought with a grin as he tossed the note on the bed and made his way out of the guest room.

Summerlin checked the mini-fridge behind the bar for a non-alcoholic beverage on his way out. He took a bottle of orange juice—originally intended for the mixing of "screwdrivers", no doubt—and opened it and took it with him on his way out of the suite. *Ding*. The Sam Houston elevator was going down and nearly filled to capacity, but Summerlin managed to fit in, with the elevator doors mere inches from his face.

Summerlin ventured through the casino floor, slowing only to avoid colliding with the occasional person too stuck in their smartphones to look up. Summerlin crossed the two lanes separating him from the valet shed. When he got there, he was greeted by Melissa the valet. Summerlin's original intentions were to take *any* car other than the one the Con-Man had suggested—*No telling whether vehicle two is a ride, or a test*, he reasoned. As his friend had suggested number two, he instinctually planned to tell the valet he desired the car in lot number "ten". *I guess the fun of finding out which car number ten would be worth the action of taking a trip off property*, he thought. He knew that Connor wished for him to have a day free of the casino, especially after his "gambling overdose" of the day before; but, Summerlin had no idea where to go; most of his happy memories of places in Vegas, Texas Palace notwithstanding, had been when he was accompanied by Sarah. As he walked up to the window, Melissa greeted him: "Good afternoon, Summerlin; I'm told you'll be preferring the car in lot number two?" Summerlin frowned and gave out a sigh. *Great*, he thought, *he told her ahead of time—now I'll have to drive the crazy thing, no matter what it was.* Fearing the worst, Summerlin nodded and with trepidation replied, "Yeah, it looks like the car chose me." Melissa laughed lightly and replied, "It's best to just do what he wants, trust me," as she grabbed a set of keys and ran out into the valet lot. *Oh boy, what have I gotten myself into?* he wondered as he awaited vehicle number two.

Goodness gracious, he thought as an antique, high-gloss white Corvette rolled in under the massive Texas Palace canopy. *Woah, classic Stingray!* he thought with a smile. "Maybe that Yankee isn't so bad, after all," he said under his breath as he approached the driver's seat. The coupe was older than he, but had a flawless glossy coat of paint that was surpassed in reflection by only the Con-Man's mirror-mobile. "Thanks," he said to Melissa as he handed her a ten dollar bill and hopped in. Once seated, Summerlin felt the entire car shake under the raw power of its V-8 engine. "Yee-haw!" he yelled happily into the air as he zoomed off property—he didn't know where he would go, but he sure was happy to be going there.

Summerlin found himself stopped by a red light at the intersection of Lake Mead and Reata Avenue. *I guess the traffic light made the choice for me, right turn on red, here we go!* he thought as he turned on his signal and sped down Lake Mead. As he neared the intersection of Lake Mead and Rancho, he gave a quick glance over to the lot of the construction site of Rancho Palace. The cranes and bulldozers were silent and motionless, yet the sight of the place still gave him a cold chill of revulsion. The unfinished triple towers seemed *inhuman* somehow when compared to the laid-back grandeur that was Texas Palace. Summerlin hit a red light as he reached the crossing of Rancho, and decided to let the flow of traffic guide him once again.

Whether it was a subconscious choice, or by accident, Summerlin found himself driving west on Cheyenne Avenue, and slowly entering the old neighborhood that surrounded Summerlin Heights. As he drove past Rainbow Avenue, he gave a quick view to his right; *That's where the baked ziti restaurant, Taste of Sin is,* he thought as he recalled the odd dinner he had shared with friends only a few days before. He remembered that he had no socks of his own, and disliked the feel of Connor's dress socks within his boots. *I'd reckon that Super Dollar World has socks that fit a workin' man. And I probably should get a watch, since I currently dwell in a building with no clocks,* he thought as he pulled into the plaza.

He decided that in choosing a parking spot for such a choice automobile that he should honor his friend's parking code: he parked the Stingray at the far edge of the massive parking lot—diagonally. "Now that there's got to get the Connor Bentley seal of approval," he said aloud before getting out. He patted the car's hood with pride as he began the long walk to Super Dollar World.

Summerlin glanced up at the sign of the place, which had bold red lettering upon a three story façade. The letters were at least ten feet high each, and read "Super Dollar World Mega-store." The building had four sets of tinted, sliding-glass doorways; two were marked "IN" and the other two "OUT". Summerlin found himself dodging people left and right as he attempted to go through the left set of doors. Undaunted, he backed up, and went to the right pair of doors; three grown men mowed right in front of him. He looked in through the doorway as the discourteous men walked through. *My goodness, what sort of place is this?* Summerlin thought in horror as he saw the same scene repeated over and over again: the building swelled with a mass of ever-milling and ever gesturing humanity—and nobody seemed to notice that there were other people there. Summerlin witnessed five human on human collisions before he even entered the store; everyone in the store, both employee and customer alike, seemed to be scowling in irritation. There wasn't a smiling person to be found in the whole place. There were, however, plenty of fire-engine red signs with the phrase "Super Dollar Deal!" upon them. *Those signs burn my eyes like Connor's dress shirts*, he thought. He genuinely appreciated the help—and strange advice—of the Con-Man, but he knew that the one thing they would go to both their deaths without doing would be agreeing in terms of fashion.

Once Summerlin had become aware of the nature of the place, he walked ever so slowly throughout the store. He had come for a few pairs of socks and a watch; but, as is often the case in mega-stores, he ended up realizing he actually could find use of a few of the sale items—by the time he reached the checkout lanes, he was holding socks, a wristwatch, a replaceable-head razor and a CD of Bocephus' greatest hits. *Okay, I think I might have gone too far with the razor...but if Connor leaves another one of those darn disposables on my bathroom sink I'm gonna glue his hangers together*, he thought with a laugh. He enjoyed the bed, but otherwise felt the amenities of the hotel lacked the true feeling of a home. A razor would, at least, be a start.

Summerlin cast a glance at the checkout lanes and noticed that though there were at least twenty of them, only one of them had a cashier actually working the register. The procession of people waiting their turn for the lane ran almost the entire breadth of the store. Luckily, there were two self-checkout lanes available, and the lines for those were much shorter.

After waiting his turn and checking out, Summerlin headed out to the parking lot. He walked to the outer limits and placed the bags into his car. He was about to get in and drive when he noticed a sign at the far end of the plaza. It was a silkscreen, backlit sign, like those he was used to seeing on the fronts of bars back home. This particular one was well-faded by the sun, but he could still make out the lettering: "Lost Wages Tavern & RESTAURANT". *I could use a bite*, he thought, noting that he had an opportune chance to consume something from a place without a hotel license. He locked the Corvette back up and headed to the restaurant on foot.

Halfway through the lot, Summerlin saw something which made him become pale and covered in chills: a deep blue Chevy Corsica with a furry steering wheel cover and an Atlanta Brave's bumper sticker on the back. "Sarah's here," he said softly as his heart began to pound.

Summerlin didn't know what to do. He had a few options, all of which had a bad point to them: He could try to leave a note—but with Gina and Olivia around, such efforts were likely to bear little fruit. He could leave, and just be happy knowing that Sarah was alive and well; *or*, he could be bold, and wait for a chance to talk to her. *Let's be bold*, he thought— *The Con-Man would love it, I'm goin' to take a gamble*. He walked over to the car, and leaned against it, trying several times to effect a "Bentley arm glide", but the glossy paint of the car made him slide his arm down the windshield. He settled with leaning against the vehicle's trunk.

He still had a post-arm-glide grin when he saw her; she had quietly walked up on him, and caught him unawares. Yet, it was she that had the open-mouthed look of confusion. "What are you doing here?" she asked in a demanding tone. Summerlin looked terrified. *This may not have been the best of plans after all*, he thought. "Are you stalking me?" she persisted. Sarah glared in anger—he had seen that look before, but never directed at *him*. "Of course not!" Summerlin quickly replied. "Why are you here, then? It just seems to me like the moment I'm not near my friends, you show up," Sarah said. "Well, darlin', I was under the impression that this shopping plaza was for the use of the general public. I didn't chase you here—I *did* make the conscious choice to wait for you once I saw your car," Summerlin said.

Sarah lowered her head and walked *through* him to get to her trunk; Summerlin sprang hastily to the side to avoid a collision. She placed two shopping bags in it, closed the trunk and went directly to the driver's side door. "You need to go," she began to speak, "Gina and Olivia told me you wouldn't leave me be—and to think they were right!" He tried to be Connor—he only *dreamt* that he could think that fast on his feet—but no snappy comebacks or insightful remarks came to him. "Sarah, I'm not saying they're wrong. All I'm saying is that it's a little strange that they're so worried to let you see me that even by your own admittance, they are always near you. The girl I fell in love with in Blacksburg thought for herself. I'm just saying we should—" he was interrupted by the closing of the Cavalier's door. Sarah cracked the window and replied, "You need to know we're over, Andy. It's for the best. Try to go home or something." As the car began to roll out of its parking space, Summerlin yelled out, "Nothing's over if you're willing to try! I'm in the Austin Suite at Texas Palace if you change your mind!" *Why, oh sweet why did I allow myself to ever become irritated by those evil "friends" of hers*, he thought as he saw the car speed off onto Rainbow Avenue, *I'm not even saying you need to be with me...I just want to talk, without them—even just for a moment.* The possibility of relaxation was now gone. He slowly plodded back to the Corvette, and headed for Texas Palace.

Summerlin punched the steering wheel in frustration when he was at a red light before the 95 South onramp. "I can't *believe* she told me to go back to Virginia—like this is her city!" he yelled in frustration. *The whole thing was pointlessly painful*, he thought. He turned on a country music station, lowered the windows, and tried his best to vent as he drove onto the highway.

As he neared the casino, Summerlin tried to breathe slowly and clear his mind of stressful thoughts; he did, indeed, like to follow thoughts through to their best available conclusion, but this was not the time. The fact that Sarah had been so defensive against letting him have any chance to speak truly bothered him; and, the fact that Gina and Olivia had precluded any chance of him talking to her with a story about him being a would-be stalker truly disgusted him.

Zak was working the valet booth when he pulled the car to a stop under the canopy. He fumbled in his wallet for a ten dollar bill, and handed it to Zak, adding "sorry for the trouble, kinda frustrated right now." The valet nodded and said, "That's Vegas: you never can tell what you're going to experience. There's always the next play though, man." That made him feel a little bit better, though Summerlin wasn't quite sure why.

Summerlin felt that it would be best to head straight for the Austin Suite. The casino Pit was bustling with people as he made way for the elevators. He kept his head down in an attempt to avoid being greeted or seen. He was successful, and made it to the suite level in silence, and relative peace. He smiled with the thought of, for once, just being able to be alone in Vegas without anyone to bother him, or try to cheer him up. *Sometimes the only thing that can help your hurtin' is to hurt*, he thought. The smile vanished from his face when he opened the door, and saw that he was not alone.

A poker table now sat in the middle of the great room and four people were sitting at it: Connor, Xero, Jail-Bait, and a young woman Summerlin vaguely recalled meeting at hotel registration a few days ago. *I think that's the girl who gave me my room key*, he thought. There was a CD boom-box on the floor near Xero that was playing heavy metal. Summerlin scanned the table to assess what game they were playing, and it was obvious. *Each one of them is holding five cards, and there's a flopped down pile near Xero, and I just saw him deal. That's Euchre for sure*, he thought. There were several shot glasses, each filled to the rim with an amber colored liquid—A bottle of "Angry Wolf" whisky sat near them as the likely source. "Oh, Megan!" Connor yelled jovially, "This is that little boy I've been training, Summerlin." The young woman turned from her cards to face him. "I think I remember you…Megan, right?" Summerlin said. She smiled and said, "yes." After ten silent seconds went by, The Con-Man waved his hand in front of Megan's eyes and said, "Hey, the game doesn't wait for you, I wanna finish this thing." Connor looked up casually at him and added, "Hey, kid, I'd love to offer you a chair—but this is a four player game." Summerlin glanced once more at the table before replying, "I know what Euchre is, fashionisto. Turns out we play it in the sticks, too." Xero and Jail-Bait laughed loudly; even Megan was grimacing to hold herself together. "Very funny, *Summerlin*, but that goes to show you how little you know. We are playing *Extreme* Euchre. Totally different experience, trust me," Connor replied with thick courtesy. "Ex…treme? What's extreme about a card game my cousins and I used to play when we were kids?" Summerlin asked. Xero looked up from his cards and said with a grin, "Just watch, kid. If what I think is true, the Con-Man will be showing you how it's played, very soon." Connor leered at Xero and replied, "You wish, spike-top. I'm about to show you your age." Jail-Bait broke in to the conversation: "Xero, Bentley, table talk! Jeez." They resumed playing the round as Summerlin took a seat at the bar and watched.

The game which the four played seemed to be identical to its non-extreme counterpart—through the second book anyway. Xero and Megan's team were leading against Connor and Jailbait, with a score of 2-1. On the final round of the hand, Megan took the final book to win the round for their team. It was then that Summerlin witnessed the fundamental difference from the normal version of the game: After Xero and Meagan won the round, everyone but Connor grabbed a shot of whisky and proceeded to toss their contents at Connor, mostly upon his face. "What the heck is this?" he said abruptly; the words came out before he had realized it. Everyone looked at him, though they all looked to be on the laughing side of a joke. "Relax, Summerlin," Xero explained, "it's how the game is played." Summerlin remained agape. Jail-Bait, Xero and Megan all said in unison: "He had it coming!" he gave a quick glance to the now alcohol-drenched Con-Man. "I had it coming," he said, nodding in contentment as he patted down his silk shirt with a napkin.

"So getting *euchred* gets you soaked—I get it," Summerlin said. Xero pushed the deck of cards to Jail-Bait to deal, and replied, "He learns fast." Connor took a sip from a nearby shot glass and began sorting his hand of cards, adding, "We can only hope so."

The game continued for several more rounds until Xero and Megan finally won by one point, 10-9. There was no shot tossing, though Xero and Megan did give a rapid procession of strange high-fives.

Summerlin had almost forgotten the circumstances which led him to be returning to the Austin Suite so early. Connor did him the favor of reminding him: "Kid? Why are you back so early anyway? Don't mind having you, of course, but weren't you supposed to be taking the day off and relaxing? It's only two minutes past four." Summerlin's head dropped as he explained to him, "I *did* sleep in. And I even took car number two—nice car, by the way—but other issues led me to believe perhaps my relaxation would best be accomplished here. After all, it seems fine by you, doesn't it? I thought I'd find the Austin empty. Well, maybe that's what I had hoped. Don't get me wrong, I love the present company, and I'm not feeling that way now. I just hate it when—" Once more, Summerlin was cut off. "Yo, cut it off or let it pull down the boat, kid." Connor laughed and put the deck of cards on the table; "Gimme a minute, guys, gotta do the whole teacher-student conference thing." Megan grabbed the cards and began shuffling them as Connor rose and walked over to join Summerlin at the bar.

Connor took a beer out of the mini-fridge and opened it before addressing Summerlin. "First off, I can relax anywhere; you are *not* me, and have had problems controlling emotions lately. But, we'll get to that later. What's more important in the now is: what are 'other issues'?"

The Con-Man had the inquisitive leer of a TV reporter. Summerlin let out a heavy sigh. "Can we go someplace with less people?" he asked. Connor's face belied a deepened curiosity. "*That bad*? Okay, follow me then." He walked out of the Austin Suite, and headed down the hallway for the elevators, with Summerlin struggling to catch up. By the time he reached Connor, the doors on the oil derrick elevator had already opened.

"Hey, you pressed the wrong one," Summerlin said after noting that Connor had pressed the button for up, not down. "Quite observant as ever, kid, and equally as wrong as ever. We're going up—on purpose." *Why does he always have to be so aloof? It's his fault for being so odd in his ways that I ask so many questions*, Summerlin thought. They boarded the elevator, which opened its doors once it reached the Executive level. "I remember this place," Summerlin said as they strolled down the hallway, passing by the doors to the Executive Conference room. Connor nodded as he pulled a small keychain from his pocket with a single brass key on it, "Yeah, love the good ol' shuffle-board court."

"You have got to be kidding," Summerlin said as he followed the Con-Man up a flight of metal stairs to a door which he unlocked with the key. "Actually, there are a few things about which I do not kid: couture, Race Book and rooftops. Now come on, it's nice and confined up here, no distractions or ears, just like you wanted." *It is what I wanted—though I have this bad feeling that I could be made to regret that*, Summerlin thought.

The doorway deposited the two men atop the roof of Texas Palace's hotel tower. On the roof, there lay a maze-like configuration of HVAC units, and a system of ladders and breaker boxes. Summerlin couldn't escape thinking that Connor and he did *not* belong there, but he realized the futility of bringing it up to him.

"So, what's your problem?" Connor asked as he walked down the maintenance walkway, ever closer to the edge. Summerlin had to fight the subtle nuances of fear to join him; a small breeze had begun to kiss his skin, and he could see his friend's hair being blown with even more force. "Well, asides from monstrous heights, I saw Sarah today, at Super Dollar World," he said meekly. Connor had reached a three-foot tall railing which was less than a yard from the building's true edge. He turned to Summerlin and said, "You saw your heartbreaker, eh? Let me guess: you saw her and couldn't resist the temptation of approaching her?" Summerlin became awash in guilt and curiosity. *Okay, I get that this isn't his first rodeo, but how did he get the second part right?* he wondered. After a few moments of silence, Connor said, "We may live in a clock-free environment, but that doesn't mean time doesn't exist—spill it, kid."

Summerlin joined Connor near the railing, and took a look at the horizon: It was a picture perfect view of Las Vegas Boulevard from Reata Avenue, the entire expanse from the Stratosphere to the Luxor, all bathed in the amber-colored light of the setting sun. "I—I don't even know how to say it in a way that won't make me sound bad. I did not see her; however I *did* see her car," he said, half at a stammer. "Well, then, that gives me license to believe that you debated leaving a message, and then let fear of two girls from the Buckeye State embolden you to stay—breaking Lesson Three in the process, I might add?" Connor said, with a bit of annoyance in his tone. "When you put it that way, it makes it sound even worse...I honestly thought I was acting out that first rule, the one about not letting your surroundings change you." Summerlin replied. Connor wagged a finger in his direction, chiding, "That would be Lesson *Five*. The one you were pretending to adhere to is Lesson *Two*: 'only logical judgments matter—fear and wishful thinking are to be left at the door.' Though, I gotta tell you, you really *ought* to have been living by Lesson number *Three*, give negative situations time, learn to become slow to react." *Uh oh*, Summerlin thought; he felt like he had said the wrong thing in math class. "Exactly how many of these rules are there?" he asked. Connor wagged his finger again; "There are nine *Lessons*, kid, but they won't matter unless you pay attention. And, what is more, the Lessons are to be *cumulative*; that is to say, you can't do number six without concurrent observation of one through five. I thought that would have been obvious, but perhaps I've been too lenient, my young friend." *"Lenient?" This guy made me gamble for a day straight!* Summerlin thought in reaction.

Summerlin sighed while returning his gaze to the breathtaking vista that laid beyond him. He heard Connor continue talking as he focused on not letting anger steal him away from reason. "Relax. You messed up. Heck, you messed up *big* time. I bet those friends of hers are even gonna label you a stalker, even!" Summerlin took a hard gulp before replying: "Actually, they labeled me that to her before I even saw her car. She ran into her car and sped off after making reference to that fact. Those *monsters* actually told her I'd do that...I wasn't following her. I wouldn't have sought out such an uncomfortable circumstance in my life." Connor joined him in his horizon-viewing. "I know that, and you know that, Summerlin. But *Sarah* won't. It's not a train wreck for certain kid, even the Sarah parts—just hold fast to Lesson Four. This just means everything is going to be a little harder, and require more work. And now we must regroup. I hereby call phase two into session." Connor replied.

"Phase two?" Summerlin asked. "Yes, it's time. You have shown yourself to be trying hard, yet unable to avail yourself of the proper answers when found alone. It's my fault, really—I dropped the ball. I should have made you shadow me more properly," Connor replied. Summerlin looked over at the Con-Man and said, "Dare I ask how I could be shadowing you more properly? I'm not doing anything gross." Connor laughed. "Well, at least you still have your sense of humor— that's a start. I simply meant that I've been having you watch what I do, without supplying you with the vital *philosophical* elements. Look, kid," he gestured Summerlin to look once more upon the glittering Vegas horizon. "Look at that. There, beneath that canopy of chaotic architecture beats a sea of thousands of hearts, all coming here for their heart's desire. You are so young yet, Summerlin: you still have your life. Heck, I have been through all I've been through, and I still have mine! We live in a dreamer's paradise, my young apprentice. Look at it all, kid, and you'll see the constellation of opportunities at your fingertips—you can't *tell me* all roads don't lead here..." He walked back in the direction of the stairwell. Summerlin stood in deep contemplation; "Again, kid, we don't have all day," the Con-Man called out after him. Summerlin blinked and took a deep breath before turning away from the view and chasing Connor down to the elevators.

9.

Connor led Summerlin back to the card table in the Austin Suite, and planted him in the seat that faced Jail-Bait. Megan took a turn at the bar while Xero sat opposing Connor. "He's just a boy, be gentle," Jail-Bait said to the Con-Man as he was dealing the cards. They all laughed—Even Summerlin. They played two full games, with each team scoring one win. After all four participants were whisky-soaked and card-weary, they collected the deck and put the poker table away; it went into closet near the guest room hallway. Megan left, adding that she had to be at work the next day at 9am. Jail-Bait, in turn, rose and said, "I gotta go—the Shake House isn't going to DJ itself. Work calls." After Jones, Xero, too, rose from his seat and said, "Well, I'm not a DJ or anything, but I just got a text from Chris that he's calling off, and rushing downstairs will net me first dibs." "Have fun guys. Be safe," Connor said to the three of them.

Once the others had left, Summerlin and the Con-Man found themselves seated at the bar. Connor was shuffling cards repeatedly; Summerlin was sipping on a beer from the fridge. "So what are you doing this evening?" he asked Connor. "Well, I figure I'll go a-gambling. I'll still let you off the hook for the rest of the day. I do suggest accomplishing something positive beyond sleeping in late," he replied. Summerlin wished Connor luck before he departed, and he was alone. *What am I going to do?* he wondered.

Summerlin decided to relax and catch up on recent sports scores. The Braves had played an entire away-stand since he had arrived at Texas Palace, and he figured that he could deal with some light natured topic matter for a change.

Apparently, the Braves had won two in a row—Summerlin toasted the TV screen before taking a sip from his beer. He didn't sleep; but, rather, found a near-sleeplike peace in watching sports talk shows while *not* worrying about anything, except perhaps what Connor's "more proper" approach might entail. *I can find that out tomorrow,* he thought.

Later, Summerlin went to the Texasland Café and had prime rib for dinner. He laid a ten-dollar tip on the table, and headed out to the casino. As he passed through a section of slot machines, a thought dawned upon him: *Hey, it's Tuesday night. The arcade should be kid-free!* Summerlin followed the overhead signs, which led him past the Customer Rewards counter, and to the arcade.

The arcade was still open when Summerlin arrived; however, there was a sign posted outside the entrance noting that it was closing at 11pm. He checked his new watch to see that it was currently 9:29. There was plenty of time for Summerlin to play the deer hunting game he had noticed there days ago. It wasn't that he particularly enjoyed the thought of hunting—he actually had to constantly remind himself while playing such games that the cute little creatures weren't ever actually getting hurt—Summerlin merely loved the art of target practice. As a child, his older brother had taken him hunting, and while he had always bested him in competitions that involved tin cans and the like, Summerlin had found better use of his rifle as a cane in the woods than as a weapon.

As Summerlin mowed down simulated bucks, he became distracted by a few nagging thoughts: Sarah was angrier than she had been last Thursday, he was still unemployed, and time seemed to be moving way too fast for him to make an easy recovery. Winning some money on the side was great, but not a real job. He had no guarantee what the next hour would bring, not to mention what the incoming days and weeks would bring. "Shooting" electronic deer had an easy set of *known* goals and results, and didn't even require a large amount of money; the game cost fifty cents to play. The video game had indeed been the least random activity he had engaged in recently. *Then again, Con would just tell me that there's no fun in predictable things, and that prediction actually means nothing...that Lesson One sure can be a rattlesnake in the boot,* he thought as he found himself admiring the digital terrain of the "Appalachia" course. After setting a high score on the course that reminded him most of his home, he opted to call it quits. Summerlin decided to return to the guest room, and perhaps even watch a movie before bed.

The elevator doors opened, and as he was about to board, Connor disembarked. "Hey, Summerlin, I was just looking for you," he said. Summerlin replied, "Oh?" "Yeah," the Con-Man continued, "Me and a few of the guys are going out—you in?" Summerlin was debating the issue mentally when Connor answered for him, "Of *course* you're in. This could be helpful to a man in your plight, I've decided. And I know, I know, I said you could have the rest of the day; but, think of it this way: it might even be past midnight when we get there. It'll be good for you anyway."

Connor began walking in the direction of the main entrance, with Summerlin following closely behind. "So, who's goin' with us? Band members? Friends from Race Book?" he asked Connor as they walked through the Craps tables in the Pit. "A little bit of the mix," he replied as he opened the center pair of glass doors. As they exited, Summerlin noticed that there was a group of four people standing next to the valet shed. Two of the group he already recognized—Trent and Samantha from The Reason Why. Trent and a woman he did not know were smoking.

"Hey, it's the *Blacksburg Bulls-eye* himself," Trent called out to Summerlin, who waved back and said, "Howdy, Trent. Goin' to let me challenge that last win of yours?" Trent laughed and added, "Not yet; I have to wear it like a crown for a little while, you know…" Summerlin nodded and smiled; *I gotta admit, I may not have the one I love, but I seem to have fallen in with genuine-hearted friends*, he thought as he turned to Connor, who was having a conversation with Samantha and the two unknowns—one was a tall, young man with a ponytail wearing a t-shirt with a T.R.Y. logo; the other, a short woman who appeared to be in her middle thirties, who was clad in a striking denim vest with several patches depicting fire, skulls and weapons that Summerlin wagered even his brother wouldn't recognize. Connor waved for Summerlin's attention, and took the initiative to dole out introductions. "Danny, Trista, this is Summerlin. Kid, this is Danny and Trista. Summerlin is a kid who helped me, and is just plain *interesting*—" Summerlin rolled his eyes as Connor went on, "Trista is an old friend of mine from back in the day, and Danny's with Samantha, if you catch my drift." The drift was caught; Samantha had her arms around the tall, olive-skinned man's waist.

"Okay guys, I know you're not going to expect me to pluck a car from valet when we intend on drinking. We have to have a way to get home tonight, and I don't want to see any designated drivers. Besides, my autos are *non-smoking*," Connor said, leering at Trent and Trista as he spoke the last part. "*Fascist*," Trista said with a grin before putting her cigarette out in a trashcan-top ashtray. Danny, meanwhile, reached out his hand to Summerlin and said, "Good to meet you." Summerlin shook it and added, "likewise." Trista next greeted Summerlin, albeit while walking over to the taxi lane, which stood at the opposite corner of the canopy. "Nice to meet you," She didn't shake his hand, but instead flashed him a peace sign. Summerlin nodded and added, "Same to you."

There were three taxicabs sitting in a line behind a three-foot tall red and white sign that read "FOR TAXI". The first cab was an orange and white Crown Vic with the words "MOJAVE TAXI". The other two cabs were Nissan Versas with a gray and white color pattern, and had the name "Emperor Cab". "Okay guys—and yes, I specifically mean you Trent—time to get over to the cab line so we can take two of these off their radios," Connor said while pointing to the last two of the three cabs. "Yeah, yeah, I'm coming," Trent replied, joining the group by the taxis. Connor opened the rear driver's side door of the second cab in the line and jumped in.

Summerlin had been intending to get into the first cab in line, but was dissuaded by Connor, who leaned out the window of the Scion and said, "Hey, we're taking these two." Summerlin shrugged; he didn't even bother asking. Once he was inside the cab, however, he was told. "I don't trust the orange ones, kid. They'll tunnel-haul you until you're dead. And then, they'll longhaul your corpse on its way to the morgue." "Long...haul?" he replied. Danny jumped into the cab; Summerlin could hear the doors of the other cab open and close, and noticed Trista, Trent and Samantha were already buckled in. "Longhauling—that's what the crooked cabbies do to make more on a fare they consider too small for them; they'll take you eight miles out for a quarter mile trip. And if you tell them you notice, they'll blame it on construction, or a faulty navigator," Danny said after buckling up. "See, kid?" Connor said, "everybody who lives here already knows about it. And the boys and girls of Emporer don't do that, so we skipped the orange one." Danny nodded and added, "Yeah, Mojave Taxi *blows*."

Once they were all boarded and buckled-in, the cabs left the property. Connor had called Samantha to have her notify their driver to follow his before telling the cabbie, "Take us to the Class ACT, please." "Strip club? Why didn't you say so before," the driver replied with a massive smile and a thick Russian accent. "You're acting like you get to come in with us," Summerlin said with a grin. "No, better," the driver replied. Connor shook his head and looked at Summerlin; "The drivers get a per-head kickback from the stripclubs, kid," he said. Summerlin nodded and retorted, "Hey, then he *is* right—can I have a per-head kick-back instead of going in?" Danny and the Con-Man burst out laughing. "Kid, it's that off-the-wall crap you somehow come up with that makes me keep you around. Well, that and the accent, of course," Connor replied. "Gee, *thanks*. Tell me, how was the Nixon Administration? I mean, you'd know, having been alive for it and all, Summerlin wryly retorted. "And the ref takes a point away," Danny said while trying to maintain a straight face. The two cabs turned onto the onramp for Highway 95 south.

When the cabs took the Charleston exit past the Spaghetti bowl, Summerlin looked up to view the area. He saw a sparsely developed landscape which was dotted with mom and pop stores—mostly restaurants—and gas stations. There was a Super Dollar World sign in the distance, and beyond the occasional trailer home, there appeared to be little to see in the relatively dark side of Vegas. "I know what you're probably thinking, Summerlin, 'how can Las Vegas get so small and dark', right?" Summerlin nodded. "Well, it can't," Connor replied, "This is the city of Sunrise Manor, which borders the city of North Las Vegas—different city hall and everything. And, before you judge, you should know that some of the more honest people I've met in my life have come from *this* side of town. Though there are good people in any mode of living, there's a certain honesty that usually comes with squalor...but, I digress. This is the proud neighborhood of the valley's *best* girlie joint—and, one of the only two in the county to allow booze *and* full nudity." Summerlin smiled, though perhaps not at what Connor was smiling about: *If it's this dark outside around these parts, I might actually see a few stars in the sky tonight*, he thought.

The cabs pulled under a canopy clad in white aluminum siding which was supported by six faux-Greek pillars. The building itself was only one story in height, but was by Summerlin's assumption almost a football field in length, and almost as wide as the downtown casinos he had seen near Fremont Street. There was a casino-style sign in the corner of the parking lot with the words "Class ACT Gentleman's Cabaret" in twinkling white lights. As they were getting ready to disembark, Summerlin noticed a small black felt bag fall from Connor's sleeve; it landed underneath the driver's seat while the driver was busy writing something on his trip sheet. *Silly city-boy, you have so much stuff you forget when you lose* it, Summerlin reasoned as he reached to return he object to his friend. Connor stopped him and then made a finger to his lips while shaking his head. *I better just go with it, I'm sure he has some reason for it. I'm equally sure, though, that if I ask I'm not goin' to understand*, he thought with a smile as he exited the cab. He saw the Con-Man hand the driver two twenties for the fare and what looked to be a fifty as a tip. Connor patted the roof of the cab after getting out. "Top-drawer, my man. Good ride. Now go make Blue Dice Taxi regret they were chartered!" "C'mon, Summerlin," Connor said, "The rest of the guys are in line already. Don't worry about the drivers, they'll get theirs. They like the patrons to get in first." "Ohh," Summerlin replied in comprehension. "That student of yours has a lot to learn, Con-Man," Danny said as they walked to join the others in a ten-person line which ended with a bouncer and a tuxedoed man with a flashlight. Connor simply laughed and said, "Sure does". Summerlin knew that Connor would have usually agreed and then listed one of his better traits to balance things out. Somehow though, he knew that such an act wouldn't be likely. *It was the Nixon line, dammit*, he thought. He looked back at his friend to see The Con-Man give a wink before grinning and turning back to face the front of the line.

"So, all this way for a nudie joint? You know they have those near the Strip, right?" Summerlin said as they slowly inched forward towards their ID and security checks. "It was Trent and Trista's idea," Connor replied. Summerlin looked up near the front of the line to see Trent and Trista, and, sure enough, they were holding their IDs in-hand with Texas Palace-sized smiles on their faces. "Somehow, I doubt you're hating the idea," he said to Connor. The Con-Man nodded, adding, "Relax, Summerlin. What's the worst that can happen? You might even have fun. You can watch Trista put a dollar in a G-string—we all do." Everyone in earshot laughed; Trista winked and made a clicking noise not unlike that of the Con-Man. Once he had passed through the metal detector and his ID was deemed satisfactory, Summerlin was waved forward by the flashlight bearer.

As he entered the building, Summerlin's ears were immediately overcome by a combination of cheers, catcalls, and loud 70's rock. From the door, the group followed a series of brass stanchions to a large Plexiglas-enclosed cashier's counter. Beyond the counter there was a windowless door made of solid oak. The cash register was being tended by two young, attractive blondes in skimpy black lingerie. Trista and Trent raced up to the window with the speed and joy of kids entering a candy store. Samantha and Danny held hands as they walked behind them. Connor held pace with Summerlin, who was walking slowly behind the others.

"First time?" Connor asked Summerlin as they were next in line to pay for admission. "'Fraid to disappoint you, but no. I *am* twenty-five and I do have an older brother. I've been to one in Atlanta and Tuscaloosa," he replied. Connor then widened his eyes and said in an astonished tone, "No—You've been to the one in Atlanta, too? *Wow!* We got ourselves a world-wisened traveler here with us, guys!" "*Hilarious*," Summerlin replied as he took his wallet out in anticipation of paying. He then got confused when he realized that Connor had simply shown his driver's license and was granted admission without payment. "Hey, what gives?" Summerlin asked Connor as he was about to open the windowless door beyond. "You don't have an in-State ID, kid. You're gonna have to pay her twenty," he said after stopping; his eyes, however, remained on the door. "Figures," Summerlin said as he smiled at the lovely ladies and handed over the money.

Summerlin's gait stuttered when he got his first look at the place—it was massive, with three main stages and, from what he could see, at least four bars. "Relax, kid. They're just pretty girls," Connor said, giving him a pat on the back as he walked to catch up with the rest of the group, who were taking their seats at a table which sat next to the circular center stage. The Class ACT was a mélange of pink lace, endless mirrored surfaces and spinning disco lights. There was a large collection of oval tables with cushy leatherette chairs around each of the three main stages. The entire club smelled vaguely of alcohol and cheap perfume. Though all three stages currently had dancers performing, Summerlin noticed that there were also scantily-clad beauties strolling through the audience, occasionally leaning in to talk to customers, sometimes joining them at their table afterwards. Summerlin saw that at the far end of the building, there were two doors, one with a sign above it in pink flashing lights read, "Champaign Room"; the other was written in black plastic letters and read, "DJ Booth." There was a small tinted window through which he could barely make out the silhouette of a large bodied man dancing to the beat with a few records in hand.

There was a svelte redhead currently dancing upon the stage nearest him; off-stage floodlights were aimed at her as she sauntered upon the mirror entrusted stage in a bubblegum-pink bikini. As he took his seat, Summerlin noticed one of the barely-clothed performers walk with an elderly man through the door to the Champaign room. *Hopefully what goes on there will stay there. This is one time I want that darn statement to be true*, he thought with a laugh. The redhead was now topless and strutting across the stage to a group of still-suited businessmen who were waving ten-dollar bills at her. Trista walked over to the business men and reached out to place a fiver into the dancer's G-string before returning to her seat.

"Let's get some severe drinking done!" Sam yelled out as she pounded rhythmically upon the edge of the table. A well-tanned brunette in a yellow pair of boy-shorts arrived with haste to take the group's drink orders—and, most likely, to silence the drummer girl.

Drinks arrived, and the group began to assail the now nude red-head with singles as she shimmied to the tune of Heart's *Barracuda*. Everyone at the table was having a good time, except Summerlin, who sat in his chair while staring at the floor. Two strippers came and went; Samantha got a lap dance from an angelic blonde in pink lace while her boyfriend Danny watched. As the current stripper—a young Asian woman who started her dance in a skirted sailor suit—got down to her lingerie, a short, curvy brunette with curled tresses came up to the table, and headed straight to Summerlin. She squatted down to his eye level and said in a sultry voice: "Hey there sad-eyes. Everything okay in there?"

The stripper—whose name turned out to be "Diamond"—sat next to Summerlin for several minutes as he, in an utmost laconic manner, regaled the body-glitter-covered woman with his story. "Aww," the woman responded in a honeyed tone, "You're old-fashioned. And I love that l'il accent you have going there, *southern sweetheart.*" Connor was by this point bookended by strippers, and being personally served drinks by a young muscle-bound man wearing a shirt that said "The MEN of Class ACT." After hearing part of Diamond and Summerlin's discussion, Connor gestured towards him and said loudly, "Now there's a waste of a perfectly good stripper." Trista, Sam and Danny all laughed. Trent spoke after the laughter had ended, "Nah, I think he's got the right idea, Con-Man—look at how close that pretty little thing is sitting to *ol' Captain Broken-hearted* over there." As he finished speaking, he returned his gaze to the now naked sailor-girl, who was currently displaying her limberness in ways that would have made Summerlin blush had he been paying attention.

"I can tell you don't want a dance, honey," Diamond protested as Summerlin tried to give her a twenty. "I can get plenty of those later on," she continued, "I just hope you start feeling better. And hey, if that one really is done with you, maybe you can take this chance to meet a new girl. Another one, perhaps even a southern woman? I don't know any, though—sorry." Summerlin smiled and told her that he was "quite happy keeping on." She kissed his cheek and slowly walked off toward a group of tables near the far end's stage. A loud voice came over the ceiling-mounted speaker-system while the sailor-stripper gathered her tips and clothes: "Give it up for *Alexa*. Our next classy lady is a hot and tempting angel we call *Ambrosia*. Summerlin noticed that the DJ's voice had put an extreme emphasis on the pronunciation of the stripper names. Ambrosia was a tall, busty Nubian beauty who came strutting onto the center stage in a purple and pink schoolgirl outfit. Summerlin sat up and watched with feigned interest. Everyone but he seemed to be having a grand old time; Ambrosia certainly benefitted from the shower of ones and fives that Trista and Danny kept tossing at her. Out of nowhere, Connor's expression changed from gregarious to anxious; he quickly rose from his seat and, with his eyes never moving from the bar near the clubs back left corner, began to walk away. "Hey, Yankee, the girls are over here. Where are you goin'?" Summerlin asked. "Oh, it's nothing, kid," he replied, "It's just that...there's someone I just realized I gotta meet." As the Con-Man departed, Summerlin called out, "That's not normal, you know!" He wasn't sure—the loud classic rock made it tough for him to judge—but he thought he heard Connor reply, "I know!"

Summerlin tried to see if he could see anything special about the four people sitting at the bar at the other end of the club, but he couldn't make the faces out—not as well as Connor had, at any rate. It was a group of four men in dark suits with crisp white dress shirts. "Okay, four extremely professional lookin' guys who aren't even lookin' at the girls...and in walks a professional gambler that they've never met? Is that odd with anyone else?" Summerlin said. Trent put down his wallet for a moment and looked down at the seemingly far away bar; he became perplexed and replied, "That *is* a little odd. Who does that kind of stuff?" Samantha and Summerlin chimed in at the same time: *"Connor Bentley."*

Summerlin had finally found a worthy target for his attention within the Class ACT; however, it was the odd impromptu social function at the bar, and not any of the hot and bothered ladies, that kept Summerlin entertained. Connor had arrived at the bar, and was cordially shaking their hands. *Okay, that part's not that shockin',* he thought—Summerlin had seen his friend and mentor break the ice with even the least likeliest of souls on more than one occasion. What was odd to him was that Connor had not mentioned any interest in the persons involved, before *or* after he left; since when did the Con-Man ever do anything without his trademark candor? Though he was sure that Connor Bentley might have known far more words than he, Summerlin was willing to wager his life that "discretion" wasn't one of them.

Though the other four seated at the table had lost interest, Summerlin remained intrigued—he couldn't fathom what would have made a guy like Connor leave his hedonistic bookends. After the handshakes, it appeared that the men were offering the Con-Man a seat, which he promptly took. The men began to talk, breaking into periodic laughter. He couldn't prove it, but Summerlin assumed Connor was speaking like a ringleader again.

Three center stage strippers came and went before Connor returned to the table. By that point, Summerlin was back to counting spots on the floor tiles. The Con-Man resumed his seat and gestured for his strippers to return, like the whole event had not even happened. *Where did this guy come from?* Summerlin thought.

"Hey," Summerlin said. Connor turned his eyes from his eye-candy for a moment to give him a nod before returning his gaze upon the performers. *He doesn't look angry. Perhaps a little self-involved for the moment, but it doesn't seem to be negative*, Summerlin thought. Connor's strange behavior had grabbed his curiosity and never let go—after a minute or so of silence, he finally spoke up: "Not in the mood to talk, Con-Man?" *Now* it looked like anger could be at least possible in the near future. "Let's just stare at the beautiful creatures, kid. That's easy enough." He hadn't seen Connor have that look of malaise since the classical music concert. Summerlin chose not to push the issue—though he stopped bringing it up, he felt almost worried for the guy. *Though I'm pretty sure he'd tell me about Lesson Four if I brought it up*, Summerlin thought.

Later on it reached a point when even Trista, Connor and Trent were ready to call it quits. There had been several rounds of various drinks consumed—the evidence of which being the multitude of empty drinking glasses which now populated the oval table. As everyone was getting up, Connor pulled a buzzing cell phone from his pocket. *Maybe it's one of the people he was talking to*, Summerlin thought. "Right. Yeah, that was me. Oh, no, you don't need to do anything like that. Just come back to the ACT, man. I'll take care of you here. Yeah, see you in a minute. No, no, thank *you* my friend," Connor said into his phone. "Incoming company so late?" Summerlin inquired. "Don't be silly," the Con-Man replied, "It's our cab driver, from before—and don't worry he's bringing a friend." "Hey Con, you're still messing with cabbies?" Trent asked in an amused tone. "Messing's a mean word. I like *screwing* with them; and, yes. I left the good ol' 'black velvet bag' on him," Connor answered. Trent and Danny laughed—Samantha, however, did not. "That's childish," she remarked while walking for the exit. "Why is it childish, who are you talking about, and *what* in festerin' Hades is a 'black velvet bag'?" Summerlin asked as the group passed out into the parking lot.

"It's a test, kid—though not the same ones you'll be enduring," Connor began. Then, Summerlin remembered the small dark felt object he had seen his friend drop nonchalantly beneath the driver's seat.

"Actually, I think I get this one; I'm inclined to agree with Samantha, but I get it. You put something there to see if a cab driver would return it, possibly even for a reward, right?" Summerlin said with a modicum of pride. "Right and wrong as usual, kid," Connor replied, without losing a beat. "He does it for that—but he also never wants to wait in line for a cab, either. And half the time he puts those snapping firecrackers inside to give them a scare," Samantha chided, though even she had to fight off a smile near the end. "There's no pyrotechnics in that tonight though, right?" Summerlin asked. "No—and the party poppers aren't even flammable. Jeez, have a sense of humor. I put zirconia in there this time, anyway," Connor replied. *It is kind of funny...damn Yankee,* Summerlin thought.

Sure enough, the cabbie who had given them a ride to the ACT earlier arrived in less than five minutes, bringing a different driver behind him. "And, just to mess with Miss Greene's mind, I have an alternate method of conveyance for myself," Connor said, snapping his fingers. Bright lights instantly blinded the eyes of the entire group—a limousine had been sitting unnoticed mere feet from where they had been waiting for the taxis. "A limo? I'm riding with you, right?" Trent yelled out. "No, I'm afraid not, guys. I have some...*precious matters* that need attending to," the Con-Man replied before opening one of the passenger doors and hopping in. Summerlin could distinctly hear laughing from a voice other than Connor's.

The limo advanced several feet before stopping; a tinted window rolled down, and Connor stuck his head out. "Hey, kid, feel free to use the Austin—I think I'm gonna be home a little late. Oh, and before I forget, take this for the cabbie. Rules are rules, he's been a good sport," he said as he handed Summerlin a small envelope that had the words "For the honest cabdriver" on it. Summerlin nodded and took the envelope. "Have a nice night...you odd, odd man," he said. Connor winked and pulled his head back inside. As the window rolled back up and the limo slowly drove off the lot, Summerlin vaguely heard Connor's voice say, "What was your name again? Ohh, that's right, *Sandy*. I love it! Driver— Top of the world!"

"Yo, Summerlin, are you coming?" Samantha yelled. He turned to face the remaining four and said, "Yeah, I'm comin'." Danny walked to the second cab and gave him ten dollars for his trouble. "Our eccentric friend took a limo, so we can all fit in one this time," Summerlin heard him tell the driver. The four of them got in and buckled up. "Where is your friend?" the driver asked as he held out Connor's bag of fake treasure. Summerlin took the velvet bag and handed him the envelope from Connor and said, "He felt the urge to show off; this is for you." The cabbie handed him the bag before accepting the envelope. He then opened the envelope and beamed with joy as he noted a rather thick assortment of greenbacks therein. Summerlin took a peek inside the small bag and saw several tiny rocks that at first glance appeared to be diamonds; however, he knew better. Summerlin laughed as he stuffed the bag of zirconia into his jeans. "Where to, strange friends?" the driver asked. "To Texas," all four of the passengers replied.

The stars were gone from view by the time the taxi arrived at Texas Palace. After they had paid their fare—they each kicked in twelve dollars to cover the ride and the tip, the group got out of the cab at the entry doors near the Lone Star—the first doorway he had ever entered at Texas Palace. "Well, good times, good times. I gotta go though," Trista said as she pointed to a car with its headlights on, not far from where Summerlin had first met Connor. "Take care," Samantha said as Trista gave a peace sign while she walked to the car. "Have a good, safe night; heck, possibly a sane one," she said to Summerlin; Danny had refrained from drinking the last two rounds, and was jingling the keys to his car while wearing Samantha's arms like a belt. Summerlin shook Danny's hand and did his best to return a fist bump from Miss Greene.

The two remaining men hung out outside the doors while Trent smoked a cigarette. When it was almost done, he offered Summerlin a handshake and said, "Well, I'm afraid it's going to be just you—I gotta pick up our friendly neighborhood DJ from the Shake House." After the handshake, Summerlin smiled and said, "Hey, it's been fun. I'm goin' to go find out what Roulette is like." Trent laughed and said, "It's like having a relationship—you *never* know what will happen." *True enough,* Summerlin thought.

I might as well play some Roulette, Summerlin thought as he walked past the Lone Star Bar and into the Pit. He didn't fear making himself a liar—it was more a case of his deep down belief that everything happened for a reason. *If I said I was fixin' to do it, I might just as well,* he figured. The Pit had cleared out since his visit to the stripclub; there was only one Roulette table currently open. A tall, bald man in a red vest stood behind the wheel. Summerlin put a hundred-dollar bill on the table and requested five-dollar chips. He was given twenty orange colored chips. The chips looked similar to the white ones he had used while playing poker, except Summerlin noticed that they didn't actually have a denomination amount printed on them. He noticed that there was a color chart near the wheel, and that the dealer had placed a white chip with the number five on it upon the orange section. "Time to get lucky or go home whinin'," he said to the dealer as he slid two of his chips onto red. The metal ball was released upon the spinning wheel, and danced about the rim before clattering several times upon the numbers. "Double zero, no winner!" the dealer said. "If at first you don't succeed, keep going until you know better," Summerlin replied with a smile as he put four chips on black. The ball landed on *single* zero this time. After a sigh, Summerlin decided to just play the remaining fourteen chips on various numbers—most of them related to family birthdates—and just see what fate had to say.

Roulette might not be the game for me, Summerlin thought as he walked away from the table empty handed. *And time for the Austin Suite,* he thought as he slowly wended his way towards the elevators. The casino floor was all but vacant. Aside from a few half-asleep gamblers and the occasional cigarette-butt hobo, everyone Summerlin saw was wearing a nametag and being paid to remain there. The vacuity of the floor made his stroll to the elevators an easy one. As he neared the elevator lobby, Summerlin became aware that he was not alone.

As he neared the elevators, Summerlin could hear two men engaged in conversation. Once he entered the lobby, he saw that he had indeed seen the two men before. The taller of the two men was a pot-bodied man with a gold tooth; *That's Mr. Ruckford from the benefit at Akerman Hall,* he thought. The other was an older, thin bodied man with the tiniest amount of gray hair left on his nearly bald pate; *And that's one of the men I saw with that security supervisor in that odd cluster near the Lone Star.* The men seemed to be having a less-than-friendly exchange of words; Mr. Ruckford was the louder of the two, though Summerlin couldn't discern what they were actually discussing. He kept walking, but found that the elevator had opened, and both men boarded before he could get in. *Probably for my own good. Snoopin's never been a vice of mine,* he reasoned, *Fishing, beer on weekends, perhaps even the occasional Waylon Jennings album marathon—but never snooping.*

The next elevator came in a matter of seconds; it didn't take long to get an elevator that late on a Texas Palace weeknight. George Strait's *Blue Clear Sky* played on the Sam Houston elevator's speakers for the duration of the elevator trip. "Love songs, right now, really Sam?" he said sarcastically before shaking his head. By the time he had reached the Suite, Summerlin felt both tired and mopey. *Diamond the stripper would definitely disapprove,* he thought.

Summerlin headed straight into the bed of the guest room, taking only his boots off before diving in and grabbing the nearest pillow for his head. He didn't need to think his current problem—sadness over a lost love—through to its clearest possible conclusion; he and the brunette stripper with a heart of gold had already done that earlier, to no avail.

It was nearly noon by the time Summerlin awoke and rose from his still-made bed. He headed straight for the restroom and took a long soothing shower. A visit to the Connor Bentley lending library netted him a pair of jeans which had the words "CON-WEAR" running down the side in reflective letters, and a red and white t-shirt with the words "Security Officers Lie". *There's definitely been an increase in the Con-Wear lately,* he though as he leafed through a few of the hangers before exiting the closet. There were a few more pairs of jeans than before—most of them bearing some sort of Con-Wear marque. There were several new t-shirts each having sayings like "Remind Summerlin to Remember His Lessons", "Ruckford SUCKS", and "THE EGG SALAD HAS FEELINGS TOO". Once again, Summerlin skipped over Connor's suggested pile of shoeboxes in lieu of his boots.

He walked out into the great room to find the Con-Man sitting on the plush white couch on the lower section, watching an old black and white movie on the massive flat-screen. Connor looked tired, drunk, or a combination thereof, and his clothing and hair were uncharacteristically disheveled. *A normal Connor would go insane at the thought of a wrinkle in his pants,* Summerlin thought. *This* Connor seemed to be exhausted and filled with what he had previously called "don't give a damn".

Summerlin sat next to the Con-Man, saying, "Hey, what's up?" Connor did not turn his eyes from the television, though he did reply, "Sorry. Not really in a talking mood right now—we'll talk later. I've got big people problems, kid." Summerlin responded with a stern look,

"Well, I'm a little preoccupied with a dilemma or two—" for once, it was Summerlin cutting off the Con-Man: "I wish I had your problems. Horse race too close to call? Did they run out of size large Texas World shirts?" He hated having to rib his friend, but Summerlin figured that if he gave Connor a reason to lecture him, at least he would be return to being the spirited man he had come to know—and usually enjoy. The Con-Man looked troubled, and lowered his head. "Just give me a few hours, I'll be fine," he said.

Okay, that didn't go at all as planned, Summerlin thought. Yet, he wouldn't be so easily dismissed. "You don't have to just help me—I can help you too, you know. And not just with protecting your high-fashion behind," he said. A moment went by where it seemed possible to Summerlin that Connor had not paid attention at all: he was wordless and without a single change of expression. Then, lightning struck—the Con-Man's eyes widened and what looked like the vestiges of a smile formed on his lips. "I just realized something, kid," he said. "What?" Summerlin inquired. Connor's response was cryptic: "I think. Yeah, just maybe...Yep, we got something here!" He rose from the couch and raced to his room, muttering something along the way; *At least he sounds positive—about what, I'm sure I'll be scared by soon enough,* Summerlin thought.

Though Summerlin did not follow Connor into his room, he could vaguely make out the sound of a few drawers being rapidly opened and shut. "So, what's goin' on Yankee?" he inquired, hoping that the Con-Man would be able to hear him from his side of the suite. Connor's head popped out of the left hallway and he replied, "You will see, dear child, you will see. Meet me at the valet. Though Connor re-entered the great room, he had started punching in a number on his cell phone, and headed for the bar while retrieving a small notebook from his bright red sports jacket's pocket. Summerlin opened his mouth to speak, but Connor waved him off; he placed the phone between his cheek and shoulder and added, "Off now—I'll see you downstairs."

As he walked down the hallway to the elevators, Summerlin couldn't help but think of how excited his previously morose friend had appeared. *Should I be worried?* he wondered.

Summerlin stood waiting for about ten minutes before Connor came through the tinted main doors and walked up to meet him at the valet shed. He was dressed in a brown cotton three piece suit, complete with a pocket-watch chain and spats. "Good, Summerlin, you're here," Connor said. Summerlin gave the valet shed a glance—Zak was inside the shed, drumming the top of his desk with pencils while death metal played in the background. "What car are we taking today?" Summerlin asked. Connor grinned and replied, "Well, that has yet to be decided. *You* will be of the greatest influence on which method of conveyance you will be using."

Curiosity began to rear its often punished head; "What's the contest, then?" Summerlin inquired. Connor gestured for him to calm down. "Woah, hold on there Georgia-Pacific, don't go derailing yourself by running too fast. *This* test won't be about winning or losing; nor will it be about right and wrong. You can't and won't get an A on this, kid, so don't even ask," he said. Summerlin rolled his eyes and said, "You always do this. You're *trying* to get me to ask too many questions. No dice, card counter." Connor looked surprised. "Wow, you actually caught on. Keep learning things and we'll actually get somewhere, Old Dominion," the Con-Man said before winking and continuing, "You said you wanted my problems—yet, nobody would actually want someone else's problems if they actually knew them. My problems might sound a little less stressful than those of a man of more modest means; however, your perception of my problems being lighter doesn't make them lighter on me, now does it?" Summerlin had intended to answer him, but he only managed, "But I—" before Connor cut him off, "Nor would my perception of your problems change how *you* feel about them. Therefore, I posit that the only person whose opinion can actually change their perception is *one's own*. So, how does one do that? Through experience, my lad, through experience. Maybe dealing with some of my problems will help cure you of your ignorance, kid. I doubt you truly understand the plight of a poor man, though, either. I propose, Summerlin, that you are neither here nor there."

The Con-Man had finished speaking with an air of confidence. "Okay," Summerlin began, "I can honestly say that I've never slept in an alley. And, I've never even *seen* a mansion. But isn't that true of most people? And what could you or I *rationally* do about that?" Connor nodded as he Summerlin had neared the end of his sentence; "Well, now that we're on the same page. This leads me, of course, to the idea I just came up with in the Austin Suite." Summerlin paced for a moment before turning to face him and saying, "What's the idea?"

Connor took a seat on a red wrought iron bench which was near the valet shed. He folded his fingers together as he began to speak: "It's a capital idea—no pun intended. And, it goes along very well with your 'education'." "I learned the lesson about too many questions, remember? Just out with it," Summerlin replied. "Ah, well, can't fault me for trying. Anyways, it's simple, really," Connor said, "I said you knew neither here nor there. And, to wit, you even agreed that your sorrow was rather limited in perspective. I intend to show you *here* and *there*." *This is goin' to either be very confusin' or very frightenin'*, Summerlin thought.

Connor rose from the bench and put his hands in his pockets. After a moment, he pulled both hands out of the pockets, but this time they were clenched as fists. He extended his fisted hands towards Summerlin. "It'll be just like the kid's game. Pick a fist; its contents will outline what awaits you," he said. "What happens after I pick?" Summerlin queried. "Twenty-four hours of whatever you picked, of course," Connor replied triumphantly. Summerlin apprehensively reached out and gave Connor's left fist a tap. The Con-Man put his right hand back into his pocket and emptied it of whatever it had contained before turning his fist over and opening his hand. Two quarters lay on his open palm. "Okay, does that mean I'm goin' to jail and goin' to need money for a phone call?" Summerlin asked as he took the two coins. They were the old style of US Quarter—the one with a heraldic bald eagle on the reverse. Connor gave a sarcastic laugh and said, "Don't be facetious. It means that you, until tomorrow at this time, at least, are a vagrant. The time on my watches is currently 12:10, if you are interested. You are going to have to depart property—can't be letting anyone who knows you feeling sorry for you. Real street people don't get that privilege except but amongst themselves. Oh, and before you go, I'm gonna need your wallet, too." Summerlin begrudgingly handed over his wallet and said, "This better lead to something good." "Oh, don't worry, it will. Oh, and I *hate* to ask for it, but I'm gonna have to have the twenty you keep folded up in your left sock, too," The Con-Man said, "You'll find in life, Summerlin, that the best taught lessons are the immersive ones. Consider these next two days and the tests thereof the principle foundation of Lesson Eight: Go all in. Summerlin pulled the stashed twenty and handed it to Connor. "Go all in when...?" he asked. The Con-Man shook his head reaching out and splitting the collar of Summerlin's t-shirt. Connor then said, "Not 'Go all in when.' Just simply: *Go all in.* If you're doing the lessons cumulatively, you'll know when and how. Sorry about the shirt—breaks my neck to harm Con-Wear...but you know, authenticity's the best. Now off with you. Get going. And, no sneaking back or I'll have the front desk block out channels airing Atlanta games in the Austin Suite." He patted Summerlin on the back gently as he turned to leave. He *wanted* to believe it was a reassuring back-slap, but he knew better: Summerlin felt a freshly scooped grip of Vegas sand land upon his shoulders, spilling beneath his now-torn neckline.

He had many questions to ask, but Summerlin had a feeling that Connor would have found a way to make the ejection from property more formal had he persisted. As he left, a thought weighed heavily upon his mind. It was not hunger, shelter, nor the scorching, hot desert sun overhead; *What was in his other hand?* Summerlin wondered.

10.

Hours became labor, and thoughts had become torture. For hours, Summerlin had mindlessly wandered the streets of central Las Vegas; he never saw the Strip, though he did see the Stratosphere's tower looming ominously overhead throughout the entire day. His instincts told him that he would be best served by staying out of the sunlight, and nearby a free source of water. The endless dabbling of strip malls along Rancho Drive provided him ample sources of shade, and there were water fountains and public restrooms in every saloon he passed; there was one on about every other block.

By the time the sun began its descent beneath Sunset Mountain, Summerlin's hunger had grown to an extent he had never before known; with each rumble of his stomach, he began to feel more and more light-headed and was on the verge of a headache. *Walkin's never been a problem for me, but I've yet to find somewhere where my fifty cents would get me supper,* he thought. He had noticed throughout the day that as long as he kept in motion, nobody seemed to mind—or even notice—his presence. If he stopped to rest at any one spot for too long, however, Summerlin became acquainted with shop owners or contracted, weaponless security "guards", who wished him semi-politely on his way.

I hate to admit it, but Connor was right—I have absolutely no idea how to get supper when there's nowhere to work for a meal, and all I got is two quarters, he thought. The only conclusion he could reach after five minute's solid contemplation was to walk south, toward the blurry colored lights of downtown, where he knew there to be at least more vagrants than himself present. *Even if they don't want to help me, I can at least watch them and maybe get a clue how to eat, not to mention sleep,* he reasoned. He had seen a few homeless people out in the open get awakened by Las Vegas City Police nightstick-pokes throughout the day, and knew that if he could see a place, it probably wasn't a good choice for slumber.

The casino-laden thoroughfare that was Fremont Street glimmered, yet not by natural means—*I don't reckon nature knew such hues before the Golden Gate*, he thought as he passed walked past the 4 Queens. He had remembered Connor telling him during their downtown "tour" that the Golden Gate was the first casino to open in Las Vegas. It was now early evening, and with the end of the desert day large crowds of people were just beginning to pour out of the closely clustered casinos. Though Summerlin saw several street performers, unofficial doormen, and a wide variety of people offering to sell tourists things ranging in price and size from generic wristwatches to Schwinn bicycles, Summerlin had yet to locate a person who seemed to be in similar straits as he.

Summerlin slowly walked off Fremont St. *Well if I'm goin' to see anyone struggling with no wares or skills, it's not goin' to be here. I can't even tell who's actually in need and who's here sellin' things to buy a BMW,* he thought. Indeed, on Fremont Street, there were merchants of every grade, from fencers to sheltered outdoor boutiques. It was a place where one could indeed buy a diamond or a zirconia within a five foot radius. He held his two quarters in his hand and contemplated giving them to a casino fountain when a group of teenagers ran by him; one of the taller of the group, a lanky boy with long, green hair smacked Summerlin's hand from underneath as he yelled, "Rob the bum!" Another one of the group grabbed the coins before they landed. Summerlin felt the desperate urge to follow after them, but his stomach cramped as he tried to run. *That's what teenage boys do down here?* he wondered in dismay.

Exhausted, overheated and famished, Summerlin slumped against a light-pole near The D. *Sweet mercy, I believe I'm in a pickle here,* he thought as his eyes blearily began to close. Time passed—though at what rate, he was uncertain. It could have been seconds, minutes or hours which had advanced while Summerlin lay unconscious; all he knew was that it was a male voice shouting which awoke him: "Hey! Get up! Hurry up, man—You don't want to collapse while you're hungry, it's bad for ya." Summerlin's eyes opened, and as they were yet slits it all seemed blurry. "How do you know I'm hungry?" he groggily asked the man he couldn't yet fully see. "Dude. When you see a guy grasp his abdomen while he collapses to the ground, you know. Besides, this is a classy joint. They'll get the security after you if you pass out there," the man answered. "Fair deal," Summerlin said as he slowly rose to a standing position, "I'm Summerlin—and you?" At last his *Good Samaritan* slowly came into focus: he was a shirtless man with blond shaggy hair and a beard to match. He was man of medium height, but had such a sinewy musculature as to appear huge in presence while being smaller in the waist than your average high school cheerleader. His jeans were threadbare, and had been torn several times over. He had a thick chrome necklace with a small replica of a spinner hubcap on his chest. Though the man was dirty—his skin was pale around the edges, but was thickly covered in a desert *patina* of tan, sand and dirt—there was a gentle, peaceful dignity to his posture that belied a tremendous sense of self-worth. "Name's Bling-Bling; but you can call me *Bling* 'til we get some food in you—save's some energy, right?" the man said as he grabbed and steadied Summerlin by the arm. He nodded as he struggled to keep his head up. It was at this time that Summerlin noticed that Bling-Bling had no shoes on. The man had what Summerlin thought were two pairs of treaded, hospital-style socks on each foot, though holes were predominant on both feet. "Eye's up here, gotta stay upright. Look at the lights if you have to," Bing-Bling said as he walked him southward.

After they had gotten onto Main Street, Bling-Bling stopped, and helped Summerlin to take a seat on an old concrete-encrusted planter. "Here, eat this—" he said to Summerlin, offering him half of a stale glazed donut he pulled from his pocket. Summerlin waved his hands weakly in protest. It wasn't that he was too good for the food offering; it was merely a matter of Summerlin detesting getting something without having earned it. Though he didn't actually have the energy to express his morality, Bling-Bling seemed to glean his intent wordlessly, by posture alone. "Hey, it ain't charity, you can owe me. We're about to work for a night's wage anyway. Can't help you earn your survival if you're falling over 'n shit," he said. Summerlin finally acquiesced, and wolfed the morsel down before he could give himself a chance to refuse it. After he had swallowed, he said, "Thank you. Really." Bling-Bling nodded and replied, "Don't mention it. After you feel up to it, you're gonna help me with what I do—and that means we'll get more done. By helping you, you'll help *me* earn more. Long story short: we're gonna eat beef tonight." *Beef.* There was a word that made Summerlin smile without hesitation. He rose and said, "Okay, as long as it's legal and decent, I'm in." Summerlin's downtown benefactor began walking again, heading southward; he called out after Summerlin, "Well let's get going, time's a wasting!" *You don't have to tell me twice*, Summerlin thought as he walked briskly to catch up with him.

The walk was relatively short. Bling-Bling had led Summerlin to a small shopping plaza at the corner of Main Street and Hoover Avenue.

There was an anchor store in the plaza, but it was a neighborhood grocery store; there were four other businesses in the strip mall, though they were all far smaller. Summerlin noticed that the first three—a wig store, a coffee shop, and a used book store—were all closed for business, and had simple signage. The fourth and final store was a twenty-four hour Laundromat, which had a large back-lit lithograph above its open doors reading "Lucky Flamingo Laundromat and Laundry Service." Beside the store name there was a logo which consisted of a cartoon flamingo wearing sunglasses and holding four aces while leaning against a sud-filled washing machine.

Bling-Bling walked up to the metal-framed glass doors of the Laundromat. The doors gave a clear view of the well-lit assemblage of stainless steel coin-operated equipment within. "Are we in need of dry cleaning or alterations?" Summerlin asked wryly, reading the services offered from a sign near the door. "No, but it's good to see you got a sense of humor; dying people wouldn't have that, I suppose," Bling-Bling replied. There was a neon green sign beneath the services sign that was written in black marker: "Coffee is always free—come on in!"

Bling-Bling opened the door. Summerlin stood where he was and asked, "Why are we here?" Bling walked closer to him and replied, "Look, I know you must be going through a lot, especially since it's obvious you're new to this life; but, you're gonna have relearn how to trust people, or else you're not gonna make it. This is Mr. West's store—he actually doesn't mind us folk going in and keeping hydrated at night. He's always saying weird stuff, and going off about 'angels on people's shoulders' and whatnot, but trust me, we center-city dwellers call him the *Angel of Hoover Avenue*." Summerlin nodded and followed Bling-Bling into the Laundromat. As he entered, Summerlin felt two things: the breeze of an air conditioning duct, and a sense of world tumbling shock.

The store was very well kept—fresh paint and recently grouted tile may not be noticed by most; but, as Summerlin had recently been ensconced in a little *desert patina* of his own, they were instantly recognized and appreciated. To the immediate left of the entrance, there stood several vending machines. At the back end of the Laundromat, there was a small wooden desk with a computer and a cash register atop it. Behind the desk sat Thomas, the man whom Connor had introduced him to at Texas Palace. Summerlin's jaw nearly fell through the floor. *So this is his business,* he thought as his brain made desperate attempts to reconcile the smiling, laid-back store owner in the Barcalounger with the faded husk of a man he had encountered near the Rail Yard.

"Hey Mr. West," Bling-Bling said. Thomas rose from his chair and walked over to meet them. "I can see that you brought a friend, Mr. Bling," he said. "Yeah," Bling replied, "Found this one over on Fremont. This is a newbie—calls himself 'Summerlin'. Thought maybe you might let me borrow a few again..." Thomas smiled and replied, "No problem." Bling-Bling gave Summerlin a thumbs-up and said, "Thanks, Mr. West; as always, you're the best." Thomas walked behind a counter which stood to the door's immediate left and returned with two buckets in hand. Bling-Bling grabbed one and handed it to Summerlin before taking the other for himself. Summerlin looked inside the bucket to find three washcloths. "I know how you feel about charity, Bling," Thomas began, "so, use these well, as always. And don't forget to bring back the spray bottles this time." He reached behind the counter and handed Bling-Bling a spray bottle half-filled with a blue liquid. Summerlin didn't know what to say; *Am I allowed to tell him? Does accepting help from Thomas outside the auspices of Texas Palace count as breaking the rules? What must he be thinking about me?* he thought.

As Thomas handed Summerlin his spray bottle, he remarked, "I'm to believe that you'll be helping?" There was an *indelible* wry look about him. Summerlin's mouth attempted an awkward syllable, but Thomas put a finger near his lips and then said, "Don't worry, *Summerlin*, I won't ask. It's Connor's work, no doubt." Summerlin nodded and responded,

"I won't even ask why you're here instead of Texas." Thomas grinned and replied, "That's right. You won't." *Did he take lessons from the Con-Man or something?* Summerlin thought—even he had to laugh at Thomas's unexpected brandishing of wit. Thomas leaned against the counter and said, "Well, Whatever he has you doing out here, at least you had the serendipity of meeting one of the decent ones." Summerlin nodded and said, "Oh, he's been very kind—" Bling-Bling cut into the conversation: "'Course he has. I'm *pimpaliscious* to the nine's, bro." Summerlin had to think it through for several wordless moments before deciding it was best just to nod, and to not even ask what in *tarnation* Bling's statement meant. Thomas laughed. "All right, clean-face, time to get to making the world shine one wheel at a time," Bling-Bling said as he walked outside. Summerlin turned as he grabbed the door handle, and said to Thomas, "Hey—See you at The Palace?" Thomas replied, "Only in a while—got my recharge this past week; sorry if we didn't notice you." Summerlin shook his head and replied, "It's ok, the old man had me running *the Gauntlet*." Thomas began to have trouble containing his laughter. "I was wondering who he'd get to do that next. After the whole Xero incident, I was curious if he'd ever do that one again." *Ugh,* Summerlin thought. "What happened with Xero's turn?" he couldn't help but ask. "Xero bet all the money on *double zero* on a Roulette table, and hit it. They gave him 'Nobility' status on the spot. Connor swore he'd never let a person bet anything but coin-ops after that," Thomas replied. Summerlin's jaw was once again floor-bound. "Hey, ain't got a millennium out here!" Bling-Bling yelled in through the now opened doorway. "Better be off, kid," Thomas said. Summerlin smiled and nodded before running out to join Bling-Bling.

Bling-Bling took Summerlin to the corner of Main and 4th Street. The intersection was bathed in casino lights from both downtown on the north side, and the Strip to its south. "So, what are we doing, offering red-light carwashes?" Summerlin asked. "Well, sorta," Bling replied, "We offer cars at red lights the best rim shine in Vegas! We're here, and hamburgers are the goal. And, one rule, my man: no asking for, or demanding, tips. If they pay, they pay and you thank them; if they don't, you remind yourself how happy you are to be alive to have done the service." Summerlin nodded and grabbed his spray bottle out of the bucket.

The two of them worked hard for more than three hours. When Summerlin and Bling-Bling had emptied their spray bottles of their entire contents, they had raised two dollars and twenty cents in gratuities. "Outta shine-sauce, and tired to boot!" Bling said enthusiastically after they put their supplies into their buckets. "Where to now?" Summerlin inquired. "Well, a word is as good as a promise—so we return Mr. West's gear; then, we go north, to Crazy Burger, home of the late night one dollar 'Insanity Meal'. It'll be great—you'll love it, new-pants." Summerlin replied, "It's *Summerlin*; Andrew if you don't like that one." Bling-Bling laughed and replied in a poetic fashion: "Tomato, tom*a*to."

Summerlin and Bling-Bling returned their cleaning gear to the Lucky Flamingo. When Summerlin entered to deposit the buckets, he noticed that Thomas was nowhere to be seen; there was classical symphony music playing from behind a closed door behind the desk. *Classical in Vegas seems like a crawdad with antlers to me*, he thought as he exited the store, *But, then again, unexpected mixtures of chaos seem to be one of the things that makes this city what it is, good and bad.*

Crazy Burger was located at the corner of Owens Avenue and Martin Luther King Boulevard. From the parking lot, Summerlin could see the glow of Texas Palace in the distance. "Okay, let's eat!" Bling-Bling yelled joyfully as if a grand banquet was awaiting them.

It might not have been *grand*—and no living being has ever confused a dollar combo meal for a banquet—but, Summerlin enjoyed every delectable bite. He extended his small cup of cola, and said, "to a hard night's work." Bling-Bling tapped Summerlin's cup with his own and added, "to any night's work." They both smiled and finished their burgers and fries in short order. After finishing their food, Summerlin and Bling refilled their soda—free, courtesy of Crazy Burger—and walked out to the parking lot. "Might as well finish our drinks at a table with a view before we head out," Bling-Bling said. Summerlin nodded and they sat at a pebble-textured table which resembled a park bench, and reclined to gaze at the nearly starless sky.

"So, tell me—how did you get here? We all got a story," Bling-Bling said as his straw began to rattle with air. Summerlin didn't know what to say. He doubted that his new friend would view him favorably upon hearing that he was, in fact, a *temporary* homeless person. He decided, instead to just go with something closer to the heart; Summerlin told Bling the story of how he got to this most recent, sad, phase of his life. "Sounds like you aren't broke after all, Summerlin," Bling said. "How's that?" Summerlin asked. "You still have hope. That makes you richer than most," Bling replied. Summerlin wanted to rebuke the notion, but on this long night's end, he remembered what Connor had said about "poverty having a certain honesty." His shoulders relaxed their tenseness, and Summerlin sighed as he nodded and said. "You know what, after today, I can honestly say I agree with you."

"What about you, Bling? You seem smart enough, why are you livin' like this?" Summerlin asked him. Bling raised his hands in dismissal, replying, "It's not about being 'smart enough' to avoid this kind of life. I'm not choosing anything; this just matches my piece of mind. If I wanted different, I'd do what I always do when I want something, man: *go get it*." *Wow*, Summerlin thought. A while back, he would have probably defended "normal life". *Something tells me that maybe there is no* "normal"—maybe it's a good thing that there isn't. The world would suffer if we all wanted the same things. The world needs Bling-Blings and Con-Men, he thought.

"So, where are you goin' to go later?" Summerlin asked Bling. "You say that like you'll have anything better to do," Bling replied. He felt guilty—Bling-Bling had been a truly honest and upright man, and Summerlin felt embarrassed to admit the temporal nature of his misery. I never said I was homeless, but I don't think it will be fun admitting I can go back to steak dinners and big screen TVs, he thought. "Hey, it's no biggie," Bling-Bling cut into the awkward silence that had developed while Summerlin's face had slowly formed into a grimace, "It's okay, really. We all rove around a little—I'm sure whatever your state, we'll see one another. Later if not sooner, you know." Bling sat up, and Summerlin followed suit.

It was then that Summerlin really noticed Bling-Bling's footwear: his outer layer of hospital socks was all gone, and there were small holes developing on the inner pair, as well. Summerlin had an awakening: he realized that he would rather learn the experience of enduring several hours of Vegas without shoes than bear the knowledge that a man who had been so kind and helpful was going to be living as such *every day*. Call it "Southern Hospitality", call it human decency, or whatever one will; Summerlin reached down and took off his boots. As he was removing his footwear, Bling-Bling said, "Hey, man. What are you doing?" Summerlin finished removing his boots without answering Bling's question. He then handed the boots to Bling, who was attempting to push them back. "Woah there. You remember what Mr. West said—I don't take charity," he said. Summerlin pulled his hands back and replied, "Neither do I. I owe you for the donut, anyway." Bling-Bling looked at the boots, and smiled warmly. He glanced at Summerlin and said, "Thank you." Summerlin did a Connor-esque wink-and-click and said, "Don't mention it."

The two shook hands, and Bling-Bling headed off, in his words, "to find a good comfy place to meditate." Summerlin felt the cold dry ground with every step, but as he walked in search of a place to sleep a for few hours that was concealed enough to avoid being seen. As he walked towards Texas Palace, Summerlin noticed the older, much smaller locals joint *Macho Grande* sitting on the corner of Reata and El Paso Lane. He waved at Texas—ostensibly at Connor—as he walkned further east on Reata Avenue than he ever had before.

Summerlin awoke in a back alley which lay between Macho Grande and a neighborhood tavern named *Greg's Place*. As he rose, he shook free a few pieces of paper trash that had drifted upon him during his early-morning slumber. Summerlin stretched his back and then took a glance at his watch: 12:03. *Damn, I better hurry or the Con-Man will never let me hear the end of it,* he thought as he made way through the small, single parking lot of Macho Grande.

11.

Summerlin arrived at Texas Palace to find Connor at the valet shed awaiting him. The Con-Man was wearing a sky-blue button-up shirt with deep beige slacks. A quizzical look from Connor was accompanied by a question: "Summerlin, good to see you. How are you doing? Have any...*footwear* problems lately? Summerlin laughed as he looked down at his now-ragged socks; his right big toe was sticking out in its entirety. "Just had a few things to deal with," he replied as he headed for the main doors. "Ah ah ah, kid. Come back here," Connor said. Summerlin stopped dead in his tracks and returned to the valet shed. "We're not done yet," The Con-Man informed him, "You made it through a day of destitution relatively unscathed, and for that, I applaud you. However, I can't go having you think that only homeless people suffer; that wouldn't be right. We're not through yet, kid. You still have a fist remaining to tap, sir."

Summerlin looked at Connor and waited for the other shoe to drop. The Con-Man put his right hand into his pocket, and pulled it out as a fist, just as he had done before, but with just the right hand option. Summerlin sighed and said, "Can't I go upstairs and get a pair of your god-awful shoes on first?" Connor shook his head no and gave a chiding glare. *"Fine"* Summerlin replied. Summerlin tapped his right hand.

Connor turned his hand over and opened it, revealing a set of keys on a simple stainless steel ring. "Keys?" Summerlin asked, not being able to discern their intended use from their appearance. "Yep," Connor replied as he pocketed the key-ring, "of course, these are only the keys to a Metroplex Lanes shoe locker—your real key is a plastic suite key which awaits you at *The Jungle Hotel & Casino.* I felt that the metal keys looked better in terms of overall effect." Summerlin nodded and said, "I'm to believe that's a Lesson Seven type decision?" Connor patted his back and smiled, adding, "You actually got one right, bluegrass."

The Jungle...Summerlin thought with a hesitation that almost neared reverence: even country-music-loving Virginia boy Summerlin knew about The Jungle. Located at the cross streets of Flamingo Road and Vegas Vic Drive, The Jungle was a hip, happening "place to be" for hip hop and techno loving twentysomethings. The place had been mentioned in a couple movies Summerlin had seen, as well as a few hip hop songs he had been forced to endure while shopping with Sarah. He had never thought that he would actually end up there. *Doesn't really strike me as my kind of place; but, then again, I wasn't really desirin' to sleep in an alley, either,* he thought. "So, they like guests lackin' shoes, do they? Must be high fallutin'," Summerlin quipped. Connor laughed. "Don't be foolish, kid," he said, "they don't give a damn if you've got enough clout."

"Clout?" Summerlin asked. The Con-Man replied while reaching into his back pocket, "Yes. This is the second of your 'here and there' experience-slash-tests. Yesterday, you endured the problems of those who have very little. I'm guessing that by living through such an endeavor, even you won't deny that you have learned something, and thereby enriched yourself in the process." Summerlin sighed and replied, "As much as I love to deny the things your metropolitan-ass comes up with, no, I can't." Connor nodded and continued speaking, very much like a school teacher giving a lecture, "Well then, today you are going to endure the plight of those who have many. It's already all been arranged and everything." Summerlin was apprehensive; *approach with caution*, he thought. "Okay, I'll even spend one of my limited number of tolerated questions on this one: *What* has been arranged?" Connor waved at Melissa, who was standing behind the valet window, and called out, "number nine, please!"

Connor took a seat on the wrought iron bench. He waved for Summerlin to join him and began, "You are to spend twenty-four hours, same as yesterday, but this time, you are going to be a high roller—as high as they come, really. I had to pull a few strings, but let's just say, for all intents and purposes, the staff at The Jungle are going to treat you as if you were me. Well, maybe a thick-accented, lesser-dressed version of me..." Summerlin tilted his head and cut the Con-Man off: "*Really*? Get to the actual point, Yankee." "Oh, sorry," Connor continued, "kind of got carried away there. Well, the point, kid, is that you are going to have a new set of rules and challenges. You are to go to the hotel-casino, and you are to find a way to spend two hundred fifty dollars. Sounds simple, huh?" *That's what makes it scary*, Summerlin thought. "Yes. What's the catch?" he asked Connor. "Ah, the catch. I racked my brain yesterday in the Austin about how I could make you feel a prominent person's pain without groupies, entourages and the like, and I believe I came up with a pretty fair, simpler replica of the experience. I'm going to make you hate money. As I previously stated, they are gonna treat you as if you were me—and, you'd be surprised how hard it can be to actually pay for something when you are *Obsidian* Tier at The Jungle. After that, there are only three simple rules. First, no leaving the property, unless given expressed in-person permission by *moi*. Second, none of the two-fifty is to be spent on gambling; this is not an exercise in gaming. Third and finally, whatever you attempt to do to spend the money, you must actually *do* whatever it is, even if you learn that they won't let you pay for it. Simple, really...right?" The Con-Man was beaming as he reached for his wallet and began to pull out greenbacks. "Wait, Con—what's this about 'the two-fifty? I don't know how many times I have to say it, but no charit—" The Con-Man: "You won't be *able* to spend it, Summerlin. So you can return it to me later. Yes, you heard me right, this test does technically have a pass-fail. Hunt for that golden A-plus that we both know you want so badly." Summerlin pushed the money back to Connor when he offered it to him. "Fair enough, fancy-man—if your lesson is so important, I'll spend some of *my* money on it. And you'll congratulate me when I outwit you," he said. "Feeling awfully cocky, aren't we?" Connor responded. "Well, let's just say I'm up against a guy who would bet *against* Secretariat," Summerlin said with a grin. "Hey," Connor said while pointing his finger in the air, and then following through with a hatchet-like motion, "Eclipse first—and all other's *nowhere!*"

A flawless GMC Delorean pulled up beside the wrought iron bench. Connor rose, and walked over to Melissa, handing her a twenty in exchange for the car keys. "You'll find The Jungle not too far off from the Flamingo exit on the I-15, kid. It's not far from the Gold Coast. Do I need to write you some directions?" Connor said. "No time for shoes, but I get directions? Great," Summerlin responded. "I'll take that as a *yes*, then," The Con-Man said. Summerlin nodded and waited for his directions, which came complete with a very poorly crafted map, all upon the backside of an advertisement flyer for the Class ACT. Connor returned Summerlin's wallet with a grin as he rose from the bench.

The moment the Delorean's tires made contact with Flamingo Boulevard, he could see it: a sleek, skyscraping tower which bathed itself in twelve rainbows worth of light. Though the premise of The Jungle had failed to amuse him, even Summerlin found the structure of the building somewhat impressive. There was a massive casino sign which was taller than the one at Macho Grande—it was comprised of four palm trees which held at their crossed apex a high-definition digital screen which occasionally flashed the hotel-casino's name in large rainbow covered lettering amongst ads for the resorts various clubs and restaurants. Summerlin pulled in to the valet parking drop-off, which, like Texas Palace, was built into a pillar supporting a massive canopy. He tipped the valet a ten-spot before heading through a gargantuan entrance which featured etched glass panels which were each individually larger in size than his college dorm bedroom had been.

After he had cleared the doorway, Summerlin headed straight for the reception desk, which sat to the immediate left of the grand entryway, beneath a large bright hanging sculpture of stylized bananas and coconuts. Though it had been less than a thirty-second journey, he noticed at least ten pairs of eyes staring at him and his now nearly ragged socks along the way. He rang the bell for service, and a very apprehensive-looking clerk walked up to greet him at the counter. *To be fair, I am basically barefoot now*, Summerlin thought. "Howdy," he said with a smile. The clerk sighed in relief and smiled. "Are you...may I ask your name, sir?" he said. Summerlin shook his head and thought, *Let me guess, he told them to expect me, and I'm sure it included some statement about where I was born, et cetera, etcetera*, Summerlin thought. "The name on my license is probably not the one you're lookin' for; I'm *Summerlin*, he said." The clerk did a fist pump reminiscent of an athlete before accepting a trophy and then stopped abruptly to politely say, "Oh, sorry, forgive me. We just had a little competition on who would get to hand you the key—I chose the one to one thirty slot. Anyhow, I was told to give you the key to the 'Rat Pack' Suite, and this." The clerk walked away towards a set of shelves which were made of inch-thick glass. He returned with a mirror-like suite key and one of the crisp white stationery envelopes that Summerlin had recently become accustomed to receiving—especially at the commencements of Connor's "tests".

"Oh, one more thing," the clerk said while Summerlin was about to open the envelope, "I'll need to actually see the *Cadoret* ID for the room paperwork." *So the crazed cardsharp does know my last name*, Summerlin thought with a mixture of irritation and amusement before giving the man his ID.

Though it all had seemed strange to his eyes, Summerlin arrived at the top level of the suite floors at The Jungle without any footwear whatsoever. The soles of his feet felt the bitter, cold sting of the stainless steel floor partition once he stepped out of the brass-lined glass elevator. He noticed that the suite doors had nameplates done in the same style as at Texas—each nameplate bore not a number, but the capitalized name of the suite itself. Summerlin passed "The Goodman Suite", "The Fremont Suite, and even an odd one entitled "The Maldonato Experience Suite" before he found the door to the "Rat Pack" suite near the end of the hallway, on his right. He did the usual key-slide that he had perfected on the Austin Suite door, and opened the door. Summerlin was nearly overcome by the sight.

The "Rat Pack Suite" was massive, elegantly appointed with postmodern art and furniture, had two floors with a working elevator, and was larger than the house in Blacksburg where Summerlin grew up. The landing which greeted his bare feet was half the size of a basketball court, and done entirely in wood parquet. He took a walk through the suite, slowly stopping every so often to admire the massive windows, posh furniture, and myriad assortment of high-definition electronic goods. Aside from three regular rooms and a master bedroom, he noticed a game room, a high-tech dinette, a personal gym, and a small art gallery. After taking in all that the suite had to offer, he returned to the landing. *Whoops, almost forgot*, Summerlin thought as he pocketed the suite key and looked at the envelope Connor had apparently left for him; his ragged-sock foray through the four star resort had distracted him from ever opening it.

Summerlin opened the envelope, the front having simply the word "Summerlin". Enclosed was the usual calligraphy-laden sheet of parchment paper. Also enclosed was a black card—a player's card for The

Jungle, which was matte black, and had the word "Obsidian" upon it above the name "Summerlin". He unfolded the note, and it read, "Reading notes while you have company is rude, you know. Sincerely, Con." Summerlin looked up from the note to see, indeed, that the Con-Man was standing mere feet from him, and holding an oblong black box.

Though his eyes were stretched as wide as they could go, Summerlin managed to speak, "How the *heck*, Yankee!" Connor beamed with pride—between laughs. "Well, kid, you don't get where I did in this town without having a few tricks up your sleeve," he said. "Is that Lesson Nine?" Summerlin inquired. "No, no—and, besides, you aren't really ready for that one yet," the Con-Man said. "What's in the box, everything you've ever owned that was tasteful?" Summerlin retorted. "No," Connor informed him, "It's the collection of everything tasteful you've ever worn." Two seconds of straight-faces was followed by both men laughing. "No, really though, this is actually for you. You handled yesterday really well, without a complaint, and I wanted to give you something to commemorate being such a good sport. And gifts aren't charity, so—" Summerlin grinned and spoke louder: "Okay, alright. Let's just give me the box and accept my thanks ahead of time before you go off on my policies on charity and ruin the whole thing." He opened the box and lifted a thin layer of gift box tissue to reveal a pair of ornately-tooled chestnut colored boots with a note atop. It read: "I don't know what the heck you see in long footwear, kid, but I thought these hand-tooled Lucchese custom twelve-inchers would be appropriate. Sincerely, Con. P.S.—*Don't scuff.* They were made of thick, smooth leather, and gave off a sheen endemic to a recent high-gloss polishing. As Summerlin took one from the box, he realized that the ornate tooling on the boots was actually crafted to resemble the Las Vegas skyline. There were pyramids, castles and Stratospheres—even the Eifel Tower replica of the Paris was fit in. Each leather outsole had the word "Summerlin" carved in a manner matching the Con-Man's calligraphy. *Holy Moly*, he thought. "Con—I...I don't even know what to say," he said. Connor patted his back and said, "just say you'll handle your loss tomorrow well." "I'll handle any outcome well. I just intend to outdo my teacher," Summerlin replied with a wink.

The Con-Man began slowly to pace, and gestured for Summerlin to follow. Connor took a seat at a bubble-shaped translucent-purple sculpture which served dual purpose as a bench in the center of the art gallery. Summerlin sat next to him and pulled out the boots to see a pair of Wrustler brand cotton socks which lay beneath. After putting on the socks, Summerlin pulled his boots on—a perfect fit. "I don't even want to *know* how much this cost you," he said in disbelief. "That's right, you don't" Connor replied, almost musically. *Such an odd, strange, wonderful guy*, Summerlin thought as he got up to take the boots for a test lap around the bench.

"So, what's up? You coulda just come with me, you know," Summerlin said after giving the boots five laps. "And risk not being stylish? *Never*," Connor replied, "Besides, you needed to experience the barefoot suite entry alone—made more sense that way. And nothing is *up*; just wanted to see the ol' place. Great place for indoor Hibachi, by the way. At any rate, I do digress. I came partly because I have business down here, the other was to congratulate you on achieving top tier status at The Jungle. Heck, took me at least a week." Summerlin pulled out the black player's card he had received in the envelope. "Gee, thanks. Again, I don't think you understand the point of a 'no charity rule'," he said. Connor wagged his finger and responded, "Actually, Alabama-Slammer, I *do*. I said that I had to 'pull some strings'—I never said I paid for anything. The clout I was referring to, my dear child, was my own. I could get the headless horseman of Sleepy Hollow a suite and Obsidian here." Summerlin managed to suppress his laughter long enough to say "You know, I'm not from Alabama. I'm from—" Connor cut him off wryly, "I know, I know, land of cotton, look away, all that good stuff—close enough." Summerlin could have brought up that he knew his friend remembered more about him than he admitted, but he was still in awe of the supposed rambling-man's surprising display of sentiment to say. *'Sides*, he thought, *'Bama's not too shabby, either.*

"Though..." Connor said as he rose to pace the room. "Though? Though what?" Summerlin asked him. "I also came for one other reason. You see, I had to make sure that your day of high-rolling had the normal pratfalls and hazards of the everyday—rich—Joe," the Con-Man replied. Summerlin stood up and looked over at Connor, who had stopped to admire a lithograph of 19th century London. "How's that?" Summerlin inquired. "Simple. I just replicate what we all endure, albeit on a smaller scale. For example, right now I'm providing you with the role of the 'friend who takes up your time with idle chatter while you should be attempting to accomplish the goal set before you. In fact, I wasn't even the first thing a rich person has to deal with to dismay you—I watched you waste at least five minutes pacing the place in wonderment before you returned to the landing to read my note. Actually, I'm doing it even more so in this sentence right here—listen, I can go on and on and on about nothing at all without ever reaching a point if I were to—" "Enough!" Summerlin yelled, cutting off his friend's intentional run-on sentence. Connor winked and added, "Point is, kid, you don't realize what other distractions or hindrances you might have to face—celebrity status is harder to deal with than one might think. I gotta go have a meeting over lunch at *Bellagio*. I'll bid you—for now, at least—good day and good luck." He patted Summerlin's back, and exited the suite.

"Okay, time to beat the Con-Man at his own game—literally," Summerlin said to himself as he walked over to a telephone which sat atop a white marble countertop near the entryway. He picked up the receiver, and his hand froze as he realized there were no buttons on the phone; the phone connected directly to the bell desk. "VIP guest interactions, this is Kyle," a young male voice with a British accent answered. "Uh, howdy Kyle. This is the "Rat Pack Suite"—was wonderin' if you could call for a tailor to do a house call? I need new clothes desperately, and tried to find a phone with numbers, but that dog won't hunt. Just make sure it's the fanciest, most expensive guy you can find," he said with particular relish. Summerlin was crestfallen when Kyle politely replied, "Why would you want that, sir? We have an in-house tailor—it's a gratuity for our high-end guests, such as yourself." *Oh crap*, Summerlin thought, *Now I'm goin' to need to sit for a tailoring session*. And so he did.

An hour-long fitting was followed by an hour of on-the-fly tailoring on a portable sewing machine by a silver-haired, well-dressed man named Cecil. Summerlin spent his idle minutes debating with the tailor over the athletic accomplishments of the SEC versus the Big Ten. By the time Cecil rose from a kneeling position and declared, "We're finally done!" at least two hours had passed, and Summerlin was the new possessor of a slate-gray cotton suit, complete with a deep navy dress shirt and a steel blue tie. Cecil grimaced when he saw Summerlin complement the suit with his new boots. Before the tailor departed, Summerlin asked him, "Hey, is there anything you have on you that *isn't* free to VIPs?" Cecil closed his sewing machine carrying case before replying, "I'm sorry to disappoint you, but no; however, I was instructed to give any guest who asked me that *this*."

The tailor handed Summerlin a crisp white envelope. Summerlin opened the envelope. It read: "I'm a little disappointed that you'd even attempt this one. Nice try, but, you should have known better, kid. Sincerely, Con. PS—remind Cecil that I love the maroon three-piece." *I have a bad feelin' that Connor might be tougher opposition than I had previously anticipated*, he thought.

Summerlin gave Cecil a twenty dollar tip on his way out. He knew it wouldn't count towards the two-fifty; but, he felt it wrong to not show some form of appreciation for a man who had just tailored him a suit on the spot.

Okay, take two, Summerlin he thought as he went to take a brief shower before donning his new—and only other—set of clothes. Having swung and missed on his first attempt, Summerlin was determined to make his next move count. His stomach growled as he was putting on his suit. The desire to foil Connor's plan combined with Summerlin's new-found hunger to form the basis of his new, two-step plan: he was to find the cheapest, lowest price level fast food restaurant in the hopes that he would be unnoticed and charged for the meal like a regular paying customer. After his meal, successful or no, Summerlin planned to visit the gift shop in an attempt to purchase something he felt would not be given to him for free—and, just in case he would be wrong, the service had to be one that wouldn't consume too much time.

The glass elevator deposited Summerlin on the ground floor, and from the moment he disembarked he began searching for an overhead sign that would guide him to the food court. He ordered two items off the dollar menu at *Enchiladas del Diablo*—A beef-and-cheese enchilada and a root beer. He *did not* get to pay; "It's our pleasure to supply your meal," the cashier kindly informed Summerlin. After he threw out his garbage, he set out for the gift shop. As before, the overhead palm tree adorned signage led the way.

Summerlin's trek took him past a theatre, two nightclubs and half of the casino Pit before he reached the gift shop area. Contrary to his expectations, Summerlin found that there was no gift shop to be found— not in the singular sense of the word: the "Amazonian Esplanade", as the signage referred to it, was actually a conglomeration of boutiques, all featuring brilliant, high-definition digital signage. *Well this sure is confusin'*, he thought, *but, this might just work out to my advantage, there being more than one place.* Summerlin headed through the large domed shopping area towards a purple-signed store called "Emporium of Wonders"—*Sounds like there's somethin' pricey in that one*, he thought. Before he made it, though, he was stopped by a severe sounding voice that called out, "Sir, I'm going to have to ask you to halt and turn around slowly."

Summerlin turned to see a uniformed police officer with his arms crossed and a serious look on his brow. He seemed somewhat lacking in size for a policeman; he had short, side-parted brown hair, and angular features to his face that made it possible to believe that the man hadn't laughed since 1975. His badge number was 544081, and his uniform had a small brass bar atop each shoulder. "Okay," the officer said while giving him a gentle pat-down, "Alright, Mr. Cadoret, you're coming with me."

Summerlin was in a state of total shock: he had never been questioned by a cop in his life, and definitely did not expect to be arrested by one. *Oh man, what have I gotten into? Is it the Obsidian trick Connor pulled? Could they be after me for fraud? Or maybe called on grounds of common decency because of the shoeless thing?* Try as he might, Summerlin couldn't think of anything to say. He meekly raised his wrists to the officer, who cuffed him, and began to lead him to a set of exit doors which lay between "The Congo Bar" and "The Emporium of Wonders".

There was a beige and brown Las Vegas City Police cruiser parked at the curb within direct sight of the exit. The policeman walked him to the car, and upon reaching the rear passenger door, gestured for him to stop. Summerlin was still too nervous and confused to take anything in—at least in any rational meaning of the word. "Okay, Con, I did it— now what's this all about," the officer said, in a complaining tone which seemed far less authority like than the one with which he had addressed him. Summerlin lowered his head in disbelief and simply thought, *he didn't. Oh no—he did.*

Sure enough, the Con-Man emerged from behind a nearby light pole, grin on face, and lit cigar in hand. "Good work, Bradley, *love it.* I didn't tell you to arrest him though; isn't that illegal?" he said.

The officer shook his head and responded, "I didn't *arrest* anyone. I told him he needed to come with me, and put his arms up like he wanted to wear cuffs—I figured, why disappoint him?" The two men laughed. Summerlin, on the other hand, did not find his current situation nearly as funny as they did. His grimace was aimed at Connor, but it was the policeman who spoke, "So, what did you have me 'isolate and question' this kid for, anyway? Does he owe you money or something?" Connor wagged the finger of his non-cigar-holding hand and added, "No, nothing like that. I don't lend—you know that well, *Nathan*." "Watch it with the first name crap, Con-Man, I still got an extra pair of cuffs," officer Bradley said. Connor walked over and patted Summerlin on the shoulder. "This, kid, is the lovely part of an every-day high echelon individual like a celebrity or myself when the plans or goals you have are blocked and slowed down by the actions of over-scrutinizing police and media who persecute you while you're just trying to do your daily affairs..." he said. Before the Con-Man could continue, Summerlin glared at Connor and replied, "That's not even a *real thing*, Con!" Connor smiled and politely replied, "Ah ah ah—in the eyes of high society it is; and all that matters is not if something is real, when evaluating life experiences, it's the internal perceptions that really matter, remember? Don't make me repeat a discourse." Summerlin shook his head and said, "No—anything but that. Okay, you've kept me from being on the floor and spending money for a few minutes. Jokes over, let me go."

Connor laughed after taking a long drag on his cigar; his mouth spewed thick, bluish smoke in chuckle-sized increments. Officer Bradley walked over to Summerlin, reaching for a set of handcuff keys from his utility belt as he did so. "Okay, must be another one of your weird *philosophy* things again. I *am* going to have to release him now that he actually asked, though," he said to the Con-Man. Connor raised his left hand and waved; "Not yet, my dear lieutenant, I think about sixty seconds would prove more prudent," he said. "Let me go," Summerlin reiterated his complaint. "Just one more moment, kid," Connor answered; officer Bradley nodded in consent, asking the Con-Man, "So, where did you find this one?"

Connor turned towards Lieutenant Bradley, and began to speak as if he were giving a narrative on stage, "He...*he* is a poor, desperate *wight*...A wounded, pathetic youth who, out of the thick, dense, allegorical confines of—" Summerlin had had enough. "O*kay*, Yankee! I get it, I think he gets it, *sweet mercy!*" he said. Connor nodded with an impish grin. Bradley looked to Summerlin with widened eyes; "And? So what is it?" he began to say; yet again, Summerlin still had a bit of frustration in his voice—more than before. He turned to face Connor, not Bradley, and raised his voice: Okay! I got dumped. I got dumped *good n' hard*! I was insensitive to my sweetheart at a time when she needed my patience and allowed my immature ass to get aggravated by her evil firebrand friends so much so that she wouldn't even believe me rational by the time I was done!" after his outburst, Summerlin leaned against the police cruiser and let out a sigh—a sigh which, at last, was followed by deep breaths of relaxation. "See, kid? Was that so hard?" Connor asked him, reaching out to help him up. "Let me out so I can yank his massage parlor-visiting head off," Summerlin said to lieutenant Bradley. "Nah, better not...Now I see why you wanted the cuffs on, Bentley. I still say it was worth a steak at Bellagio, though," he replied.

Summerlin wanted to get up the strength for another barrage of yelling, but he couldn't. The Con-Man observed, "Now, that's the first time you've ever been honest with yourself about your pain since you arrived at Texas, kid. Doesn't it feel better now?" He squeezed his eyelids shut as if revulsion to the fact, but he swallowed hard and replied, "Yes. It does. Now I have to get back to showin' you a thing or two. So, if you don't mind..." he shook his wrists. Officer Bradley walked over and uncuffed him. "No hard feelings, uh Dixie?" He asked Summerlin, who, in turn responded, "No hard feelin's on one condition. You tell me *how* a *lieutenant* in the City Police Department fell in with the Con-Man?" Connor and his friend laughed. "He's got good taste in strippers, kid!" Connor said. *Why is it that doesn't surprise me none?* Summerlin thought as he shook his head.

"Well, come on, kid, you gotta get ready. Test or no, we have The Reason Why Thursday recital to go to," Connor said to Summerlin after he fist-pumped the departing officer Bradley. Summerlin froze in place and jerked his head to face him. "Wait one cotton pickin' moment, you said that I got to stay here—and you've actually taken time away," he said. Connor opened his arms wide and said with a smile, "I said that you couldn't leave property unless given express *in-person* permission. I'm officially here, and granting you permission. And, ordering you to do so as your teacher. Besides, consider it representative of how a celebrity would need to pause his or her affairs to support their performer friends. I'll let you take the car you came in so you can return even if I drink. No stopping for gas, though, I'll have the Texas valets refill the Delorean free-of-charge." *Argh*, Summerlin thought. It wasn't that he disliked the band—he actually found himself to be liking some of their numbers; it was simply a matter of his competitive nature. He wanted to accomplish the task at hand. *Might as well enjoy it—I'm still goin' to beat him*, Summerlin thought.

Summerlin pulled into the valet lane at Texas Palace to find it nearly full. "Don't worry, Mr. Summerlin, the Con-Man's reserved spots are never given out. And I understand you will be needing a courtesy fill-up as well," a smiling Zak greeted him. Summerlin tipped the valet a Lincoln before heading for the doors. He checked his watch before entering: it was already 3:16pm.

The curtain to the Rail Yard was open, and though there was no attendant with a podium, there was a security officer checking IDs on the way in. It didn't take long for Summerlin to find Connor: he was at the table on the dance floor which was closest to the stage, sitting with Danny, Trista and Chris the bartender. The other tables were half-filled with groups eating lunch brought to them from the Texasland Café, and there were a few sporadic beer drinkers seated in the theater seating area. The band was just then setting up their equipment. Xero carried two large speakers at once while Trent and Blake were handling the unpacking of the instruments. Samantha somehow pulled her entire drum kit into place without anyone's assistance.

"You made it," he heard Connor call out. Summerlin nodded and pulled a chair from an adjacent table, joining the Con-Man and the others. "Howdy," he said after sitting down. Trista waved, and Danny gave him a brief handshake; Jail-Bait had just finished plugging in the amps and speakers. Xero and Trent had their guitars in hand, and Blake stood, microphone in hand, with his back to the audience. Trista waved her arms and put a finger to her lips. "Shhh," she added before returning her eyes to the stage. Connor and Danny were likewise transfixed, so much so that viewing their wonder led Summerlin to stare at the stage as well. The soft roll of a drum began to slowly increase in speed and volume.

"First of all, from the bottom of our hearts, we'd like to thank you for being here this early Texas evening," Blake began as a spotlight hit him, "And secondly, may I take this opportunity to let you all know that we came here this fine day to for one very specific reason. I don't think I need to tell you though. You already know..." He walked to the stage's rim and knelt before rising with an extended fist and shouting "The Reason Why!" The band then began to play one of their own songs, "Don't Break".

A waitress from the buffet greeted the table and took their orders. Everyone but Summerlin had beer—he knew he'd have to drive back to The Jungle after the concert, and decided that drinking a cola would be a far safer thing to do. "You hungry, kid? *I'll pay*," Connor said to him smugly. "No, Yankee, I'm just fine. But what is all this? I thought T.R.Y. rehearsed on Thursdays and performed on Friday nights," Summerlin replied. Connor took a sip from an Old Fashioned before replying, "Their Friday night shows sell out, and Saturday nights at the Rail Yard are set aside for visiting acts—Jackie Jackinson's here in two days..." "The point, Con, *the point*," Summerlin said. "The fans begged

238

Mr. Moroni for an extra show. And, seeing as how even the band-hating club owner couldn't resist the idea of getting extra money out of an already-in-use venue, he let them raise the curtain, so to speak, and let people in during the rehearsals. He gets to run his bar, and the buffet gives him a percentage for the rights to the customers. There's no cover, and the fans love it. Fair deal, even if one that was offered by a scoundrel," the Con-Man said. Summerlin nodded and took a sip from his soda.

Summerlin listened to the band play their set list—it was the same as it had been the Friday before with two exceptions: Xero played keyboard for several songs as Jail-Bait took her turn at playing bass, and Trent, not Blake, led the audience in a sing-along of "Don't Mess With Texas". Though he knew it to be a song about Texas Palace, Summerlin being a southern son loved listening to the tune, from the Jail-Bait's faux organ intro to Samantha's song-ending solo. The sing-along nature of the song's performance caused Summerlin to hear the words more clearly than he had before:

> *Don't mess with Texas, we are warning you*
> *Don't mess with Texas, it will be the last thing you do.*
> *We got ourselves a Palace and we know it very well*
> *If you don't like the Palace you can just go to Hell.*
> *While chillin' at ol' Texas, you'll learn a point of view:*
> *That when you're in dear Texas, it's best to just be you.*

The song went on for three verses, but Summerlin lost track of the words once the song reached Trent's guitar solo that followed the second chorus. After that, the band did a practice round of Xero's hacky-sack exhibition; though this version was done with Jail-Bait joining in, and without music, save for the rhythmic chanting of the fans. After the hack-off—Xero 27, Jones 20—Blake approached the center microphone stand and said, "Okay guys, it being a Thursday, you know the tradition: The Reason Why is now open for requests." Several song titles were yelled aloud by various fans; but, it was Connor's request that was the most salient—He walked up to the stage, and, as the crowd began to cheer "Con-Man" repetitively, he yelled up to Blake, "Hey, I think we owe the l'il one some country!" Blake nodded and said, "You don't have to tell me twice."

Blake clutched his guitar and looked out into the audience before saying, "This is for Summerlin." The band began to play Lynyrd Skynyrd's *Sweet Home Alabama*. Summerlin shook his head while smiling and said, "You know, I'm not *from there*." Nobody even noticed he said it; and, after a moment, he had forgotten the utterance as well—*It is a great song, and probably the closest I'll get—I'll take it!* Summerlin thought as he listened to Blake's vocal rendition of the tune.

Not bad. Not bad at all, he thought as the song came to an end and the small but vocal crowd clapped readily in their seats. Summerlin alone rose and gave the group a standing ovation. Blake winked back from onstage, and The Reason Why went on to play Elton John's *Tiny Dancer* before wrapping things up in their customary fashion. "We are The Reason Why," Trent said over the mic, "and we love you. See you awesome souls tomorrow!"

Most of the people exited the Rail Yard; a few fans walked up to the stage to ask for autographs and pictures, to which the five band members were more than happy to oblige. Connor and Summerlin even posed together with them. After the band had walked backstage, Connor got up, and Summerlin followed suit. He followed the Con-Man through the stage corridor that he had passed through when he first met The Reason Why. The band members were just entering the communal back room when Summerlin and Connor arrived.

Jail-Bait went straight to the table near the wall with the Jackinson poster, and plopped a large stack of sheet music upon it. Xero put his arm around Trent and convinced the lead guitarist to join him in the corner of the room to, in his words, "smoke some *serious* trees." Summerlin declined Xero's offer to join them. *I'll let Willie have it—there's no way I'm doin' that in the land of lights*, he thought.

Summerlin took a seat on the faded floral couch, and Connor joined him. The Con-Man began inspecting his various wrist devices while Summerlin watched the rest of the band enter. Blake came in alone, carrying two instrument cases on each arm. By the time that Jail-Bait had helped him set the cases down, Samantha and Danny had arrived, holding hands as they entered the room. Blake took his acoustic guitar out of its case and sat on the vinyl couch, strumming a slow but peaceful melody. All of a sudden, a voice came calling out from the entrance Summerlin and Connor had used—It was Mr. Moroni.

"Gentlemen—and I am using that term *very* loosely—I have just received a letter addressed to you. Perhaps more of that odd fan mail you seem to inspire; and I warn you, if its more joints being anonymously donated to your bassist, I'm going to call the *police*," Mr. Moroni said as he politely yet angrily thrust the sealed envelope into Jail-Bait's hands. He then glared over at Xero and Trent; after a few silent seconds passed, Xero stepped forward and said, "Yes, Master?" Mr. Moroni scoffed and swiftly left the room, saying, "You are under contract—you will cooperate!"

"Xero, *really?*" Jail-Bait chided him before looking at the letter. Xero grimaced and said, "Sorry...that guy just sucks, though." "He pays our checks," she replied. Blake turned to face her and added, "at least for now. What's it say, Jasmine?" *Jasmine? Who is...oh yeah*, Summerlin thought. He had almost forgotten Jail-Bait's real name due to the fact that he had only heard it once before. Jailbait opened the envelope and unfolded the paper it contained. She donned a pair of purple-rimmed reading glasses, and began to read the document aloud: "To: The Reason Why, care of Rail Yard management...From: Alexander Collins, Executive Producer of *Altered Note Records*..." The room became an anxious sea of smiles as she continued to read the letter, "I am writing you to inform you that we here at Altered Note have an interest in pursuing a potential record contract with you at this time. We have sent a scout several times to your recent performances, and are interested in seeing if The Reason Why will fit well with our catalogue here at Altered Note. However we will need to do a final audition, and due to the fact that our label produces primarily live albums, we feel that viewing one of your Friday shows will tell us all we need to know. Please ensure that there are five front row seats reserved for April fifth." Jail-Bait paused. "that's two weeks from tomorrow," Trent said before she continued reading: "Look forward to hearing from us in the future. Your's truly... etc." Xero, Samantha and Trent all began to cheer fanatically. "We're gonna get it, bro!" Xero shouted happily while mussing up Trent's hair. "Well, I'll be," Blake said as he stroked his chin, looking like he found the news too good to be true. "We haven't 'made it' yet, guys. It's a shot, though," Jail-Bait said before putting the letter back in the envelope, and tossing it atop the sheet music pile.

Summerlin smiled to see the guys so happy. "Hey, kid," Connor said after tapping his shoulder, "We love having *y'all*, but you did your job here, and have important matters to attend to—*remember*?" He had almost completely forgot his test, and the challenge it included. Summerlin nodded. "You're right," he said to the Con-Man before addressing the rest of the group, "I hate to go, guys, but I gotta go show this card-slinger a thing or two about *redneck ingenuity*." Xero, Connor and Trent laughed; Blake and Jail-Bait gave him the thumbs up and simultaneously cheered, "Right on!" Connor shook his head dismissively and said, "best of luck, *Green Acres*," as Summerlin left the room.

Summerlin sped back to The Jungle in the Delorean. He pulled into the valet lane and tipped the attendant a ten-spot on his way inside. He walked with a brisk pace to the shopping area to find that the boutiques had closed for the night. The only store left open was a low-end convenience store called "The Unending Summer Supply Shop", which sold only mundane, inexpensive items like candy, cigarettes and beer—and there was no way that Summerlin would have been able to, as the rules suggest, use everything he would have had to buy there to constitute a two hundred fifty dollar sale. *The concert; he was keeping me away on purpose—that miserable conniving...oh, wait, forgot who I was talking about here,* Summerlin thought as he walked back out onto the main casino floor.

Connor had not fully trapped him, but he could see the fences closing in on him; Summerlin had run out of conceivable ways of distributing his wealth without leaving the property or gambling. He decided to take a walk outside. *Fresh air can't ever hurt,* Summerlin reasoned. He found a one-door exit near the entrance to a club called *Kawaiiko.*

Summerlin took in a breath of fresh air—the Vegas version thereof, at least—and looked skyward. There wasn't a single star visible within the pink-stained nightscape. Aside from the vague rumblings of club music, there was an odd silence. *It's funny how somethin' as simple as peace and quiet can feel like an exotic experience here. It's also a place that has yet to bore me, though,* he thought as he followed a slender sidewalk towards the rear side of the hotel tower—the side of The Jungle that the Strip has never seen.

"That one's mine, Down-Low," Summerlin heard a man's voice say as he rounded a corner. He turned to find two men, both well over the drinking age. They were standing next to a dumpster with its lid left open. The taller of the two looked at the piece of pizza that his compatriot held and said, "No, Seven, we had an agreement last night that *I* had the rights to any Italian." They were dressed in suits that had an array of patches, non-sequitur buttons, and holes. The only thing that the men had on them that looked new—or whole—was their footwear; both were clad in Army boots, the kind that you'd find at a military surplus store. *These guys are older than Bling, I bet they learned from experience which piece of apparel matters most out here*, Summerlin thought as he walked towards them. "Seven" and "Down-Low" may not have sounded like the names of two men to *Andrew* two weeks prior; but, "Summerlin" had gotten used to the convention—to his chagrin.

"Since when is pizza frickin' Italian?" Down-Low said. He had pronounced the word in a fashion similar to Connor; Summerlin cringed. "Since *forever*, numb-nuts—It's mine, DL. Fair and square." "Seven, I say I found it, and I thought it was American when I—" Down-Low stopped speaking when he became aware of Summerlin's presence. Both men stared at him, and "Seven" appeared to be contemplating a dash. "Now, don't look at me like that. And runnin' isn't necessary, either." Seven and Down-Low looked at each other and did a series of nods before Down-Low turned to Summerlin and said, "Yeah? Well, what is it you want, fancy boy?" Summerlin had forgotten that he was wearing the suit that Cecil the on-staff tailor had tailored for him.

"Okay, I know what it looks like, but believe it or not, I slept in a gutter last night myself. Not here to judge you—heck, not here to do anything, really. I just realized that the man who inadvertently gave me this silly suit beat me in a game. I thought myself to be of equal talent in this game to the Con-Man, and I've just recently realized that there wasn't a marked deck: there has only ever been the appearance of cards. He had me from the moment I said I'd win," Summerlin said. Down-Low's head turned to Summerlin the moment he heard mention of Connor Bentley's name. "What's Mr. Bentley got to do with this?" he asked Summerlin. *Goodness gracious, I'm not even goin' to ask*, he thought.

Summerlin replied, "I know him. He's also the reason for me sleepin' in an alley, actually. I met a guy named Bling-Bling of all things, and he took me to the *Angel of Hoover Avenue*." The two shabbily-clad men stood close and mumbled things amongst themselves. At last, Down-Low looked at Summerlin and said, "I dunno, Seven, he looks honest to me—*and*, he knows about Bling and the Lucky Flamingo. 'Bling-Bling' might have been just a guess—but he knows about the *Angel?* That's not something you can know about unless you've walked in the deepest parts of the city past nightfall in desperation. The paying customers come during daylight hours." Seven walked closer to Summerlin and looked him over head to toe. "Well, I do find him bein' a fake at wealthy, that much in his words is true—no whale would be wearin' cowboy boots with a suit like that," he said.

Down-Low walked up to Seven and pointed at a flattened cardboard box which sat near the dumpster, and the group took a seat. "Okay, hillbilly, you got my attention, and the garbage truck ain't coming for an hour or so—tell us something amusing, and we'll see if we can help," he said.

Summerlin regaled the dumpster divers with his tale. Down-Low shared a bottled water amongst the three of them, each having a café mug with a broken off handle for a vessel. After Summerlin was done explaining his current feeling of failure, Seven stood up and faced him, saying, "Sounds like you've been through a bunch, kid." Summerlin nodded and took a sip of water—it was not even daylight anymore, but in Las Vegas, even the night time heat can dehydrate. "Sounds like you also don't know much if you assumed that only poor people suffer. Heck, I wouldn't trade places with the worries of a CEO or lawyer for all the money in the county," Seven continued, "Everyone—everyone in the entire world suffers—without pain there'd be no joy. Do yourself a favor and lose that suit soon as you can; it's poisoning your judgment or something."

He didn't know what to say—The vagrant who had been arguing 'who gets the thrown away pizza' was, indeed, making more rational choices than he. Summerlin never thought of something to say to Seven and Down-Low; he did, however, think of something he could do.

Summerlin could still hear the two men cheering his name as he left the alley that led to the back side of the building—he felt confident that he hadn't needed to walk and see it after all. He happily reentered the casino after securing a small white folded piece of paper. *Lesson One all over again...My plan had nothin' to do with my goal*, Summerlin thought, *I guess, to be fair, Connor's Lesson Four also applies, the part about everythin' happenin' as it should. The Con-Man's darned advice might actually be cumulative.* Summerlin rushed up to the Rat Pack Suite and slept on a sofa on the landing, with his watch alarm set for eleven-thirty. He didn't care about comfort, he didn't care about style— all that mattered to Summerlin that night was that he had won, and he couldn't wait to tell the Con-Man himself.

PART THREE:

HOUSES OF CARDS

12.

Summerlin arrived at the Austin Suite at two past noon to find it empty. He had raced the Delorean past the ever-busy Rancho Palace construction site with a smile thinking that he would use his suite key to unlock what was, to him, *a three-tiered-cake of "I told you so."* It is often that even the simplest of plans seem to go astray. "Oh well, so much for playin' darts while braggin'," Summerlin said to himself as he headed to the guest wing for a shower and a change of clothes.

Once Summerlin had finished showering and shaving, he left the suite. He had decided to begin his casino-level Connor-search at the Lone Star Bar—*I stand a good chance of meetin' up with him there, and if not, Race and Sports Book isn't even a holler away from there,* Summerlin decided.

The Lone Star Bar was packed—a young blonde bar-back ran frenetically, passing glasses and mugs to Fugi and Jim as they took drink orders. Connor, however, was nowhere to be seen at the Lone Star; Summerlin decided to try finding him the Race Book area. The Con-Man wasn't in his VIP Race Booth, nor was he in the general seating of the Race Book, either. "There you are," Summerlin said to Connor upon finding him in the front row of the Sports Book chairs, staring up at a basketball game that was playing on the center and largest of the big screens overhead. It was Boston versus New York.

The seats in the Sports Book were placed out in a formation befitting school desks, each lining up rank and file, for several rows. The chairs themselves were old, patched and scuffed beyond repair, and the room smelled of stale cigar smoke and beer. A slew of smaller televisions surrounded the three main big screens, and they were displaying a variety of programming that ran the gamut from golf to competitive scuba diving.

A commercial for Crazy Burger came on the center big screen. Connor turned to face Summerlin and said, "Hey kid, how was your failure?" The Con-Man was wearing lime green dress slacks with a sports jacket to match; beneath which lay a Jackie J. Jackinson promotional t-shirt. Indeed, the shirt sported a picture of the "Rockabilly Legend" himself, quite unlike the staged photo in the backstage room of the Rail Yard: He was a pale, gangly man wearing trousers and chaps, with a yellow "Don't Tread On Me" flag as a cape. Jackie J. was holding an electric guitar with a fierce, crazed-yet-happy look on his long-bearded face. Beneath his name, the shirt text read: "You know it!" *Actually*, Summerlin thought, *I don't think I do.*

"Actually, Con-Artist, I won—and don't you *dare* go blamin' that musician on the south! I actually like Rockabilly, but *that*..." Connor laughed and said, "No, actually, Jackinson's from out here. Quite a cult following; it's not for young ears, though. Wait—What did you say?" Summerlin plopped into the seat next to him and pulled out the folded piece of paper he had saved from the night before. He handed it to Connor, saying, "Here's all you need to know. Oh, but if I may request, for personal satisfaction 'n' all, that you read it aloud?"

Connor unfolded the note and read: "Dear Mr. Bentley, we met this kid at The Jungle—he's drinking fountain water with us in a suit and all he wants is for me to write a receipt. Yes, he did give me and Down-Low a hundred seventy-five dollars each. He also wanted me to tell you that DL and I have better taste in clothing than you do. Thanks for the coffee the other day—you're awesome. Sincerely...'Seven'." The Con-Man shook his head slowly as it hung low. "Summerlin, I gotta tell you, I'm—I'm *impressed*. You even got a receipt. Excellent work—you proved me wrong in my opinion of your spending talent. Technically, you cheated by going outside the auspices of The Jungle...And you didn't—technically—buy anything with the money. But, that being said, I applaud the initiative, and we'll count it as a win. But, fair being fair and all—admit it, it wasn't easy with all that hoopla. You couldn't even do the simple act of spending less than three hundred dollars—and those were miniature examples," he said.

Summerlin nodded and said, "Actually, it was impossible. I couldn't get anywhere. Was there a secret, a planned strategy you knew could work, may I ask?" Connor took a sip from an Old Fashioned and looked back to the basketball game as he replied, "Yeah, kid—movie theatres. Trident Cinemas doesn't honor VIPs. All you would have needed was the courage to say no to everyone and risk your entire day watching movies." *Argh!* Summerlin thought. The movie theatres were the one place he *hadn't* considered; and, he never realized that there wasn't a rule forbidding him from declining to indulge Connor's "celebrity challenges". "Touché. How's your fantasy camp of a life goin'?" he inquired. Summerlin knew he was taking a risk in asking—he didn't know for certain if the Con-Man's "silence during 'business' hours" policy extended to the Sports Book general seating area as well.

Apparently, it did not: Connor replied without taking his eyes off the screen, "Not bad, a lot of the usual. Got twenty large on Boston." Summerlin's jaw nearly hit the floor. He had recently become accustomed to seeing large amounts of cash being played around like it was play money; however, Summerlin was still not used to seeing so much money—twenty thousand dollars—bet on a team winning or losing one game.

Summerlin gave a look up to the center big screen and noted the score: New York 85, Boston 83. It was the fourth quarter, and there was less than ten minutes left remaining on the game clock. "How can you not be nervous when the score is that close?" he asked Connor. "Now, I couldn't go doing that," the Con-Man began, "That would mean that I'd be letting a situation or condition affect who I am. Remember Lesson Five, kid? Never let anything—positive or negative—change how you feel or choose to act." Summerlin replied, "Okay, I'll have to remember that," He meant it—*letting circumstances change my core behavior was what got me into the whole mess*, Summerlin thought.

"Besides," Connor continued once another set of commercials began to air, "with the point spread, I only need Boston to win by three or more." Summerlin's eyes widened; Connor remained cool as a cucumber, as always.

Summerlin leaned back in his chair and began to watch not the basketball game overhead, but the fearless gambler beneath who seemed to be at greatest peace when the dice were still being rolled. "The best part of a race is when nobody's won yet, kid," Connor had told him a few nights before in between drinks at the Class ACT—It all seemed to make sense now: The Con-Man had somehow developed the ability to have his favorite part of a sports or race bet be the part that regular people dreaded the most. Summerlin almost wanted to see the moment that would make the Con-Man lose his cool—not out of anger or jealousy, but more in an attempt to finally place this strange personality within everyday human parameters. A dark, immature part of him wanted to see if there would be a moment where Connor, not he, would be the weak one, and he could finally repay his friend for his support. That moment never came.

Connor remained laid-back for the entire remainder of the game. The final score of the game was New York 102, Boston 105. The Con-Man had barely won, and you'd never have known it to look at him. "So, you won?" Summerlin said inquired. "Yep," Connor replied before rising and casually walking to the Sports Book betting counter. There were two women waiting in line ahead of him, but after a Connor ice-breaker, the ladies were laughing and waved him ahead. *Maybe he told them what he won?* Summerlin thought.

The Con-Man returned and resumed his seat. "Hey—you're not asking what we're gonna do. And, you're not crying or talking about right and wrong. I must declare, Summerlin, you're beginning to seem like a new man." He smiled and gave Summerlin a thumbs-up. He thought for a minute and said, "You know what, Con? I'm not bad, Can't say that my problems have been fixed; but, for the moment, I have no complaints." Connor winked and replied, "Good! Because we have things to do now that you're here." Summerlin raised an eye brow; "Oh?" he queried. "Yeah," Connor began, "And I don't think I need to remind you *The Reason Why.*" He winked and gave his used-car salesman-like clicking sound. *Oh yeah, it's Friday,* Summerlin thought. "So, it's up to the Austin for your 'change of threads', then?" Summerlin said wryly. Connor replied as he rose and made way for the casino pit, "Now there you go asking questions again. But, yes, we are going upstairs." Summerlin grinned the entire way up.

After Summerlin had visited the guest room closet and chosen his clothing from what was rapidly becoming *The Con-Wear Collection*™, he exited the room wearing a silver dress shirt and a pair of Con-Wear jeans that were ash-gray. His boots were breaking in, ever so slowly; Summerlin still winced a little as he put them back on. While he was still getting his hair combed he heard Connor call out, "See you down there, kid—you know where I'll be."

Summerlin rode an empty elevator down to the ground floor and walked in a casual, laid-back pace towards the Rail Yard. He had to give it to the man—Connor's methods had placed Summerlin in two distinctly different stressful situations. After the survival game of destitution and the grand stress fest that was temporary wealth, life somehow seemed to flow at a slower, more peaceful pace for him than it had before his recent change of address. *Heck*, Summerlin realized while crossing the Pit, *I haven't even thought of Sarah in two days.*

As he walked past the entrance of the Rail Yard, Summerlin turned and headed for the entrance line, which stretched halfway to the hotel-casino's main entrance. "Hey!" a voice well-known to Summerlin called out—it was Xero: he was standing to the immediate right of the night club's doors. The young bassist was clad in his usual torn jeans and biker jacket, though this night he had a pair of shoes that matched—a pair of dark orange Chuck Taylors that matched the Texas World shirt beneath his jacket. Xero gestured for him to join him. "Hey, I'm comin'," he replied at a louder-than-usual volume. Xero shook his head and grinned before gesturing again, this time yelling out twice as loud as he had before, "Get your *igno* ass over here!" *Hate to leave the line*, Summerlin thought, *But this might be the only chance I get to ask what in Sam Hill that word means.*

"Hey, what's up? You made me lose my place. Gotta ask something: you said "igno" before...what does that mean?" Xero laughed before looking at Summerlin; he patted his back and said, "It means you're one of us, Summerlin—now get your butt in there."

As Summerlin walked into the Rail Yard that night, he felt *accepted*— like his company was actually wanted. It was a feeling which he had not truly felt since he had left his country home. Things were starting to look better: he was beginning to actually *feel* better. *There must be something to all this*, he thought as he walked through the curtained passage to the communal backstage room.

When he arrived, Summerlin found Connor sitting in a deep recline upon the faded floral couch. The members of T.R.Y. were all there as well, though Xero, Trent and Blake were hurriedly unpacking the instruments from their cases. Samantha and Jail-Bait were sorting through clusters of sheet music. Meanwhile, the Con-Man was looking at the ceiling while humming the tune to *Shut Up and Hold the Wheel*.

"You know," Jail-Bait said to Connor while hustling about, "you're gonna be forced to sing if you keep on hanging out here before every show." Jones then noticed Summerlin, and added, "And now he's getting as bad as you!" The rest of the band was laughing loudly as Jail-Bait's chiding look at Summerlin began to waver. "Not funny, guys," Blake said after seeing Jail-Bait sigh, "We got a lot of things goin' on—let's take it easy on our poor worryin' matriarch, huh?" Blake himself had only managed to stop laughing just before he spoke. Connor looked at Jail-Bait and said, "Sorry, JB, just trying to show my support." Jones had already returned to sorting the music packets for the show. Her face softened and Jail-Bait replied, "Fine, just try to do it from the *audience*, or back here after the show, okay?" Connor replied while resuming his view of the ceiling, "I'm *trying*." Jail-Bait rolled her eyes and said, "Okay guys, let's do it." She ran for the exit, leading the charge to the stage. Connor rose and walked up to Summerlin. "Well, time to take in a show," he said.

Summerlin found Connor at the same VIP table location as last week—Again, there was seating for two with a white stock paper sign reading "Reserved." The Con-Man gave him a nod of acknowledgement, and the two men turned their eyes to the stage, which had become bathed in lights. The band went through their usual intro, which culminated with Blake shouting "You already know...The Reason Why!" to the adulation of the crowd.

The band's set opened with Go West's *King of Wishful Thinking*, which was followed by the band-written composition, *Don't Break*. The Friday night show followed, for the most part, the same formula as the show that Summerlin had viewed a week before; Xero scored a thirty-six during his hack-fest this time. Another difference of note was that the band performed the Michael Jackson hit, *The Way You Make Me Feel*, with Xero singing solo as he selected a "Bride of Xero" from his dedicated fan seating section and took her onstage for a stanza-long dance. Summerlin noticed that before his solo song-and-dance, Jailbait mussed Xero's hair affectionately and said, "Go get 'em." The crowd was raucous, and, by the time the band got to *Don't Mess With Texas*, the cheering and applause had reached a level that made Summerlin swear the place might fall down.

Near the end of their set, at the point where Summerlin had become accustomed to hearing the band-written ballad *That's Just Life*, he was given a pleasant surprise. The guys performed a more polished version of the *Skynyrd* cover from the night before. The crowd loved it; Summerlin gave an even more emphatic standing ovation than he had done the last time.

Connor and Summerlin left right after they heard Trent voice the band's closing, "Thank you. We are The Reason Why, and we love you!" The band members had already taken seats in the backstage room by the time they arrived—except for Jail-Bait, who was stacking sheet music and rearranging the instrument cases. Xero and Trent were sitting on foldable chairs in a corner smoking next to a large sign that read, "No Smoking". Samantha and Blake were sitting on the vinyl couch.

"Nice job," The Con-Man said while giving Jail-Bait a look-over, "capital legs there, old chum." Jones was wearing a bridesmaid's dress with a large slit up the side with denim shorts and a bustier beneath. "Capital questionable taste in clothing there, old pal," Jail-Bait retorted.

"*Feminist,*" Connor responded. "*Drifter,*" Jail-Bait snapped back; both of them then laughed. The Con-Man extended a fist to Jones, and she retaliated with her own, resulting in a delayed-action fist pump.

The main topic of conversation for everyone assembled back stage was a discussion over how the night's show had gone. This topic inevitably to a debate concerning the contents of the playlist for their performance in two weeks that would also serve as their audition for Altered Note Records. There were differing opinions on what would serve as the best content for the show, which was now less than two weeks away. Jail-Bait and Trent felt that their set should be modified to showcase the band's self-written compositions, and included The Reason Why playing a song which Blake and Jail-Bait had been tinkering on entitled *Pull Me Away.* Blake and Xero endorsed a strategy of keeping their set relatively the same as normal, but with a few changes to emphasize the band's ability to "play up the crowd". Samantha abstained from the topic, noting, "I like our old set, but, I think either of those ideas would be killer."

After all sides were chosen, The Con-Man put in his two cents: "I don't know if it'll be of any worth to you, but I think you guys should do *either of those set lists*; *but,* with the swing shift security supervisors handcuffed in their underwear behind you on the stage." Everyone but Jail-Bait laughed loudly—even Jones smiled a little.

The band decided to "agree to disagree", for the time being at least. "We have almost two weeks to figure that out," Blake had said. They agreed to put it on the back burner so that more pressing issues—such as where they should throw a post-show celebration—could be attended. Connor declared that the Austin Suite was "always open for fun and frolic". Connor and Samantha left first—Summerlin had volunteered to do the work in her stead; the rest of the band agreed to reconvene at the Austin after the band's gear had been properly secured.

Summerlin checked his watch as he rode the elevator upwards—it was 11:03. Normally this was about the time where he would be getting tired and seeking rest—but, due to his enjoyment of the evening, Summerlin felt nowhere near out of energy. He strolled down the suite level hallway, admiring the glass-domed light fixtures on the ceiling as he did so.

The door to the Austin Suite had been left ajar; Summerlin could hear several voices being drowned out by classic rock blaring from a stereo within. He entered to find that the sounds of talking and music were coming from the elevated section of the great room. Summerlin joined the group, most of which stood around the pool table. Xero and Blake were playing a game of 9-Ball. Trent was at the bar mixing margaritas while singing *Pull Me Away* and being *very* liberal with the tequila bottle.

Blake won the game. He next played Jail-Bait, though in 8-Ball this time. Connor had taken a seat on one of the nearby red velvet-backed chairs. Summerlin joined him, sitting on an identical chair cattycorner to the Con-Man. "Hey, kid," Connor said. "Hey," Summerlin began, "I goin' to have to ask, seein' as I thought it was a small prank at first, but it seems to be taking a firm hold on the world 'round here..." Summerlin gestured at his shirt and pants before continuing, "What is 'Con-Wear'?" The Con-Man grinned as he stretched his arms. "It's just this little thing I do. The 'custom t-shirt stores' in the valley insisted on putting tags on the shirts—and, I *loathe* neck tags, kid—they're worse than a cold six-deck shoe. So I had to get a small warehouse and a silkscreen press...and well, I didn't expect people would *offer money for* it. Started as something small like you thought; just seems to keep growing and growing, though. Thinking about making *shoes*..." *Oh, boy*, Summerlin thought—he didn't know whether to encourage or discourage him. "I know you give out the Texas World ones—where are people *buying* these?" Summerlin asked. Connor snapped his fingers before winking. "At every fine men's boutique and indoor swap meet in the City, cottonseed," he added. Summerlin was honestly surprised; he didn't have a single comeback, even when his friend had baited him with an obvious "south equals cotton" reference. "You can close your jaw, kid—you don't want it stuck that way, a fly will move right on in there. Summerlin managed to shut his mouth, but his eyes remained as stretched open as they would go. "I can get you a pair of—" Connor's words were cut short by Summerlin, who said, "No—that'll be *okay*. Thank you very much, though."

Jail-Bait defeated Blake in 8-Ball, and went to the bar to help Trent serve everyone one of his "Trent's special margaritas". Summerlin found the neon-green concoction to be a bit salty, and rather heavy in its tequila content. A dart game was in the midst of forming; Summerlin rose the moment he heard the word *darts* and walked with haste to find Xero and Samantha already grabbing the tips. "Southern boy wants a toss," Xero said with a grin—his fake southern accent was almost as bad as the Con-Man's, "What should we do?" Trent walked up to join them and said, "I'd say drop the accent and let him play—he beat *my* ass." The game was set with Samantha, Trent, Summerlin and Xero playing Cricket. Summerlin threw six 20's before even bothering with locking the other numbers up.

The game resulted in a lopsided victory in favor of Summerlin; he scored thirty points, but Trent had seventy, and Xero and Samantha each had over a hundred points. "*Damn!* How'd you learn to play like that?" Xero asked after the game of Cricket had ended. "Nothin' special," Summerlin said, "I just practiced really hard every time a musician doubted my dart skills." Trent and Samantha laughed—Samantha laughed so hard she fell down. "Very funny; I'm still the resident smart-ass though, even if you did totally destroy me in darts," Xero said with a nod and a smile. "Fair enough," Summerlin conceded.

Connor applauded a game well played. "It was like watching *Barbaro* all over again," he said. "Watching *who*?" Summerlin asked said. "Oh,"

Connor replied, "nevermind, Summerlin. We'll talk ponies someday when you're gray. I'm in the next game!" The Con-Man rose from his seat and walked over to the dart line.

Summerlin took a seat in his velvet-backed chair from before, and watched—with amusement—as Connor and the entire band debated who would play in the next game. It was not a childish argument like one Summerlin would have expected at the hands of Gina and Olivia. No, it was more of a back and forth of playful banter interrupted a few times by volume-raising contests. Summerlin enjoyed merely being in the presence of such genuine camaraderie. He liked it so much that he, an avid darts player, opted to sit the next two games out to enjoy simply being a sedentary observer to the current amicable, happy nature of the Austin Suite. It was not childish—child-*like*, perhaps, but not childish.

Everyone then took turns to see who could get the top score on one of Connor's cabinet-style arcade games entitled *Shooter of Destiny*. The game had been made in the late 90's, but one would have never known it from the excited reactions and trash-talking sessions that ensued. Connor ended up getting the second-best score—Xero got the top score and typed his initials in as "o" before doing a post-game victory dance. Summerlin's score had been somewhere between Jail-Bait and Samantha—he was having too much fun to care.

After the *Shooter of Destiny* competition had ended, everyone decided to conclude the night with a final drink. Trent mixed up some strawberry daiquiris. They turned out to be every bit as strong as Trent's "special" margaritas had been; however, Summerlin found the daiquiri to handle the liquor flavor better than the first cocktail had. After a group-wide toast to everyone's health, the group began to part ways: Blake and Trent left to take a taxi; Sam and Jail-Bait were picked up by Danny. Xero didn't feel tired—*naturally*—so he decided to "go for a walk and listen to some *Floyd*".

And then, there were two. Connor was sticking darts back into the board when Summerlin spoke: "Wow, that was fun." The Con-Man finished sticking the darts into place before responding, "Yeah, we always have some good times. Hey kid—you up for a little *late night Blackjack*?" Summerlin didn't spare a moment in replying, "Heck yeah I am." Connor walked over to him and said, "And the boy is becoming a man. Let's go!" Summerlin had rolled his eyes upon hearing the "boy" comment; but, it didn't take him long to regain his smile: he knew that not all of his troubles were solved, but fact was no longer impeding him from relaxing anymore. Summerlin decided that when it all came down to it, he could always worry about his troubles *tomorrow* just as well as he could today. *You know what*, he realized, *I think I'm beginnin' to like this "shadow" thing.*

The next day served as a template for those that would follow; waking would be followed by a Race Book session—one which was held in total silence, and often filled with Summerlin improving his new hobby of Oragami on a day to day basis. He had found a book entitled "Oragami Makes Paper Human" in the gift shop, and actually found the art to be somewhat calming. Connor tried his best to push the daily assemblage of handmade swans, whales and boxes away from his gambling area without showing his obvious chagrin.

Lunch would be at the buffet—Connor seemed to really love the Texas Buffet—the man seemed to eat there at least once a day. Afternoons were devoted to Pit games. Summerlin noticed that Connor played all the games in the pit with one exception: Roulette. When he finally got the nerve to ask him about it, the Con-Man replied, "I don't like that the two "zero" slots can tank your gaming strategy, I guess. I just don't fancy it. Everyone's allowed to have a game or two that they don't like." Summerlin instantly quipped, "Or to not want to gamble altogether?" Connor's face looked like he had just been told that frogs speak in Lithuanian backwards. After a wordless minute of craps play, he responded, "Now why would any normal person want to choose that path? Gambling can be a subject of acts and deeds beyond the negative ones. In moderation, gambling can almost be a little *therapeutic*. Life needs a little risk—you can't win in life without a wager, kid." Somehow, in some weird way, it all made sense. Summerlin nodded, still attempting to put his fast-talking friend's words into perspective.

Evenings varied. The next six days held a wide variety of activities performed between 6 and 11pm: on Saturday, it was a night club, where Connor got Summerlin a VIP table to himself, just like the one he had—Summerlin felt a little awkward during the whole event; he couldn't dance, and wasn't used to seeing so many half-naked women in one place. Sunday it was Keno, and Monday evening was, as the Con-Man put it, "Race sheet reading time" at the SFC, which turned out to be a lovely place with an open bar and complimentary cigars and several high definition big screens. Tuesday night, Connor took Summerlin down to the Shake House, a local's nightclub where Jail-Bait DJed on the side. Wednesday and Thursday evenings were devoted to poker.

Night times consisted of clubbing with celebrities, mocking security personnel and risking large amounts of money downtown. Connor somehow even got Summerlin to make a high limit sports book bet on a baseball game on Wednesday—Atlanta over New York— for three hundred dollars. Summerlin won four hundred fifty dollars that night.Late nights often included Xero, who never appeared the slightest bit drowsy.

Six days and six nights passed, with Summerlin becoming ever so relaxed and positive in his train of thought. He also began to become known for accompanying the Con-Man; the security staff had begun to call Summerlin *"Protége,"* though he was sure that they didn't mean it in the *good* way. The security staff started showing verbal and visual signs of their dislike for him. Another strange thing also happened: Summerlin, for some reason, never had to pay for a drink at Texas Palace again—even when Xero wasn't serving.

Six days and nights of laughing amongst friends and gambling alongside Connor came and went. After the near-week was over, Summerlin found himself to be up two thousand two hundred fifty dollars from the experience. He had only thought of Sarah or his unemployment twice during the entire six days. Both times his rationale for dismissing worry was "I'll get back to it later." All was going well until Friday morning, when Summerlin and Connor had decided to go see a movie...

13.

C onnor and Summerlin were waiting their turn in a line which filled almost the entire brass-stanchioned "stockade". It was then that Summerlin was reminded that all dreams must eventually end—his sanguine state ended that Friday morning when Connor and he were waiting in the ticket line at Trident Cinemas. Pain became possible once more, when Summerlin saw Sarah standing in line only a few spots away.

She was wearing a Blue t-shirt that said "I Heart Old Dominion," with the "heart" being a cartoon heart rather than the letters for the word, that had originally belonged to Summerlin; her long silken hair was bound with a bowed blue ribbon. *Love the irony, she's wearing my favorite color*, he thought. Summerlin grimaced and his heart began to race. He was unsure of how to handle the situation—he still felt every ounce of love for Sarah, but had gotten accustomed to avoiding thoughts of her in order to continue "letting the good times roll". *What do I say? Wait—maybe I shouldn't say anything. Aww, man, this sucks—if I bring it up to Connor it's goin' to throw a shadow on our whole day*, he thought.

He decided that he had no choice; when he took a second look at Sarah, Summerlin noticed that she was accompanied by Gina and Olivia. He was going to have to ask Connor, whether he wanted to or not. "Con—Con!" Summerlin whispered as loud as he could to rouse his friend's attention; the Con-Man was reading the various movie posters posted on the walls surrounding the theatre. "I'm busy admiring capitalism—what is it, kid?" Connor asked. "That's Sarah, right over there," Summerlin replied in a whisper as he pointed her out to him. Connor stood on tippy-toes and leaned to the left and right. "The long-haired brunette. The beautiful one," Summerlin added.

Connor's eyes widened and he smiled as he said, "*Wow*. Nice taste, kid." Moments passed without words, and the two men advanced several positions before a frustrated Summerlin turned to Connor and said, "What do I do?" The Con-Man patted his shoulder and replied, "Tsk tsk—You haven't even brought her up in days." Summerlin didn't seem to understand Connor's lack of enthusiasm. "Connor, she's *standing right there*," he responded. Connor sighed and said, "You can do what you want at this point, kid. I'd suggest giving thought to the broad, open universe that eludes the monogamous—but, hey, you're a big boy now, do what you wish." Summerlin smiled and enthusiastically replied, "Wow, is that Lesson Nine?" The Con-Man wagged his finger before saying, "No sir. You're not ready for Nine yet, but trust me, it will come."

Summerlin nodded and got out of the line. He walked up to where Sarah and her friends were standing, and addressed her from beyond the stanchions: "Hey—Sarah." She turned to face him, and almost for a moment seemed to be smiling. Summerlin didn't know what to think; from what he had last seen, he thought that she despised him. Sarah's mouth opened, but to her shock and Summerlin's horror, Gina turned to face him as well, and said, "What is your Billy Bob corn-pone ass doing here? Don't you know stalking's *illegal*?" Summerlin felt the blow, but remained cool; *I am not goin' to be broken by former decisions—what matters is what happens the next time*, he decided.

By this point, Olivia had turned to face Summerlin as well. "What's he still doing here?" she chimed in. Summerlin merely shook his head and said, "Sarah, if it'd be alright with you, I think we should talk." It became evident to him that his patience under fire was irritating Gina, whose face had become redder in the past few moments. Olivia simply crossed her arms and huffed. Sarah took a step away from her friends. Her eyes seemed softer, somehow happier than they had just two minutes prior. She began to speak, "Andrew! I had no idea I'd see you here," she made a gesture with her shoulder towards Gina and Olivia, and continued, "I was just coming to see *Old Hickory*—you know how I am with my love of historical films..." Actually, Summerlin did not; quite the contrary, in fact: Sarah never judged any of his hobbies that she didn't share with him save for one: Sarah *hated* history movies. She didn't even like movies that required her to remember what time period the film was set in to enjoy and understand it.

Comprehension hit Summerlin like a truck loaded with bricks— *She's saying that on purpose—what's she tryin' to let me know*? He wondered. "Uh, yeah—I know how you are...especially with movies about Andrew Jackson," Summerlin said, thought it was hard for him to say it with a straight face. "Andrew, I—" it sounded like Sarah was actually about to say something positive; however, Summerlin was not given the chance to find out: Gina stomped her way in front of Sarah and glared at Summerlin. She then said with her hands upon her hips, "Look, *hoss*, I think you left your tractor-trailer double-parked." Though he bought it with great internal frustration, Summerlin was maintaining an even-keeled sense of peace. Just then, Gina, Olivia, Summerlin and Sarah were all stopped wordlessly. Connor Bentley had walked outside the stanchion, and was standing next to Summerlin, with a defiant look in his eyes.

"Pardon me, but I don't think someone wearing last year's pumps should be allowed to even *criticize* the land of someone's upbringing. And besides, don't you two have a witchcraft convention to be attending or something?" Summerlin bit his lip to hide his laughter; Sarah followed suit—Gina and Olivia, however, were furious. "Look, *old man*, I think you're sticking your over-styled head in where it doesn't belong," Gina chided. Connor looked her up and down before giving her an eye-roll, adding, *"Please.* I was staying out while my friend was being bashed and the playing field was at least level—you two miscreants look like you don't even understand the concept of courtesy: you lambaste a man who is peaceful and polite over his homeland. Let me tell *you* something you insignificant child, if *your* homeland is a place where people aren't reared to be polite anymore, I'd rather be from *anywhere else."* The Con-Man had spoken; after that, he didn't seem to deign Sarah's two friends worthy of his attention. Connor gestured to Summerlin and mouthed the words, "Now's your chance, kid."

Gina and Olivia moved forward with the line. Sarah initially stayed back, and fought the forward progress of the line. "Look, Sarah," Summerlin began to say to her; however, Olivia stomped back to Sarah and grabbed her wrist. Sarah tugged her hand free and stepped a half-foot closer to Summerlin. She began to speak, "Who is your friend?" However, Gina had joined Olivia, and this time, she was smiling. "He's 'the Con-Man'—apparently a celebrity of local sorts. That don't matter right now, darlin' I want to—f" Summerlin had apparently at last crossed his boundary in Gina's eyes. She whispered something to Olivia, and then grabbed Sarah's wrist, with Olivia's help this time. "Andrew. Don't—" was all she had managed to say before her friends began to tug her wrist in the direction of the ticket counter. Gina grinned and finished Sarah's sentence for her—though, not in the manner that Summerlin, or Sarah, would have anticipated: "...come around anymore, psycho stalker."

Summerlin instantly regretted that both he and his mentor had passed out of the line. As Sarah's companions urged her to the counter, he realized that he couldn't follow and continue talking to her without facing the wrath of approximately thirty as-yet ticketless moviegoers. As Sarah was pulled through the dark doorway to the theatre screens, he could hear Olivia saying, "Girl, you gotta be more careful—you don't know guys like that like we do..." Summerlin's heart was enraged: he knew that every minute the two women who spited him had with Sarah would make his case for reconciliation all the more difficult. There was one good thing out of the scene: *I know I might not know this right for sure—but, it sounded almost like she still had feelin's for me. If it weren't for those evil disrespectin' creatures I would have at least been able to communicate with her and find out,* he realized.

Summerlin walked several feet from Trident Cinemas to lean against one of Texas Palace's many faux-brick pillars. The Con-Man lit a thick cigar and casually walked up to join him. He gave Summerlin a soft, lamentful look, like the one he often brandished when a bet didn't end up paying out the way he had planned. "She wanted to talk to me—I think," Summerlin began. "I know, kid, I could tell. At least you know that the ending of the conversation was through no failure on your part. You can be proud of that, really," Connor replied. The consolation might have been a like a soothing balm for someone like the Con-Man, but to Summerlin it was of little solace.

"Now what do I do?" Summerlin asked Connor in a voice which was slowly heading towards panic. "What do you mean, Summerlin? *You be you.* Remember to relax, and—" He didn't bother cutting Connor off—he simply turned his back and walked off. Two security officers who were standing nearby gave the Con-Man the evil eye. Connor shrugged and then went in search of his friend.

Summerlin's emotion filled stomp-off led him to the Arcade, which was next to Trident Cinemas. When Connor found him, he was half-way through the *Appalachia* course on the hunting game, *Super Buck Hunting Bonanza.* He didn't seem to be enjoying it—Summerlin was shooting away at simulated deer more out of catharsis than recreation. His aim never wavered, even when Connor walked up to his side and waved his hand in front of the videogame gun's scope. "Hey, Summerlin, it's not that bad," he said. Summerlin kept playing with an intense look on his face.

"I know setbacks can be painful. Trust me, I know," The Con-Man said told him. The game had ended—Summerlin placed the plastic rifle back in the cabinet's sling. "Setbacks?" he replied, "Her friends took her away right as we were making progress—*and*, I can be pretty sure they're goin' to spend the next movie-length increment of their lives pursuadin' my girlfriend to believe their *lies*!" Connor shook his head and leaned against the adjacent machine, doing what amounted to a compact version of his arm glide as he said, "Sarah's friends don't concern you. If she's everything you've told me she is, she'll begin to see the cracks in the veneer. You gotta give good people a chance to show they're good in life sometimes, kid." Summerlin sighed and slumped his shoulders. He responded in a tone which had transformed from angered frustration to stoic lament: "Don't you see my worry, though, Con? They're goin' to convince her to *hate me*." The Con-Man smiled reassuringly and replied, "I do see your point of view, but do you see mine? If she's the true-hearted girl you've told me about, you have no worries. Besides, we can't rush the situation and *do anything* anyway..." Summerlin lifted his then-lowered head and asked Connor with curiosity, "And why's that, Yankee?" Connor rose from his arm-glide lean and thrust a finger forward, gesturing like a professor. "That's simple," he began, "If you go all 'guns blazing' after her—even if it's to prove that you're correct— you'll only be giving Gina and Olivia all the ammo they'd ever need to paint you as some easily-angered Neanderthal redneck. Remember the lessons I taught you about perception? The only person that can change a given person's way of seeing things is *the person themselves*. So, it's all simply a matter of this: would you bet on the love you two shared?" Summerlin knew his answer immediately, and with such conviction that he didn't even feel the need to respond vocally. Summerlin nodded without a second thought. "We'll think of your options as prudent timing allows: always remember Lessons Three and Four. Situations need time, and everything will happen in the end as it should. I'm hungry, how about you?" the Con-Man asked. Summerlin nodded and said, "I'm so hungry my belly thinks my throat's been cut." "That one's so *country* that I don't even have a response. Intentional walk—*take your base*," Connor replied with a laugh as the two men headed out of the Arcade.

Connor took Summerlin to the buffet, where they had lunch. The Con-Man had a Caesar salad, pizza, Chow Mein and a side of roast beef, which he washed down with a glass of apple juice. Summerlin ate only breadsticks. The meal was spent mostly in silence, though Connor tried to initiate several conversations, such as the weather, *The Reason Why*, poker, and even *why southern states are good*. It was all to no avail; Summerlin was too busy brooding to talk to anyone, even the man who had inadvertently made it so he could afford to be consuming bread-sticks with soda.

After lunch, Connor led Summerlin to the valet shed. Zak waved to the Con-Man, who waved back and said, "Number five, please!" Melissa gave Connor a confused look, like she was double checking to make sure what she heard was—and could even be—possible. Connor nodded and said, "Yes. Five." Melissa skeptically grabbed a keychain from the pegboard inside the valet shed and slowly walked out into the valet lot, looking very confused. "What's with her?" Summerlin asked. Connor grinned and replied, "Oh nothing. Say kid—you ever been 'drop-topping'?" He shook his head no—*of course* he hadn't. He wasn't even sure he knew what it meant; *something to do with convertibles, I reckon*, he thought. Connor's grin had passed the line dividing playful and devilish. "Well, you're gonna today," he said as a loud engine roared to life in the distance.

It was *not* what Summerlin had been expecting. He soon found him-self and Connor sputtering along Las Vegas Boulevard in a solid black topless car which Summerlin assumed to be a mechanized "horseless carriage". "*Nobody* drop-tops like the Con-Man, kid—nobody," he said happily while maintaining control of the vehicle's *rudder*. "What in tarnation is this thing?" Summerlin inquired as they were stopped by a red light. There was a line of unhappy motorists who had been stranded behind the slow moving vehicle; several of the cars piled up in the passing lane, and were in turn blasted with the ancient auto's exhaust. "Hey, don't be disrespecting the Packard," the Con-Man replied.

The light turned green, and the car was once again surrounded with a symphony of irritated drivers honking their horns as they lurched slowly forward. "Don't worry about them," Connor said with a relaxed smile. Summerlin couldn't help but laugh; *This crazy gambler gets relaxed by making the irritated people angrier*, he thought. It was a comic display—he was sure that the Con-Man was merely being so zanily eccentric in an effort to cheer him up; but, it was actually the fact that he had a friend who cared enough to try that made him stop worrying and finally smile. "Hey Metropolitan," Summerlin said, "what does this thing take, *leaded* gasoline?" Connor replied in a tone befitting *the Queen's English*: "Yes. What exactly *is* malarkey, again?"

Connor took Summerlin downtown in the not-convertible-yet-still-roofless Packard. Once the ancient car had been stowed safely at the *Plaza* valet, he took Summerlin for a short walk, which deposited them at the doorstep of an old brick building with a green and white sign that read "Sergio's Place." There were tiny red and white barber poles painted on both sides of the name. The Con-Man entered, with Summerlin following a moment thereafter. A bell attached to the hinge of the door gave a light, silvery *ding* as the men entered.

The barber shop appeared to Summerlin to be a running joke of what barbershops from old TV shows in the 50's looked like, from the black and white checkerboard laminated floor to the tall barbacide-filled cylinders filled with combs and shears.

"Connor Bentley!" a tall, gray-haired proprietor who was sweeping up stray clumps of hair looked up and exclaimed. The Con-Man nodded and said, "Sergio, my man. This is a young man in need. We call him Summerlin." Sergio spoke before Summerlin had a chance to greet him: "Summerlin, welcome! You're a friend of Mr. Bentley, and that makes you a friend of mine. Come, sit down. How can I help you two today?" Summerlin sat in one of three brown vinyl swivel chairs that were placed beneath a wall-mounted ten inch TV that looked like it had once broadcast the Reagan Inauguration. Currently, the venerable television was showing a UNLV baseball game. Connor, however, did not sit.

"Well, Sergio, this one's not for me—we have a man here with us who is in desperate need of *smooth*." Summerlin's head twitched away from a double steal with two outs to retort, "Wait—*me*?" He had only taken a seat because there was a baseball game viewable from it; Summerlin had been assuming that the visit was for *Connor's* hair.

"Me?" He asked once more, staring the Con-Man in the eye. Summerlin then came to the realization that it had been at least two months since his last hair cut. He stood up and took a glance in the mirror. As he was inspecting his appearance, he heard Connor and Sergio shout out in unison, "*Yes!*"

Summerlin sat begrudgingly throughout the duration of the hair-cut, griping the entire time about how his hair had been good enough. Sergio simply laughed and kept on cutting. Connor had taken to lounging in the chair to Summerlin's right. He didn't say anything, he just watched the baseball game with a grin on his face.

After the two of them had exited Sergio's, Summerlin ran his fingers through his now-inch-shorter hair. "You look *fine*," Connor reassured him as they returned to the Plaza valet and boarded the Packard. As they rolled onto the street, Summerlin noticed that Connor had begun to show a more serious expression. He couldn't take it anymore—*I get that he doesn't like to let his emotions control who he is and all that, but if he keeps getting suddenly glum without reason like this, I'm goin' to scream,* Summerlin thought. Though, indeed, the Con-Man had retained his regular—for him, at least—behavior of constantly enjoying life, Summerlin had noticed a change in him: ever since the symphony at Akerman Hall, Connor had taken to sporadic moments of stoic, almost poetic sadness. When asked, his mentor always assured him that he had been mistaken. The only cure he had found that worked at all was to pretend he didn't notice and try to get Connor interested in something else. *It's funny how teachers can learn from students— heck, students can learn a thing or two about how teachers can benefit from students, I s'pose,* Summerlin thought.

Summerlin couldn't take it anymore, and finally asked: "Okay, Con-Man, I got a question." Connor gave him a glance after stopping at a red light. "Sure, kid," he replied. Summerlin looked out to the side of the road as he said, "What is it that seems to keep botherin' you? You routinely handle the most extreme cases of stress with no sweat—I've *seen it.* But lately, you keep havin' these little 'moments'. Don't lie to me and say it's nothin'. I can help you, too." The Con-Man pulled the Packard to the side of the road and put it into park.

"Okay, Summerlin, I really didn't want anyone to be bothered by—or get involved with—this..." He paused for a moment before continuing, "They're gonna take her down, kid." Summerlin's face could be found in the dictionary under the word *confusion.* He gestured with his head, giving an inquisitive nod in the hopes that the Con-Man would elaborate. "The Place. The Palace. *Texas,* for crying out loud."

Summerlin's jaw fell. "Why?" he asked immediately. Connor's eyes rolled and he replied, "Because apparently, Palace Casinos has made its choice: the company intends to eschew the glorious things of old in favor of an 'ultra-chic', 'vibe-driven' casino for trust fund babies near the Spaghetti Bowl." He watched in horror as the Con-Man continued, "They're gonna tear our heaven apart and sell the scrapped lot to Super Dollar World."

Suddenly, it all began to make sense to him—Summerlin remembered the group of businessmen he had seen near the side exit that one day. He remembered learning later that one of the men was Robert Ruckford, the guy in charge of the *Rancho Palace* movement. He also remembered that Lonnie the swing security supervisor had been there as well, standing next to a tall, tan-skinned man whom he was not familiar. There had been a wide-bodied man with a gaunt face wearing a black suit; but, he couldn't actually remember if the man had anything to do with the men who were talking. The only other unknown, for Summerlin, was the bald-headed man he had seen arguing with Mr. Ruckford over a week ago. He didn't know how the man figured in, but he was sure that he had something to do with the overall equation.

"Okay, Yankee, I know I'm running the risk of being told I am too inquisitive 'n' all—but I got one more question for you," Summerlin said. "Go ahead," the Con-Man replied with little sense of enthusiasm. "Do you know of any short bald men in suits that might not like what that Mr. Ruckford might have to say?" Summerlin asked with curiosity. Connor didn't respond—his head sunk low and he began to breathe extremely metered breaths. *He must really have hated what I just said. He only does the "count your breaths" thing when he loses at Blackjack past 2am*, Summerlin thought.

After several minutes of watching cars zoom past them, Summerlin finally broke the silence. "Con, look, it went like this: A while back I saw that Ruckford guy, you know the one involved with that Rancho Palace?" Connor didn't reply verbally; all Summerlin got was a nod. He continued, "It was him, the security supervisor you despise so much, and a tall, skinny guy with a goatee. There was another suit in the same general area but he never talked and was standing a foot away from everyone else." The Con-Man's eyes went panoramic—suddenly, he looked like he was beginning to not feel too well.

"When was that, kid?" Connor asked. Summerlin had to think for a second before replying, "About two weeks ago. It was a few days before that fancy shindig—and that was only a couple days before I saw Rob Ruckford yelling at that old man…" The Con-Man grimaced at his last two words. "Oh," Summerlin said after noticing, "I didn't mean it in a bad way. I mean I make fun of you for—" Connor put up a hand and gestured him to stop.

"It's not that, Summerlin. It is that the *old man* you describe as being Mr. Ruckford's verbal punching bag—was Cid Peterson. *My* mentor, kid. Or at least a guy who kept a transplanted twenty-two year old's Vegas dreams from destroying him. He's the General Manager of Texas Palace. He is also the man who unlocks the door to the executive conference room for me. *So that's what that was all about,* Summerlin thought. "And, furthermore," Connor continued, "if you were to go to the Super Dollar World on Rainbow and Cheyenne and asked for *their* GM, you'd be swiftly introduced to your tall man with a goatee. This is horrible. It means that they've had more time at it than I thought. When I saw the assistant clerk for the Clark County City Planning Department at the ACT, I had assumed his 'hot gossip' about the soon-coming fall of Texas Palace to be fresh news, not a work already well underway. Now that Palace Casinos has everybody excited about Rancho Palace, they'll be announcing the new shelf life of our favorite hangout any day now."

"So what does it all mean?" Summerlin asked. Connor started the car back up and put it into gear. "What it *means*, kid, is that we're gonna need to step up our game." He could only begin to wonder what the Con-Man's intentions of "stepping up their game" could mean or entail. Summerlin's mind didn't dwell on the old-time car's speed, nor did the long line of honking cars behind them tarry long in his thoughts. His mind was preoccupied with all of the information he had just been given.

Summerlin lowered his gaze and thought: *That GM from the megastore chain was with Ruckford when they were discussing future plans…that means that Super Dollar World was in on the discussion from before the soon-coming Rancho Palace had been announced; before Connor found out about Texas' impendin' destruction, even. And, I've noticed that nobody has a better ear to the ground of Sin City than him. If he says he heard the Palace is doomed, this could be bad.*

The Con-Man had reverted to wordlessness, but managed to maintain composure as he piloted the Packard's rudder while they turned onto Washburn Avenue. As the car passed Maryland Avenue, Connor's face had changed from sadness to determination. "Hey Con, I have to ask. You said something about 'stepping things up.' But, realistically speaking, what exactly can you or I—or *anyone*—hope to do about—" Connor cut him off: "Don't worry about it. Not for now, at any rate. I've got a few ideas. Speaking of which, I wonder if our friend Thomas is still at Texas; all of my recent concerns with the data gathering and all, I've neglected to check up on him."

Summerlin smiled as he realized two things: first, that he could actually be of use to the Con-Man. He knew that Thomas had only spent a few days at Texas Palace—He had personally been told so by Mr. West himself while working a late night at his downtown Laundromat branch. Secondly, Summerlin finally knew something that Connor did not. The fact that the news he had to offer was of the not-depressing variety only served to make the moment the sweeter. "Nope," he said to Connor, "I know about that, too." The Packard was once again pulled over to the side of a road; this time, it was at the intersection of Washburn and 15th Street. "How do you know where he is?" the Con-Man inquired. Summerlin grinned and replied, "Speed this thing above two miles per year and I'll tell you."

Connor's face mirrored that of Summerlin during his haircut at Sergio's Place as he pushed the century-old automobile as hard as it could go. Upon hearing the engine roar, Summerlin nodded and said with a grin, "I saw him when I was a bum. He was at the Laundromat me and Bli—this bum I met and I were at the Laundromat. He helped us earn some supper money. 'Lucky Bird' or somethin' like that."

"Lucky *Flamingo*," the Con-Man said in an crisp, defining tone. Summerlin replied, "That's the one. What about him, though? I know you said he had some cash, but I doubt a guy with a couple Laundromats could have enough money to help you do what I think you're doing." Connor stuck out his hand in the same manner he had while defending *Eclipse—Nobody* can stop the dauntless, kid!" He then took a deep breath and calmed down before continuing, "Besides, Tommy isn't just a laundry man; not anymore, anyway. He was always so ambitious, the most ambitious of all of us, actually. He had a plan for everything. Problem was—as we know—life didn't go the way the plans were written. However, his business acumen never actually faltered. His initial successes were used to buy new branches, which in turn raised capital for his business investments. Heck, I *believe* the Palace Casinos laundry is done on a service contract via his commercial center on Industrial Road. I don't doubt his *ability*, kid. I just worry that he may not have it all held together enough to be of use: I need him *rational*. But what you said's a good sign." Summerlin couldn't help but ask: "Why's that, pinstripe?" Connor cleared his throat and replied with a casual smile, "Because if he helped you and Bling-Bling—*yes*, I know who he is—then he might be approachable for my—heck, our—needs."

"Approachable for what? Are you goin' to ask him for a few *mil* on the side or somethin'?" Summerlin said. "Don't be crude," Connor replied, "I'm going to ask for his advice, connections, and any other help that the Texas World movement can avail itself of. He really is—in lucid moments, at least—very talented at what he does." "Do you really think anything could be done to save Texas?" Summerlin asked with a tone of worry. "Kid, I honestly wish I knew. And, what is more, you ask far too many questions," Connor replied.

The Con-Man was lost in deep thought as they turned right onto 16th Street. The moment that the car began to drive on the road, Summerlin noticed an immediate change in scenery. There were no more single and double leveled stores, nor was the block bathed in casino lights. In fact, there were no houses, buildings or trees: there was nothing here. Houseless plots of land sat next to one another divided only by chain-link fences. Summerlin felt it odd that there were no "FOR SALE" signs in any of the empty lots. The entirety of 16th Street from Washburn to Hoosier Avenue was a hodgepodge of lots in varying states of overgrowth and decay. Near the end of the block, there stood the only man-made structure on the block that wasn't made of chain-link.

The house at the corner was a faded gray wooden-paneled two story home that seemed somehow eerie—the faded, bluish gray paint was cracked to the point of being a pattern, and the patina-covered beams showed signs of oxidation Summerlin had only ever before seen in a junkyard car. In the absence of any other structures, the Victorian styled house seemed even more bizarre. *A house's shadow sure becomes noticeable when it's the only one around*, Summerlin thought.

A disheveled patchwork of shingles covered the canopy-style roof. The Packard slowed to a stop directly in front of the lone house. Summerlin got out after Connor and slowly followed him towards the front door. Once out of the car, he caught a better look at the place: it was a house built before World War I by Summerlin's estimation; he had only taken one class in architecture at Virginia Tech, and it was a class in modern works of architecture. A structure built before the birth of his grandparents seemed odd and surreal to his eyes—he had gotten used to living in the city where ten year old buildings are often deemed archaic, and backhoes never seem to be out of work.

There was an old-style porch with rusty chains dangling off the side-beam of the house, hinting at the former presence of a porch swing in times gone by. There were two windows on each floor. These portals were not the single-paned kind which Summerlin had become accustomed to seeing in all around town. The four street-facing windows on the ancient house were nine-paneled, old fashioned works—the kind of windows he hadn't seen on a building since Blacksburg. *Someone who was once an apprentice made those,* he noted as they neared the door.

Summerlin made an attempt to see through the house's windows, but was only able to discern that the windows all had their shades drawn. Connor had arrived at the door by the time Summerlin climbed the short wooden staircase to the porch. Floorboards older than Summerlin creaked beneath his booted feet as he joined the Con-Man who was knocking on the deep green front door.

"Not home," Connor said as he turned to Summerlin, who was still giving the fish-out-of-water house a dedicated once-over. "That's odd," the Con-Man said as he walked back to the car, "Tommy usually goes to do business stuff in the evenings—he was always the night owl, even in better times. He then reached the car and hopped in the driver's seat and revved the engine to life. Summerlin was halfway to the car, walking backwards while staring at the ramshackle house when he heard Connor yell, "Summerlin! It's just a house—You've seen them before. Let's roll."

The sun was dipping low into the mountains as Connor and Summerlin drove back to Texas Palace. They pulled under the canopy just as the hotel-casino's lights were coming on. The valet lane next to the Packard had a brown 80's model Chevy truck with a white stripe down its side. The license plate read "SYLS." Summerlin admired the truck—it was in excellent condition. he poked Connor and gestured toward the vehicle. Connor shrugged like it was an everyday affair to see such an older utility vehicle from decades ago in showroom condition. "Is it that I'm a country boy and you don't notice beautiful trucks?" he asked Connor. "No," the Con-Man replied while shaking his lowered head, "I know the owner."

14.

Later on that evening, Summerlin and Connor were in the Austin suite for Connor's ritualistic pre-T.R.Y. change of clothes when an unexpected knock came on the door. Summerlin had just exited the shower when he heard the first knock, and managed to hurriedly put on a gray silk shirt and khakis before he grabbed a pair of socks and his boots and ran to the great room.

Summerlin had hoped to find Connor on the landing answering the door. He did not. Summerlin arrived in the great room to find it—and the landing, empty. He tried to peer through the peephole, but its view was blocked. Summerlin began to feel the mild tingle of worry creep up his back. He decided that he would risk allowing the knocker to know that someone was inside the suite if there were a chance that the person behind the door might be amicable in nature. *The potential benefits outweigh the risks*, he decided.

"Xero? Trent? Jail-Bait? Is it one of you guys?" Summerlin worriedly asked. There was no response. Connor was managing his coiffure as he walked down to join him on the landing. "Who is it?" he asked Summerlin in a whisper. "I had hoped you'd know," he replied, equally as softly. Connor made a clueless shrug of his shoulders and whispered,

"I wasn't expecting anyone; it's Friday." The knocking came again—this time it was so loud as to cause the unmoving second door to the suite to rattle.

"What do we do?" Summerlin mouthed the words without any volume whatsoever. "We do what anyone normally does when a door is knocked upon: we answer it," Connor said, raising his voice as he finished his statement. He walked to the door and withdrew its deadbolt. After unlocking the door, the Con-Man gripped the door and swung it open before making a spry leap a few feet away from the doorway. It was a maneuver performed so quickly and with such skill that Summerlin was led to wonder—*was that instinct—or was it habit?*

Connor's little hop-away was proven to be warranted—two tall, broad-chested, muscular men in black suits came through the doorway. They didn't so much rush in with terrible speed as they *strolled* in with non-stop momentum. *He'd've been blindsided*, Summerlin realized. The two men both had pale, gaunt faces with heavy stubble. *Wait a minute—I know that face!* Summerlin thought—it was the wordless man in the suit standing a few feet away from the rest of the group who were discussing Texas's future. The other man was a little pudgier than the one Summerlin recognized; though, both men strongly resembled one another in terms of facial features.

Summerlin took a few cautious steps backward, being eyeing on what he deemed to be a potentially violent situation. The dark-suited men did *not* look happy. Connor did not retreat. He strolled in cavalier fashion to the angry duo until he was inches from the fatter of the two. "Good evening! My fine gentlemen, may I inquire as to the nature of our little get together here?" he inquired. It was bordering the impossible, but Summerlin believed the men looked even angrier than they previously had. "Mr. Bentley," the man Summerlin recognized began in a raspy baritone, "we represent certain concerned parties, and have come with a simple request." Connor grinned and said, "Well, your success will totally depend on what you're after." The man shook his head and began walking further onto the landing, his companion following not far behind. "Let it go. Leave Texas Palace to its fate. Our...'friends' are even willing to return the six hundred large you spent to have a lifelong ownership of the suite. Just drop your crap, Bentley, before things get *uncivilized*," he said. Summerlin saw the Con-Man go from his usual cucumber-cool to a teeth-grinding display of raw aggression in less than ten words.

"Ah! I was wondering where I recognized you—you're the *Calvert* brothers. I get it now," Connor said. Summerlin kept quiet and kept his eyes intentfully upon his friend; he was prepared to jump in at any needed moment. "You're awful smart, dumbass," the pudgier man said as he pulled out a switchblade and flipped it open. The rules had suddenly changed. Summerlin was no longer standing in the sidelines but walking, slowly at first, towards the Calvert brothers.

"So, are the *whatever brothers* bad at Poker, too?" Summerlin quipped as he stood to Connor's right side. "Actually," the Con-Man replied, "I have no clue, and we don't have time to find out, either. I know them from their *non-gaming* reputation." Summerlin looked to the Calverts and then back at the Con-Man; "Yeah, I know the thinner one from that group at the side exit I told you 'bout," he said. "Oh?" Connor replied as he and Summerlin began pacing slowly backwards to widen the ever-shrinking gap between them and the Calvert brothers. Their exchange was cut short—"Look, you keep denying us and those we represent the respect we deserve and Louie and I are gonna have to remind you how the real world works, Bentley," the skinnier, slightly taller man said as he too brandished a blade identical to his brother's.

"I know how the world works, Joseph Calvert. And, yes, I'm well aware of who you and the *'concerned parties'* you represent are. The world I know lets foolish hired muscle like yourselves do foul deeds to reputable people and institutions—but, in the end it will also always throw such worthless offal as you and your brother to a fate you truly deserve," Connor said, his eyes unflinching and his posture defiant. *I think it's safe to say the man doesn't get intimidated by knives,* Summerlin thought as he turned to keep an eye on Louie Calvert.

"Let's drop the crap, philosopher. You drop your crap, and you and your hick buddy here can live a scar-free life," Joe Calvert said. Louie remained quiet with his eyes and knife aimed at Summerlin. "We don't need any trouble, understand?" Summerlin said boldly while staring Louie Calvert in the eye. Connor looked at his protégé—he was standing with his fists clenched, and trembling like he was set to strike without a moment's hesitation.

The Con-Man gave Summerlin a dismissive head nod. He then walked closer to Joe and said, "Okay, okay. There's no need to be ruining the furniture. Tell your concerned parties that you can't keep me at knifepoint twenty-four seven. And, furthermore, you *really* shouldn't go threatening people's lives when you're on closed-circuit surveillance..." Connor pointed to two different ceiling corners as he finished speaking. Sure enough, there were two small cameras, both with red blinking lights indicating that they were functioning. *Do I really know a man who is involved in these kinds of things often enough as to necessitate having security footage? I can't believe I never noticed them before,* Summerlin thought as he glanced from the cameras back to the situation at hand.

Both of the Calverts looked up to see the cameras. Joe flipped his knife closed and made a gesture to his brother. "Let's go, Louie, I think he's heard our point," he said. Connor made a playful "bye-bye" wave as the Calvert brothers walked slowly but steadily to the landing, and then out the door. They left the Austin Suite doors ajar in their departure.

After a few moments of silence, Summerlin decided that he had waited long enough to ask: "Con—who were those guys?" The Con-Man replied, "They were the Calvert brothers, but I thought we already covered that." *Argh. Who does shtick at a time like this,* Summerlin thought. "I meant," Summerlin reiterated, "who are they *to you*?"

Connor straightened out a floor rug and then stood back up to address him: "Well, I didn't actually know at first that I'd ever meet them. I first heard of Joe and Louie Calvert in a little byline on the local paper; it was something about 'questionable business practices' being employed towards some of the mom and pop places that used to surround Texas Palace—the chained up lots you'll see on the other side of Reata..." Summerlin nodded and gestured for the Con-Man to go on. Connor plopped himself on the couch near the big screen and continued, "The Calverts ended up becoming more important to Palace Casinos when Cy Lancaster married their sister, Margaret."

"Wait—Who's Cy Lancaster? I don't think I've heard of him, but that last name seems familiar," Summerlin said. "It should, kid," Connor replied, "Tyler Lancaster founded the Palace Casinos empire when he opened Vegas Palace back in 1984. *His sons*, Cy and Dominic, are set to inherit the reigns now that he is beginning to take more time off to enjoy his golden years with his wife, Nancy. Dominic oversaw the original purchase of the Texasland Casino back in '89—he was the man who made my mentor who he was; Cid" Summerlin was confused; "I don't get it, Con-Man, why would an in-law of Dominic be involved in stoppin' you from helpin' Texas stay alive?" Connor shook his head and replied, "Well, kid, that's where it gets messy and becomes believable..."

Summerlin joined the Con-Man on the couch. "The Calverts aren't Lancasters—and that's the problem. Old Tyler Lancaster is a good man; however, his intent to leave control of the company to whichever son served the bottom line best, has had unforeseen consequences," Connor said. Summerlin waited a moment before asking, "Like what, exactly?" "Well," he began, "It caused Cy and Dominic to not get along. The competition had always favored Dominic; afterall, Henderson Palace and Texas Palace make way more of a combined gross than Vegas Palace and Silver Palace do, any day of the week. The problem arose when Cy Lancaster decided he didn't want to lose. His brothers in law, while not having to answer to Tyler, were more than willing to answer to him, so long as the price was right. So they go from two-bit thugs hustling center-city dwellers to the right hand men of a man with a plan—a plan that he seemingly hopes to use to promote his new protégé, Robert Ruckford, to the GM of the property that will shut down half of Dominic's profits. Two birds with one stone, I guess."

"Okay, I get the sibling rivalry and all that—but where exactly do the Calverts come in on the Texas side of things?" Summerlin inquired. "Oh, that. Well, that part's simple, actually. The word on the real estate gossip line is that the Calvert family had their eyes on the property location way back when Harry Stevens, the original owner of the Texasland Casino before Palace Casinos, bought it. The Calverts have a share of ownership in—guess what—Super Dollar World. Joe and Louie had all along been pursuing their now-passed father's prerogative: to control, one way or another, the center-city, Spaghetti-Bowl area of town. When the Lancaster family bought Texasland and converted it to Texas Palace, the Calverts had to stick to harassing the mom and pops. Fast forward two decades and you see the Calvert brothers *somehow* become in-laws to the Lancaster family. And, when one of the brothers decided that he was willing to pursue less-than-ethical methods to achieve their father's legacy..." Summerlin gulped before nodding. He said, "You get a pair of vengeful Calvert brothers ever willin' to help him...and Super Dollar World?" Connor folded his hands together; he replied without looking up: "Super Dollar World was only barely out-bid by the Lancasters—they simply want to get the lot so they can open a Spaghetti-Bowl area location. It wouldn't surprise me to discover that they have intent to clear Texas's lot as soon as they can, though. A buzz going around town is that the Calvert brothers have each been 'mysteriously' given a minor stake in the new Rancho monstrosity for their help. I must admit, I've been talking to high-ups in the civil planning department, but I never thought that those two would actually show up at my doorstep. They must have been watching me and decided that my wanting to save Texas would prove a threat. Tyler Lancaster is being tricked by his own son into thinking they're simply selling a failing edifice to make money to buy a more profitable casino locale. He doesn't realize that Dominic's 'poor performance' as of late has actually been due to various Cy and Calvert-related treachery. I've even heard rumors that the club manager, Drew Moroni, was on their take. Wouldn't surprise me any."

Summerlin tried to take it all in. He tried to figure out why such persons at corporate level would even concern themselves with Connor Bentley. Yes, it was obvious that if Texas's future were threatened, the Con-Man *would* be a person one could expect to protest the closing— or even, as indeed he was doing, to try and find any way he could to keep the Palace operational. But, what he couldn't fathom was why Cy Lancaster would have it in for his teacher and friend; *I love his never-give-up spirit, but even I know that places like this cost more than even a small millionaire can afford*, Summerlin thought. "The scary thing, Con," he said, "is that if what you say is true, those guys who visited us tonight have two reasons to hate Texas." "And, therefore, two reasons to hate my guts," Connor said. Summerlin stood and walked over toward the bar. After pulling a beer from the fridge he said, "Before you showed them your closed-circuit cameras and scared them off, that Joe Calvert said somethin' about you needin' to 'stop your crap.' What exactly have you been doin'?" Summerlin asked.

Connor rose and joined him at the bar, mixing himself an Old Fashioned as he said, "First off, those cameras aren't real—they're cheap replicas from a truck stop. Look real, don't they? But sadly, I'm sure they'll have surveillance called and be informed the truth, so that's a trick that won't work a second time. And to answer to your question: What have I been doing? I've been looking around, as I said—I'm trying to form a strategy. I only hope that if the money can somehow be levied, Tyler Lancaster could be approached by Dominic and someone extremely versed in Texas Palace and common sense, perhaps he could be convinced to see reason and let Texas survive, or be bought out by someone with the intent on renewing the gaming license. This place doesn't just belong to Lancasters, Calverts or shareholders: Texas belongs to us—the customers and our neighborhood. There's been a

Lone Star and an Old Glory flying over the top of the buffet's exterior dome for over twenty-five years," Connor said.

"Wait a second—You're going to *purposefully* keep doin' what those large thugs told you *not* to do?" Summerlin asked. The Con-Man gave a short laugh before replying, "Well, kid, you can't go through your life doing everything everyone tells you to do; especially if a knife's involved. Besides, I might actually succeed here. Thomas being on one of his 'sadness trips' hurts things a little, but I've still got another trick or two up my sleeve." He then walked to the still-cracked door. "Where are you going?" Summerlin inquired as he put his beer down and joined Connor on the landing. The Con-Man turned and replied with a grin, "Kid, it's Friday evening at Texas Palace. Do I really need to give you another clever usage of the band's name?"

"We're still goin'?" he asked Connor. "Of course we are," the Con-Man replied as he walked out into the hallway. Summerlin didn't bother asking any further questions—he was still digesting everything he had learned. He followed Connor wordlessly to the Rail Yard. The usual long line of regulars awaited them at the entrance.

They, of course, didn't wait. When Connor and Summerlin arrived in the backstage room, they found The Reason Why together in a circle near the two couches, and looking somewhat dejected. The sight seemed unnatural; something was wrong. "Hey gang," Connor said as he approached the band's huddle. *Somethin' don't seem right—even Xero looks sad 'n' serious*, Summerlin thought as he approached the group. He waved to the cluster as he sat down on the vinyl couch near the huddle.

Connor stood within the huddle and, within moments, assumed the same somber expression that was shared by the rest of the group. *What's goin' on? Did somebody die?* Summerlin wondered. After a few minutes of soft, near-whispered conversation, Connor waved for Summerlin to come over and join them. He got up from the couch and apprehensively walked over to the group. Everyone said "hi," after being greeted by Summerlin's customary "howdy". The band seemed perhaps a bit too melancholy for *howdy.*

"Bad news?" Summerlin asked while looking to Connor and Jail-Bait who stood in the center of the informal huddle. "You could say that again, a thousand times," Blake replied. Seeing these individuals who were usually so cheerful turn sorrowful deeply troubled Summerlin. *What could be that bad?* He wondered but dared not ask. "Don't feel bad, Summerlin. It isn't you," Jail-Bait said. "What's the matter guys, has someone passed away?" he asked. "Someone may as well have," Xero replied as he sat down in a chair near the wall, still holding his bass. He then began to play an unplugged riff from Chopin's *Funeral March.*

"It's the band, man," Blake began, "You know the audition we're scheduled for with Altered Note Records next week?" Summerlin nodded and replied, "Yeah." Blake shook his head and said, "I wouldn't bother saving the date." Summerlin responded immediately in shock, "What? Why?" Blake didn't get the chance to answer his question—Xero cut in. "Because of that rat bastard Moroni, *that's why!*" he said as he rose from his seat angrily and stomped off towards the stage with his guitar. "We still have a show, you know!" Jones called out to him as he left the room.

"Hey, kid," Jail-Bait said while looking at Summerlin. He had gotten used to hearing the Con-Man calling him that—hearing the sobriquet from a voice that was not Connor's took Summerlin by surprise. It took an extra moment for him to realize that Jail-Bait was in fact speaking to him. "Yes?" he responded with a mildly confused expression. "It's gonna be okay," she replied as she patted his shoulder, "It just sucks. Moroni, in the guise of 'cross-property promotional event,' has scheduled The Reason Why for a performance clear across the valley at Henderson Palace *at 7:15 on Friday.*"

"Wait, doesn't that mean he's breakin' the contract he likes to flaunt so often?" Summerlin inquired, trying to be helpful. "Well, ordinarily, yes," said Samantha, who had until then remained silent. She shook her head and continued, "The problem is that Drew Moroni owns the night-club at Henderson Palace, too. He's even scheduled the show at a different time than our regular one so it looks like he didn't double-book us." Blake sighed and added, "And we all know there isn't a snowball's chance in the Mojave of us getting an hour long set done and still driving across the valley to Texas Palace before 9pm." Summerlin couldn't believe it. "Why would he do a thing like that? Is it because you didn't play *Your Cheatin' Heart*? I mean, forgive me, I like that song, too—but isn't he bein' a little bit harsh?" he said.

"No, it's more an issue of our band doing too well for Mr. Moroni; he's grown spoiled," Xero replied as he re-entered the room. He appeared calmer—still angry, but he seemed to be more in control now. Connor walked over to Xero and said, "The problem is, Spikey, the band seems to be doing too well for the liking of Palace Casinos—they are threatened that if you guys get a recording contract, they might lose their club-filling act. And, I'm pretty sure that my irritating Cy Lancaster and his buddy Drew isn't helping things."

Blake spoke immediately after the Con-Man: "He's right. We pack the house, every Friday, and Moroni knows that. That's why he gave in and let us invite fans in to watch our Thursday rehearsals. However, it appears that same popularity will be the reason they won't even let us have an audition without a fight."

"Relax," Jail-Bait said, "he can't keep us locked in forever—" Xero cut her off. "Our audition with the record company won't last forever." Jones let out a sigh and resumed speaking to Summerlin, "Mr. Moroni wants to keep our leash short. I don't know if we're going to be able to get out of this. Blake and I've checked the contract—the only provisions we could even find didn't help us much. There's a provision barring our group from being forced to play at non-Palace Casino venues...not much else." Blake nodded and added, "There was a thought that we'd petition for a half-hour to forty-five minute show; *but*, the contract states that we have to do a full performance. The darned document defines a 'performance' as being a 'musically and tonally pleasing session of auditory entertainment to be considered as full and done when the audience has been satisfied.' The problem is, that's goin' to be a Henderson crowd, mostly—and I'm willin' to bet that there's no chance of convincing people *pre-show* to devalue their tickets." Summerlin sighed; Connor and Trent did likewise.

"So, what are you guys gonna do?" Connor asked. Jail-Bait responded, "What else *can* we do? We're going to play out our contract. For the legality, yes—but for our fans and regulars, too. They don't deserve to suffer by being caught in the middle of all this." Blake walked over to his guitar case and picked it up. "She's right. We can't let Drew Moroni's cruelty turn us into angry, negative people." Samantha walked over to her drumsticks, which were sitting next to Jail-Bait's sheet music pile, and picked them up. She twirled a stick in her left hand and added, "It does suck though. Hard core. But the audience won't ever know—I suggest we rock the joint, *for* the fans, whatever may happen." Jones checked her watch and said, "Okay guys, it's 8:50. We still have a show to put on, let's do it right." As they gathered their things and headed out toward the stage, Summerlin could hear Trent say, "Sam and Jail-Bait are right guys, let's make it one to remember!"

After the band had departed, Summerlin and Connor went to their VIP table. The Friday night set remained essentially the same as the show a week before, save for a few minor changes in song order, and some severe ad-libbing on Trent and Xero's part. Xero didn't perform his hacky-sack routine this show. Instead, Trent wowed the crowd by juggling five hacky-sacks at once for four minutes straight as the band played *Flight of the Bumblebee.* Everyone in the crowd applauded loudly and Summerlin and Connor even heard a few people talking about 'a nice change of pace'—but they knew the real reason for the temporary switch: *Xero was too angry to concentrate.*

The show went well; the crowd never seemed to notice any sign or show of negativity on the band's behalf. It was a regular standing-room-only Friday night performance. That is, until the end of it. Rather than follow the end of the set with their cover of Elton John's *Tiny Dancer*—as was the norm—the band instead remained silent. The stage lights went out, save for one shining upon the currently-unmanned center stage microphone.

Jail-Bait approached the microphone and tapped it a few times in an attempt to get the attention of the now-murmuring crowd. She was wearing a full length evening gown with a Hawaiian floral print one-piece swimsuit underneath it. Once a hush had fallen over those seated within the Rail Yard, Jones began to address the crowd: "Hey guys. How are you doing out there tonight?" The audience erupted into a series of boisterous cheers. Jail-Bait continued with an enthusiastic smile, "Good. Good—we like to hear that. Now we love playing music for you guys, but we here of The Reason Why need to get a little serious here for a moment..." The crowd's roaring died down, but did not diminish entirely. "You see, the thing is," Jones continued as she grabbed the microphone from the stand and began to pace the rim of the stage while addressing the audience. " When we close our show and say 'we love you,' we aren't kidding—we never have nor never will take the people who help us *survive* jokingly. If there's no you, there is no *us*. But we also feel the need to be honest with you—" The audience stirred restlessly at her words. "No," Jail-Bait continued, "No, don't worry—it wasn't a lie from us. But, it is a lie that concerns you guys as much as it concerns us, really. It goes like this, my friends: We love sharing our music with others. *But* the ownership of this very nightclub is not a fan of losing money—so, instead of us doing our weekly thing here next week, they have scheduled us to play at Henderson Palace. We had no say. So, instead of giving you guys some fun, and instead of playing for a live audition with *Altered Note Records*, we will be playing at The Island Room at Henderson Palace, while Mr. Moroni schedules someone as a 'backup' should we miss our nine o' clock show here—and trust me, he made it so we won't be able to help missing it if we want to avoid prosecution for breach of contract..."

Boos and catcalls filled the theatre-nightclub to the brim. Jail-Bait hopped down to the floor from the stage and raise her hands overhead towards the crowd. She then said, "Listen guys, because we're going to need your help now more than ever. We need you all to share your voices. We need you to let the powers that be know that we *shall not be kept down*!" The other band members joined her at the foot of the stage—during Jones's speaking, they had gone behind the curtain and all changed into Texas World t-shirts.

Thunderous cheers erupted. Many rose from their seats—some of which were also wearing orange Texas World t-shirts—to applaud Jail-Bait and the band. The Brides of Xero raised large poster-board signs overhead. Summerlin noticed two: one reading "WE ARE THE REASON NOW!" and "NO XERO NO PEACE." The band went on to play *Don't Mess With Texas*. The song, intended or not, was converted to a sing-along, as the crowd was fervently reciting every word. Near the end of the tune, Blake yelled out, "Now give 'em your Texas salute!" The entire audience was standing by this time—They all turned toward the exit doors to face the security officers posted there, and raised their middle fingers high overhead.

The band then went on to play their usual ending song, but this time as an encore to which the crowd of fans cheered, but did not turn to see. After the encore, the band took their bows and walked off stage. The audience was still wild. Summerlin got up in anticipation of following his friend backstage; however, that wasn't what happened. The Con-Man got up from the table and climbed onto the stage. A few of the cheering patrons turned and noticed that Connor Bentley had taken the stage, and the word spread; within moments, they began to chant "Con-Man" over and over, getting louder with each repetition. Summerlin watched nervously from the VIP table. *Okay, now what's that crazy Yankee up to?* he wondered.

Connor grabbed the microphone and said, "Okay guys I can't stay here—yes, thank you. I love you too. At any rate, I just want to let you true believers know that I stand for Cid Peterson, and I stand for the noble Lancaster family name. They gave us Texas, our *home*. And, what is more, there are efforts out there to besmirch the legacy of Tyler and

Dominic Lancaster. So, if you could please, in the loudest, most repetitive manner possible, let *every ear in the zip code hear your dismay.* Can I get a Texas World?" The crowd began to repetitively chant "Texas World." The two security officers near the entrance were already on their way down the aisles to depose the Con-Man; several fans had slowed their progress. "Thank you!" Connor shouted with a showman's smile as he replaced the microphone and ran towards the backstage corridor. Summerlin rose meekly and then darted after him.

Summerlin and Connor rushed to the communal backstage room. The band was clustered again, but this time Trent, Blake and Samantha were sitting on the floral print couch while Jail-Bait and Blake sat on the floor. They were spirited, perhaps a little stirred-up from the chanting of the crowd—which was still going quite loudly. Indeed, the chants of "Texas World" could still be made out from inside the room.

Connor spoke as he approached them: "Hey guys. Killer set, really got the crowd's energy up." Samantha was spinning a drumstick in her hand as she replied, "Yeah. Maybe a bit too much." Xero playfully nudged her shoulder and added, "There's no such thing as too much crowd excitement. 'Sides, the establishment is mad at us, not the fans. They're paying customers, even Moroni knows not to bite the hand that feeds; they'll be fine."

Summerlin couldn't believe how alive the room felt. The band members were all abuzz, splitting into two distinct mini-groups. Xero, Samantha and Trent were discussing how thankful they were for the support of their fans; Jail-Bait, Summerlin, Blake, and Connor were still near the floral couch and were talking about Henderson Palace. Ten minutes had passed, and everyone could still hear the persisting, undying chants from within the Rail Yard.

After a few minutes of backstage conversation, Connor and Trent left the room. It wasn't until ten minutes of Summerlin sitting alone on the vinyl couch that the two men returned. Connor came in lugging a cardboard box filled with orange t-shirts. He doled them out, giving each band member a shirt. Summerlin expected Connor to hand him one; he did not. "Hey, bullseye," Trent said from the corner of the room where he and Xero were standing. Summerlin looked over and got up to join them. Xero was smoking his customary contraband; Trent held out a rolled-up t-shirt to Summerlin. He took it and unrolled it: It was a Texas World shirt, like the countless ones he had seen around the Palace. This one was different, however. It had, in bold oversized letters, the phrase "YOU CAN'T KILL TEXAS." Above the Texas World logo on the front was, in small blue cursive, the words "Summerlin, Igno For Life." He looked down at the shirt and smiled before returning his eyes to Trent, who was smiling with an apprehensive look in his eyes. "The Con-Man and I decided that if they want to make it personal, so shall we. You in?" There wasn't a shadow of doubt in Summerlin's mind. He took off his ash-gray sports jacket and put the shirt on without a second thought.

Within two minutes, everyone in the room was wearing the new, personalized versions of the shirts. Connor patted Summerlin's back and smiled like a parent being proud of his progeny completing a rite of passage. Summerlin then laughed as he noticed the blue cursive on Connor's shirt: "Con-Man, Future King." Summerlin shook his head and smiled as he said, "You know, Con—you are without a doubt one of the oddest people I've ever met in my entire life." Connor checked his hair and hems in a mirror on the wall as he replied, "I get that—a lot, actually. And, as always, I shall take it not only as a compliment— but as a major one." Summerlin smiled—*You have to admire his resiliency*, he thought. "I admire your positivity. Perhaps you could spread it to our beloved *The Reason Why*," Summerlin said. Connor sighed before responding, "Sadly, I believe that they will have to play this thing through on their own. Trust me, kid, we *all* have problems: you, me,

Xero; heck—even Texas itself." It was then that the rest of the room came to an immediate, unexpected quiet. *Uh oh,* Summerlin realized, *They didn't even know…*

All eyes turned to the Con-Man, whose eyes instantly lowered in regret; he had obviously not intended to put another set of troubles upon the band's already heavy plate. He took a few slow breaths before looking up and addressing the room full of concerned ears, "That's right, guys. Sorry you had to hear it this way, but they're gonna close Texas Palace. I heard through the grapevine that the company intends on making it public this week sometime. The group looked more horrified than when they were speaking of their potentially-doomed audition. Xero lowered his head into his hands, saying, "I thought we were rallying against Moroni—now it's the entire company trying to end the only home I've ever known."

Samantha stood and turned to face Xero. "Wait, we still have a contract with Mr. Moroni, and he owns both of the nightclubs…That means this 'cross-promotion crap—We're going to have to actually *play* at that Henderson dump?" she said with a small grin. "I think we all have bigger problems than that, Sam," Blake said. Connor looked apologetically upon the faces of the band and said, "For what it's worth, I'm sorry: I had no say nor choice in the matter. I *am,* however, not completely helpless. I have a few ideas." *Ideas—to save a casino?* Summerlin thought before looking to the Con-Man. "Love the optimism, Con, but even *you* don't have casino-buying kind of money. Connor winked and replied, "Nothing's impossible."

Summerlin and the Con-Man hung out with the band members in the backstage area for a while, but did not adjourn to the Austin Suite as they had the week before. Trent had a girlfriend wanting to go out on the town. Blake needed to go home because Samantha needed to, and couldn't reach Danny for a ride. Xero had a shift, and Jail-Bait left with the intention of further studying the band's contract with Drew Moroni.

When the room had cleared, Summerlin addressed Connor: "Hey, if we're not hangin' out with the guys, where are we goin'?" Connor picked a few pieces of lint off of his trousers as he replied, "Well, kid, *I* am going to go kick plans up a notch. *You* are going to do whatever it may be that you would wish to do past eleven at night on a Friday." Summerlin had not expected such a response. *What does he mean? What could he possibly get done this late?* he wondered.

"Really? You're ditchin' me?" Summerlin said. The Con-Man pulled out a comb and began fixing his hair, adding, "Yep. You're fun, kid, but there's work to be done, and it's best that I do some parts alone. It's futile work, I'm relatively certain, but I've always considered myself a person who follows everything through. No bravery, no victory, I always say." And he was off.

Summerlin could still hear distinct isolated groups of patrons and former audience members cheering "Texas World" as he crossed the Pit—much to the security staff's dismay. The elevator lobby was empty, and the Oil Derrick elevator opened its doors the instant that he pressed the button. Summerlin's brow's raised when his elevator began its ascent; he noticed an orange metal sign that looked to be cemented upon the now-closed doors. It read: "SAVE TEXAS."

15.

"Kid! Kid! Wake up!" Summerlin woke to the sound of Connor's raised voice. He rose to find the Con-Man scurrying around the suite in a half-dressed state of panic. Summerlin quickly pulled on a pair of jeans and joined Connor on the landing. "What on Earth is going on?" he asked while bracing his eyes from the light pouring in through the great room windows. "No time! No time! Come on kid, we gotta go!" he replied. Summerlin had never seen Connor in such a state of anxiety; What could possibly make Connor Bentley wake up early and rush out of his suite not fully dressed? The man would take ten minutes to adjust his hat, not to mention every other detail, Summerlin thought as he followed Connor out the door and down the hallway towards the elevators. Connor pulled out his cell phone and pressed a few buttons before placing the phone up to his ear. "Yeah. On our way now—is he still inside?" he said while Summerlin pressed the "down" button. When they got inside the elevator, Summerlin reached to touch the Lobby/ Casino button when Connor interjected, "Wait Summerlin, stop at floor fifteen." He pressed the button for floor fifteen, and the elevator soon gave off an overhead "ding" and opened its doors.

The two got out, with Connor briskly leading the way. There was a large group of people, several of them security officers, filling the half-way point of the hallway to capacity. Connor's face became wild-eyed, and he ran to the group, yelling, "Cid! Cid!" as he did so. Summerlin walked at a quickened pace, and as he approached the scene, he got a better picture of what was occurring: Lonnie and Allison were standing next to the older man Summerlin had come to know as Cid Peterson, and they had three uniformed security officers with them. Connor pushed one of them, the older bicycle officer Summerlin had remembered asking what time it was in front of the Rail Yard, to make his way through to Cid.

"Cid? What's going on here? What are they doing, man?" Connor asked. The nearly-bald man looked up at the Con-Man and replied, "They woke me up. I've been tol—" Allison, assistant supervisor of security, cut him off: "Mr. Peterson has been notified of the termination of his contract; he has also been given the warning that he is to gather his possessions and leave the property, whereupon he is to be formally barred from entering all Palace Casino Properties." She was positively beaming. *Wait a second—why does he live under the suite level, and why are they—*Summerlin's train of thought changed instantly as he realized what was happening: *It's like Connor said last night: they're taking away anyone who would fight for Texas.*

The Con-Man got within inches of Lonnie's face. His eyes were wild with resentment, and for the first time ever, Summerlin saw his friend show actual rage. "He might not live on the suite level like me, but that's because the man never wanted anything more than a clean Queen bed and a view of our paradise. How *dare* you do this—and how dare you follow it through in such a pedestrian manner. Peterson hired you two suit wearing badge-bearers, you know," he said while leering directly toward Lonnie. "Unfortunately, sharp tongue or no, your words have little bearing here," Lonnie replied, "And though I cannot stop you from helping him out, I will have you removed from property if you attempt to impede." Mr. Peterson exited the room—number 1526—carrying a briefcase in his hand and a faded khaki raincoat over his shoulder. He walked over to Connor and said, "It's best just to humor them, Bentley my boy, they'll only get less dignified if we rebel." The Con-Man sighed and took Cid's briefcase in his hand. Summerlin followed the cluster of people as they went to the elevators. It took two elevators to accommodate everyone involved.

Connor insisted on sharing the elevator that held Cid Peterson, Allison and Lonnie; Summerlin road the Sam Houston elevator down with three security officers who eyed him suspiciously the whole time. "Yeah, that's right," he said as he noticed them staring at his Texas World shirt.

The elevators reached the lobby at the same time. The doors opened to reveal Mr. Robert Ruckford standing with a grin and his arms crossed several feet in front of the elevators. He had a Vegas Palace security officer standing at his side. The uniform was identical to the Texas officers, but was gray with gold trim. "How did I know I'd find you here," Connor said with disgust upon noticing his presence. "I could say the same about you," Ruckford replied. Cid Peterson looked up at Mr. Ruckford and then sighed before shaking his head and slowly walking forward.

"Don't you think this is a little bit of over-kill? I mean he's one man, and he doesn't exactly look dangerous enough to necessitate a GM, two supervisors and four armed officers escorting him out?" Summerlin said in a polite and earnest manner. Ruckford replied, "They aren't here for him. Me and Ms. Schwartz could have done that: the extras are for you two. We somehow knew you'd come." Connor walked forward from where Cid was walking and grinned. "You should know. After all, it was one of your security detail that warned me ahead of time—how's *that* feel, beluga?" The Con-Man once again had his usual effect on Allison

Schwartz: she clenched her fists and her skin began to grow bright red; she kept walking, however.

Lonnie and Allison lead Mr. Peterson to the employee parking lot, which sat on the back end of the property near the east side valet. The procession came to a halt upon reaching an old red Coupe De Ville. Cid opened his trunk and threw his jacket inside. "I would at this point like to thank you—*yes*, I am actually thanking you two—for the years of dedicated service you have given to our company. For the many times you have acted with upright, hardworking honesty. Current dishonor and turnabout aside: I hired both of you because you were both good people. Thank you." Allison scoffed and turned her face away from him; Lonnie, on the other hand, must not have seen Mr. Peterson's honesty coming—his eyes seemed misty, though it was hard for Summerlin to tell beneath the blistering desert sun.

"Mr. Peterson," Mr. Ruckford began to read from a folded sheet of paper he pulled from his smoke-gray sports jacket, "You are being hereby notified that in addition to your termination and severance, you are henceforth barred in all legal terms from returning to any Palace Stations property, this of course includes, but is not limited to locales in Las Vegas, Reno—" Connor had had about all he could take. He walked over to face Mr. Ruckford and waved his hands in front of the paper he was reading and said loudly, "You cannot be doing this to him—he's a *Vegas icon*, for goodness sakes! He made this place fun, you worthless yuppie trust-fund degenerate!" Robert Ruckford shook his head mildly and replied, "Tsk tsk. Sticks and stones, Mr. Bentley. And don't think we won't be charging you for the removal of all those Texas World placards you installed. Connor laughed. "Ha ha. I didn't put them up, and your own surveillance will prove it. Actually, it's supposed to be Cid's surveillance. Don't you have better things to do over at Vegas Palace, or perhaps down at your Rancho hipster complex? You could have let him retire with the Palace. Forgive me saying, but I honestly believe that you are incapable of even the basest level of human dignity. You are the prodigy of a *lesser Lancaster*. And if your boss's father and brother only knew how you were conducting business they'd—" Ruckford raised his hand and said, "Now that's just about all I'm willing to take from a man with no degree and no permanent address save for a hotel. Might I remind you that your deal with the company concerning your 'permanent suite' is to be dissolved with the impending closing of this property. I would take your out-of-town friend and leave peacefully and quietly, lest I as new interim GM for the closing of Texas Palace decide to end it sooner." Connor slowly stepped back to where Cid and Summerlin were standing, muttering, "*scum*," as he did.

When the Con-Man returned, Summerlin asked him, "What in blazes is goin' on here, Con?" Connor took a glance towards Mr. Ruckford, who had resumed reading his legal decree and said, "It's Cid. They gave him the axe, and didn't even let him sleep in to find out about it. Tyler Lancaster himself hired him upon purchasing *The Texaland Gamblin' Hall*—and Dominic was always smart enough to let him do his thing. Of course, he doesn't have much say recently...His brother's sick maneuvers have charmed the company into believing his 'direction' will be more profitable. If Tyler weren't nearly ninety and half-blinded by age, he would have figured the lot out and be firing and ejecting *Ruckford*. Cid's a guest's best friend, and a local legend." Allison said, "He *was*," under her breath before giggling. Several of the security officers surrounding the car thought it was funny, as well.

Connor turned her way and rebuked, "I don't know what you're so happy about, Schwartz. It's not like the death of Texas will be benefitting you. You may be enforcing the will and wishes of Cy Lancaster and Rob Ruckford, but that *doesn't* make you important to them—they're having the most important man on property kicked off, remember? All this means for you, my dear morbidly obese assistant supervisor, is that you'll be making yourself feel important from the tacky confines of Henderson Palace by mid-summer." Allison hissed with bared teeth.

"That will do, gentlemen. You may watch Mr. Peterson depart, if you wish; but, from over near the casino where we can keep you on camera," Lonnie said while standing next to Rob Ruckford with a proud smile. Summerlin began to walk to the casino, but stopped and turned around when he realized that Connor wasn't following him. The Con-Man hadn't budged an inch, in fact. He was standing near the trunk of the car with his eyes hatefully locked upon Ruckford. Cid patted him on the back and said, "Look, kid: they got me. It's alright, I'll get a severance, and I'm old, so there's always social security to look forward to. Well, that and senior appreciation night at the Class ACT..." Connor turned to face him; Summerlin could tell from several feet away that the Con-Man was indeed on the verge of tears. He stood there facing Cid Peterson, beginning to tremble. For once, Connor Bentley was at a loss for words.

"It'll be alright, Connor my boy. I'll be fine," Cid said. Summerlin could see that there was a strong bond between the two men—it almost seemed like a wronged father was comforting his son. Connor's face was pale, and he had yet to speak when Cid said, "You just take care of the Palace. Keep her from being ruined, even if it's just until they tear her down—we owe that much to the area. You'll rise, kid. You ought to know that by now!" The two men hugged before Mr. Peterson got in his car. Connor slowly walked to join Summerlin, and they regrouped on the sidewalk near the fenced-off pool area.

As Cid's car was driving off property, he briefly pulled to a stop near the two men and rolled down his window. Summerlin couldn't see in due to the car's height, but he heard Cid tell Connor, "Don't let them change you, Connor. Don't *ever* change for anybody." Summerlin patted the Con-Man reassuringly on the back as they watched Cid Peterson's red Coupe De Ville slowly drive off onto Austin Lane, a small back road which lead to the east valet.

Connor and Summerlin re-entered Texas Palace and headed straight for the Lone Star Bar. When they arrived, they took seats facing the Race and Sports Book area. Summerlin waved a hand overhead in an attempt to summon a bartender. *Con definitely strikes me as a man who could currently benefit from the numbing properties of alcohol—and I don't blame him*, he thought.

It didn't take long for Summerlin's request to be answered. Xero walked up to them and said with a wink, "Whaddup Igno—How you chillin'?" *I'm not even goin' to ask*, Summerlin thought. The Con-Man raised a single finger and twirled it in the air while his head remained lowered upon the bar. Summerlin finally realized what Xero had asked and replied, "Not much—hard day's mornin', really. I th—" Connor's voice broke through Summerlin's words like a battle axe: "Cid's gone, Xero. They booted him, and we're all next."

Summerlin didn't know what to think; he had never seen his friend so hurt, so offended. *I don't even know how to handle him like this— how can I be expected to know how to fix somethin' I've never seen?* For the better part of a month, Connor had always been there to help him when sadness took hold, yet despite his best wishes, Summerlin felt woefully inefficient, and guilty for being so.

Xero tapped the bar in front of Connor's still lowered head and said, "So, what'll it be, Con-Man, same as always?" He gave Xero a slight nod. When it was Summerlin's turn to order, he said, "I'll have what he's having."

Two rounds and four international drag races later, Summerlin took a moment's pause at his game of video poker to see how the Con-Man was doing. "You doin' alright now?" he asked. "I will survive, kid," Connor replied, "Can't let these circumstances change who I am, right?" Summerlin nodded—something deep down told him that it would best serve Connor for him to listen and not speak. *The man need's a pair of ears, not another mouth*, he reasoned.

The moment didn't come quickly; but, eventually, Connor opened up. His words came, at last, after he finished his third cocktail. The Con-Man took his eyes off the drag race channel and looked to Summerlin. "It's just not right, how they're going about doing all this—I know that the owners have the right to use their property as they see fit. But, there has to be a better way. Quietly and ruthlessly shanghaiing the GM who helped *make* this place, coupled with behind-closed-doors escapades: It just seems so cheap, so inhuman. They owe more than that..." *Wait,* Summerlin thought, *is he talking about Cid, or Texas?*

Summerlin raised an eyebrow in curiosity, but remained silent. He knew that the only way to let Connor vent was to let him get there on his own pace. *If I'm too inquisitive, he might see my intent and cease lettin' go of anything,* Summerlin thought. The Con-Man glanced at the TV on the far end of the bar, which was airing a golf tournament, before resuming his words, "When I came to town, I wasn't all that different than you, kid. Skipping all the wherefores and whys, I came to this valley with a knapsack and an open heart. Can't say I've ever met a nicer, good-hearted man...You've always reminded me a little of the old man, actually—Maybe that's why you seem so different than most of the people I've met. A man can have many acquaintances, Summerlin, but few real friends. And Cid helped me out, he showed me this fine, sweet abode of the dreamers we call Texas. My *home,* kid. Look out there, see all those *real people*: they are living, loving and giving—in this *real* place. They have no clue that the honorable Lancaster name has been tricked by an unworthy descendant; they have no clue that the company they think appreciates them has already signed the death certificate of their oasis. All for Cy's dream: a 'move forward,' to a place with glass towers, filled to the brim with 'boutique' amenities offered by venders with foreign-sounding names—all an attempt to glorify the *nouveau riche.* Except, Dominic knew better: if people want a Strip-like experience, they're going to go to the Strip—and there's *nothing* wrong with that, that's what the Boulevard is *for.* The Palace wouldn't fit in on the Strip, either. Texas is supposed to be a place for locals, a place for the savvy visiting conventioneer and, above all else, a place where Vegas's own can come and enjoy being themselves. Even if Cy gets all his glorious *Rancho Palace* dreams fulfilled, it still won't succeed, it's trying to be a Boulevard Resort where only a local's beloved dive would go. Look, kid, unless it's fashion-related, the rule stands: if I can't pronounce it, *I don't want it.*"

Summerlin took a sip from a freshly delivered soda and replied, "From what I've seen, you're right. There is a genuine heart to this place—a hidden goodness here. And despite having good ownership, one sour apple is ruining the bunch. That shady brother who hired that Ruckford guy—he's intent on destroyin' it all. What can we do, though?"

Connor sat in silent contemplation for a moment. He took out a cigar and replied after lighting it, "Well, that's the thing. I only know how to live one way." Summerlin looked curiously at him and said, "Oh? Dare I ask?" Connor nodded and replied, "Certainly. I only know one way, and you should know it's related to Lesson Eight: go *all-in.* I'm going at this full speed ahead, and with no intention of looking back." Summerlin watched as Xero handily dodged Fugi, who had turned backwards while holding two mugs, and nearly crashed into him. Several patrons cheered. Summerlin turned back to Connor and said, "And what, exactly, is that goin' to entail?" The Con-Man leaned back and grinned; "You ask way too many questions, kid," he said.

Later that day, the two men reconvened at the Austin Suite. It was Saturday, and Connor wanted to go out. Summerlin wasn't too enthused by the idea—he dreaded the concept of being a wallflower at any club that began with "strip" or "night". The Con-Man had left Summerlin at the bar to go change clothes when a knock came upon the door.

Summerlin approached the door with caution—he didn't know if it was a friend or a Calvert who awaited him on the other side of the door. Another knock came before his hand had reached the door handle. He then heard a voice come through the door: "Relax, Summerlin, it's me." It was Xero. *Thank the Lord,* Summerlin thought as he undid the dead-bolt and opened the door.

Xero walked in and yelled, "The X-factor's in effect! Xero has entered the building!" Connor's voice came shouting from his side of the suite: "You rolling with us, bro?" Xero took an orange soda from the fridge before plopping down on the couch and replying, "You know it." Xero was wearing a black duster with an *AC/DC* t-shirt and jeans. The Con-Man entered the great room in what appeared to be a red velvet tuxedo.

Summerlin stared with awe at his friend's ridiculous getup and said, "Wow—startin' a circus are we?" Xero laughed; Connor did not. "Jealousy is such an ugly emotion," the Con-Man said while running a comb through his hair. "Where are we goin' tonight anyway?" Summerlin asked. Xero took his eyes off the fish tank to grin and say, "Still haven't weaned him of the 'too many questions' thing, eh Con-Man?" Connor nodded with Xero as if they were agreeing on a matter of science. Summerlin sighed and resigned his Saturday night plans to the unknown.

Within minutes, the three men were driving towards the Strip in Connor's champagne-colored Cadillac coupe. The stars vanished overhead as they drove ever closer to the neon heart of the city. Summerlin didn't know how to feel. It was at a red light at MLK and Las Vegas Boulevard that he came to a realization and thought, *What are we doin'? Releasin' stress, or runnin' from trouble?*

"Problem, kid?" Connor asked after noticing Summerlin had become quiet. Summerlin didn't want to tell him the real reason for his silence—that he had been worrying about *him*. Instead, he opted to go with something a little more believable and much easier to deal with. "Me? Only the same as usual," he replied, "I doubt that she even—" Connor honked his car horn to silence Summerlin; "And *that* will be enough of *that* for this evening." Summerlin was confused. "I thought you were wonderin' what was botherin' me?" he asked while gazing at the pinkish Vegas horizon. "I care—trust me. But tonight's not a night for hearing about the long-term problems we have in life. We don't have time for that right now. Besides, you're doing fine, kid. Making progress, even," the Con-Man replied.

"Makin' progress? How?" Summerlin inquired. The Cadillac came to red light at Las Vegas Boulevard and Sahara Avenue. "Simple, kid," The Con-Man replied, "time is passing, and today notwithstanding, you've gotten a lot calmer lately. Summerlin didn't want to inform his friend that it was seeing him vulnerable was what had set him off on a negative train of thought. Connor had been too good to him to blame— even if the negative mood had originated from him. "I guess you're right," Summerlin said, "If I'm doin' well, can we go see Sarah instead of whatever extremely well-lit place you had in mind?"

It was not Connor, but Xero who replied this time: "No, man. Don't search her out. If it's meant to happen *it will happen*. The Con-Man simply nodded. Summerlin reclined and closed his eyes. *There's no point in arguin'. And, at least I got his mind off his friend bein' kicked out*, Summerlin thought.

The champagne-colored Cadillac continued to navigate the city roads as they made their way ever closer to the grand cluster of buildings which gave the city its famous skyline. By the time Summerlin opened his eyes, the car was rolling to a stop in a valet lane. "Where are we?" he asked groggily as he sat up. Both Xero and Connor answered at the same time: *"Rome."*

Summerlin followed Xero and Connor into the casino, which had massive white pillars supporting a canopy over the entrance. They led him through the lavish casino floor to a pair of double doors that were tinted heavier than the entrance doors of Texas Palace. He felt extremely out of place amidst the sea of well-dressed people waiting in line to get into the establishment, which, from the loud techno music echoing from within, Summerlin determined to be a nightclub. Hurry up, Summerlin, or we'll leave you out here with the bottle rats!"

Connor yelled out as he and Xero had a quick "conversation" with the bouncer. The tall, massive man was dressed entirely in black and wearing sunglasses inside; he smiled and waved for them to go in. Summerlin raced to catch up with them, feeling completely awkward the entire time.

What Summerlin found inside the club defied all logic he had previously known. There were multi-colored flashes of light coming from everywhere, yet most of the heavily-populated dance floor was dimly lit. Summerlin didn't notice any signage denoting the name of the club; he shrugged and thought, *Doesn't matter I s'pose. I probably wouldn't be able to pronounce it, anyway.*

Connor led Xero and Summerlin to a roped-off section of tables which were near the rear of the nightclub. Summerlin saw people whom he had only seen prior on televisions and movie screens as they reached the Con-Man's reserved VIP table. Xero gave Summerlin a nudge as they approached their seats. "Just pretend that they're impersonators, and not the real people, it's what I do, he said with a smile. *Whew. It's a relief that I'm not the only one to feel out of place,* Summerlin thought.

They passed several hours in the loud, light-pulsing confines of the nightclub. Summerlin spent the time sipping sodas and contemplating ways to get to talk to Sarah without having Gina or Olivia around. Xero danced with a few women in skimpy dresses, both young and old, before relaxing at the table with a tropical cocktail that was larger than one of Summerlin's boots. Connor, on the other hand, barely ever saw the table—he spent almost the entire duration of their stay dancing and having conversations with a multitude of people, famous and regular alike. *Apparently, this relaxes him,* Summerlin realized. Summerlin clinked his glass of soda against Xero's über-cocktail and said, "What sort of man gets his *relaxation* while dwellin' in chaos?" Xero replied without hesitation, as if he were reading it aloud from a text book: "Connor Stephen Bentley."

Another hour or so of reverie passed, and the three men slowly walked out to the valet. Being that Summerlin was the only one of the three who had not consumed alcohol while inside the club, Connor allowed him to drive his Cadillac rather than the group paying for a taxi that would necessitate a next-day return to pick up the car. "Don't *Virginiafy* it," the Con-Man said after handing him the keys. "I'm not even askin' what that means," Summerlin responded with a grin as he started up the car and drove onto the Boulevard.

As the car neared Main Street, Connor turned down the radio—Summerlin had tuned it to a classic country station—and tapped Summerlin on the shoulder. "Hey, kid, stop at the Nugget, will you?" Summerlin instinctually tried to come up with reasons why they should, in fact, *not* visit the Golden Nugget; however, be it providence, fatigue, or maybe even a little bit of he having become "more mellow" as the Con-Man had said—Summerlin instead nodded and said, "*Yessir*, Golden Nugget, comin' up."

Summerlin pulled the car into the Nugget's valet lane. Connor got out before he did and handed the valet a twenty. Xero got out of the car and yelled out to the sky, "How's it hangin', Sin City!" Summerlin got out of the car and walked over to the Con-Man. Before he could reach him, Xero began to run towards the massive Fremont Experience dome, with Connor following behind. Summerlin was genuinely curious as to the intent of their detour, but had grown tired of being told that he asked too many questions. *Sometimes*, he thought, *it's just more fun to not know, I s'pose.* He ran after his friends, yelling, "Okay guys, I'm comin'!"

The streets were still busy with half-drunken tourists wending their ways back to their temporary Vegas homes. Fremont Street was every bit as densely packed as the Strip had been earlier in the night, but the people were of a totally different universe altogether. Everywhere he looked, Summerlin saw a sampling of every walk of life, both poor and wealthy alike; tourists were mingling readily with locals, and even street people, without any discrimination or bias. He smiled as he looked at the extremely varied crowd. *I guess if there's one altruistic trait this town has, it's unity and acceptance*, he thought.

As the three of them neared the corner of Main Street and Freemont, a voice cried out from across the street: "Hey, Con-Man, all right!" Connor turned to see the source of the words, and walked spryly across the street, gesturing for Xero and Summerlin to follow.

Connor waved at Summerlin and Xero again, saying, "Hurry up or you're buying your own." The Con-Man was standing at a small metallic minibar on wheels which had several patrons surrounding it. Summerlin instantly recognized one of the customers as Seven, the vagrant who had helped him with advice over a week ago. "So, what's the fun?" Xero asked as he and Summerlin stepped up to the bar. "Champagne toast, bitches!" Connor joyfully exclaimed; the svelte brunette merchant/ bartender poured out enough flutes full of bubbly for all six people present—plus herself. Summerlin walked over and shook Seven's hand as everyone else was getting their glass. "Hey—thanks for the other night," he said. "Hey, man, it's no problem, you know. Everything always comes back to ya," Seven said before raising his glass. Everyone else followed suit. Seven then turned to Connor and said, "I say we toast to the one thing we all adore: to *Vegas!*" They all agreed, and repeated, "To Vegas!"

And so it was that Summerlin found himself enjoying a toast near Fremont Street. Downtown Vegas at 3:30 in the morning seemed an odd place and time for a champagne toast, but he barely noticed the novelty. *You can get used to random, strange things in a city like this very easily*, Summerlin thought. "I say we toast again," Connor declared, "and, this time, we do it to the thing we all love as much as our city: to life!" The group cheered and then imbibed their sparkling wine. "Always a silver linin', huh, Con-Man?" Summerlin said. Connor smiled and replied, "You're damn right, kid."

Loud pounding upon the guest room door awoke Summerlin. *What in blazes is goin' on?* he thought as he rose from the bed. As he got up, he realized that he was still fully dressed. Summerlin noted his unshaven, disheveled appearance in a wall mirror on his way to open the door. It was Connor.

"What the heck, kid? You're not ready for Bingo." *Oh, crap,* Summerlin thought—he had forgotten about Connor's tendency to wake at 8:45 am on Sunday mornings for the nine o' clock Bingo match. It was promoted as *Sunday Bingo Madness*. "Sorry," he said to the Con-Man, "not really feelin' the early morning stuff right now." Connor displayed his typical grin. "Shame, Summerlin. But, you're still going."

Summerlin tried to go back to bed, but Connor remained at his door and began to very poorly croon his personal version of Kenny Rodgers' *The Gambler* until Summerlin could no longer take it; he caved in and got back up by the second verse. "Comb, kid?" the Con-Man offered as they exited the suite for the elevators.

The Bingo hall was cramped, and Summerlin felt sleep-deprived and perhaps a little bit hung-over. "Twelve cards, my man," he heard the Con-Man say as he reached the oak-paneled counter. "And how many for you, sir?" a kind octogenarian asked Summerlin from behind a large cash register. "Four, I guess," he replied as he pulled out a twenty dollar bill.

The two men sat down near the back of the hall. Summerlin took a moment to examine Connor—It was as if the Saturday night bender hadn't ever happened. The Con-Man was dressed in a clean, crisp white suit and appeared perfectly coiffured and refreshed. Summerlin couldn't fathom his friend's resiliency.

Connor arranged his twelve Bingo cards and procured several card stampers from his sports coat. "Hey, Yankee," Summerlin said; the Con-Man looked up from his cards. "Can I borrow one of those?" Connor grinned before replying, "You know what you have to do, Summerlin." *Oh darnit, I forgot*, Summerlin thought. What he had neglected to remember from the prior Sunday was that Connor Bentley only shared his Bingo stampers if you were willing to make a recitation of what the Con-Man referred to as "The Lament of the Unprepared." Summerlin sighed and rose from his seat to face the sea of gamblers.

"Ahem. I am an inconsiderate person. I have to bum a marker from the Con-Man because I didn't have the common sense to bring my own. The world is truly a better place when everyone remembers their own utensils," Summerlin said in a manner dripping of lip-service. Connor laughed and slid him a pink circle-stamper.

Sunday Bingo Madness came and went, with Summerlin losing on all four of his cards. Connor shared the second round's Bingo with two blue-haired ladies. "It wasn't a pick-six," he noted, "but I'll take it. I've been feeling positive all morning, kid. I came to a few post-toast revelations." Summerlin looked interested, yet dared not ask an unwanted question. "No, no—you can *ask* that one," the Con-Man informed him.

Summerlin crumpled his losing cards and threw them in a waste basket before asking, "Okay, this oughta be good: what realizations did you get when you were walking with Xero and I through the downtown alleys and gutters?" Connor replied has he rose from his seat, "Come. Walk with me, talk with me." Summerlin followed suit, and the Con-Man began to speak as they walked out of the hall.

"I realized that the object which motivates our enemies might be a salvation to our cause." Connor glanced at Summerlin awaiting one of his usual questions; though, he didn't ask anything; Summerlin knew that the Con-Man would either explain on his own, or not say it at all; *No use askin' too many questions*, he reasoned. Sure enough, as they neared the buffet, Connor continued. "And what is that, you ask? It's simple: greed. It's greed which has compelled the board to suggest Cy Lancaster as the heir to the empire—and they gave their recommendation to Tyler based solely on that. And you and I personally know that all parties are currently being fooled by Cy's less than honorable business practices. This greed has led the board to be convinced that it's a good idea to sell of their Texas treasure in order to pursue a glass towered monstrosity with the hopes of luring the kids of foreign leaders, or whoever it is they hope to pull three miles from the Strip. But, worry not, my young apprentice—I have a plan," he said.

"Okay," Summerlin responded as they reached the buffet entrance, "skipping whatever strange title you have for your plan, what is it?" Connor smiled at the hostess as she led Summerlin and he to their table. The Con-man arranged unwrapped his silverware while he said, "Skipping my glorious plan title—*Operation: Get 'Em With Their Own Guns*, by the way—my plan is to use the moronic greed that Cy has installed in his father's advisors *against them*. Palace Casinos doesn't have feelings of love or altruism for Super Dollar World—If I, and a few co-signers, can raise the funds to out-bid the mega-store chain, then even Cy's advisors would be telling him to take it. And if he didn't, Tyler would be informed. One way or another, kid, old Mr. Lancaster will need to be informed. But don't worry, a friend of mine and I have a plan for that, too."

Summerlin gave the idea some thought before responding. The Con-Man got up to fill his plate, and returned with a thick slab of roast beef with a salad. Summerlin took the break in silence as an opportunity to get his own food as well. He loaded up his plate with biscuits, bacon, fiesta corn and an omelet, and was halfway through consuming it before he finally responded to Connor's plan: "It's not a bad idea, Con—but, what about competition? Even if you could convince Palace Casinos to *not* implode Texas, and let it remain a hotel-casino under new ownership, I severely doubt that they'd want a competitor casino so close to Rancho Palace." Connor was washing the former contents of his empty Lone Star plate down with a glass of milk. He wiped his mouth and said, "You see, Texas wouldn't need to be seen as a threat. It would be a venue conducting the same order of business as Rancho; however, the vibe of the two properties couldn't possibly be different." Summerlin nodded and added, "Well, I can't argue with you there. "Hey," Connor hastily retorted, "don't go knocking my baby, Summerlin." They both laughed a little.

"So, what's goin' to be your first move, then?" Summerlin inquired. The Con-Man pushed his empty plate to the side of the table and said, "We finish here, and chill later with the gang. Banks aren't open until tomorrow. Tonight is for generating good mojo."

Their night of gathering good will passed with Summerlin and Connor spending a large portion lounging at the Billiard Bar. Everyone made it—the entirety of The Reason Why was there, as were Megan and Danny and Trista. They drank beers, shot pool and established a solid three-hour period of jukebox domination.

Around midnight, the group adjourned to the great room of the Austin Suite. Samantha and Connor played each other in an alcohol-related match of Midway's *NBA JAM*; they tied at two wins each. Summerlin, Jail-Bait and Trent played several games of *900*.

The assemblage of gamblers, hotel staff and band members kept the Austin Suite active until the early hours of Monday morning. Summerlin didn't exactly remember when he fell asleep, or how, exactly, he came to wake up on the top of the bar in the great room. He felt his neck pop as he hopped off the bar and stretched mid-yawn. The great room was empty—he was alone. Summerlin slowly ambled to the guest room, where he grabbed a change of clothes to be worn after his shower and shave. *I guess the Con-Man's out doin' his bankin' thing—whatever that is*, he figured.

After his shower, shave and redress, Summerlin went to exit the suite and found a note waiting for him on the door. It wasn't the usual crisp white stationery card stock, but a simple sticky-backed note that looked like it came from an office desk. It read: "Take a car, and do something positive!" "So, valet it is," Summerlin said to himself as he headed down to the main entrance. When he reached the valet shed, Zak the valet greeted him and said, "Con-Man says you can have the pick of his litter. It's spaces two through eighteen, if you want to do a visual inspection first." Summerlin nodded and stood on tippy-toes in an attempt to survey the valet lot. He was unable to get a clear view; the canopy, and cars driving by impeded any attempt. He smiled and said, "Okay. I might as well go give it a look-see." What he actually was thinking was: *Alright, let's go see which one is the least ridiculous.*

A row by row inspection of the valet lot led Summerlin to the cars nearest the Reata Avenue side; he found the lot which had a number two at the front, and began to take in the Con-Man's motley assortment of automobiles. He found his friend's taste in methods of conveyance to be quite varied: There were several cars which Summerlin recognized from seeing before—the mirror-coupe, the Delorean, the Stingray and the Maybach. It was the vehicles which he had never seen before that blew his mind: a black Rolls Royce *Phantom V,* two additional Cadillac *Coupe De Villes*—one blue, the other gray—a World War II army-style Jeep, and what appeared to be a Surrey awaiting fresh horses in space fourteen. Then, Summerlin saw it—the *non sequitur.*

Amongst the stylish and the sleek, buried beneath the flashy and the memorable sat an old, beaten down Dodge *Aries* that predated Summerlin's birth by at least five years. It was a muddy shade of brown, somewhere between taupe and chestnut, and obviously well-faded by years of Las Vegas sunlight. The car's body had several small patches of rust, and Summerlin could see a small crack near the corner of the windshield. It was a beacon of humble modesty amidst a throng of objects which were built and bought to impress. *Gentleman Zak, I believe we have a winner*, he thought as he returned to the valet shack.

"Did one catch your eye?" Zak asked Summerlin. "Yeah," he replied, "I want that old borin' plain one—the Dodge." A distressed look came over the young valet. "I'm afraid that's the one thing I can't do, sir," Zak informed him. "Really?" Summerlin replied in confusion. Zak pointed out towards the valet lot and said, "I was told by Mr. Bentley himself that you are to be allowed access to any of his cars that you want; however, I cannot let you take that one—we don't even have its key, actually." *Now what in tarnation?* Summerlin wondered before inquiring, "Well, then how do you even fuel or service it?" Zak looked out towards the lot as he spoke: "The Con-Man gasses it up personally; he only drives it two or three times a year—so they tell me, anyway." *Wow*, Summerlin thought, *the luxury cars are all fair game, but the busted-up relic is untouchable? Only Connor.* "I guess I'll take the stainless steel lookin' one, then," Summerlin said. "I'll have the Delorean for you right away Mr. Summerlin," Zak replied as he ran with a set of keys to the valet lot.

Summerlin took the Delorean north bound on Reata. *I don't suppose there could be any harm in drivin' around the old side of town*, he thought. He hadn't seen his old neighborhood for the better part of a month. *Connor would hate the idea*, Summerlin thought as he stared at the red light above him. "Screw it," he said to himself softly, "Connor *isn't here*." He hit the gas pedal as he merged onto Rancho Drive.

The sky was a brilliant blue when Summerlin slowly rolled to a stop near the gates of Summerlin Heights Apartments. The name "Summerlin" on the complex's stucco sign seemed so strange to him; last time he has seen the word in print, it had been the name of an upscale community on the northwest side of Vegas, not his name. He left the stainless steel sedan parked outside the gates and walked into the apartment complex on foot.

Summerlin instantly regretted that he had not brought a pair of sunglasses with him. He resorted to raising his hands to block the intense sunlight from piercing his eyes. He walked around a tight left turn to see unit 2145. But, as Summerlin would soon discover, he was *not alone.* The bright red hatchback which was parked in front of the unit was all too familiar to him and meant only one thing: Gina Martin was on property as well. *Well, she don't have any more of a justifiable reason for bein' here than I do*, Summerlin thought as he headed for the front door.

Summerlin was not exactly certain what he would do at his former residence in the presence of Sarah's dark-hearted friend—he hadn't been totally sure of his intentions with the place when he had previously thought it unoccupied. Perhaps he thought there would have been a chance to talk with Sarah. Perhaps any number of things—it didn't matter anymore.

He opened the front door and immediately saw Gina. She was heading out the doorway with two small cardboard boxes in her arms and several clumps of her red hair in her face. Upon seeing Summerlin, her face erupted in anger. "What are you doing here?" she demanded. He took a page from the Con-Man's book and replied, "Annoying *you.* Didn't see any signs around here bannin' my presence...but, of course, that wouldn't have helped me none, seeing as how I don't *know how to read* or nothin' like that." He grinned and stood blocking the doorway.

Gina became a red-faced ticking time bomb in the form of a lanky, curly haired short woman. She said nothing as she rammed with full momentum through the doorway, bashing Summerlin square in the jaw with a box as she did. "Now I thought you and Olivia were Sarah's *polite* friends," he said as he stood back up from the blow. *Wow*, he thought, *I never got a word in on her edgewise before—maybe old Con was right about my progress.*

Gina hustled over to set her boxes on the ground and open the hatchback. Summerlin walked over as if to help—but, regardless of his true intention, Gina looked at him and said, "Just go. She isn't here, and she won't be, either." Shock overcame Summerlin. "What do you mean?" he asked brusquely. Gina beamed with confidence as she said, "Sarah's moved, Andrew." He didn't reply—he couldn't; he was at a loss for words.

Gina turned to face him and said, "I'm leaving. And, don't you dare follow me; if you do, I'll call the cops." Summerlin, who had been wordless upon the news of Sarah moving, suddenly found himself equipped with a reply that was bursting in *Bentleyness*: "I wouldn't be worryin' about that. I don't have the intent nor the desire: followin' you would be like chasin' the *plague*." Sarah's emaciated, red headed friend drove off in a huff, leaving Summerlin standing alone in a cloud of desert dust.

Originally, he had intended to go inside unit 2145; now, it seemed sadly pointless to Summerlin. As he walked slowly back to the Delorean, the excruciating sunlight bathed him the entire way. With the new information he had just obtained, Summerlin's strongest wish would have been to talk with Connor about it. He needed perspective above all things. *But*, Summerlin thought, *he's got his own problems right now.*

Summerlin didn't know what returning to Texas Palace would do to cure his pain—he headed back to the hotel-casino not out of a specified need, but more because he knew of nowhere else to go. When he arrived back at the valet shed, Zak was standing at the curb waiting for him.

"Decided to trade it in?" he asked Summerlin. "Nah, just keep it," he replied as he handed Zak ten dollars and went for the main entrance.

The casino floor was a ghost town. Gone were the bums, the grannies and regular Monday morning stragglers; there wasn't a person in sight. As he walked through the Pit, Summerlin noticed from afar that the curtained entrance to the Rail Yard was open. From the Roulette tables, he could tell that the stage was lit, and he could hear faint applause coming from within. *I've never even heard of the Rail Yard bein' open on a Monday mornin'*, Summerlin thought. Curiosity, along with a bit of his now often-displayed "don't give a darn" led him to get closer. *Heck*, he figured, *why not crash the party?*

Summerlin found the entrance to be blocked by the plump, gray-haired officer whom he had first encountered the night that he met the Con-Man; he felt it odd to see an uniformed outdoor officer standing duty inside, but Summerlin didn't see the point in inquiring. He approached the entrance to the Rail Yard and greeted the officer with a kind "howdy".

"*Not* gonna happen, Texas Worlder," the grumpy-toned officer replied. *My reputation precedes me*, Summerlin thought. "Is the event goin' on inside there open to the public?" he asked the officer. "Yes," the pudgy badge-bearer replied, "but if you cross the doorway, I am to call the supervisor and have you *trespassed*." Though Summerlin had heard the term be used before, it had never been directed at him. "Tresspassing" someone meant a verbal trespass warning, and offense which bears with it a twenty-four hour period of being kicked off property. *What the heck? What'd I do?* Summerlin thought. He was rather curious as to what was transpiring within the nightclub, and leaned in as an attempt to find out. The security officer pulled the curtained entrance shut. "Now look, I have done nothin' wrong here—correct?" Summerlin queried. The officer put his hands on his vinyl basket-weave utility belt and responded, "That's not it. You associate with the wrong crowd. There's to be no riff-raff in there today, they're doing something important. Now out of here—*beat it!*"

The Austin Suite now seemed to be the only destination that made any sense. If for no other reason than to don his Texas World t-shirt. *Don't be tellin' a southern boy what not to do*, he thought as he reached the elevator lobby. Summerlin was staring at the portrait of a bucking cowboy when the terror finally hit him: he no longer knew where Sarah lived anymore, nor did he have her phone number—he had lost her. "Now what do I do!?" he yelled out loud as the elevator opened to the suite level. Even if Summerlin devised a perfect plan to get Sarah back, he'd now never have the ability to execute it—the thought petrified him. His heart felt like it fell a thousand feet, and tears began to well in his eyes.

Summerlin slowly plodded down the hallway toward the Austin Suite, his mind and body feeling ever the worse as he went. He opened the doors and slunk instantly down upon the chair nearest the entrance. *Things are goin' way too fast*, Summerlin thought as squinted his eyes shut. *Try to think of anythin' but this*, he thought. But, as fate would have it, a rapid knocking came upon the doors.

"Con! Connor! Con-Man!" the voice cried. He didn't need to check the peephole—he knew the voice to be Blake's. It seemed odd to Summerlin to see the man alone, though. He had only ever seen him in the company of Jail-Bait, and had somehow gotten the silly impression that they always accompanied one another. *But that*, Summerlin thought, *is just plain ridiculous.*

Summerlin unlocked and opened the door. Blake was wearing a frayed jean jacket over his Texas World shirt; his custom front moniker read, "Blake: Symphonic Conductor of Smooth." The man seemed nervous—a shade of emotion Summerlin had never thought possible for "good ol' Blake." Summerlin shook his hand and opened the door widely, adding, "Come on in, man."

16.

The two men took seats at the bar. Summerlin offered Blake a beer, and he accepted. "So, what's your horror?" Summerlin asked. Blake rested his head full of thick brown locks upon his folded arms between beer swigs. "I can tell you're hurtin' with all of the stuff you've got goin' on in your own life, Summerlin. I don't want to bother nobody with my worries, but—" He was cut short by Summerlin, who had pounded the bar with a gavel-like fist and interjected: "The point, Blake. I can't help you if you don't get to *the point*."

Blake took a deep gasp of air and said, "Beg your pardon, Summerlin. See, here's the thing—the 'point' as you call it: Jasmine called the record company, and they're unwillin' to reschedule. Equally unwillin' to accommodate is Mr. Moroni's crooked ass. Altered Note insists that the performance begin sharply at nine. And, to make matters truly worse, there's *this*." Blake withdrew a folded piece of high-gloss paper from his jacket and flopped it open upon the heavily varnished bar top. It was a promotional flyer advertising the "hot new house band of Henderson Palace"—*The Reason Why*!

Now I know why he's so astir, Summerlin thought. He noticed that Blake's honey-brown eyes were staring right at him—the man was expecting advice and understanding; Summerlin wasn't sure he could offer him either. "Wow. This is worse than just one person, I'll be the first to admit that," was the best that Summerlin could do. It wasn't that he didn't care—Summerlin had grown a great appreciation for all of his friends at the Palace. It was simply an issue of him feeling overwhelmed and undertrained to help his friend in a way that he believed only the Con-Man could. "We both need Connor, huh?" Blake replied. Summerlin nodded before grabbing a beer for himself out from the fridge.

"So, what's your trouble, Virginia?" Blake asked. "Well Arkansas," Summerlin replied, "my girl's gone. And I mean *long* gone. No number, no address, and no chance that pair of harpies who call themselves her friends will ever let me even write a post card to her ever again." Blake tossed his empty beer bottle at a waste basket that lay at the foot of the bar; it missed, and splattered a few droplets upon the nearby wall and floor. "Well damn," Blake said, "Yep—I'm as bad at the philosophy thing as you are. We're an English teacher-to-be and a carpenter. We need a professional gambler. Summerlin nodded in agreement and got up to fetch Blake another round when a new set of knocks came upon the Austin Suite doors.

"This is quickly becomin' the place to be, I guess," Summerlin said as he opened the doors to let Xero inside. He was still wearing his collared bar-back shirt, only there was a hole torn in it near his left armpit, where his nametag usually was. "Thought you were workin' today, X-factor," Blake said. Xero shook his head and replied, "Yeah, well, I quit." Blake and Summerlin stared in wide-eyed shock.

"What happened?" Summerlin asked. Xero took a soda from the fridge before taking a seat at the bar. "Oh, you're gonna have to get ready for this one," he said. Summerlin and Blake both nodded and waited for him to continue. "That conference they're having at the Rail Yard—they have news cameras and everything. The bastards scheduled me to bar-back for Jim at the Lone Star during it." Xero paused, and Summerlin took his moment of reflection to add his perspective on the event: "I saw there was somethin' different goin' on in there, but the security officer called me a 'Texas Worlder' and turned me away. What was it, Xero?"

"What was it?" Xero replied, "It was our 'friends' at Palace Casinos announcing that Texas Palace only has ninety days to live. Cy Lancaster is there to personally announce the 'great news', bad wig of his and all." Blake and Summerlin became crestfallen; they knew that things at Texas weren't looking up, but neither man had assumed that the end of the Palace would be coming so soon. "They're closing' it up?" Blake inquired. Xero took a long gulp of his soda before responding. "They are not only closing the place, but they're *celebrating* it, too. 'We're making way for the proud new addition to the Palace family,' Lancaster told the news crews." Xero finished his statement in a disgruntled, bitter tone.

"I understand your anger, but are you sure you should have quit? I'm sure that they were going to help you guys find jobs at one of the other Palace Casinos, if not at that newfangled one," Blake said. Xero replied right back, "Oh, they did do a lot of talk about how 'very few jobs will be lost'—that part was done for the cameras. I'm *sure* they're gonna put my name as a top priority on that list." Summerlin wanted to contradict Xero, but he had just recently learned that Palace Casinos viewed all friends of Connor Bentley as enemies of the state. Blake rose from the bar and replaced Xero's glass soda bottle with one containing fermented barley and hops.

The three of them drank in quiet until an hour had passed, and the Con-Man entered the suite. Blake, Summerlin, and Xero all turned in their seats to see him the moment he entered the great room. Connor was wearing a simple black suit with a red carnation pinned to the lapel. Whatever he had experienced, the gambler held his poker face well. Blake nudged Summerlin, who responded in a whisper, "It's not gonna be *me*. Everyone says I ask too many questions." The Con-Man walked up to join them at the bar. "It's okay, fellas, you can talk," he said. The silence persisted. "Alright, then," Connor continued, "it seems that we are going to accomplish nothing until someone here gets me to talk about the bank—am I right? Is that it?" The three other men gave him a resounding synchronized "Yes!"

Connor took a deep series of breaths before he began, "Well, guys, it didn't go well, I'm afraid." He looked around the bar to find that everyone was still silent. "Okay, I guess you need more than that. We struck out. Tell a banker that you want a business loan and they're all ears. Tell them you're a professional gambler and they show you the door." Summerlin knew it couldn't be true, but to him, it felt like the temperature of the room had just dropped by ten degrees.

"Sorry, guys," the Con-Man said, "this sucks for me too. Unless I can find some major credit or cosigners, and I mean soon, this will all have been for naught." Summerlin rose from his barstool and walked over to Connor. "What about your boy? You know, Thomas?" The room went quiet—silent enough to hear cells divide. Xero got up and walked out of the Austin Suite without saying even a word.

"What did I say?" Summerlin asked in confusion. "Blake, a moment for me and the kid alone, please?" Connor said. Blake nodded and got up. "Sure," he said, "no problem; someone should check on Xero, anyway."

Connor took off the jacket to his suit and proceeded to serve himself an Old Fashioned. He remained behind the bar, pacing back and forth slowly. "A few things, Summerlin," he said, "First off, you should have learned by now not to bring up one's name when the other is around—it never bodes well. Indeed, during the week prior, Summerlin had witnessed two minor scuffles when the two men, Xero and Thomas, were even in the same *casino* together. Neither seemed evil or eagerly combative—in fact, both seemed to be quite polite, in their own ways, when not in each other's company. However, whenever the two met in person, it resulted in events such as Thomas shutting a door in Xero's face, or with Xero making snarky remarks such as, "Ah, Mr. West—how's your *health*?" Summerlin acquiesced to the Con-Man's first point and nodded.

"Beyond that," Connor continued, "it's just bad timing, kid." Summerlin hadn't seen that coming. "Bad timin'? Why?" he eagerly inquired. The Con-Man approached the bar closer, and braced his hands upon its edge. He then said, "Well, as you have pointed out, I do have a close friend who is also at times a business power to be reckoned with. The problem is that I don't think he's gonna hear the proposal."

"Too many questions be damned—I'm askin', he thought before looking Connor in the eye and asking, "Why not? So he's a little weird and talks to himself and occasionally confuses the plurality of the first person. Like you've pointed out before: Thomas does great for weeks on end without the Texas visits." Connor refilled his glass; he walked around the bar and sat on the stool Blake had been using. "First off—nice use of the whole 'objective person' stuff; I genuinely believe anyone who can memorize that annoying stuff deserves to be an English teacher. That being said, back to the point at hand. I don't think he's holding up as well as we'd like. Trust me, I'm the one ducking out all the time to check up on the guy. His 'Texas trips' are becoming more frequent, Thomas is getting worse and we all know it. He dwells openly with his pain when he's here, kid. Jail-Bait, Trent and I call it his *'muck-raking.'* It seems after Sylvia died, his made-for-business mind needed a way to categorize things. He comes here, under the auspices of relaxation, and this is where I help him, when I can. Two bad things though: neither he nor I seem to have any control on when he will come or go, or be coherent in business matters at all, these days. Yet, if he didn't have his moments of bittersweet vulnerability here, he probably would never make it. He's a great guy, kid—he's broken, though. Don't worry, he's far too polite to let it show too much."

Summerlin didn't even have a clue what to say. He instead attempted to ask a question relating to the topic at hand, rather than dealing with the actual situation they were discussing. "Why does he come here? Just to be here? That don't make no sense. I never see him eating here, nor have I seen him gamble even a nickel. He's vulnerable here? What does that mean?" Connor sighed and replied, "It's not so easy to define such things—we're discussing matters of the mind, heart, and soul here, not cooking or architecture. Tommy West is a person, one whom I still hold quite dear, actually. He was there for me in times of need. I know, few people would ever believe that 'Mr. Party' could ever *need* anything; but, he was always the guy you never even needed to ask. I included your 'bum day' in your training for a reason, kid. I've seen at least three of those myself for every one I've gotten at the Palace. There was once an angel I had met, who set me down in Texas Paradise. Introduced me to my mentor, even. My past hasn't always been so lucrative, Summerlin..."

The Con-Man went on, but for once, Summerlin wasn't listening. All he could do was picture what it must have looked like. *Connor Bentley was once just like Bling, Seven and Down-Low*, he realized. And long ago, back before he himself was old enough to drive, there was a man, looking so much like the *Angel of Hoover Avenue*, but without any of the stoic pain held deep. The Con-Man's once non-Italian shoes did scuff a Lucky Flamingo's tile after midnight.

Connor's eyes locked in on Summerlin, and he raised his voice in order to regain his protégé's attention: "And now when you, Thomas, the band, and Texas Palace itself are in dire need, I have to go and try to talk to the husk I see so often to see if there's any of my friend left in there."

Summerlin's eyes had navigated to the bar top; "That's horrible," he said. Connor took another sip from his drink and replied, "You and I both know it. Apparently, if your luck and his are any symptom, I haven't been that good of a role model lately. See, that's the thing about ol' Tommy Pastrami, kid: he was never the life of the party, though he so often fueled it. Thomas wasn't the Con-Man and all his distractions—he was Connor Stephen Bentley's friend. He was the guy who stood behind the magic act and set the real pace. You'd be surprised how much you'd miss that guy when he's gone, too."

"But he's *not* gone! He's right here at the Palace." Connor dismissed his point with a head shake. "You didn't know the man we got to—maybe you won't be able to understand." Summerlin pounded his fist on the bar and raised his voice, "Then let me try to help you, Bentley. You're at least tryin' to help me. Allow me the favor likewise." The Con-Man's face had gone from lively enthusiasm to near-deathly pallor. "He always talks to her," Connor began, "but, I'm gonna have to try to reach him." Summerlin waved his hands in protest. "No, Con, I meant what's makin' Mr. West worse? And why in Hades do he and Xero hate each other?"

Connor sighed and downed the entire remaining contents of his glass before speaking. "That's right, you don't know about that part," he said. Summerlin immediately said, "Don't know what?" The Con-Man laid his hands on the bar and leaned in towards him. "Xero is Sylvia Sanford's brother."

Summerlin's face turned pale—"Damn," was all he could think to say; and, really, it sort of slipped out. "Thomas's Sylv—" he began before being cut off in draconian fashion by Connor: "They've feuded since the car wreck. It's so strange to think that five years ago, they were think as thieves—I think Spike-Top actually viewed him as an older brother figure. After he reached eighteen and moved out, it turned out that Blake's band needed a bassist, and the young kid fit right in…talent must run in Sanford veins: Xero's sister made me cry when she played kid, even the happy, beautiful pieces. The topics and reasons have changed, but since that horrible, life-changing tragedy, the twain has never met. But, as to your other question: why does Thomas West come to Texas?" Summerlin replied with his own inquiry, "Yeah, especially if he—" The Con-Man ended his words yet again. "It's for two reasons, kid. First off, the band and the Palace are two of the only things he has left of his past—his golden age that ended so coldly one December night. His time, when he showed us and the world all that a properly motivated ambitious young man could achieve. Believe it or not, Summerlin, *love* was once that man's motivation. Now it lies mostly with the second reason. It's the same reason he attends our monthly baked ziti fest at Sylvia's best friend Sally's restaurant—for the same reason he still drives that POS truck and he still lives in that house even though all the other lots have been torn down to make way for a school and a strip mall, kid. For the act of keeping tradition and promises made. Several companies have offered him the moon and back for that last remaining plot on that block of 16th Street, kid—he just always refuses; that was his home, that was where he and Sylvia and Blake and Trista lived. I spent more than a handful of nights there myself, kid. No, there's more likelihood of me giving birth than there is of Thomas selling that plot, nor of him missing a scheduled date at A Taste of Sin, even if it means sitting near someone he currently loathes. It seems, even in severe disrepair, he still has some honor left."

Connor grabbed a bottle of water and took several gulps. As he began to comb his hair, he turned out of nowhere to face Summerlin. "Hey, kid, wait a sec—what are you even doing back here so early? You're supposed to be 'Lesson Eighting' the world to your delight right now." Summerlin lowered his head and replied, "It's Sarah. I lost her; she moved." Summerlin expected Connor to get angry and chide him, but he didn't. The Con-Man looked at him with a cool, collected disposition and said, "I see. Well, that's even worse than we'd planned for. Give me a few hours and we will work on that one. I have to go and try to rouse my old friend. And, no offense, but a person who hasn't gotten to Lesson Nine would only hinder the situation, no matter what their intention." Summerlin retorted, "No offense taken. I truly hope he hears you. And I'm ready for Lesson Nine whenever you are. Connor put his suit jacket back on as he headed for the door. "I honestly hope he hears me, too. If he doesn't, he'll lose his safe haven, now won't he? Oh, and, when you're *actually* ready for Lesson Nine, life—not I—will tell you, kid." After the door closed behind the Con-Man, all Summerlin could think was, *Now what is that supposed to mean?*

Summerlin did wish that he could see Connor's attempt—*He is the only hope we have of getting to hear Thomas discuss much beyond the weather and wine,* he thought, *Texas Palace or not, I really hope the Con-Man can reach him.*

He found himself frantically pacing the great room. Summerlin had been able to restrict the level of his despair when his mentor had been present. But, in Connor's absence, it returned. He wanted to see Connor succeed, but he rationed that even if Thomas was of sound mind, any pitch that the Con-Man made would have to avoid any reference to the hotel-casino's house band or former bartending staff. *And, should Connor fail, I doubt he will be willin' to even try helpin' me,* Summerlin thought, *I understand him feelin' awful over the Thomas-Xero thing—but the "Sarah and I" thing could still be aided to success.* He slammed his fists upon the bar in utter pure frustration.

Hours passed. Several hours. Summerlin had begun to slow his circuitous march of the great room when he heard the sound of a hotel room key being accepted by the Austin Suite's key reader. When the door opened, it was thrown with such force as to leave the handle stuck in the drywall after its collision with it. It was Connor, and he looked *horrible.* He walked in with mussed hair and a pale, tear-streaked face which sent terror into Summerlin's heart. He dared not say a word until the Con-Man did; Summerlin stared vacantly at the Prince of Ponies poster.

"Well, kid," Connor began as he walked over to the bar, "I don't think we stand a hooker's chance in Henderson on this one. Thomas wouldn't hear me...he only wanted to discuss the nature of *pinot* grapes. Texas is dead. I only hope that we can get Thomas someplace safe when the time comes. Also, we need to try to see if there's anything we can do to help the band's situation. I dunno if I can get them to that audition by 9pm, though—that one's tough. I'm guessing that you are as ill-equipped with a musical instrument as I?"

Summerlin answered, "Yessir, Yankee, just as worthless as *you* on that one." He had said it in a joking tone, hoping to cheer him up a bit, if at all. The Con-Man shrugged his shoulders and then cleared his throat. "Okay, last issue at bat. Let's see what we can do with that mangled l'il heart of yours. What's up with Sarah?" Summerlin couldn't tell if he was being blasé or serious; *I better assume "serious" until proven otherwise*, he thought. "She moved."

"Where?" Connor asked. "I got a feelin' that she's moved in with Gina and Olivia. That's a bad thing though: I don't know where they live, and even if I did, those girls won't even let me send a prayer to her, no less a letter or phone call. Heck, they're so evil, I wouldn't put it past them to convince her she needs to get a restrainin' order should I actually figure out where they live. Sarah's not a bad woman, Con, she's just young enough to be fooled by the wrong people. She's too good hearted to 'see the cracks in their veneer,' as you call it. I'm losin' all hope, Connor," he said.

Summerlin waited. *I don't like discussin' my pain, but if you make me bring it up, I at least deserve some sort of an answer*, he thought. "Anything?" Summerlin asked after several minutes of silence. Connor fixed himself another Old Fashioned from the bar; Summerlin grabbed an orange soda. Noises came from the doorway of the suite—Sam, Xero, Blake and Danny had been standing in the doorway, though Summerlin had no clue as to how long. Connor didn't look, nor seem to currently care.

332

"Well, kid, then I got bad news for you," Connor finally said. "What's that?" Summerlin asked. The Con-Man put his drink down and walked over to where Summerlin was standing, near the pool table. "The bad news is, it's time for Lesson Nine. Sadly, I can't be the initiator of the actual learning act like I've been with the others: you'll only truly know yourself that you've learned it once the world shows you that you have." Summerlin's brow raised—he was praying above all else that his friend would have some supreme, sublime panacea to work his misery undone.

"Lesson Nine, kid: take each loss as well as you would a win," Connor said before putting his hand on Summerlin's shoulder and continuing, "And, if you can do that one, kid? You won't have to worry about the other eight, because you'll already be doing them all correctly." Summerlin's head sank low; he felt not a let-down, but a betrayal brewing.

Summerlin's eyes were as wide as saucers. Connor took his friend's shock as an opportunity to continue: "I'm afraid you're gonna have to let that one go. Don't worry, though, this city's a sea of many fish—we can find you an even better girl; heck, maybe even one who moved here from your beloved Southland. I don't mean your Buckeye dream any insult here, it's just that it's reached the point where our efforts will be guaranteed to produce very little fruit, and any 'fruits' of our labor would probably be poisoned ones, if you get my comparison." Summerlin's eyes were beginning to tear, yet Connor continued nonetheless, "Don't worry about it, kid. You're a great person, very diligent, pure-hearted and, heck, *almost* as good looking as I am. You have a great future of possibilities ahead of you—we'll get you a job if that'd make you feel better; heck, we can get you back in school so that you can teach a class of your own someday. And, if that's not what you want anymore, just chill with me—I bet two guys like us could *run* this city given proper time and ambition."

Summerlin could see Connor's intent; however, it was *not* what he had been wanting to hear. He shook off his friend's hand and rebuked, "I can get a job on my *own*, Con-Man. I was here—I've been here *this whole time* to supposedly have my life fixed under your 'wise' tutorage. Well, I know you're hurtin' over other stuff, but my pain is real, too. I could have solved this all on my own by now, this is gettin' ridiculous! I'm tired of toleratin' the claims of others; I'm tired of bein' told that when I feel uncomfortable it means I'm bein' helped. And, what is more, I'm sick and tired of living with what I have come to see as a direction free life—I should have known you'd go straight from tellin' me to ignore my pain to orderin' me to destroy it completely!

Connor shook his head and added at a near-whisper: "I'm sure time will change your mind, kid. It's all a matter of perspective." Summerlin shook his head and said, "I came to you because you offered to fix me, not *change* me—pick your battles!"

"You?" Connor began in a manner in which his volume raised the entire time he spoke, "Do you have any idea how it feels to be a leader and to discover that you *suck* at it? You're failing? How do you think I feel? I can't do shit in life except make money." Summerlin gritted his teeth and walked over towards the couch. After a moment, he turned to face Connor and said, "I'd respond to what you've just said, only, I know what you'll say—somethin' about how I don't understand the problems of your tax bracket. Nice smoke and mirror, plate-spinning monkey on a unicycle circus sideshow you've got goin' there." Connor, utterly dejected, plodded miserably to the bar. When he reached it, he turned, exposing a ferocious scowl and said with words that seemed to drip with venom: "*Fine*! Let's whine about *everything* that bothers us—*Me*? I hate tourists!" After he finished his yelling, Connor grabbed Xero's mostly-empty beer bottle from before and threw it with great force. The bottle crashed and exploded within inches of Summerlin's feet.

Summerlin erupted. The deep, painful hole in his heart was replaced with a dour vile hatred for the man whom until that moment he would have called his dearest friend on earth. As before, when the two had first met, Summerlin saw not persons, deeds, nor consequences; but, rather, he saw raw facts. It was shadow versus light, water against fire— It was not a specific anger but, rather, an amalgamated rancor which drove Summerlin to charge at the Con-Man with fists bared, yelling, "That's it, screw you!"

What followed was chaos. Connor raised his fists and began to charge at Summerlin, who was already a foot or so from him. The two men collided and fell to the ground amidst a rapid back and forth of fists upon each other's torsos. Connor pushed away and stood up; by this point, Summerlin was rising from the ground as well. The Con-Man stomped on his foot, and in the confusion, landed a punch straight in Summerlin's face. It hit him well and hard, directly beneath his left eye. It hurt Summerlin, but it did not daze him, nor knock him off balance. He was too amped up to remember how dirty of a fighter the Con-Man was, nor to notice that perhaps Connor would have never actually needed life-saving that night a month ago, after all. Likewise, the Con-Man was far to inebriated to remember how strong his friend could be when blinded by anger: a second after Connor landed his face-crunching blow, Summerlin struck him with a heavy right cross to his chin.

Summerlin had spared Connor a head wound—the blow knocked him over nonetheless. He pulled back; something within him eased up enough to enable him to be restrained enough to not kick a man when he was down. As the Con-Man rose, Summerlin, whose chest was heaving deeply, and whose nose was now a flurry of blood, said amid rapid gasps for air: "So, tell me somethin' Connor Stephen Bentley. *Why* did you even give me the razzle-dazzle? Why did you even want me here? I'd like to know, since it's obvious that you never really had an endgame prepared for my goal."

Connor got up slowly and stared him straight in the eye as he replied, "Because I saw something of value! Because...I saw someone who could actually achieve something. Unlike a person who spends his life winning money and little else. You see, kid, I'm not like you, Cid, or Thomas—I've never been able to inflict a positive effect on anything in my life except the odds on a horse race." Summerlin shook his head and said in a raspy tone, "Don't feel too bad, I recently learned that my friend pickin' skills are *crap*."

The Con-Man clenched his fists; his face was redder than he had ever made Allison Schwartz's. "Then why don't you get the *hell* out of my suite. I don't want you—*nobody wants you*, you arrogant snake in the grass son of a bitch!" He turned with his back to Summerlin and those assembled at the Austin Suite's doors.

Summerlin turned his back to Connor. The assembled band members near the doors stood agape. Summerlin powered through the doorway and took the emergency staircase down to the lobby—all sixteen floors of it—hammering every step with anger as he went. And, with that, Summerlin left Texas Palace alone.

17.

Sarah Crawford looked Gina dead in the eyes and said, "Wait—what did you just say?" Gina cut open the top of one of the two cardboard boxes on the coffee table and replied, "I said that the brutish oaf tried to get in my way, but I knocked his block off with your box of flower pots and plowed right through his hillbilly ass." Gina's words had begun jubilantly, yet, she switched quickly to an almost-regretful tone when she noticed that Sarah wasn't finding her story funny in the slightest. "Was he complaining in that atrocious drawl of his?" Olivia said as she entered the room, her long blonde hair tied up in a bun that almost seemed to make her face appear stretched out. Gina smiled at Olivia— she had received backup without ever even requesting it. Despite her opinion of the story being outnumbered, Sarah's frown had not diminished an inch.

"Was he alone, or with that flashy dresser?" Sarah asked, almost impatiently. The question struck Gina *and* Olivia by surprise. "I don't get your priorities, girl. But he was alone. I thought that he'd come on foot, but there was a car that looked like it came from a time traveling movie near the leasing office. That car *had* to belong to that other guy. Why do you care about that?" Sarah didn't respond. "You should

be smiling, really. You finally got that problem out of your life for good."
She could have recited the entirety of the US Constitution for all Sarah
cared—she was no longer listening.

Sarah's souring opinion of Gina's advice had not been sudden. In
fact, it had been growing exponentially ever since she went to the movie
theatre at Texas Palace. Behind her friends' backs, she had carefully for-
mulated a plan. What Andrew had told her near the Lost Wages Tavern
had been rattling around in her mind for over almost two weeks; she
needed to know if what he said about her friends lying to control her
was true. And, to do that, she would have to devise a plan that would
enable her to reach Andrew without Gina and Olivia even knowing
about it. *All I have to do in order to accomplish that*, she figured, *is go
somewhere they would be loath to go.*

Sarah spent several days looking through the local paper—she
needed an event that would both be well advertised, yet also be *at* Texas
Palace. She wanted to talk to Andrew, but knew no other lead to pursue
in looking for him than that he slept at the Austin Suite. That info would
surely not be a reason to be going near downtown—not in Olivia and
Gina's minds, at any rate. Sarah struck gold on Thursday evening when
she was looking at the movie ads for Trident Cinemas, and found what
she had been looking for: There was a showing of *Old Hickory: The Tale
of Andrew Jackson* early Friday afternoon. It was listed as a one-time
showing. *Andrew's nuts over old musty history films like that*, Sarah
thought. She got her iPhone and checked to see who, in fact, Andrew
Jackson had been.

After learning that he was a former president and that he had been
born in Tennessee, Sarah thought, *It's the best shot I'm going to get.* She
thought that telling Olivia and Gina about the movie—and its nature—
that she would have been given a clear pass to go to Texas Palace, *alone.*

That was not, however, what occurred. "We love history!" the girls assured her—a fact that she remembered from their days in high school to be false; they hated such movies more than she did.

Sarah was undeterred; she decided that she'd simply take her friends with her. *I can ditch them in the theatre, and then go out to the casino. Andrew people might not know how to find, but that Con-Man guy sounds like he'll be easy to locate*, she thought. Of course, the plan had failed—a blessing and a curse occurred when she met Andrew in the line that day. *He wasn't supposed to actually be in line*, Sarah had thought. She was very happy to have located him so easily—but Gina and Olivia were there in person, and would never have allowed them to talk.

In the end, the seeds of doubt were planted by Gina. After she had been "guided" to the ticket window, when she and her friends were walking through the darkened hallway toward their theatre, Ms. Martin said, "I'm surprised that they let illiterates in here anyway." The comment shook her fundamental notions to the core. It was not only a heartless remark for meanness's sake—but, beyond that, it exposed Sarah to how idiotic her old friends could be. *He's read more books in a month than I ever have in a year*, she thought, *and he's going to be an English teacher, for crying out loud.*

Sarah's moving out had not been by intentional design. She simply didn't have enough money to make the rent; Andrew's absence meant that there would be no way for her to cover the bills at Summerlin Heights. Gina and Olivia seemed happy to take her in. *Almost too happy*, Sarah recalled.

In the days after the Trident Cinemas incident, Olivia tried, on several occasions, to set Sarah up on blind dates. Each potential suitor was given the same response: "I don't do blind dates—I'm not interested at all." As the days progressed, Sarah began to worry: *Perhaps I've made a terrible mistake...*

"Hey—earth to Sarah, do you hear me?" Olivia said, pulling her mind's focus back to the present. "No, sorry," she replied, "my mind kinda ran off there for a second." Olivia helped Gina unpack the flower pots from the box; several had been cracked. "I was saying that we should forget all this nonsense and go to the Red Manhattan in Henderson," Olivia said. Sarah grimaced as she found that several of her favorite knickknacks had been destroyed by her friend, all in the name of being spiteful to someone she didn't even really know. *Gina and Olivia were a grade ahead of me in high school, I had always assumed that they were wiser and knew better. I'm starting to think that maybe even back then, they really didn't know anything at all...except, maybe how to be spiteful*, she thought.

"No thanks," Sarah replied. Then, she had an idea—*let's see what doing this does*, she thought, *if they have no ulterior motives in wanting to go out, they'll still want to go out, even if I'm not going to accompany them. Will my "friends" let me stay home—and, free from their control—while they go out dancing? I truly hope so.*

Sarah's hopes had been in vain. Gina dropped a pot back into the box and replied, "Nah, I think that we should, like, stay together—right Olivia?" Olivia enthusiastically agreed by nodding her head with a smile. *I'm beginning to think Olivia would nod even if Gina suggested we all went down to the sewage plant for a swim*, Sarah thought.

"No thanks, I'm feeling a little tired, and I think it'd be fun for me to just hang out, maybe catch up on some sleep I've lost lately," she said. Sarah hated going out to dance. It wasn't that she hated dancing; she had simply gotten bored with it, as her two new roommates liked to go out to clubs four days a week. Sarah had lost her job at the library branch for falling asleep at work twice the week before, and she felt that the seemingly-mandatory all night dance outings were to blame.

Gina did not look happy about Sarah's persistence. Olivia, however, maintained her smile, and said in sugary words, "I think she might be right, Gin. Why don't we hang out in here tonight; we could call over some of those freshmen we met at the Shake House!" Gina and Olivia high-fived before turning to observe Sarah's reaction. "Sure, you girls go ahead and party all you want, I'll just go book a room at Texas P—" Gina waved her arm and yelled, "What the *hell*, Sarah?" "Woah," Sarah continued talking with a confident stare upon Gina's face, "don't be using such words in reference to me. I've never had to tolerate that before—and, I'm certainly not going to go starting now. Olivia's hands moved to her hips; her face began to contort into a wicked grimace. "Who taught you that, your country boy?" she sniped. "No," Sarah said as she stepped within an inch of Olivia's face. The rest of her response came in a scowling yell wrought of fury: "my *father* did!"

Olivia looked hurt, yet Gina seemed truly disgusted. "You know what, you little traitor, I think we might have made a mistake when we let you move in. You're starting to sound like someone we wouldn't even want to hang out with." Sarah's volume lowered, but her tone remained the same, "I'm acting like myself. And I wouldn't even have to be here if I would have never listened to you guys about my boyfriend." Gina scoffed and said, "It's not our fault your lazy stalker ex-boyfriend didn't offer to help." And that was the straw that broke the neon camel's back.

"My Andrew has never been lazy a day in his life—he grew up on a farm for crying out loud. And, *stop* calling him a stalker! He told me to contact *him* if I ever wanted to talk. Stalkers don't tell you where they'll be, Gina—they *stalk*! Or maybe you didn't know because you're the one who dances every fricking day instead of reading something once in a while." Gina didn't retort; Olivia stared at them wordlessly.

Nobody spoke for several minutes. The apartment was filled to the rafters with an extremely tense silence that was almost palpable. Gina opened a compact and preened herself. Olivia had her iPhone in her hands and appeared to be giving all of her current attention towards an application on its screen—whether she was actually using her phone or merely pretending to be so that she could avoid being noticed was anyone's guess. "I think you should leave, Sarah," Olivia said out of nowhere, in a calm, yet resentful voice. Sarah gave her a defiant look and replied, "I think that's the one thing you've ever told me since we've met that I can actually believe in. And don't worry about my stuff—I'll send someone you *hate* to come pick it up for me. That is, the things you haven't already broken in your immaturity." Sarah didn't look back as she pulled away from the Sandy Meadow Lane apartments. As her blue Corsica sped off southward, she thought, *At least I have one silver lining. I don't have to figure out where to go.* Sarah made for Texas Palace as fast as her car could carry her.

The sun had begun to set into the purple-pink horizon as she ran two red lights and made several questionable slow-downs at stop signs on her way to the Texas Palace valet. Melissa asked her, "What name, ma'am?" to which she responded, "It doesn't matter!" She gave her keys and a five dollar bill to Melissa and ran through the entrance.

Sarah Crawford had many fine traits—patience was not one of them. With guilt further compounding her sense of haste, she opted for the stairs after three fruitless clicks of a button in the elevator lobby. Sarah was thoroughly exhausted by the time she made it to the suite level. She sprayed herself down with a light spritz of perfume and tried to fix her hair as she arrived to the doors of the Austin Suite.

Knocking on the door yielded no result. *Guess I better try harder*, Sarah reasoned. She knocked louder than before and yelled, "Andrew! Andrew Cadoret!" There was no immediate reply; as she was turning away to dejectedly for the elevators, Sarah heard a door open behind her.

Sarah entered the suite to find a dreary looking Connor Bentley lurching his way back to the great room bar. There were several empty

Old Fashioned glasses atop the bar, as well as several origami animals and a framed color photo. Sarah didn't know when it was taken, but she could tell it was of the man before her and Andrew, and they were happily posing with a band on stage.

"Now," Connor began, "I've made a living figuring things out before other people...but, please, help me Sarah: tell me why *you* would come here to my door. It's the only reason I let you in—I need to understand this curveball before I strike out." The Con-Man was bruised, messy-haired, and his clothing was torn in several places; several tear tracks betrayed any sense of pride he might have had in his greeting to her. *I don't know what he thinks—he's probably right, even—but I really hope he can help*, Sarah thought as she walked closer to the bar.

"Look, Mr. Con-Man," She began. "It's Mr. Bentley, to you," Connor cut in before gesturing for her to go on. "Mr. Bentley, I know I've caused some painful moments. I understand that there's suffering that my own ignorance has set in motion; I'm not here to fight. I'm here to apologize to Andrew—if he'll hear me. I know I've been—" Connor cut her off: "You know? What do *you* know? Besides how to make a dear friend hate me? Besides your obvious skill at breaking hearts and starting fights, I mean. Tell me, child—*Tell me* what it is that 'you know'."

Tears began to flow freely down Sarah's cheeks. She had been used to defending what she thought was right in her life up to this point. She had never been in an argument before where she knew that her original stance had been wrong; she felt too guilty to even try to defend her-self: she knew he was right. She wiped her face off with her hands and replied weakly, "I'm here for Andrew. Is he here? If not, have you seen him?" Connor gave a sarcastic eye roll before responding, "Oh yeah, I've seen him. He left because of *you!*"

"Because of me?" Sarah eagerly inquired, "Is he trying to find me?" The idea did confuse Sarah somewhat, being as Andrew didn't have an address at which to find her, but she was hopelessly optimistic. Connor began to pour another drink at the bar; he was stumbling a little, and clearly smelled of whiskey. "No, he left because we had words," he said.

It appeared, from the thrown over chair, torn clothing and beer bottle shards, that there had been more than just words on Monday evening in the Austin Suite.

"Okay, I'm sorry you two had words—can't you see I'm trying to help fix what I did? You can't tell me that's not a noble act, at least?" Connor spun in his barstool and then put his drink on the bar. He rose and said, "Actually, young lady, I'm grown, and this is my place, at least for the next ninety days or so. I can do whatever the hell I please." *Oh man,* Sarah thought, *I got a bad feeling that the only way I'm gonna find him is to look for him myself.* "Look, I didn't come here looking for a fight. Are you going to help me or not?" she asked. The Con-Man shrugged and replied, "He wouldn't have had a reason to be mad at me if you hadn't been so closed off to him. You took the words of little known 'friends' over someone you had known for more than a year—he was always really hurt over that, you know. I ended up telling the poor kid that he'd be better off with somebody else. Maybe if he's truly lucky he will be."

Sarah's tears persisted. Her eyes strayed to see the picture on the bar—how happy Andrew seemed to be, smiling with his friend and the band they adored. It was her fault, and it was destroying her. She tried to find something to say but found herself mute; Sarah's own conscience had silenced her. Sarah lowered her head and simply walked out the door. She heard a robust door slam on her way to the elevators.

As she drove the Corsica off the Texas Palace lot, Sarah began to contemplate her next move. *I don't know how I'm going to do this— but I need to. Actions speak louder than words, and words won't help me, anyway; whether I can find him or not, I'll go down swinging,* she thought. She began to drive aimlessly southward. It wasn't until her car reached the intersection of Rancho and MLK that she realized something of vital importance. *Wait a sec—he didn't want to help me, but I think he just may have, anyhow. He said that he and Andrew had a fight, and brought up that he told him to get someone new. Now, I am pretty sure that the last part was put in for my benefit.*

*But, like my grandma always used to tell me when I was little, "If you're careful with how you treat things, even trash will be treasure." Is there a fact hidden there? Was the fight over the new girl concept, or a disa—oh no...*Sarah thought as she came to the conclusion: *he's looking for me.* She tried frantically to think of where Andrew would go if he were trying to find her. She drew a blank, and pounded the steering wheel in frustration. *I guess I'll have to just drive around the streets surrounding Texas Palace, and work outward from there,* she concluded.

Hours passed without sight nor sound of Andrew. It was early Tuesday morning when Sarah, no longer acute nor alert in her search, gave in and found a place to sleep. She drove her car to the leasing office for Summerlin Heights. *If he goes back to Texas Palace, that Bentley guy will be there for him; he might even tell Andrew that I'm looking for him. And, if he goes by our old home together, I'll be here,* she reasoned.

Sarah awoke to the sound of car horns blaring. She roused herself to find cars parked on both sides of the Corsica. A Las Vegas City Transit shuttle was honking; she had been so tired in the morning that she hadn't thought to check for the placard that wasn't far from her current eye-level: "LVCT VEHICLES ONLY." There was a short, angry looking man covered in stubble honking the horn and gesturing rudely for her to get out. Sarah rolled down her windows to apologize and explain, but the driver beat her to the punch. "You can't park that thing here, sweetheart! Get your makeup on already and get out," he said. She had been prepared to eat crow over her parking violation; but, she wouldn't stand for chauvinism while still groggy and being honked at. Sarah pulled out, but before she did, she gave the driver the finger and said, "I'm not your sweetheart, jerk!"

"*Great,* he didn't show," Sarah said to herself as she drove southbound on Craig Road. She had been hoping that Andrew had been hiking to Summerlin Heights. *And that means forget checking on Texas Palace, either,* she thought, having realized that Andrew would have taken a car to look for her if he had returned to patch things up with his friend. *So, where now? Where would he—a person not from here—go; and, how am I, equally non-native, supposed to find him?* Sarah wondered. She ended up deciding on heading downtown. *Well, if he could be anywhere in Vegas, I might as well start near the center. Downtown it is,* she reasoned.

She was hungry, still a little tired, and in desperate need of a shower; but, she didn't care. She had no home address, no money, and had accidentally left her iPhone behind at Gina and Olivia's. But, it didn't bother her. Nothing bothered Sarah Crawford at this moment, not as long as there was still a chance of getting to Andrew and making things right. *He may not even want to ever be with me again, for all I know...And I'd deserve it, whatever happens. The least I can do is apologize and show my honest intentions,* she thought.

The 95 South was congested; it took Sarah nearly a half hour to reach the Downtown-Fremont exit. The downtown casinos were bathed in rays of mid-morning sun. She took the opportunity to stop at every red light, and prayed for good luck as she took a series of loops that always seemed to end on 4th Street. Downtown was quickly becoming a disappointment.

As Sarah drove northbound on Main Street, she began to panic. She had spent most of Tuesday looking at every vacant corner she could find. There weren't many people on the streets near Fremont when she had left it, though she theorized that it wouldn't matter anyway. Tourists hanging out downtown were not very likely to know Andrew Cadoret from Adam.

Sarah awoke the next morning with her car parked in front of the leasing office of Summerlin Heights. She had been extra careful to avoid parking in the shuttle's designated parking spot this time. She groggily sat up straight and looked at herself in the rearview mirror—she had seen better days. Beyond lacking makeup, Sarah's hair was getting greasy and she had bags beneath her eyes. "I'll buy a toothbrush if I can find the money for one," she told herself reassuringly. "But," she said softly as she turned her key in the ignition, "I have more important things to do right now than go searching through the seat cushions for quarters."

As she drove south on Craig Road, Sarah spotted what appeared to be a man walking alone with his head hung low, about a football field away. Her heart raced and she pressed the gas harder in anticipation. When she got near enough to get a better look, she realized that she did recognize the man, but it was not who she had hoped to encounter on the side of the road. It was Connor.

"What's wrong? Maserati having transmission problems?" She asked him. The Con-Man shook his head and said, "The *Rolls* ran out of gas while I was looking for the kid, actually." Sarah sighed. Connor slowly began to shamble southward on foot. Sarah caught up with him again, and this time honked her horn to get his attention. He looked at her with confusion in her eyes. Sarah said in the closest she could manage to a friendly voice: "Get in."

"Turn left on Tenaya," Connor told Sarah as they drove down Craig. "Why, is that a place Andrew would go?" she asked sanguinely. "No, dear child, it's the nearest possible Left Aid convenience store. You, miss, need to get cleaned up a little." Sarah couldn't believe her ears. She gritted her teeth, but consented with a nod.

After a quick trip to recoup supplies at Texas, the oddly formed team that was Sarah and the Con-Man departed freshly fed, recently showered and eager to search for the man whom they had only recently agreed to both call "Summerlin". Connor had donned a new white tux, whereas Sarah became the proud owner of a pair of bedazzled jeans bearing a tag reading "Con-Wear for Ladies-and Bad Girls." The tag didn't make her grumble, but the t-shirt that Connor gave her to wear did. It read simply: "I AM A CHILD." As a consolation for wearing it, the Con-Man let Ms. Crawford choose the car that they would use in their quest. She opted for the mirror-coupe.

Wednesday came and went without the two of them seeing hide nor hair of Summerlin. Their travels took Connor and Sarah through-out Summerlin and central Vegas, through every major street and side alley that the Con-Man could conjure. At one point Wednesday evening, Connor pulled the coupe to a slow crawl on 4th Street. There was a pair of raggedly dressed men walking with sandwiches in their hands. "Seven!" he called out towards them. They turned, and the taller of the two men walked up to the car after Connor stopped it and put on the emergency break. "What's happenin' Bentley?" He asked. "Not much, old codger, just living the life. Say, you wouldn't have run into my friend Summerlin lately, would you?" Seven shook his head and said, "Nope. Me and Lenny here have been living rather large ourselves, taking in the lights and eating dollar sandwiches. Haven't seen 'im, or I'd continue to bestow my thanks." Connor nodded and said, "Thanks anyway, old pal." The car began to drive away when Seven called out, "You should go uptown, back near Texas; that's where Down-Low said he'd be headed. Maybe he's seen something." Both Connor and Sarah gave repeated thanks to the two men before departing.

"I want to eat, I'm hungry," Connor said about an hour later as they cruised beneath the Spaghetti Bowl. "I'm not. I want to find 'Summerlin', remember? I'll take my stomach hurting: I earned it." Connor laughed and replied, "Trust me, young one, there's no point in learning a les-son if you destroy yourself doing it. Come with me inside Crazy Burger and eat something. We wouldn't want to have Summerlin find a girl that resembles a skin-covered skeleton, now would we?" Sarah looked as if she were honestly debating the question. Connor pulled the car into the Crazy Burger parking lot and said, "Come on, we're eating, and that' that." Sarah sighed and went in to have an Insanity Meal beside the Con-Man. Though she wouldn't admit it, she thought to herself while eating, *He's awful nice. I don't think we'd ever get along if we didn't have Andrew—Summerlin in common, but he's being a lot more mature about this than I would have expected. Andrew and I both chose older friends when in need of advice; go figure he'd pick an eccentric gambler and would be the wiser for it.*

"The problem is," Connor said to Sarah while finishing his *Psycho-Shake*, "the dear boy likes to walk long distances when he's pissed." Sarah nodded. "Yeah, he's prone to that. He always said it was his way of keeping himself from saying something he would later regret." Connor hung his head and remained silent until Sarah said, "Hey—I wasn't trying to remind you of what happened or anything. We both know I'm the guiltier party..." Connor wagged his finger and rose his head to respond, "We both did a few wrong things, Miss Crawford. We only need remember those for when we apologize. Apart from apologizing, you'll find in life that right and wrong don't matter—what happens the next time is what counts." She smiled and nodded before rising from her seat. She adjusted her ponytail and stretched her arms before exclaiming, "Okay, let's go then!" Connor rose slowly, grinning. "There may be hope for you yet, Buckeye."

18.

Summerlin rose from the faded black daybed and stretched as he rubbed his eyes. He wandered to the window nearest him, which faced out towards a green plot of overgrown grass. There was grass as far as the eye could see. Thomas's place had not been Summerlin's first choice for sleeping. Actually, his temporary residence at 16th Street had come about by complete chance. Contrary to the intuitions of Sarah and the Con-Man, Summerlin had headed away from the city, not into it. His late Monday walk took him to the corner of Aldebaran Avenue and Dean Martin Drive, where a Lucky Flamingo Laundromat branch enticed him to take a breather. As Summerlin walked to the kitchen, he recalled the fight he had with Connor several nights prior, and how he had come to wake in the purple-gray house that time forgot.

The image of an ice-cold bottle of soda may not have been the cure for all that ailed him, but, he thought—*It sure is a good place to start.* He would have just kept walking; Summerlin had no real sense of time or distance that night. His anger had cooled down by the time he arrived at the Lucky Flamingo. Summerlin didn't intend on tarrying long, however, it did on some level feel like he was near something familiar when he walked inside. He expected to find a large soda machine to the left of the entrance—and did. What Summerlin did not expect was to hear a voice call out behind him as he put a dollar in the soda machine.

"Hey, Summerlin," the voice said. Summerlin turned around. It was Thomas. "Wouldn't have thought it would be so easy to surprise a country boy. Having trouble, Mr. Cadoret?" he said with a grin. At first he didn't answer—Summerlin hadn't expected to see Thomas this far south of downtown—*What would make an Angel abandon Hoover Avenue?* he wondered. "Yeah," Summerlin replied, "I s'pose I am. I didn't know you'd be here, but I'm kinda glad you are." Thomas walked back to the desk near the rear of the store and opened a desk drawer. He tossed Summerlin a bag of pretzels.

Summerlin said, "thanks," before opening the bag and wolfing down its contents. "Actually, I was just about to leave Texas for Hoover; but, someone told me that I should come here." Summerlin sighed; *I'm glad he cares after our fight, but how'd the Con-Man know I'd be on this side of town*, he wondered. "I heard about the fight, and I'd like to help," Thomas said as he put four quarters into the drink machine. "I don't know if I feel like acceptin' help anymore, no offense. It's seemed to cause me some awful headaches in the past," Summerlin said as he stared at the floor. Thomas leaned against the counter near the machine and said, "I wouldn't go saying things like that—trust me, I know a lot about such things. Besides, you will need someone to help your honest soul survive out there. You won't find Mr. Bling; he rarely wanders down this far south. Real street people usually stay away from the Boulevard."

"Well, I don't know. You aren't goin' to try and fix my life are you?" Summerlin asked. Thomas laughed and said, "No, I don't think that's my forte. I'm afraid all I can do is offer you a bed." Summerlin agreed, and Thomas took him through the back of the building to a small parking lot that barely contained the large old brown pickup truck he had seen parked near Connor's Packard at the Palace. "Thomas got in and opened the door for Summerlin. "Where are we goin'?" he asked. Thomas's voice became a shade more poetic as he started up the pickup and said, "To 16th Street, and all that remains of paradise."

Summerlin's only request was that he not inform the Con-Man where he was. He didn't hate Connor, but wanted a breather before he attempted mending a friendship that he feared might have been stretched to the limit. Thomas obliged, and provided him with a roof over his head and two square meals a day. On the first two nights, Thomas played Summerlin in chess before departing for Hoover Avenue. By Wednesday, he was going along for the ride with Mr. West, and helped load the transient peoples' wash while the proprietor served late night coffee.

Summerlin knowingly kept the topic matter of their conversations light—there was no talk of death, Texas's bankruptcy, Sarah or the fight; instead, they had discussions about quality tobacco, baseball and blue-grass music. There were a few times where Thomas seemed to vanish from reality, and simply talk to himself out loud—almost as if he were disagreeing with himself; but, Summerlin felt there was no point in bringing it up. *Can't go livin' life by judgin' people by their weaknesses,* he decided.

By the time Thursday night's work at the Lucky Flamingo had ended, Summerlin had nearly memorized the melody of thirteen classical music pieces. Tommy played the stuff all night long, and often, at a barely-bearable volume, at least as far as Summerlin was concerned. They left the Laundromat around 4:30am. When they got home, Thomas went upstairs seeming wide awake. Summerlin crashed on the black daybed that sat in the living room. And then, hours later, he woke.

And that places me here, Summerlin thought as he finished the cereal he had poured during his contemplation of what had led him to be eating alone—literally, alone on the entire block—in the late afternoon. Thomas was nowhere to be found.

It was a quaint wooden house with faded walls and dark wooden moldings running the span of almost every wall. There was a stale air about the place which made the house seem vulnerable amidst the desert city; *usually they tear down buildings 'round here way before this*, Summerlin thought as he walked around the lower floor. Though he had been a resident there for the better part of a week, he had yet to climb the stairs. *Mr. West is a very nice, but very private seemin' man— it would be best to respect both facts 'bout him*, Summerlin reasoned.

Further wandering led him through the dining room and to a room with a tile floor and an empty bookcase that Summerlin assumed had at one time been a den or study—all of these rooms were empty and lacking of any furniture: dust was their only tenant. The rooms beyond the kitchen made Summerlin find his living room quite well appointed: it was a wooden paneled, square shaped room with a window facing the front yard; the other front facing wall lay to the left of the doorway, near the houses archaic hand tooled staircase. The living room had a single black daybed with oddly fresh-smelling sheets, a coffee table with a chess board and Bible on it, and a metal roller cart with a TV-VCR with a cable box on it that Thomas had brought for Summerlin on Tuesday morning when he came home.

Summerlin checked his watch: it was 3:49pm. He walked to the foot of the stairs and yelled out, "Mr. West? Tommy!" several times, but to no result. *Where could he be? He's usually up by now*, Summerlin thought. He decided to climb to the top of the stairs and try calling out Thomas's name again. At the top, he yelled, "Thomas?" There was still no response. He didn't go up any further, but an odd sight caught Summerlin's eye: There were four sets of doors, two on each side of the short, flowery-wallpapered hallway. Three of them had brass door handles, but the one on the far right seemed silver, and looked unlike the others: that knob had a key-hole, and was rounder than the others. *Snoopin's still not my thing*, Summerlin thought as he walked down the stairs.

Summerlin sat back down on the daybed, and began to wonder what he was supposed to be doing, in Thomas's absence. He was alive and physically well—the rest of his life, however, was still completely up in the air. His financial future was in chaos, a detail he had until then ignored in the face of greater circumstances. Summerlin was going to have to get ahold of his family back home to let them know where he was and that he was doing okay. He had gotten used to making such calls on the Austin Suite's free long distance line.

And then, there was Sarah. Despite the near month-long separation and angst, Summerlin's heart was still ever hers. *I'm not the kind of guy to throw away years of happiness for a month worth of mistakes*, he reasoned. All he ever had to do was get her attention for a few minutes, Summerlin was sure of it. But, he had not, in more than three weeks, been capable of getting even three second alone to speak with Sarah. *If only I had seen this comin', I would have warned her of my similar mistakes*, he thought.

Summerlin was thinking of the time when he was seventeen, when he dumped his then-girlfriend Jenny at the advice of his "friends", Those same friends ended up stealing and selling his 1996 Atlanta Braves team signed baseball. He thought, *true friends won't dictate your life. Real friends would never interfere in matters of the heart. Of course, even I had to learn that one.*

After brushing his teeth and showering in the bathroom that connected to the dimly-lit kitchen, Summerlin put on his clothes—a pair of Con-Wear jeans and a Lucky Flamingo t-shirt. "What can I do today?" he asked himself while looking in the bathroom mirror as he fixed his hair. As it was a Friday, finding employment seemed unlikely. Summerlin then endured a brief mental barrage of all the good, nice people he couldn't go see right then: Xero, Trista, the rest of the band—even Connor. They were all either at Henderson Palace, which Summerlin had no clue how to get to, or at Texas, a place where he wouldn't feel right about even stepping foot inside until he'd smoothed things over with the Con-Man.

Summerlin found himself pacing the hardwood floor in circles as his mind addressed his worries individually. He made a point to keep his body busy while he recalled every instance since the evil Thursday which had set him upon Connor Bentley's doorstep. "Oww!" Summerlin yelled when out of nowhere, his elbow bashed into the corner of the wall molding in the dining room. His instincts pulled his gaze to the minor scrape on his elbow. But, after a moment's glance, his eyes met the wall that had injured him, and the secret compartment within the wall he had just unknowingly dislodged.

The cavity beyond the false wall panel was filled with unpainted wooden shelves which appeared to hold nothing but dust. Then, he saw it—there was something flat and small deep within the recess. Summerlin put his hand on the third shelf down and reached as far as his arm would go. His fingers loosely pulled upon a plastic object; he adjusted his grip and pulled it out. It was an old VHS tape with a homemade label. The words were in alternating colors as to have the effect of a rainbow. The penmanship appeared feminine—and very happy. It read: "The Best Days!" and had several smiley faces on its front and top labels.

Curiosity can be a near-lethal force, especially when all subtler avenues of thought are absent. *Mama always told me 'don't go openin' closed doors without a reason'. Well,* Summerlin reasoned, *I didn't open it. Fate did. And seein' as how I was strangely gifted with a television that plays only tapes—Maybe it's s'posed to be played?* Summerlin felt a little guilty as he carried the tape into the living room. He debated the deed, and came to the conclusion that he'd rather make a losing bet than none at all—Summerlin turned on the television and pushed the tape into the VCR.

Lines and white noise were followed by a chain of home video clips. Several youngsters playing board games on the coffee table on which

Summerlin currently had a bottle of soda. The group of youngsters sung, danced, and were having a good time. Then came a scene which reverberated throughout Summerlin's mind and body—the kids were playing *Extreme Euchre*!

Summerlin rewound the tape and started it from the beginning. This time, he was looking at not what the group of college-aged kids were doing, but at their faces. His search did not leave him waiting— Summerlin's hypothesis was proven correct within thirty seconds: he recognized three of the four euchre players. Thomas, Jail-Bait and... *Connor? What in blazes?* he thought. Clearly, this was a very important video to have been stowed away when everything else on the main floor save the kitchen and a daybed had been removed.

He watched the happy moments roll along. They hacky-sacked, play-fought and even had a sing-a-long to the piano playing of a curly-haired woman whom Summerlin did not recognize. *They all seem so happy*, he thought as he continued watching. There was a scene where the Con-Man, wearing ragged clothes, hopped out of a rust-free and undamaged Dodge Aries with a smile on his face—"My first car guys! I love it!" Connor seemed happy to tears, and for some reason hugged Thomas after getting out of the vehicle.

Summerlin rewound the tape again, intent on figuring out who the fourth euchre player had been. The problem was, the kid didn't look old enough to be living there—*wait*, he thought as he pressed play during a hacking scene, *that's...Xero!* Indeed, somehow the old spikey haired rebel had convinced Thomas to hack in a circle with him. To his credit, Mr. West was somewhat agile, but not that good at foot to sack contact; he smiled joyfully nonetheless. *Wow*, Summerlin thought, *night and day...*

After Connor's car moment, there came a scene unlike all the others before it. The video quality for this portion was more stable than those in the preceding portion of the tape—the audio quality even seemed to be finer. It was the front steps of the house, and Thomas and the curly-haired young lady were in focus. Tommy was kneeling before the piano girl. He said in a manner most clear and eloquent: "Sylvia Sanford, you have long been the great joy of my life—the epitome of all I hold dear. You, my friend and loved one, are water to my desert, food to my soul and light where else there had been darkness. Asking to spend a life with you is a tragedy: an abuse of sad proportions, considering that a full life of days is not nearly time enough to appreciate you. Will you do me the fine honor of making me the happiest man to ever stand this earth, and be my wife?" The girl exclaimed "Yes!" with jubilation and rushed to embrace Thomas. The two kissed as the picture began to get fuzzy.

Summerlin's heart fell the height of the *Stratosphere*. Upon hearing Sylvia's answer, Thomas's face had lit up with pride and happiness that he hadn't thought possible. Mr. West had, at all times, been a gentleman to Summerlin, but he'd always shown such a faded, polite distance, emotionally speaking, and he was having trouble reconciling the *Angel of Hoover Avenue* with the man proposing on the tape. Then, the tears came. Not tears for Sarah, poverty, or pain, but for the noble, once passion-filled man with whom Summerlin could only become acquainted with through the confines of history. *No—That man has to still be in there*, he thought. Summerlin had a soul-reviving moment of realization: *My fate may be screwed, but I can still be of use—if not for myself, then for these genuine, good people. I need to do something.* His thoughts drifted instantly to Thomas and Xero...

When Tommy came home, he found Summerlin laying on the day-bed with a distressed look upon his face. Thomas sat next to him and said, "I know you don't want to hear this, but you are going to have to talk to our friend Connor. When Blake came by to pick up the band's clothes for today's show, he said that the Con-Man was looking for you, and very upset. You got him scared. Word of your guys's fight has spread far and wide. Even the street folk on 4ᵗʰ Street have heard of it." Summerlin hung his head low and replied, "I'm sorry this has all gone like this—I never had any idea my leaving Connor's place was news." Thomas patted his shoulder and replied, "Of course it is—you're one of the family." Summerlin had yet to discuss the topic—or anything even approaching its depth—with Thomas; he had figured that the man had his own problems and didn't need any more. Summerlin wanted to tell Mr. West the absolute truth about what had occurred between Connor and he. Summerlin desired deeply to go into the topics in great detail. But, as fate would have it, he couldn't. Instead, for the first time in his life, Summerlin was about to intentionally tell a true friend a lie.

Instead of telling Thomas about the tape; rather than discussing Sarah, or the actual fight with Connor, Summerlin began to undertake the plan that he had crafted during the early evening hours. He told Thomas about the fight, but changed several details. Summerlin told Tommy that the fight had been started by Sarah's friends Gina and Olivia—that they had called the Austin Suite and bragged that they had decided to move back to the Ohio river valley, and that Sarah was indeed going with them. He told Thomas that the three girls were flying out of Henderson Airport—he wasn't even sure if such a thing existed—on Friday, and would be staying at Henderson Palace until then. Summerlin listed the phone call as the reason Connor told him to get a new girl. He was depending strongly on the fact that Xero had been watching his fight with the Con-Man, which meant that Thomas wouldn't have been anywhere near to know any better. Blake telling him something was a risk, but Summerlin was no longer scared by risks. *They're all I have now*, he surmised.

The plan wasn't happenstance: Summerlin spent over an hour thinking through the particulars. He knew that he had to get Xero and

Thomas to talk, and he knew that he wanted to help the band make their audition. Summerlin carefully devised his story to Thomas as to include a flight departure time of 8:30, so that he could attempt to convince the man to take him there. This would enable Summerlin to be there at the show; of course, he still hadn't figured out how the show could be cancelled or curtailed. It was only minutes before Thomas came home that he realized the solution—*It's that contract, it's the way out. We just need to make sure the audience is satisfied*, Summerlin thought. The act of helping the band would also force Xero and Thomas to get along and be together for something that wasn't Italian food. *On that end, I'll just have to make it up as I go, I s'pose*, he figured.

He checked his watch: it was 6:40. "Why didn't you tell me this before," Thomas asked him in a cautious tone. Summerlin had seen this one coming; he replied in a faux sadness: "I didn't want to trouble you none. I also was just too thankful to be a bother. But now the end-game to this sadness is just about broken all chance I'll ever know to be happy." Summerlin wasn't *fully* lying—he was using real emotions relating to his equally real pain; he was merely changing terms to make the act work. *I'm no actor, and I've never been much for dishonesty— I'm taking a big gamble here, and I can only pray that the ends will justify the means*, Summerlin thought. Thomas sat contemplating what Summerlin had said before standing to face him.

"I don't know what to say kid—maybe Connor does know best. Trust me, love and relationships can be the torture of a man's life. How about we just go try and fix things between you and him instead?" Summerlin shook his head and thought of when his childhood dog Casey died in order to muster up the tears necessary for his plea to work. "Tommy, I need help, desperately. This is my last chance at redemption."

Thomas thought silently for what seemed like ages. "I don't know kid..." Summerlin stood up and implored him, "Please? I thought maybe you'd understand. You loved your g—" Thomas waved his hand dismissively and replied in a cold tone: "That's *different*, Cadoret. You don't even understand what I've seen and been through—" Summerlin likewise cut Thomas off. "But—one thing, Mr. West: what if I told you I do? What if I told you I'm every bit as certain of my love for her as you ever were for your angel?" Those were the first honest words to pass Summerlin's lips in fifteen minutes. The sentiments and feelings for Sarah were true, but, as far as he knew, she was already lost to him. He was trying to re-purpose his angst. *It might as well serve somebody well*, Summerlin thought.

Thomas's eyes began to well up with unshed tears. He knelt and closed his eyes for several moments before rising and staring Summerlin in the eye. He asked, "For love?" Summerlin nodded and answered with an emphatic "Yes!" Thomas grabbed his keys from the kitchen and said in a defiant tone, "Then come, we shall *not fail!*"

The old truck roared to life, and the tires burnt rubber as Thomas and Summerlin sped off for the highway. Summerlin checked his watch again—it was now 6:58. "You got a strategy, Summerlin?" Thomas asked as they neared the highway ramp. "Yeah, but it's kind of hard to explain. Just promise me you'll follow my lead, no matter what." Tommy nodded and said, "It's your show, cowboy." Summerlin replied, "I'm a farmer's son, not a cowboy." Thomas grinned and said, "Same difference."

They didn't get far on the 95 south—rush hour had set in, and the cars were racked up bumper to bumper. "Oh, great, now what do we do?" Summerlin said as he began to feel anxiety and fear creeping in. It would all be for nothing if the two of them did not make it to Henderson Palace in time. "Ah, well I'm glad you asked," Thomas replied, "Now, we *improvise!*"

Thomas revved the truck's engine and pulled the car onto the shoulder of the highway. The truck then began to do a combination of lane-skipping, weaving, and all out disrespect of every highway transit law ever written. Summerlin nearly had a heart attack. As he clutched his seat for dear life, he said, "Don't you think this might be a little bit... dangerous?" Thomas's eyes widened and he and replied with devout passion, "Don't worry, child—we have *angels on our shoulders!*"

The old Chevy pickup pulled into the Henderson Palace valet at 7:34. Summerlin threw a twenty dollar bill on the driver's seat as they ran out of the truck. "Keep it in the lane and there's another bill in it for you!" he shouted to the confused looking valet.

Summerlin's heart began to race as he called out to Thomas, "Just follow me no matter what!" After they had entered the Pit, Tommy yelled out from behind him, "Hey, what are you doing? The bell desk is back there!" *Thank God*, Summerlin thought as he continued to run without slacking in pace, *if I can hear him, it means he's still behind me.* He didn't actually know where he was going. Summerlin's only hope was that Texas Palace's sister property would also have it's nightclub connected to the end of the gaming Pit. Luckily, it was. Though he was running very low on oxygen, Summerlin sped up his gait once he saw the curtained entrance in the distance—"The Red Manhattan" was only a few more yards away.

Summerlin began to hear music—it was The Reason Why, and they were halfway into Journey's *Don't Stop Believin'.* All sense left his mind—*This is goin' to be about bravery and guts, I just gotta stop the music, no matter what*, Summerlin thought. There was no time to wait; Summerlin ran full speed through the entrance of the nightclub, leveling the clipboard holding attendant who was stationed at the podium near the curtains.

Inside the Red Manhattan, there was a standing room only crowd, and The Reason Why was playing on stage, all five members were clad in their personalized Texas World shirts. As Summerlin ran towards the stage, he noticed that there were several veil-wearing Brides of Xero in attendance, as well as a few regulars from Texas Palace. One group was holding a sign that read, "NO FAIR STEALING TEXAS!"

Summerlin didn't look for the backstage entrance. He didn't care where it was—the only act he could come up with to halt the music on stage would be to climb onstage himself. And, so, he did. Summerlin lept on top of the stage while the band continued to play the Journey song. He flailed his arms wildly and yelled, "Guys! Guys! Stop it, already!" The band's playing stopped immediately upon Blake and Jail-Bait noticing what had occurred. Summerlin heard Thomas yelling from off stage, "Cadoret—what are you *doing*?!"

Blake Blanchard, ever the showman, never lost a beat, or his composure. He smiled and walked up to Summerlin, mic in hand and said, "Looks like we got ourselves a huge fan here!" The crowd roared. The band members walked over to Summerlin; Thomas was currently flailing his arms in an attempt to stop two security officers who were marching for the stage.

"Woah! What the hell's up, Summerlin?" Jail-Bait asked. "I came here because I had to," he replied. "What?" Blake, Sam, and Xero said in unison. "Look," Summerlin said, "I know this sounds odd—but you guys need to go to Texas. Your shot to fame awaits." A security officer made it onstage, but was waved off by Trent, who said, "He's with us, old sport." Thomas took the backstage staircase to join the group onstage. The audience became a sea of murmurs and confusion. Thomas had a very grave look on his face as he approached Summerlin. "Mr. Cadoret, I believe we need to talk." Summerlin lowered his head and said, "Yes, I s'pose we do. I lied to you; but, if you give sufficient time to review my motives, I hope that you'll find forgiveness possible—I'd never intentionally hurt you." Thomas nodded and replied, "That much I already knew kid—I know you must have some good intention, you're too pure hearted to do otherwise. However, next time, no lies. Especially ones that would bring me to be near hi—" Jail-Bait grabbed a microphone and turned it on to overpower Thomas: "Okay, that'll be quite enough of *that*." "You need to make things up with Xero. He loves you, and you love him—you were practically brothers for goodness sake," Summerlin whispered. Thomas shook his head and replied, "Whether or not that is even humanly possible isn't the point, Summerlin. What are we doing on the f-ing stage?" Summerlin smiled and nodded before walking over to Blake.

"Hey Blake, remember that contract you and Jail-Bait were perusin'?" he asked. Blake nodded and said, "Yeah, what about it?" Summerlin said, "I thought of somethin'—and, I'm pretty sure it's goin' to work. Guys: Bail. The contract says music needs to be played, not that you have to be doin' it. Thomas and I can do somethin'." Jail-Bait shook her head with a frown before adding, "I love the spirit, Summerlin, but the contract also defined a show as 'a performance of music which is appreciable in its nature to its intended audience."

"Yes. And these are T.R.Y. *fans*. They don't have to like me and Tommy bein' tone-deaf to appreciate lettin' you guys get your chance." "*You guys*?" the band said more or less at the time. "Sure," Summerlin answered with a grin, "I'm not Waylan Jennings, but I can sing the Blacksburg High fight song." Xero laughed and replied, "Okay, I'm not even gonna ask what that is." Xero nudged Blake and pointed to the mic, which Blake then handed to him. Xero smiled and began to speak to the crowd and the stage at the same time.

"I think I get at least part of what our friend here is trying to do. Ladies and gentlemen, we here of The Reason Why have a problem, and we are hoping that maybe you can help us out." The audience cheered until Xero gestured for them to calm down so he could continue. "As many of you, our fans especially, are aware, we love you guys. But, we've been scheduled to play here at Henderson Palace. It's a nice place—we like it, a lot; but, we were sorta sent here against our will." Jail-Bait walked up to where Xero stood during his address. She smiled and made a gesture for the microphone; Xero bowed and handed it to her.

"Hey guys. Like my buddy Xero was saying, our contract holder— Drew Maroni, he's nearby somewhere, guys—put us here so that we wouldn't be able to make our audition with Altered Note Records at

Texas Palace tonight. Seems a certain club owner is afraid that we'll buy out the contract and lose him money if we get our shot." The crowd began to roar with boos, hisses and a litany of curse words. "That's right," Jones continued, "but, it's going to be okay—our young friend here has just brought up a very important fact: our performance here can be considered over, done and fulfilled. That is, if you guys agree that you've already been 'satisfied' by our act. You guys could really help us tonight, what do you say?"

Ballparks rarely sound so enthralled: a resounding chorus of cheers echoed throughout the Red Manhattan. Many of the fans were chanting "Texas World" or "The Reason Why." "Well," Blake said with a smile, "I do believe we got our answer." It was then Drew Moroni entered the nightclub, surrounded by four security officers. "Stop! Stop *right there!*" he said as he approached the stage. "You are bound to my contract, and I demand you play on until the end of your allotted playing time. And I mean it," he said, gesturing for the officers to get on stage. "You're losin' it, man," Xero said while staring at Moroni, "What are you gonna do, make us play at gunpoint?" The crowd began to yell loudly, several wrappers, cups, and other pieces of trash were hurled upon the club owner and his security detail.

"One more favor, guys," a voice said over the speakers. It was Samantha—she had finally found a reason to speak on a microphone, after all. "We need to get to the doors. We need some help, *Texas* style." Miss Greene may have been small in stature, but her words caused a massive effect: the entire audience rose to their feet and turned to face Moroni. His officers were no longer trying to climb the stage; rather, they were beginning to look a little nervous.

The crowd began to slowly chant in an oddly coordinated harmony; Summerlin couldn't tell at first what they were singing. The audience members began to slowly but steadily enclose around Mr. Moroni and his officers. Then, he recognized it: They were chanting the University of Texas's alma mater—*The Eyes of Texas*. Two of the four officers bolted for the exit. Summerlin couldn't tell from all the commotion if they ever made it there. He did, however, hear Moroni shout to the remaining two: "What are you guys doing? You are supposed to protect me!" One of the officers yelled out, "You're on your own!" They ripped their badges off and raised their hands in defeat as they walked towards the curtained exit. To the crowd's credit, they let the two now unemployed men flee without even a hindrance. The band was too busy leaving the stage to look down. The last thing Summerlin saw as they were hustling to move the equipment offstage was Mr. Moroni's hand reaching out above a swarm of orange-shirted fans who had engulfed him.

They arrived at the valet lane five minutes later. Everyone, non-musicians and band members alike, was carrying musical equipment. Danny joined the group to help carry Samantha's drum kit. "I'm goin' to have to call a cab for the equipment," Blake lamented, "I highly doubt that Palace Casinos will be sendin' a shuttle for us after what just went on in there." Thomas walked up to Blake and thrust his valet ticket out toward him. "Here, take my angel's chariot." Blake grabbed the ticket and shouted, "Thanks! You're a paragon, Tommy!" he yelled. Before going to the valet shed, Blake handed Thomas *his* car keys. "You guys get there before us and distract the crowd if need be. Just don't sing, either of you. You'll need speed. Just don't wreck my baby. It's the dark blue Lebaron in the lot near the Paseo Grande entrance," he said. Summerlin followed Thomas as he ran off towards the lot bordering Paseo Grande. "I'll drive," he told Summerlin, "you just buckle up and hold on to something."

"When we get there, just let me handle it. Do that, and we're even on the deception thing," Thomas said to Summerlin as they made their way back onto the highway. "Am I to assume you're goin' to deceive me in a few minutes, then?" Thomas grinned and replied, "I know now what must be done, and I'll see it done. Just trust me." Summerlin grabbed onto his seat cushion as the car sped faster and faster, and began to weave through traffic once more. "Fine," he said, "as long as you promise me you'll talk to Xero." Thomas nodded in acquiescence. "Fair enough, if you talk to Connor."

The old blue car zoomed with all haste towards Texas Palace. The casino was but a speck on their horizon when Thomas and Summerlin took the Rancho Drive off ramp. "You know," Summerlin said as the car began to run red lights and careen dangerously near light poles and peo-ple, "we can only be of use if we arrive *alive*." Thomas smiled peacefully as the wind ripped through his hair. "Don't worry so much, Summerlin. Everything happens for a reason—we have—" Summerlin cut him off: "I know, I know. Angels on our shoulders; I only hope you're right."

No red light, stop sign, nor pedestrian was going to stop the Lebaron as it raced northbound on Rancho Drive. Nothing could halt the two men on their desperate race to the Palace. Nothing, except for Summerlin spotting Connor's mirror-coupe oddly parked alongside the corner of Rancho and Washington; it was wedged between two black cars with heavy window tinting. "Hold on," he yelled to Thomas, "It's Connor—and Sarah! What is goin' on?" Thomas took the corner rather hard, but ground the car to a halt within feet of the black cars. It was then that Summerlin noticed the men standing outside the black cars— it was the Calvert brothers, and they were advancing upon Sarah and the Con-Man.

"No doors, no fake cameras, and no witnesses," Joe Calvert said as he stared at Connor. The Con-Man had a nonchalant grin, but Sarah was cowering behind him and looked genuinely frightened. "Geez," Connor replied, "I'm kind of busy; got things going on, you know? Can't you come bother me and threaten my life after ten? I'm also open on Sunday...Hey! Summerlin! Guys!" Connor's face lit with joy at the sight of his friends. "Couldn't miss the party, Sarah!" Summerlin called out to her as Thomas and he walked up to the cluster of cars and Calverts. Sarah yelled back, "*Andrew*! I'm here. I'm so sorry, baby, I—" She was cut off by Summerlin, who said, "We'll be fine, darlin'—we got bigger problems right now." She appeared to be crying as she replied, "But I'm so sorry, and if we don't make it out of this I want you to know that—" Once again, Summerlin mimicked his teacher and cut her off, saying: "Baby it's not goin' to happen like that. And besides, where is my place if not beside you?" The two nearly-star-crossed lovers looked one another in the eye. It was a beautiful scene, until Joe Calvert ruined it. "Yeah, you do have some more important details to attend to—your funeral, unless you give up Bentley there. Wait a second, I remember *you*—you were with that piece of shit last time, too."

"Yeah, and what of it?" Summerlin responded defiantly. This time, it was Louie who spoke, "That makes you as dead as him in my book." Joe shook his head and waved his brother off. "Louie, Lou—shut it. Let's do this the easy way: we only came for Connor Bentley." "Oh yeah?" Summerlin replied, "What are you goin' to do to get him?" Joe Calvert flipped out his switchblade and reached out to grab Sarah; he hastily put the blade to the young woman's throat. At this time, Thomas gave an anxious glance to his wristwatch. After a moment of what looked like intense panic, Thomas ran to the mirror-coupe and jumped in it. The engine started, and the coupe peeled out in reverse before correcting itself to go northbound on Rancho.

"Tommy...Why?" Connor cried out. He looked genuinely hurt—and confused. The Calvert brothers laughed. "Your odds are dropping, shit-pile." Summerlin stomped over to within a foot of where Joe stood and said in a calm, but rancorous voice: "Let her go, or spend the entirety of your existence in regret." There was no kidding in Summerlin's eyes: he was deadly serious. "Fine, you got me, boys. Just leave Summerlin and the girl out of it. By the way, kid, stellar on the daring assistance to the band," Connor said. He winked before raising his hands and walking slowly over to where Louie Calvert stood. *How did he*, was all Summerlin managed to think before he saw the Con-Man make a phone gesture with his hands. *Oh*, he thought, *Jail-Bait or Blake must've called him.*

Summerlin was trembling; he didn't fear the Calvert's nor their threats to Connor—but, he wasn't willing to take any chances as far as Sarah's safety was concerned. He walked up to Joe Calvert and said, "Let the girl *go*." Joe looked from Connor to Louie and replied, "It's okay, he's a piece of crap, but I do trust his word." Sarah was released from knife-point and pushed towards Summerlin. She was within inches of him, but Summerlin couldn't stop to think of his happiness. As Sarah collided with him, he whispered in her ear: "Baby, do you trust me now?" She quickly replied, "Yeah, now more than ever, why?" He didn't answer her question; instead, Summerlin pushed Sarah as hard as he could, as to make her collide with the Con-Man like a cue ball. "Sorry love," he whispered as he regained his composure and eyed down Joe Calvert.

As Sarah collided with Connor, Summerlin took advantage of the fact that the Calvert brothers had turned their eyes from him. "Yeehaw!" he screamed as he bum-rushed Joe *into* Louie, and the three men tumbled over into a knot of confusion. Connor helped Sarah up and looked in bewilderment towards Summerlin. "Get Sarah out of here! Go, Connor!" He screamed to them as he tried his best to keep both men down long enough for Sarah and the Con-Man to escape. "Run!" he cried, "Run like *Ecclipse*!" Connor Bentley didn't need to be told twice—as Summerlin found himself pretzeled with Calverts, the Con-Man pushed Sarah into the Lebaron and peeled out for Texas Palace. "You stupid, ignorant son of a bitch!" Louie yelled as he, too brandished a knife after breaking free from Summerlin.

Summerlin's odds of survival had fallen significantly, but he was at peace. No matter what, his best friend and the love of his life would be safe. It was then, as the Calvert's rose and began to close in on Summerlin with their knives drawn, that it hit him: a sudden, knife-proof happiness rose within his heart. He remembered what his mentor had taught him about Lesson Nine, and how the world, not he, would be the one to let him know. *I do believe I've lost...but I couldn't be happier,* he thought as he began to smile widely.

The Calvert's slowly paced towards Summerlin as he backed himself into an alley between Macho Grande and a small bar called "Greg's Place." "What the hell is up with you, hick?" Louie demanded as they pressed ever forward. Summerlin glanced behind to notice that he was being backed into a wall—an eight foot, sleek wall that would be too difficult to scale unscathed. "Oh nothin', fellas," Summerlin replied peacefully, "I just realized that there's nothin' you guys can do but kill me. You'll never kill my heart—that will live on no matter what your dark-suited, ill-mannered buffoons intend. But, don't worry, I can 'fight back' if you want it to be more sportin'."

The end had come; Summerlin felt the smooth, cold press of the wall against his back. He lowered his head and closed his eyes, intending to say his final prayers and wish for the health and happiness of his friends and family. There would be no witnesses to see his undoing—and he doubted that the Calverts would leave behind any trace of him for his folks back home to mourn. A scurrying noise came out of nowhere from behind the wall. The scurry was followed by the sound of something hitting the pavement. Summerlin opened his eyes and saw only footwear—but, that was all he needed to see. His former pair of black ropers was now between him and the Calvert brothers.

"Bling!" Summerlin yelled. The vagrant rose from his post-landing kneel, and stood with his fists bared. Another sound soon followed; two more street people found themselves between Summerlin and the suited thugs. The two men were shabbily dressed, and one of them was holding a broken bottle—it was Low-down; he was wearing a rainbow kerchief, and had a wicked look in his eye. Low-Down's companion held a brick, and looked every bit as fierce.

"Now who the hell are you?" Joe Calvert said, stepping forward a foot with his knife pointed towards Bling-Bling's sculpted muscles. "My name's Bling—and if you lay one hand on that man's head, *you aren't leaving this alley alive.*" Louie and Joe gave Bling-Bling a cold stare and continued to press forward. "No? You're funeral, then," Bling said casually before making a series of almost inhuman crowing sounds. Within seconds, the Calvert brothers jerked their heads from side to side: a new set of unidentified sounds was occurring—this conglomeration of scuffles, stomping and footfalls was, however, coming from all directions.

Bling turned toward Summerlin and said, "S-man, glad to see I could return a favor. It's truly been an honor, but, I'm gonna have to ask you to run away, and never look back." The alley was slowly beginning to fill with the shadows of a multitude of vagrants, bums and hobos, most of which were wielding knives, broken bottles, or whatever other makeshift weapon they could procure. Summerlin nodded and made a break for it on foot. The Calverts didn't bother touching him—their now-pale faces were too focused on the swarm of humanity that was descending upon them. Summerlin kept to his word, and didn't even look back when he heard a series of exasperated cries in the distance. Summerlin's future was his once again.

19.

Thomas's knuckles were white, and he was imperiled with fear. It wasn't the threat of physical harm which scared him, but fear of the future. "We'll only get one shot at this, love," the curly-haired young woman said as she leaned into Thomas as he drove the coupe as fast as it could go. "Darling, I want to do this—*I do*—but, I just don't know." He was trembling in a cold sweat. All that separated him from becoming a gibbering heap of jelly was the devoted girl at his side. "Thomas Leonard West, you have never shied away from a challenge that mattered in your life. You were raised to be a gentleman, and if you ever act anything but that, there will be hell to pay."

Thomas gulped, but it did not relieve him of the butterflies in his stomach. "As always," he said to her, "I give my trust to you, my love." The woman kissed his cheek and then lovingly replied, "No, baby, this time I'm gonna need you to put your faith in *you*."

Blake gave the truck a lead foot, and managed, despite all the traffic-related odds, to arrive with band gear in tow at the valet shed

of Texas Palace. "Time?" he anxiously called out to the shell-covered bed of the truck. "8:54," Trent replied. "Boy, this is goin' to have to be quick. I hope we don't lose our chance here," Blake said before stopping the truck and putting it in park. He ran to the back of the truck and opened the tailgate. The band members got out while Blake and Trent began to unload their gear. Jail-Bait checked her phone and said, "It's already 8:55—they're expecting a curtain rise at 9pm sharp. We need a vanguard." Sam, Blake and Trent all replied at the same time: "Xero!"

Xero had been pushing the equipment forward from the back of the truck bed; he slid out and faced Blake and Jail-Bait. Jones looked at him with determination and said, "Hey, we're going to need those young legs of yours..." Xero nodded enthusiastically before exclaiming, "I'll be your huckleberry!" and running for the entrance.

The young bassist ran full speed for the Rail Yard. There was a sign near the bell desk advertising the Rail Yard as having a Friday show: "T.R.Y. OR KARAOKE MADNESS." He took an unmarked side door near the Lone Star Bar which led him through a tiled back service hallway which in turn led indirectly to the backstage of the nightclub. He ran to the wing of the stage and his heart nearly stopped. The curtain was up, and the crowd was hushed by a piano being masterfully played. Xero couldn't move; he was immobilized by what was unfolding before him: There sat in the middle of the stage the piano which the band occasionally rolled in on Fridays for Jones to play. There was a hand-written sign bearing a simple phrase written in green marker: "The Reason Why." It was Thomas, and his hands were a dervish of music and grandeur. He was playing—and singing rather poorly—Five For Fighting's *100 Years*.

Xero couldn't move a single cell of his body. He was bearing witness to some sort of miracle: gone was the sad reject whom he had come to despise, and, in its place, a beacon of light—a pallbearer proudly standing in the face of adversity. He saw not a wretch, but a the last standing remnant of all that Xero had known of decency from the earlier, happier days. His eyes began to tear up, not from sadness, but from awe. Thomas continued to play expertly, glancing every so often to a spot to his left.

It was only when Jail-Bait elbowed his side that Xero came to his senses. "Xero! He isn't doing this for nothing!" she attested. Xero gathered himself and replied, "Yes ma'am!" as he grabbed his guitar from Blake and walked towards the stage. Thomas, through it all, kept playing...

Summerlin didn't even try to get a ride, nor did he worry about the fate of Sarah, Connor or the band. He knew that he had given everyone the best shot at their ends that he could. And so, Summerlin slowly sauntered into Texas Palace: tired, covered in sweat, but with a positively uplifting smile upon his face. *To the Rail Yard, and all that I hold dear*, he thought.

He walked past the bell desk and kept his eyes ever on the Rail Yard entrance at the end of the Pit. Summerlin was walking briskly when he was halted in his tracks. "Summerlin! Thank God!" It was Connor; he was leaning against a brick pillar in his usual fashion. "Oh? You believe in him now?" Summerlin asked as he turned to face Connor, who replied with a grin, "I never said I didn't, kid. By the way, I believe I have something for you..." Summerlin's curiosity was answered when the Con-Man took a sidestep, revealing Sarah, who was smiling brightly and wearing a Texas World shirt. The blue cursive title read: "Sarah, Buckeye Firebrand."

"Hey, kid," she said with a wink. And then, not even the laws of time nor physics could separate them; Sarah ran to become enveloped in Summerlin's welcoming arms. "I'm so sorry—I failed you, Andrew," she said as she kissed his neck. "We failed each other, darlin'. We've known each other for a long time now; if there ever were really somethin' that could tear us apart, it would be a problem between you and I, not outsiders. We're stronger than that." Sarah nodded and cuddled against his chest.

After a few happy moments had passed, Sarah looked up at Summerlin and said, "I have to ask, Andre—err, Summerlin...How did you not give up on me?" Summerlin kissed her forehead and replied, "Simple, my sweet. I didn't give up on you because you never gave up on me when I got caught up in bull crap back home." Sarah shook her head and said, "Your good ol' boy friends wanted to ruin your *career*, Summerlin. "Then we're even, love," he said. "Still, I feel like you were in the right—" Summerlin silenced her, not with words, but a sweet kiss on the lips that was a month in the making.

"Who's right and who's wrong don't really matter, anyway, Sarah," Summerlin said. Sarah nodded and added, "You're right—what happens the next time is what counts." Connor grinned and said, "I couldn't have said it any better myself. It's an all's well that ends well, kids. You gotta take those where you can get 'em in life." Summerlin nodded emphatically. "I intend to. Speaking of which, how'd it all go?"

Connor pointed toward the Rail Yard—just outside the entrance curtain was Xero and Thomas. They were talking, and, it appeared, hugging. "Don't mind them," Connor said, "they're just getting around to some things they should have done five years ago." Summerlin gave the two men a look and waved to them with a smile before returning his attention to Connor. "And the band?" Connor pumped his fist in the air and said, "They rocked the place, kid. They won't know Altered Note's verdict for a couple days from now; their future looks good, though. Jail-Bait actually sang lead on *Don't Break*!" Summerlin replied in shock, "Wow. That just leaves you and the house that Texas built."

"I wouldn't go worrying about that. Several of my more famous friends wanted in on my buy-in after they heard that I had a major co-signer turned silent partner...Possibly the best business mind in the

Silver State, really..." Summerlin smiled as he noticed Connor throw Thomas a wink. "And, to make it even sweeter," the Con-Man continued, "Old Cid went down to Tyler Lancaster's for me, and has been talking his ear off for two straight days; seems he didn't know about Cy's transgressions. Needless to say, Dominic is being restored to power, and all is right with the Palace Casino family once more. Of course, they don't want cross competition, so Tyler was kind enough to offer my consortium a good deal. Only two hundred million for the gates, games and the Austin Suite. But I digress..."

Summerlin watched from afar as he saw Xero and Thomas; they were talking with smiles through tear-streaked faces. "I have to know, Yankee..." Connor replied, "Yeah, what's that Kentucky-Fried?" Summerlin's smile diminished and he asked, "Does he still see..." Connor grinned and said, "Her? He sure does. Thomas gave a performance for the ages; he can't sing worth a shit, though. He played the ivories like he had been born on one."

"Really?" Summerlin inquired, "I didn't ever get the inclination that he had any musical talent." "Well," the Con-Man replied, "that's because he didn't. Thomas West? Are you kidding? He couldn't even play *Guitar Legend* on the Q-Box." Confusion struck Summerlin. "What? How then? Wait—" A cold chill ran down the length of his spine. Summerlin said, "You don't think he actually—" Connor cut him off: "I'll stop you right there, kid. You're asking the wrong question." Even Sarah seemed intrigued by this one. "The wrong questions?" Summerlin inquired, "I'd think it's the *only* question..."

"Nope. Now bear with me, I know I've sorta lost the right to wax philosophically, but gimme a just a second of your contemplation: Does it really matter how he did it? The way I see it, there are only two real possible explanations. One, that Thomas was in fact guided by his long-beloved's hand, or two, that Thomas has spent years in secret learning how to emulate his girl's love of music. Can you honestly tell me that either outcome would be less fantastical or heroic? Either way, their love can go down as one for the record books." Summerlin had to give it to the old gambler—he had a point. "I'm...I'm at a loss for words," he said to Connor and Sarah with a smile. "Ah," the Con-Man replied, "I see you've learned all nine of them, then. *Excellent.* Now let's go hang out with our friends—Do I need to tell you the reason why?" The three of them joined the remaining band members for toasts at the Lone Star Bar.

EPILOGUE

Summerlin awoke in the guest room, but for the first time ever, he was not alone. He awoke to find the woman of his dreams by his side. Connor Bentley had already left the Austin Suite; it was, after all, a Saturday, and the Con-Man never missed a Saturday morning in the Race Book. A simple, yet elegantly penned, note was pinned to the door. It read: "Come meet me at the Lone Star when you're ready." Sarah and Summerlin took their time.

On the way down to the Lone Star Bar, Sarah stopped at a bank of Dixie Dollars machines. "Hey babe, look at this one. Why don't we give it a shot?" Summerlin looked with anxiety for a moment before he grinned and pulled out a twenty from his wallet. "Ah, what the heck, right?" he said. Sarah smiled and took a seat at the machine. Out of nowhere came Connor, saying, "Now there's a bold move followed by a wise decision." He was smiling like a proud father. Summerlin smiled and gave Sarah a kiss before replying, "You can't win in life without a wager."

Before the Con-Man had a chance to add anything, the machine which Sarah had just started to play blared triumphant music as its lights flashed: she had scored three US flags, and the three of them watched in joy as the balance on the machine continued to climb ever higher.

www.ingramcontent.com/pod-product-compliance
Lightning Source LLC
Chambersburg PA
CBHW071158250626
47159CB00001B/129